Illuminated Boundaries

Mila King

Published by Mila King, 2024.

This is a work of fiction. Similarities to real people, places, or events are entirely coincidental.

ILLUMINATED BOUNDARIES

First edition. October 25, 2024.

Copyright © 2024 Mila King.

ISBN: 979-8227867858

Written by Mila King.

Chapter 1: A Candle's Glow

The warmth of the candle's flame dances against the windowpane as I pour wax into molds, letting the scents of sage and lavender fill the small studio apartment. Each swirl of melted wax creates an intricate masterpiece, a reflection of the vibrant chaos that is Brooklyn life outside my door. I revel in the ritual, the quiet satisfaction of crafting something from scratch. With every flick of my wrist, I'm not just pouring wax; I'm infusing my dreams and desires into the mixture, watching it harden into something that radiates warmth and comfort. The candles, once mere vessels of wax, come alive in the glow of the flame, glowing brighter when people hold them close and make a wish.

There's a magic in this moment, a power humming just beneath my skin, teasing me with whispers of what could be. My little studio feels like a sanctuary amid the urban sprawl, a place where creativity intertwines with hope. Tonight, I'm preparing a new batch for the weekend market, which always buzzes with the promise of possibility. Just as I'm about to add a few drops of rosemary essential oil—a personal favorite—the sound of paper sliding under the door interrupts my concentration.

I glance toward the entrance, my curiosity piqued. What could possibly slip through that threshold uninvited? I set down the glass dropper and wipe my hands on my apron, the fabric already speckled with a kaleidoscope of wax remnants. As I pick up the stray flyer, my brow furrows at the sight: a bright, bold announcement of a grand opening for a tech startup down the street—the very building that has turned parking into a nightmare with its never-ending construction.

My first instinct is to crumple the paper and toss it in the trash. I have no reason to go; I'm perfectly content wrapped up in my candle-making, with its calming fragrances and soothing routines.

But as I read the details—"Innovative technology, creative minds, a new vision for the future"—I feel a tug in my chest. Perhaps it's the thrill of curiosity, or maybe it's the ever-present itch for change. Brooklyn has always been a place of transformation, and it's no wonder my magic has been growing here.

I slip off my apron and pull my hair into a messy bun, a practiced move that somehow makes me feel more adventurous. A glance in the mirror reveals the remnants of candle wax dusting my cheeks and a satisfied smile curving my lips. I grab my favorite vintage denim jacket—a little frayed at the edges but packed with stories—and slip my feet into well-worn sneakers. Stepping into the evening air, I am greeted by the sounds of a city alive with energy.

The streets pulse with the heartbeat of humanity, each step pulling me deeper into the vibrant tapestry of life unfolding around me. Food carts steam with fragrant offerings, laughter erupts from a nearby bar, and somewhere, a guitar strums a familiar tune. The air smells of possibility, an intoxicating blend of autumn leaves and street food, with a hint of the unexpected just around the corner.

As I approach the tech startup's entrance, my excitement swells, mingling with apprehension. It's a stark contrast to my cozy studio, all sleek glass and steel, buzzing with the energy of the young and ambitious. I take a breath, allowing the electric atmosphere to wrap around me like a warm embrace. I step inside, and the soft hum of conversation greets me, filled with the laughter of new beginnings and the promise of connections yet to be made.

A crowd has gathered around a table displaying innovative gadgets that blink and buzz with the vigor of a new dawn. I wander further in, absorbing the sights and sounds, my senses dancing with curiosity. My eyes scan the room, landing on a young woman with vibrant blue hair, passionately explaining a device that promises to revolutionize daily commuting. Her enthusiasm is infectious, igniting a spark of interest within me. I find myself inching closer, not just to hear her words but to feel the electricity of her dreams radiating through the air.

"Who knew you could create a smart umbrella that tells you when it's about to rain?" I remark, a grin slipping across my face as I lean closer to her demonstration. She turns, eyes sparkling with delight at the interaction.

"I know, right? It's like having a personal weather assistant that's also a fashion statement!" Her laughter rings out, a melody that seems to harmonize perfectly with the rhythm of the night.

"Can it also tell me when I need to put on more layers? Because I swear, the weather has been playing games with my sanity."

We share a knowing chuckle, and in that moment, it's as if the world outside fades away, leaving just the two of us tangled in this moment of connection. A small voice in my head whispers that this is the kind of magic I've been searching for, the kind that goes beyond wax and wicks, igniting passions I didn't know existed.

As the evening unfolds, I find myself mingling with strangers who feel less like mere acquaintances and more like potential friends. Each conversation threads into the next, weaving a rich tapestry of laughter, ideas, and dreams that hang in the air like the scents from my candles. I revel in the stories they share—of late nights fueled by caffeine and ambition, of failures turned triumphs, and of the risks taken in the pursuit of something greater.

But then, just as the night seems to shimmer with possibility, my gaze lands on a figure across the room—a man with dark hair, tousled as if he's just stepped out of a storm, and eyes that seem to hold the mysteries of the universe. He's talking to a small group, his hands animatedly gesturing as if weaving magic into the air. I'm drawn to him, an inexplicable force urging me closer, despite the swirl of activity around us.

In that moment, the familiar warmth of the candle's glow and the electric buzz of the startup collide, igniting something deep within me—a longing for connection, adventure, and perhaps even love. With every step I take toward him, the flame of possibility flickers brighter, promising a night filled with unexpected twists and layers of tension that could change everything.

The crowd ebbs and flows around me, an energetic river of conversation and laughter. I'm swept along, the warmth of connection pulsating through the air like a familiar tune. The man across the room, with his tousled dark hair and captivating gaze, stands as a beacon amid the chaos. It's as if he's a magnet, drawing me in with an invisible force. I watch as he leans closer to his group, his voice smooth like dark chocolate, and a sudden urge to know him sends a flutter through my stomach.

"Excuse me," I say to the blue-haired dynamo beside me, who's engrossed in her own animated discussion. "I need to go find out if he's as interesting as he looks or if he's just really good at being mysterious."

She shoots me a conspiratorial smile. "Good luck. I'd place my bets on the mysterious part. Those types usually are."

I take a deep breath and weave through the crowd, navigating the sea of bodies and conversations, my heart beating a little faster with every step. When I reach him, he's explaining something about algorithms and user interfaces, his hands dancing through the air, punctuating each point with flair.

"Right, because nothing screams 'trust me' like a complicated algorithm," I interject, my voice laced with playful sarcasm. "What's next, an app that predicts your coffee preferences based on the last five dates you went on?"

His eyes flicker with surprise, then delight, as he turns to face me fully. "If only! I'd be rich and, ironically, much more socially awkward."

"Ah, but isn't that the tech world in a nutshell? Brilliant ideas paired with a distinct lack of social skills."

He chuckles, a rich sound that seems to wrap around me like a warm blanket. "Touché. I'm Evan, by the way."

"Carmen. Professional candle maker, part-time fortune teller," I say, holding out my hand. "I predict a lot of late nights filled with caffeine and coding in your future."

His grip is warm and firm, a spark zinging through my fingertips as we connect. "You might be onto something there. How does a candle maker end up at a tech startup launch? Sounds like a setup for a terrible joke."

"Trust me, I've got enough terrible jokes stored up for a lifetime. But it's simple, really. I'm here for the ambiance, and you were the most interesting thing in the room."

"Flattery and a sense of humor? Now I'm intrigued," he replies, his smile widening. "What kind of candles do you make?"

I take a breath, diving into my passion as easily as I slip into my apron each morning. "I craft them from all-natural wax, infused with essential oils—think sage, lavender, and a hint of rosemary. They're not just candles; they're little spells of comfort. I've had customers tell me they can feel the magic."

"Magic, you say?" He leans in closer, genuinely interested. "What's the secret ingredient?"

I lean in as if sharing state secrets. "If I told you, I'd have to charge you double."

We share a laugh, and I feel the distance between us shrinking, the air thickening with possibilities. The night continues to unfold, filled with lively conversations and laughter, yet there's an unmistakable focus on Evan. He listens intently as I talk about my craft, asking questions that reveal a curiosity beyond surface-level interest. There's a rhythm to our exchange, a back-and-forth that feels both effortless and electric.

But just as I'm settling into this newfound connection, a woman with sharp features and a perfectly tailored blazer saunters over, her expression a mix of annoyance and curiosity. She plants herself next to Evan, offering a saccharine smile that doesn't quite reach her eyes. "Evan, darling, there you are! I've been looking everywhere for you."

"Oh, hey, Laura!" He straightens, his body language shifting slightly. The easygoing demeanor I was just enjoying tightens. "I was just—"

"Just chatting up a storm, I see. Always the social butterfly." Her gaze flicks to me, a trace of condescension threading through her tone. "And you are...?"

"I'm Carmen, just a humble candle maker," I reply, injecting cheer into my voice, hoping to disarm the tension.

"Right," she says, dismissing my introduction with a wave of her hand. "Evan, we need to discuss the investor pitch before it's too late. Can you step away for a moment?"

He hesitates, glancing between her and me, the warmth from our conversation wavering under her icy demeanor. "Uh, sure. Just give me a second."

I feel a pang of disappointment, but I nod, forcing a smile that feels strained. "Of course, work calls. Nice to meet you, Laura."

Her lips curve into a smile that could cut glass, but I refuse to be intimidated. As Evan walks away, I shift my focus back to the crowd, determined to enjoy the evening despite the interruption. A little voice in my head whispers that perhaps I should just leave, that this was a fleeting moment in a vibrant city filled with possibilities. But I push it down, letting the ambiance of the event wash over me like a soothing balm.

Minutes slip by, and I find myself mingling with a group discussing innovative food technologies. I'm drawn into their excitement, sharing ideas and laughter as the world around me becomes a blur. But every so often, my gaze flits toward Evan, who seems to be trapped in a conversation with Laura, her fingers dancing over his arm in a way that sends an unexpected pang of irritation through me.

When the crowd begins to thin, I decide it's time to make my exit. I want to grab my bag and make a quiet escape before I drown in the sea of my own emotions. Just as I turn to leave, I hear Evan's voice calling after me, cutting through the background noise.

"Carmen! Wait!"

I turn back, heart racing. He rushes over, his expression a mix of urgency and something else—determination, perhaps. "I'm really sorry about that. Laura can be... well, let's just say she's very dedicated to her work."

"Dedicated? Is that what we're calling it?" I can't help the wry smile that breaks through, and he laughs, the tension easing between us.

"I was really enjoying our conversation. I didn't want it to end." His sincerity sends a jolt of warmth through me, the night suddenly feeling full of promise again.

"Neither did I. But you have to admit, this was quite the dramatic entrance."

He shakes his head, an amused smile dancing on his lips. "How about we grab a coffee sometime? I'd love to hear more about your candles—and maybe share a few bad jokes."

The unexpected invitation sends a thrill through me. "Coffee sounds perfect. But I warn you, my jokes are terrible."

"Then we're a match made in heaven," he replies, his eyes sparkling with mischief. "I'll see you soon, Carmen."

As I step outside, the cool night air embraces me like a long-lost friend, the city alive with sounds and scents that promise more adventures to come. The flame of possibility flickers brighter within me, igniting a thrill that feels like the first spark of a new candle. I glance back at the tech startup, a smile creeping onto my face. The night hasn't ended yet, not for me.

The city hums around me, a comforting melody that blends the sounds of distant sirens with the laughter spilling from open windows. The night air is cool against my skin, a refreshing contrast to the warmth I left behind in my studio. As I stroll, the anticipation of a potential coffee date with Evan sends ripples of excitement through me, mingling with the scents of street food and the faintest hint of rain lingering in the breeze. I catch myself smiling like a giddy teenager, a flutter of hope and possibility swelling in my chest.

Each step toward my apartment feels charged with energy, the glow of streetlights illuminating the way. I can't help but replay our conversation in my head, the banter we shared a delightful dance of wit and charm. The way his eyes lit up when I spoke about my candles lingers in my mind, a warmth that propels me forward. It's been ages since someone truly listened to me, and Evan, with his magnetic presence, seems to have a way of making me feel seen.

Arriving at my door, I fumble for the keys, still lost in the thrill of the evening. The familiar scent of sage and lavender wafts from within as I push the door open, a comforting embrace enveloping me. I drop my bag on the table, my fingers brushing over the half-finished candles, remnants of the evening's tasks. But my mind is too abuzz to focus on them now. Instead, I pull out my phone, heart racing as I type out a message to Evan: "I had a great time tonight. Let's definitely grab that coffee soon!"

As I send the message, a strange sense of foreboding flickers at the edges of my mind. I shake it off, dismissing the nagging feeling. There's no reason for worry; this is the start of something promising, isn't it? Just then, my phone buzzes, jolting me from my thoughts. The screen lights up with Evan's reply, and a rush of anticipation floods my veins.

"I'd love that! How about Saturday morning?"

Perfect. The excitement spirals again, and I reply with an enthusiastic "Yes!" as I sink into the familiar comfort of my couch.

But as I settle in, the earlier unease creeps back. The flickering candlelight feels less inviting now, shadows dancing along the walls like secrets whispered too closely. I glance around the apartment, taking in the cozy clutter—the wax remnants, the jars of essential oils, the sketches of new designs pinned above my workspace. All of it feels like a cocoon, and yet, there's an unsettling tension wrapping itself around me.

Just as I try to shake it off and focus on the warmth of the moment, there's a knock at the door—sharp, insistent. My heart skips a beat. Who could it be at this hour? My imagination spins wild scenarios: a neighbor in distress, a lost delivery, or something far less mundane. With each cautious step toward the door, the air thickens, crackling with tension. I glance through the peephole, half-expecting to see a familiar face, but instead, I find a stranger standing on my doorstep.

He's tall, with shaggy hair that seems to be perpetually tousled, dressed in a leather jacket that looks like it's seen better days. His face is partially obscured by the shadows, but the sharpness of his features is undeniable. I hesitate, uncertainty coursing through me.

"Can I help you?" I call out, my voice steadier than I feel.

"Carmen?" he asks, his tone even but laced with urgency.

"Yes, who's asking?"

"I need to talk to you. It's important."

The gravity in his voice makes my stomach churn. I grip the doorknob tighter, ready to close the door if necessary. "I'm not sure I can help you. Can you tell me what this is about?"

He hesitates, and for a moment, I think he might turn and walk away, but then he takes a step closer, his silhouette framed by the streetlights behind him. "It's about your candles."

A rush of confusion floods my mind. "What do you mean? My candles?"

"I can't explain everything right now. Just—please, let me in. I promise, I'm not here to hurt you."

That strange instinct, the one that urged me to come to the tech startup, flickers in my gut. But this feels different, charged with a tension I can't quite grasp. "Why should I trust you?"

"I know you're not a believer in coincidence. This is bigger than just candles. It involves you—your magic."

My heart races, the shadows of doubt battling the flickering light of curiosity. "My magic?"

"Yes," he insists, urgency seeping into his voice. "There's something about your candles that they want. Something powerful."

A chill runs down my spine as his words sink in. My candles are just candles, right? A whimsical dream I've nurtured, nothing more. Yet, something in his eyes—a spark of desperation—nudges me closer to the edge of intrigue. "Who are they?"

"People who understand how to harness magic. And they're looking for you."

Before I can process his words, he glances over his shoulder, scanning the street with an intensity that makes my skin prickle. "Please, let me in. We don't have much time."

The urgency in his voice is undeniable, and a part of me is compelled by a strange mix of fear and curiosity. I wrestle with my decision, my heart pounding in my ears. Can I trust him? What if this is some elaborate trick? But what if it isn't?

I draw in a deep breath, weighing my options. My instinct tells me that this moment could lead to something significant—a turning point in my life, one that intertwines with the magic I've always believed in but never fully acknowledged.

"Fine," I finally say, pulling the door open just a crack, enough to let his shadowy form slip through. "But you better have a good explanation for all this."

He steps inside, and as I close the door behind him, I can't shake the feeling that I've just crossed an unseen threshold into a world I'm wholly unprepared for. The air shifts, charged with an energy I've never felt before, and I know that whatever comes next, it's going to change everything.

Chapter 2: The Grand Opening

The shimmering skyline of Manhattan sprawls like a sea of jewels beneath the ink-black sky, each light a pulse in the lifeblood of the city. I cradle my cocktail, a delicate blend of elderflower and gin, its froth fizzing like whispers of excitement. The rooftop, adorned with twinkling fairy lights, feels like a glamorous set from a film, complete with a live band crooning softly in the background. They strum out mellow tunes, the sound wrapping around the mingling crowd like a silk scarf, drawing them closer together. Here, amidst the sleek, glass-and-steel backdrop, the energy of ambition and innovation vibrates in the air, each moment alive with possibility.

I blend into the edges of the gathering, my eyes flicking over the elegantly dressed attendees who glide about with an effortless grace, laughter spilling like fine wine. I'm all too aware of the designer dress hugging my curves, a deep emerald green that contrasts with my auburn hair, cascading in soft waves. Yet, despite the exquisite fabric and the care I took to style my hair, I can't shake the feeling of being an imposter in this dazzling crowd. These are the titans of technology, the trailblazers who sculpt ideas into reality. Me? I'm just a cog in the machine, an enthusiastic supporter of the revolution.

And then I see him. Grant Rivers. He stands a few feet away, surrounded by an entourage that practically beams with admiration, his presence magnetic. There's something both reassuring and intimidating in the way he commands attention; his tailored suit clings perfectly to his athletic frame, and his dark hair, tousled just enough to appear casual, frames a face that seems to have been carved by the hands of the gods. Our eyes lock, and time stalls. It's as if the bustling world around us fades into a muted backdrop, a fleeting moment suspended in the air. A playful smirk dances on his lips, igniting a flurry of butterflies in my stomach, the kind that I hadn't felt since my teenage crush on the boy next door.

Before I can recover from the surprise of recognition, he strides toward me, each step deliberate and confident. I remind myself to breathe, but it feels as though my lungs are tangled in the shimmering strands of the lights hanging overhead. "You're here," he says, his voice smooth and warm, wrapping around me like a cashmere blanket. "I didn't think you'd make it."

"Surprise! I couldn't resist the allure of free cocktails and cutting-edge tech," I reply, injecting a teasing note into my voice to mask my rising nerves. "You know how it is—when the future calls, one must answer."

He laughs, a sound that feels like a melody all its own, and suddenly, the air thickens with an unspoken understanding. "Well, I'm glad you did. It's been a long road to get here, and tonight feels... monumental." His gaze drifts over the crowd, a mixture of pride and excitement glimmering in his blue eyes.

I take a sip of my cocktail, trying to anchor myself in the moment. "Monumental? It's a full-on spectacle. I half-expect the building to sprout wings and take flight."

"Ah, but that's the magic of it, isn't it?" He gestures around the rooftop, where laughter erupts like fireworks. "Innovation isn't just about technology; it's about the atmosphere we create. It's the spark that ignites new ideas."

"And what about the sparks between people?" I ask, tilting my head slightly, curious about the depths beneath his confident exterior. "Those are equally important."

He raises an eyebrow, intrigued. "Now you're getting philosophical on me."

"It's the champagne talking," I say, a cheeky grin breaking through my facade. "You should keep that in mind before offering me another drink."

The conversation flows easily between us, an unanticipated rhythm that feels natural and exhilarating. I find myself leaning closer, drawn in by the warmth of his presence. We exchange stories about our journeys, the ups and downs that brought us to this rooftop. He speaks of sleepless nights and relentless passion, his voice carrying an intensity that sends a shiver up my spine. I match his vulnerability with tales of my own—of moments spent in dimly lit cafés, fingers stained with ink as I mapped out dreams that often felt just out of reach.

But as the night unfolds, shadows of doubt creep into my mind. Here I am, an average girl with aspirations that could fill a small room, standing next to a man who embodies ambition and success. I find myself wondering if he sees me as an equal or merely a fleeting distraction in his whirlwind life. The pulse of the band shifts, a lively tune stirring the crowd into motion, and I'm swept along in the rhythm, a part of something larger yet also feeling the weight of my own inadequacy.

"Shall we dance?" he asks suddenly, his smile inviting. There's a glint of mischief in his eyes that I can't resist, despite the tension brewing in my chest.

"Dancing? You do realize my last dance was an awkward shuffle at a cousin's wedding?" I reply, playfully batting my eyelashes.

"Perfect! Awkward shuffles are all the rage in the tech world." His laughter rings out, infectious, and before I can protest further, he takes my hand, leading me toward the makeshift dance floor, which has transformed into a swirl of colorful skirts and sleek shoes.

As we begin to move, I lose myself in the music, my worries melting away like ice in the summer sun. He's surprisingly light on his feet, guiding me with a finesse that belies his tough exterior. Our bodies sway together, laughter punctuating the air, a delightful tension crackling like static electricity between us.

The crowd seems to fade away, and for a brief moment, it feels as though we are the only two people in this entire universe, sharing a secret amidst the chaos. The beat of the music echoes the rapid thump of my heart, and as I glance up at him, the spark in his eyes mirrors the thrill coursing through me. I want to believe that this moment is not just a flash in the pan, but the beginning of something remarkable. The world might still spin around us, but here, with him, it feels like time has finally taken a breath.

The music swells, a vibrant melody weaving through the air, lifting the atmosphere into something almost electric. Grant's hand rests lightly on the small of my back as we sway to the rhythm, the touch igniting sensations that dance across my skin like summer fireflies. His presence envelops me, a warm glow in the cool evening breeze, and with each beat, I feel myself leaning into him, my laughter mingling with the music, transforming the night into a tapestry of sound and sensation.

"You have quite the rhythm for a tech mogul," I tease, twisting slightly to catch a glimpse of his face. The band shifts into a lively tune, the kind that invites spontaneous movement. "I half expected you to have two left feet, given how serious you seem in all those interviews."

Grant chuckles, a low, rich sound that sends a thrill through me. "Don't let the sharp jawline fool you; I'm full of surprises. If you ask nicely, I might even show you my secret salsa moves." He winks, and I can't help but smile wider.

"Secret salsa moves? Now you've piqued my interest. But I warn you, my dance skills resemble those of a slightly tipsy giraffe."

"Perfect! I've always wanted to dance with a giraffe. Just think of the views!" He leans in, his breath warm against my ear, making it nearly impossible to focus on anything other than the way he makes me feel so alive, so seen.

As the song shifts into a slower melody, we draw closer, the space between us shrinking until it's filled with a breathless tension. His eyes hold mine, deep blue pools reflecting the shimmering lights around us. For a heartbeat, I lose myself in his gaze, the weight of everything else in the world dissolving. Yet, in that serene moment, a flicker of doubt crosses my mind. Can this be real? Is it possible that someone like Grant Rivers—so ambitious, so utterly captivating—would be interested in someone like me?

"What's that look for?" he asks, his voice pulling me from my thoughts. "You're not getting cold feet, are you?"

"Not cold feet, just a bit… introspective. You know, the weight of the world on my shoulders and all that." I attempt to keep my tone light, but my honesty slips through.

He raises an eyebrow, curiosity dancing in his expression. "Ah, a philosopher. Tell me more about your existential crisis while we're twirling under the stars."

"Only if you promise to share yours first," I shoot back, a playful grin spreading across my face. "I have a feeling it involves spreadsheets and startup pressure."

"Touché," he replies, shaking his head in mock defeat. "But really, it's not as dramatic as you might think. I mean, how often can you be the guy leading a revolution in tech? The pressure can be daunting, especially with investors breathing down your neck."

His candidness pulls me in deeper, and I find myself sharing my own struggles, how the chaos of life sometimes makes it hard to carve out my own space amid everyone else's expectations. "I feel like I'm always standing on the sidelines, waiting for my moment to jump in. It's exhausting."

"You know," he says, his voice softening, "you'd be surprised how many people feel the same way. Just because someone seems to have it all together doesn't mean they don't struggle. We all have our dance steps to learn."

"True," I nod, grateful for his insight. "But I don't want to be a wallflower forever. I want to leap out there, just once without fear of landing on my face."

ILLUMINATED BOUNDARIES

"Then let's leap together." His gaze intensifies, his sincerity pulling at something deep within me. "Let's make tonight a beginning. After all, the best dance partners are the ones who don't let you fall."

Before I can reply, the music shifts again, now a fast-paced rhythm that catches the crowd's attention. Grant's fingers gently intertwine with mine as he leads me back toward the center of the dance floor. The laughter and cheers of our fellow party-goers swirl around us like confetti, each person swept up in their own whirlwind of celebration.

"Time to unleash the giraffe!" I exclaim, my heart racing. We dive into the movement, twirling and spinning, letting the music guide us. In this moment, I shed my worries, my insecurities, and for the first time, I feel the thrill of pure, unadulterated joy.

As we dance, I lose track of time and space, our movements synchronizing effortlessly, and it's exhilarating. Grant matches my energy, his laughter ringing out like a beacon amidst the lively chaos. I catch glimpses of his colleagues watching us, a mix of admiration and surprise flickering across their faces, and for a moment, I revel in the attention.

Yet, just as I start to believe that maybe this night will mark the turning point I've longed for, a shadow interrupts our radiant bubble. A figure steps forward, and I recognize her immediately. Natalie, Grant's former assistant and now his right hand in the company, is clad in a sleek black dress that speaks of power and poise. Her presence commands the space around her, and the tension in the air thickens as she approaches.

"Grant, there you are!" she says, her tone a mixture of urgency and impatience. "We need to discuss the investor presentation before it's too late."

"Can't it wait?" he replies, his brow furrowing slightly. "I'm in the middle of—"

"Aren't you the one who always insists on being prepared?" She crosses her arms, her perfectly manicured nails tapping against her elbow, and I can almost see the gears turning in her head as she assesses our dynamic.

I catch Grant's eye, searching for a hint of what's going on behind his charming façade. "It's fine," I say, stepping back slightly to give him room. "We can talk later."

"Are you sure?" He looks conflicted, torn between duty and desire.

"Absolutely. Go save the day." I force a smile, though inside I feel a tiny pang of disappointment. I never wanted to be the distraction, the fleeting moment in his busy life.

"Right." He hesitates, then leans in, brushing his lips against my cheek, a soft gesture that sends a delightful shock through me. "I'll be back."

"Don't keep me waiting too long," I reply, channeling my inner bravado as he walks away.

As Grant disappears into the crowd, I can't shake the feeling that something pivotal has just shifted. I'm left standing amidst the joyous chaos, the lively dancefloor suddenly feeling a little too vast and empty without him. I swirl my cocktail, forcing myself to breathe, yet the doubt that had lingered in the shadows returns, whispering unsettling thoughts. Was it all just a spark—a fleeting connection that wouldn't endure in the harsh light of reality?

Before I can spiral too far, I take a deep breath, reminding myself that this night is still mine to embrace. The party continues around me, laughter and music flowing like a river, and I refuse to let a momentary interruption dim the glow of the evening. Time to dance like nobody's watching, even if a tech mogul's absence feels like an unfinished melody. I plunge into the rhythm, letting the music carry me forward, determined to make this night a memory worth cherishing.

ILLUMINATED BOUNDARIES 19

The air thrums with energy as the music shifts to a lively tune, one that pulls at the legs of everyone present, urging them to sway and spin. I shake off the fleeting disappointment of Grant's departure and let the rhythm envelop me, my feet finding their own beat as I move among the guests. The shimmering skyline of Manhattan provides a stunning backdrop, its lights glistening like stars that have decided to settle down for a soirée. I twirl, letting the soft fabric of my dress flutter around me like a vibrant flag, the sparkle of the evening reflecting in my eyes.

As I lose myself in the music, I notice a group of colleagues nearby, laughter spilling from their lips. They're animated, gesturing excitedly about some recent breakthrough in tech—probably something Grant spearheaded. The energy of the room is infectious, and I can't help but smile at the camaraderie that fills the air. It's a stark contrast to the little bubble of doubt that had threatened to take hold. I remind myself that I'm here to celebrate the dawn of something new, something extraordinary.

When the band transitions into a slower tune, I pause to take a sip of my drink, the cool liquid refreshing against the warmth of my skin. That's when I spot her—Natalie, standing by the edge of the dance floor, her expression a mix of determination and concern. She's flipping through her phone with the kind of intensity that suggests the world might end if she doesn't find what she's looking for.

"Are you okay?" I ask as I approach, my voice steady despite the thrumming in my chest.

Natalie looks up, startled, as if I've pulled her from an urgent mission. "Oh, hey! I didn't mean to ignore the party," she says, attempting to offer a smile that doesn't quite reach her eyes. "Just checking on some last-minute details for the pitch tomorrow. You know how it is."

"Always the overachiever," I tease gently, a playful glint in my eye. "Can't let a little thing like a grand opening distract you from world domination, can you?"

She chuckles, the tension easing slightly. "If only it were that glamorous. I just wish Grant would focus a bit more on the event and a little less on…" She trails off, glancing back toward the crowd, her eyes narrowing.

"On what?" I follow her gaze, but my view is blocked by a cluster of partygoers. "You mean me? I promise, I'm just as bewildered by this night as you are."

Natalie shakes her head, her expression growing serious. "It's not you, trust me. I just think Grant's a little too distracted. He's got a lot on his plate, and I don't know how much longer he can keep juggling everything."

"Maybe he just needs a little more fun in his life," I suggest, trying to lighten the mood. "Everyone deserves a break, especially the 'big tech guy' with the sharp jawline."

"Right, because 'big tech guy' is known for his stellar work-life balance," she quips, but her gaze softens. "I'm just concerned. He can be so driven that he forgets to take a breath. It's exhausting to watch."

"I get that." I lean against the railing, letting the cool metal ground me. "But it seems like he's surrounded by people who care. That's got to count for something, right?"

"Let's hope so," she murmurs, her eyes scanning the crowd. "The last thing we need is him burning out. He's got too much potential to fizzle out before he even gets started."

As if on cue, the music changes again, morphing into a rhythmic pulse that stirs the crowd into an energetic frenzy. I catch a glimpse of Grant weaving back through the throng, his eyes scanning for me. When he finally spots me, relief washes over his features, and he heads my way, cutting through the noise like a lighthouse beam cutting through fog.

"Sorry about that," he says, breathless as he reaches me. "I didn't mean to disappear. You were having too much fun without me."

"Hardly," I reply, a teasing lilt in my voice. "Just enjoying the view and trying to fend off the shadows of self-doubt."

He studies me for a moment, his expression shifting from playful to concerned. "You? You have no reason to doubt yourself. You lit up this room the moment you walked in."

Heat rushes to my cheeks, and I'm not sure if it's the compliment or the lingering energy from the dance floor that warms me. "You sure know how to flatter a girl."

"It's not flattery if it's true." He glances around, his gaze lingering on the buzz of activity. "Are you having a good time?"

"Absolutely! But it seems like there's a lot going on behind the scenes." I nod toward Natalie, who's still keeping an eye on the unfolding events, her phone now cradled in her palm like a precious artifact. "She seems a bit... preoccupied."

He follows my gaze, a shadow flickering across his face. "She's my anchor, really. Without her, I'd probably be lost at sea."

"Lucky for you, then." I can't help but tease again, trying to lighten the atmosphere. "I can't imagine navigating those waters alone."

"You have no idea," he replies with a laugh, the tension in his shoulders easing as he draws me back into the moment. "But I'm glad you're here. It makes all of this feel more... real."

The dance floor beckons once more, and without missing a beat, Grant takes my hand and leads me back into the swirling mass of laughter and music. It's intoxicating—the rhythm, the laughter, the warmth of his hand in mine. We move together effortlessly, as if our bodies were designed for this moment.

But as the music pulses around us, an unexpected commotion erupts at the edge of the rooftop, shattering the joyous atmosphere. A group of well-dressed attendees has gathered, their expressions alarmed, voices rising in urgency. I catch snippets of conversation—a mention of a disagreement, something about "the deal"—and the mood shifts, darkening like a cloud passing over the moon.

"What's happening?" I ask Grant, trying to decipher the scene unfolding before us.

His expression hardens, the carefree glimmer in his eyes replaced by a sharp focus. "I'm not sure, but I'd better go see."

Before I can protest, he's slipping through the crowd, leaving me momentarily frozen in place, the sudden absence of his warmth like a chill on my skin. I inch closer to the group, straining to hear the hushed tones.

"It's all falling apart! We can't afford to lose this," a voice hisses, panic threading through the words. My heart races as I realize they're discussing the future of Pulsar Co., the very foundation of what brought us all together tonight.

"Grant can't be expected to manage this!" another voice cuts in, laced with frustration. "If he doesn't come back with a solution, we're all in trouble."

A surge of unease sweeps through me. Grant had just been dancing with me, lost in the moment, but now, he's thrust back into the reality of running a tech empire, and the weight of that responsibility is palpable.

I start to edge closer to the circle when suddenly, a loud crash echoes through the air, followed by an ominous silence that blankets the rooftop. Everyone turns, their attention yanked away from their conversations, eyes wide with shock. The noise seemed to erupt from the direction Grant had gone, and my heart drops as dread pools in my stomach.

Pushing past the crowd, I reach the edge of the throng, my pulse racing with each step. I scan the faces for Grant, but what I find instead is chaos—people are moving in all directions, their faces masks of confusion. I struggle to keep my footing as I navigate the sea of bodies, each heartbeat resonating like a drum.

And then I see him—Grant, standing near the edge, his back to me, and the world feels as though it's slowed to a standstill. In his hand is a briefcase, the contents spilling out, papers fluttering in the night breeze like lost dreams, each one carrying the weight of everything we had hoped for.

My breath catches, and just as I call his name, a figure lunges forward from the shadows, their intentions as dark as the night itself. Everything hinges on that moment, the air heavy with anticipation, and as their silhouette moves to collide with Grant, I realize that the evening's joy could unravel into chaos with a single, reckless action.

Chapter 3: Misfires and Malfunctions

The gala buzzed with the energy of ambition and the clinking of crystal glasses, an opulent affair adorned with twinkling lights and the sharp aroma of exotic hors d'oeuvres that mingled with the crisp scent of polished oak. I stood at the edge of the crowd, my gaze flitting between the bustling guests in their tailored suits and glittering gowns, and the elaborate tech demonstrations that were meant to dazzle. My heart danced with the rhythm of the music, a jazzy number that intertwined with the low hum of conversation, creating a vibrant tapestry of sound.

And then, as if orchestrated by some unseen conductor, the chaos began. Screens flickered erratically, a visual cacophony that turned the sleek presentations into chaotic bursts of color. I watched as one of the drones, sleek and sophisticated, wobbled mid-air, its navigation system clearly having a moment of existential crisis. It dipped and swooped, completely disregarding its programmed path, before careening toward me with the grace of a drunken bird. I stood frozen, half-amused, half-terrified, as it hovered inches from my face, its whirring blades brushing against my hair.

"Get it together, Stella," I muttered under my breath, an ironic twist of fate not lost on me. I had spent my whole life trying to keep my own magic in check, an energy that sometimes seeped out like a leaky faucet, manifesting in the oddest of ways. My heart raced. Was this my fault? I could practically feel the collective tension of the room as guests diverted their attention to the spectacle unfolding. Grant, ever the composed host, was at the helm, trying to regain control as he flashed that charming smile that could disarm anyone, yet his eyes betrayed a hint of panic.

"Is this part of the show?" one of the guests quipped, a high-pitched laugh ringing out over the drone's increasing whirr. I couldn't help but snicker at the absurdity of it all. Grant shot me a quick, desperate glance, and I lifted my shoulders in a casual shrug, half-defensive and half-apologetic. My smirk was unintentional, yet it broke through the tension like a breath of fresh air, igniting a flicker of understanding between us.

With a sudden burst of self-preservation, I stepped back as the drone veered toward a tower of champagne glasses, the golden bubbles catching the light in an intoxicating dance. A split second later, it collided with the glass tower in a shower of sparkling shards, and time seemed to slow as the sounds of gasps echoed in the air, drowning out the jazz. My heart sank as I absorbed the look of horror on Grant's face—his meticulously arranged display now a glittering mess on the marble floor.

"Perfect," I whispered, the guilt twisting in my gut like a coil tightening around my heart. My magic had always been a wild card, an unpredictable force that manifested when I least wanted it. I wondered if my presence had jinxed the event. If I had set this off without even trying.

As Grant hurried to address the crowd, a forced laugh on his lips as he assured them the evening would continue without a hitch, I slipped away, my heels tapping softly against the polished floor. The room was swirling, a heady mixture of champagne and laughter, but the brilliance of it all was overshadowed by my internal turmoil. I maneuvered through clusters of eager tech enthusiasts, exchanging brief pleasantries while my mind raced. How could I have let this happen?

Just outside the main ballroom, I leaned against the cool marble wall, letting the silence envelop me. The twinkling lights of the gala felt miles away, their vibrancy dulled by the weight of my thoughts. A part of me wanted to sink into the shadows and disappear entirely, but the other part—the reckless, rebellious spirit that had sparked my journey in the first place—simmered just beneath the surface.

Perhaps it was a necessary misfire, a demonstration of the chaos that often accompanied my magic.

"Stella!" Grant's voice cut through the haze, sharp and bright. I looked up to find him striding toward me, his earlier composure replaced by an urgency that made my pulse quicken. "You alright?"

"Sure," I said, offering him a smile that felt more like a grimace. "Just a little... overwhelmed. You know how it is, right? One minute you're mingling, the next you're dodging drones and broken glass."

He chuckled, though the tension remained in his eyes. "It was quite a spectacle. I didn't realize we were hosting a demolition derby." His sarcasm dripped like honey, sweet yet biting, pulling a genuine laugh from me. "Though I doubt that was in the brochure."

"Definitely not in my contract," I replied, the air between us crackling with an undeniable spark. His laughter faded, leaving a moment of charged silence that stretched between us, thick with unsaid words and the weight of the night's mishaps.

"I've got to make an announcement, but..." he hesitated, his gaze lingering on mine as if weighing something crucial. "I need to know if you're okay. I don't want you to feel responsible for what happened."

I took a deep breath, the warmth of his concern wrapping around me like a soft blanket. "It wasn't just me. These things happen, right? You can't control everything. Besides, it made for a memorable night."

"Memorable, sure. A disaster? Maybe." He rubbed the back of his neck, frustration mingling with a hint of amusement. "But I'd rather have a perfectly executed evening. With you, preferably."

"Is that so?" My heart leaped at his words, teasingly playful. "You're going to have to tell me how you plan to prevent future mishaps, then."

"Easy," he replied, leaning closer, the warmth of his presence a stark contrast to the cool air surrounding us. "Next time, I'll have you wear a safety helmet."

We both laughed, the tension easing just a little as I considered the wildness of the night. I had a strange feeling that our shared experience was just the beginning, a prelude to something far more tangled and exhilarating than either of us could predict.

The night unfurled like an elaborate tapestry, shimmering with the remnants of laughter and the sweet tang of spilled champagne. I lingered near the exit, still caught in the whirlwind of the chaotic demonstration. The extravagant venue was now a patchwork of scattered glass and lingering echoes of Grant's voice, attempting to mask the awkwardness with charm. My feet, snug in their heels, shifted uneasily on the polished floor as I scanned the dimly lit space.

A myriad of emotions swirled within me—guilt, exhilaration, and an odd sense of belonging. In that moment, I was a performer, caught between the stage and the wings, teetering on the edge of something exhilarating and terrifying. The vibrant chatter faded into a dull hum as I stepped outside, welcomed by the crisp night air that wrapped around me like a much-needed embrace. The stars twinkled above, indifferent to my misadventures, their distant brilliance echoing the scattered chaos within.

My thoughts drifted back to Grant, the way his expression shifted from shock to amusement, those moments suspended in the air like the drone itself, hovering between embarrassment and delight. I couldn't shake the feeling that our exchange had woven a thread of connection—one that promised to complicate my already chaotic life. What was it about the way he looked at me that sent my heart into a fitful dance?

With each step away from the gala, my heels echoed a soft rhythm against the cobblestones, a stark contrast to the vibrant pulse of the party I was leaving behind. I made my way toward the nearby park, its quiet charm offering solace from the relentless energy of the night. Moonlight spilled through the trees, casting gentle shadows that played tricks on my imagination. The scent of damp earth mingled with the faint sweetness of flowers, creating a heady mix that felt both grounding and ethereal.

Finding a secluded bench, I sank into the cool wood, letting out a breath I hadn't realized I was holding. A cool breeze whispered past, carrying with it the muffled sounds of the party, now a distant echo. I closed my eyes for a moment, allowing the soft rustling of leaves to lull me into a meditative calm. Just as I began to relax, my phone buzzed insistently in my pocket, shattering the peace like a sudden clap of thunder.

With a sigh, I pulled it out and glanced at the screen—an unexpected text from Grant, a splash of blue against the backdrop of muted colors. *You disappeared too quickly. I hope the drones didn't scare you off.*

I couldn't help but chuckle at the absurdity of it all. The mischief that brewed inside me sparked to life again, fueled by the playful challenge his words presented. *Scare me off? Hardly. I'm just rethinking my career as a professional drone dodger.* I hit send, my fingers dancing over the screen, each tap an echo of my wry humor.

His reply was almost immediate. *I'll add that to the list of talents I'm looking for in my new assistant. Also, can I offer you a drink? Preferably one without drones involved this time?*

A thrill coursed through me, the warmth of possibility wrapping around my heart. It was a strange sensation, inviting yet daunting, as if I were standing on the precipice of something unknown. I hesitated, biting my lip, aware of the kaleidoscope of feelings swirling in my chest. *Only if it comes with a complimentary safety helmet.*

The laugh emoji that followed made me smile, lightening the tension that had settled into my bones. His responses felt like a delicate dance, each exchange a step toward something more vibrant than the humdrum of my everyday life. I could almost see the twinkle in his eye as he typed. How about I meet you at The Loft? I promise no drones, just a rooftop view and a little peace and quiet.

A flash of excitement surged through me at the thought of being with him again, even amid the uncertainty of the evening's previous chaos. I was unsure whether it was my reckless spirit or a spark of genuine curiosity about him that propelled me to reply. Deal. But if it gets too quiet, I might start bringing my own chaos.

The moment I hit send, a rush of adrenaline pulsed through my veins, exhilarating and terrifying all at once. I could hardly believe I was entertaining the thought of meeting him again, especially after the embarrassment of the party. Yet the prospect of sharing a drink, of diving deeper into the labyrinth of his mind, felt too enticing to resist.

The night air was alive with the sounds of distant laughter and music as I made my way to The Loft. Each step felt lighter than the last, as if my feet were buoyed by the excitement swirling within me. As I approached the entrance, the warm glow of lights spilled onto the street, casting a golden hue that beckoned like a lighthouse on a dark night.

Once inside, I was enveloped by a cozy ambiance, soft jazz playing in the background, intermingled with the murmurs of patrons enjoying their own conversations. The decor was a blend of industrial chic and bohemian flair, a stylish oasis high above the bustling streets. I spotted Grant at the bar, his silhouette cutting a striking figure against the backdrop of glowing bottles.

He turned as I approached, a wide smile breaking across his face, and suddenly the chaos of the earlier evening felt like a distant memory. "There you are! I was beginning to think the drones had abducted you," he teased, his eyes dancing with amusement.

"Just needed a moment to gather my thoughts—and possibly my dignity," I replied, taking a seat next to him, feeling a rush of warmth wash over me. The bartender approached, and Grant ordered us each a drink, his voice smooth and confident, a stark contrast to the fluttering nerves in my stomach.

"What are we drinking?" I asked, curious as he leaned in closer, the scent of his cologne mixing with the faint aroma of citrus from the bar.

"Something refreshing. Trust me, it'll be worth it." He winked, and I couldn't help but mirror his grin, a wave of excitement crashing over me.

As we settled into our conversation, the earlier tension began to dissolve, replaced by a flow of easy banter. We shared stories of our most awkward moments, laughter bubbling between us like champagne, each revelation drawing us closer. I found myself drawn into his charm, the way he spoke with passion, weaving his dreams into the fabric of our dialogue.

"What about you?" he asked, leaning back, his curiosity piqued. "What's your most embarrassing moment?"

I hesitated, considering the delightful misfires of my life. "Well, there was that time I tried to impress my friends with my baking skills. Let's just say it turned into a fire hazard rather than a culinary masterpiece."

His laughter echoed through the bar, drawing glances from other patrons, but I felt a thrill in his enjoyment. "Fire hazard? Now that's a story worth telling. What happened?"

With each word, I unveiled snippets of my life, a mosaic of mishaps and triumphs. The connection between us deepened, each laugh and shared glance illuminating the night like the stars outside. Little did I know, the misfires of my past were only the beginning, setting the stage for an unexpected journey that lay ahead, one that would weave our lives together in ways I couldn't yet imagine.

As the night unfolded beneath the twinkling lights of The Loft, I found myself swept up in a current of conversation that felt both exhilarating and terrifying. Each laugh we shared echoed off the walls, creating a cocoon of warmth that wrapped around us like a soft blanket on a chilly night. The initial tension that had lingered between Grant and me dissolved, leaving behind an electric buzz of attraction and unspoken words.

"Okay, spill it," he said, leaning closer, his expression a mix of playful curiosity and genuine interest. "What's the most absurd thing you've ever done in the name of love?"

I paused, biting my lip as I sifted through memories like a fisherman combing through the ocean for treasure. "Well, there was that time I decided to impress a guy by cooking a gourmet dinner. I may or may not have mistaken cayenne pepper for paprika."

"Ah, the classic misfire. How did that go?" he prodded, his eyes sparkling with mischief.

"It was a disaster," I laughed, remembering the fiery red sauce that had turned the dinner party into a scene from a horror film. "Let's just say he spent more time gulping water than actually enjoying the meal. We ended up ordering pizza instead."

Grant chuckled, the sound rich and full, as if the absurdity of my tale delighted him. "I like a woman who isn't afraid to set her culinary ambitions ablaze. Quite literally."

Our drinks arrived, the bartender placing two expertly crafted cocktails in front of us. I took a sip, the refreshing blend of flavors sending a jolt of energy through me, igniting my senses. "What about you? Any embarrassing attempts to woo someone?"

He tilted his head thoughtfully, a smile teasing the corners of his lips. "Let's see... there was a time I tried to serenade a girl with a guitar I could barely play. I thought I was channeling my inner rock star. Turns out, I was more of a cat in a blender."

I burst into laughter, the imagery so vividly absurd that I could hardly contain myself. "You? A cat in a blender? I can't picture that at all."

He raised an eyebrow, clearly enjoying the moment. "It's true! But she thought it was adorable, so maybe I should have kept at it."

The conversation flowed effortlessly, each exchange weaving a tapestry of connection. As the night wore on, we slipped into comfortable silences, the kind that spoke volumes without the need for words. I felt a magnetic pull toward him, a curiosity that tugged at the edges of my mind. Just as I was about to ask him more about his life, a figure approached, interrupting our bubble of intimacy.

"Grant!" The voice was sharp, cutting through our conversation like a knife. A woman with sleek black hair and a designer dress approached, her heels clicking assertively against the floor. She had an air of confidence that commanded attention, and her gaze flicked between us with barely concealed annoyance. "There you are. We need to talk about the event. Now."

The sudden shift in Grant's demeanor was palpable. He straightened, a shadow crossing his face as he exchanged a glance with the woman. "Of course, Eleanor. Just give me a minute."

My heart sank as I watched him. The atmosphere between us shifted, a palpable tension that made it feel like we were standing on the precipice of something deeper, and then suddenly, it was being pulled away. Eleanor's presence was a dark cloud looming over our bright moment.

"Sorry about this," Grant murmured to me, his eyes softening for a brief moment before he turned to Eleanor. "Can we discuss it over there?" He gestured to a quieter corner of the bar, his tone steady yet tinged with reluctance.

"Now," she insisted, her voice leaving no room for negotiation.

I felt a pang of disappointment, an ache in my chest at the abrupt interruption. As they moved away, I fumbled with my drink, swirling the colorful liquid and watching the ice clink against the glass. The cheerful ambiance of the bar felt suffocating suddenly, a stark contrast to the bubbling chemistry I had just shared with Grant.

After a moment of staring into my glass, I caught snippets of their conversation, the tension palpable even from a distance. Eleanor's tone was authoritative, while Grant's responses were measured, almost defensive. My stomach twisted, a strange mixture of jealousy and confusion roiling within me. Was she a colleague? A former flame?

I decided I needed air, a breath of freedom from the tightening knot of uncertainty that clung to me. As I slipped outside, the cool breeze caressed my cheeks, a welcome relief from the warmth of the bar. The stars shimmered overhead, their distant glow a reminder of the vastness of the world beyond this moment.

Leaning against the railing of the rooftop terrace, I took a deep breath, allowing the crispness of the night to wash over me. But the tranquility didn't last long. Just as I began to gather my thoughts, I heard footsteps approaching.

"Hey," Grant's voice broke through the stillness, his expression a mix of frustration and concern. "I didn't mean to leave you like that. I just—"

"Don't worry about it," I interjected, forcing a smile that felt more like a mask. "Eleanor seems... important."

"Yeah, she is," he admitted, running a hand through his hair, a gesture that somehow made him look even more handsome and disheveled. "But I don't want to talk about her. I want to talk about you."

My heart fluttered at his words, the genuine desire in his voice lifting the weight from my shoulders. "Okay, let's talk then. How do you manage to juggle all this chaos?" I gestured vaguely at the city skyline, lit up like a thousand dreams, each twinkle a potential story waiting to unfold.

Grant chuckled, his eyes brightening. "Honestly? I don't know if I do. I think I just roll with the punches, try not to let the chaos consume me."

"Roll with the punches," I echoed, leaning closer. "I could use some of that wisdom in my life."

He met my gaze, the intensity of his blue eyes holding me captive. "You've got it in you, you know. I've seen how you handle things. You've got a spark."

Just as I was about to respond, a loud crash erupted from inside the bar, the sound sharp and jarring against the tranquility of the night. We both turned, eyes wide, as a collective gasp rose from the crowd.

"What was that?" I exclaimed, a rush of adrenaline spiking through me.

"Stay here!" Grant said, urgency in his voice as he moved toward the entrance.

"No way," I insisted, my heart racing. "I'm coming with you."

Together, we hurried back inside, and the sight that met us was chaos incarnate. Tables were overturned, and people were standing, some frozen in shock, others rushing toward the exit.

"Get out!" someone shouted, and my pulse quickened.

Before I could ask what was happening, I caught sight of Eleanor, her face pale as she pointed toward the bar. Grant rushed forward, and I followed, adrenaline surging through me.

As we reached the bar, the source of the chaos became clear. One of the large glass panels behind the bar had shattered, shards of glass glinting ominously on the floor. A flicker of movement caught my eye, and I realized the drone—the same one that had wreaked havoc at the party—was hovering menacingly above the crowd.

"Not again!" I gasped, and the panic that had been simmering just below the surface burst forth like a dam breaking.

"Stay close!" Grant shouted, and I instinctively reached for his hand, the warmth grounding me amid the rising hysteria.

But before we could react, the drone suddenly surged forward, its lights flashing ominously. A gasp rippled through the crowd, and I felt the air thicken with a tangible sense of impending chaos.

"Stella, look out!" Grant shouted just as the drone darted toward me, and in that moment, I understood that my magic—whatever I had accidentally unleashed—was about to return with a vengeance.

And then everything went dark.

Chapter 4: An Unplanned Meeting

The soft chime of the bell above my door signals Grant's entrance, a sound that feels both familiar and foreign. The warm glow of my shop embraces him as he steps inside, trailing hints of crisp autumn air mingled with the fragrant undertones of the orange and clove candle he cradles in his hands. The moment seems to stretch, suspended in the light that filters through the window, painting him in soft hues of gold and amber.

"Just thought you'd like to know," he says, his voice low, laced with a gravelly warmth that makes my heart skip. "This is my new favorite." He gestures toward the flickering flame, which dances merrily in its glass jar, as if it has a personality of its own. I can't help but smile, a small twist of pride blooming in my chest.

"Really?" I raise an eyebrow, feigning nonchalance, though inside, I'm secretly elated. "You must be hard to please if that's your favorite."

He chuckles, the sound resonating in the small space, wrapping around us like an embrace. "I'm notoriously picky," he admits, leaning against the counter, a relaxed posture that hints at his confidence. "But I'm serious. There's something about it that just... I don't know, speaks to me. It's got soul."

I feel a flutter of warmth creeping up my neck at his words. A candle with soul. What a lovely thought, one I never imagined would be attributed to my creations. "I put a little magic in every batch," I tease, my tone light, but I can feel the weight of something more between us.

He tilts his head, a smirk playing on his lips. "Well, it's working. Or maybe it's just you. There's definitely a spark in here." The compliment hangs in the air, charged and electric, and my heart races. We stand there, gazing at each other across the polished wood of the counter, the vibrant orange wax casting playful shadows across his face.

Breaking the spell, I turn to busy myself with the display of candles lining the shelves. My fingers glide over the smooth glass, pretending to arrange them while my mind races. Grant, with his tousled hair and easy smile, is both a distraction and a temptation. A week ago, I was adamant about keeping my distance after our chaotic first meeting. But here he was, clearly not deterred, and now it felt like the universe had conspired to throw us back together.

"What brings you here today?" I ask, trying to keep my tone light, masking the nervous energy swirling in my stomach.

"I thought I'd come and see what else you've been cooking up," he replies, glancing around the shop with genuine interest. "Maybe I could get a head start on my holiday shopping."

A flutter of hope bubbles in my chest. "Holiday shopping already? You're either a planner or a masochist." I shoot him a playful look.

"Definitely the former," he says with a wink. "I like to get it all done early. You never know when the chaos will hit, and then it's too late."

"That's a good philosophy," I nod, secretly impressed. "I could take a cue from you."

His eyes flicker to mine, a hint of mischief dancing within them. "Or you could just take my number and let me help you out."

My laughter bubbles up, unexpected and light, shattering the remnants of my careful facade. "Oh really? So now you're volunteering to be my holiday assistant? I must say, that's a tempting offer."

He steps closer, the space between us shrinking, the scent of his cologne mixing with the citrusy aroma of the candles. "I promise I'm good at wrapping things up."

"Is that so?" I arch an eyebrow, feeling bold. "You mean you're good at giving gifts or just good at tying pretty bows?"

He chuckles, the rich sound resonating through the shop. "A little of both, actually. My mother would be proud."

"Now I'm curious about the rest of your family," I reply, my interest piqued. "What else have you inherited from them?"

"Let's see," he leans back, a mock serious expression crossing his face. "I got my father's stubbornness, my mother's charm, and an unfortunate penchant for mischief."

"An intriguing combination," I say, leaning against the counter, matching his playful energy. "Sounds like you might be trouble."

"Only if you let me be," he counters, his gaze unwavering.

The air thickens with unspoken possibilities, and I find myself momentarily lost in the depths of his hazel eyes, where warmth and challenge blend into something intoxicating. Just then, a bell jingles at the door, breaking our spell, and an elderly woman enters, her face brightening at the sight of the candles.

"Good afternoon!" I call, forcing myself to step back from the magnetic pull of Grant's presence.

"Hello, dear! I just came by to get more of that lovely lavender you had last week," she chirps, bustling toward the shelves.

As I help her select her favorites, I can feel Grant lingering, watching us with an amused smile. He eventually wanders closer, picking up a lavender candle and holding it aloft like a trophy. "I can see why you're popular around here," he murmurs, leaning in to me, his voice low. "You've got quite the talent."

"Or perhaps I just know how to charm my customers," I quip, enjoying the banter while stealing glances at the woman, who is now selecting another scent.

"Admit it," he says, his eyes narrowing playfully. "You're here to woo me with your candle magic."

"Maybe I am," I reply, unable to hide my smile.

"You might have just sealed the deal."

And just like that, the energy between us shifts again, warm and inviting, with an undercurrent of excitement that promises so much more than just candles.

The elderly woman finishes her selection, and I wrap her candles in a crisp layer of tissue paper, each fold precise and delicate, as if I'm handling something far more precious than wax and wicks. Grant leans casually against the shelf, his presence a comforting weight in the room, as though he belongs here just as much as I do. The rhythmic crinkle of paper fills the space, punctuated by the woman's delighted chatter about her granddaughter's upcoming wedding, pulling me into the world of lace and vows while Grant watches with an easy smile.

"Do you think she'll want a lavender candle as a centerpiece?" he muses, his eyes sparkling with mischief. "Or maybe something in a more, say, romantic color?"

"Lavender is always a classic, but maybe she should go for something a little more daring, like a spicy cinnamon," I reply, tossing him a playful glance. "After all, weddings should be about turning up the heat."

"Spicy and daring, huh? Sounds like you're talking about a wedding cake and not just candles," he laughs, the sound warm and inviting.

The woman laughs too, glancing back at us with a twinkle in her eye. "Oh dear, if only it were that simple! My granddaughter wants a traditional affair, and here I am trying to sneak in a few modern touches."

"Who could blame you? Tradition can be lovely, but it doesn't hurt to add a little fun," I say, handing over the wrapped candles with a flourish. "Here you go! May your granddaughter's wedding be as delightful as these scents."

"Thank you, dear! You're a gem," she replies, beaming at me before heading for the door.

Once she leaves, the shop settles into a cozy silence. Grant steps closer again, his gaze intent. "You're really good at this," he says, nodding toward the door as if it somehow holds the key to understanding me. "You make everyone feel special."

"It's just candles," I say, brushing off the compliment, though a small swell of pride rises within me. "But I guess it's about creating an experience. You light a candle, and suddenly, everything feels a little more... magical."

"See? That's it right there," he gestures animatedly, his hands weaving through the air like he's conducting an orchestra. "You've got this way of weaving in the idea of magic into something as simple as wax. And here I thought I was just buying a candle."

"It's not just a candle," I correct him, leaning on the counter with a playful smirk. "It's an invitation to a moment—like a brief escape."

He nods, considering my words, and for a moment, the room is filled with an electric stillness, a current running beneath our playful banter. "So what moment do you escape to?" he asks softly, his curiosity turning more serious.

"I think I escape to a place where life is less complicated," I admit, my heart racing a little. "Where scents can tell stories, and every flicker of a flame can remind you that there's beauty in the ordinary."

His brow furrows, and the playful spark dims for just a moment. "Do you not like the ordinary?"

I hesitate, caught off guard by the weight of his question. "It's not that I don't like it, but... it can feel stifling sometimes. You know?"

He seems to understand, a knowing look crossing his features. "Like you're waiting for something to happen?"

"Exactly," I reply, surprised by my own honesty. "I love this shop and the candles, but sometimes I wonder if I'm meant for something more, something... different."

"Like what?" he presses, his gaze steady and encouraging.

"Like adventure, maybe?" I muse, biting my lip. "I want to experience the world outside these walls. But every time I think about it, I get scared."

"Scared of what?"

"Of leaving everything behind, I guess," I whisper, a little embarrassed to lay my feelings bare. "I've worked so hard to create this, and the thought of walking away feels like betrayal."

He takes a step closer, the space between us shrinking until I can feel the warmth radiating from him, as inviting as the glow of my candles. "But what if walking away leads you to something better?"

My breath catches at the weight of his words. "And what if it doesn't?" I counter, searching his eyes for any hint of insincerity, but all I find is genuine encouragement.

"Then you come back, and you've still got this," he gestures to the shop, the warm light illuminating the array of candles around us. "But if you don't try, you'll always wonder."

For a heartbeat, time stretches, and I feel as if the universe is pushing me to leap. But before I can respond, the bell jingles again, heralding another customer's entrance. A tall figure strides in, dressed in a tailored jacket and a confident smile, which instantly shifts the energy of the room.

"Good afternoon! I'm looking for something unique, something that tells a story," he announces, his gaze sweeping the shop as if searching for a hidden treasure.

"Ah, I think you've come to the right place," I say, forcing my thoughts back into the moment, tucking away the conversation I was having with Grant like a cherished secret.

Grant sidesteps, allowing me to take the lead, but I can feel the weight of his eyes on me, supportive and curious. I launch into my sales pitch, highlighting the fragrances and their origins, gesturing toward the array of candles like a proud artist showcasing her work.

As I explain the notes of sandalwood and jasmine, I steal glances at Grant, who watches me with a proud smile.

The newcomer, engrossed in my words, seems pleased. "I can tell you really love what you do. How do you come up with these blends?"

"It's all about inspiration," I say, a flicker of excitement sparking within me. "Each scent is a story waiting to be told."

"And what's the story behind the orange and clove?" he inquires, a glint of interest in his eyes.

"That one's about cozy nights in, with friends gathered around a fire, sharing laughter and stories," I reply, my heart racing as I remember my last gathering with friends, the room filled with the warmth of candlelight and connection.

"Sounds perfect for winter," he says, nodding appreciatively. "I'll take one of those."

As I ring him up, I feel Grant's presence lingering just behind me, a quiet support as I navigate this unexpected shift in the atmosphere. With every exchange, I sense something inside me expanding, as if the walls of my little shop are not just boundaries but rather a launchpad for the adventures that await outside. And as the bell chimes yet again with the next customer, I can't help but wonder if, perhaps, that leap of faith isn't as far away as I had imagined.

As the last customer bids me farewell, I take a moment to breathe in the comforting scents surrounding me—the familiar notes of lavender, vanilla, and freshly poured wax mingling in the air. The shop feels like a refuge, a cocoon woven from warmth and light. I glance at Grant, who has settled into a corner of the room, his hands casually tucked into his pockets, but his gaze is sharp and attentive, watching everything unfold with genuine interest.

"Looks like you've got a little fan club forming," he teases, his voice laced with playful sarcasm as the last customer retreats, her laughter echoing down the street.

"Just doing my job," I say with a shrug, pretending to brush off the compliment, though a blush creeps into my cheeks. "Besides, I can't take all the credit. The candles sell themselves."

"Is that so?" he asks, crossing his arms, leaning slightly against the shelf. "So you're saying it's not you who's charming them into spending money?"

"I mean, it's a combined effort," I concede, unable to suppress a grin. "But if I'm honest, it's all about the atmosphere. Candles create magic, you know?"

"Magic," he repeats, his tone thoughtful. "You keep saying that word. Are you sure you're not a witch?"

"Not unless I've secretly enrolled in a spell-casting course," I quip back, laughter dancing in my voice. "But maybe I should look into it. I could use a little enchantment in my life."

He chuckles, and the sound ignites a warmth inside me that stretches beyond our playful banter. "There's something enchanting about this place," he says, gesturing to the cozy corners and flickering flames. "It feels like you've bottled up pieces of your soul in every candle."

For a moment, I consider his words, the truth of them resonating deep within me. "I suppose that's what I'm trying to do. Capture moments, feelings, and memories in a way that lets others experience them, too."

"That's powerful," he replies, his gaze suddenly serious. "And rare. Most people just sell things; they don't think about the story behind them."

I nod, appreciating his understanding, feeling a connection deepen between us. "It's everything I've wanted to create. A sanctuary for anyone who walks through that door."

"Speaking of stories," he shifts, a glimmer of mischief returning to his expression. "What's yours? What brought you here, to this charming little shop, in the heart of Brooklyn?"

My heart skips, the question stirring something inside me. I've rarely shared the full story with anyone, let alone someone I've only just met. "It's a long one," I hedge, glancing at the clock ticking softly above us.

"I'm not going anywhere," he assures me, settling in as if he were about to savor a fine wine.

"Okay, but promise not to judge," I say, biting my lip, steeling myself. "I grew up in a small town where everyone knew everyone. It was suffocating in a way. The expectations, the sameness... I always felt like I needed to escape."

"Escape?" he prompts, intrigued.

"Yeah. I left for college, thinking I'd never look back. I studied business, thinking that was the key to success." I pause, a soft laugh escaping my lips. "Turns out I hated it. But I discovered a passion for crafting candles in my dorm room, pouring my frustrations and dreams into each one."

"And then?" he leans in, eyes glinting with curiosity.

"I returned home, determined to find a way to share that passion," I continue, warmth blooming in my chest. "So I saved up, took a leap of faith, and opened this place."

"It sounds like quite a journey," he says, his tone softening. "And brave."

"Maybe a bit foolish," I reply, shaking my head, but there's a thrill in my veins as I share my truth. "But it feels right. This shop is my heart."

"And what do you want?" he asks, his voice suddenly serious, as though he's asking more than just about my ambitions.

"To create a space where people feel at home. Where they can pause and breathe, even for just a moment," I say, the conviction in my voice surprising even me.

"I think you're doing that," he says, sincerity etched in his features. "You're creating something special, and I can see it's making a difference."

The door swings open, a gust of brisk autumn air swirling in, carrying the scent of fallen leaves and distant city sounds. A young woman steps inside, her cheeks flushed and a scarf wrapped tightly around her neck. She glances at us, the surprise evident on her face as she takes in the warmth of the shop.

"Sorry to interrupt!" she exclaims, her voice brightening the room. "I just saw the sign outside and couldn't resist."

"No interruption at all!" I say cheerily, glancing at Grant, who is now watching her with mild amusement. "What can I help you find today?"

She peruses the shelves, her fingers tracing the jars. "I'm actually looking for something to help with my anxiety," she admits, her eyes darting to mine, vulnerability flickering in her expression. "A candle that might help me calm down?"

"Absolutely," I respond, the instinct to help kicking in. "What scents do you find soothing?"

"Lavender always helps," she replies hesitantly. "But I'd love something new, too. I'm open to suggestions."

As I begin to guide her through the array of options, I feel Grant stepping slightly back, his presence still strong but allowing me to take the lead. I pull a few candles, explaining their properties while the woman listens intently, and as we talk, the earlier connection with Grant lingers in the air, unbroken and warm.

"I think you'll find this one particularly calming," I say, holding up a soft green candle infused with chamomile and mint. "It's designed to help with relaxation and clarity."

Her eyes widen. "That sounds perfect! I'll take it."

As I ring her up, a sudden thought crosses my mind, pulling at my heartstrings. I glance at Grant, whose expression seems to have shifted subtly. He's observing the interaction, but there's a flicker of concern dancing in his eyes that makes me question if he's truly okay.

"Thanks for your help," the woman says, beaming at me as I wrap her candle with care. "You have a lovely shop. I'll definitely come back."

"Thank you! Take care," I call after her, watching as she exits with a bright smile, a flicker of hope in her step.

Turning back to Grant, I open my mouth to ask what's bothering him when the bell rings again, announcing yet another customer. This one, however, isn't a casual shopper but a familiar face: Sarah, my old friend from college, looking frantic, her cheeks flushed and eyes wide.

"Julia!" she calls, her voice high with urgency. "I need your help—now!"

My stomach drops, a rush of adrenaline coursing through me. "What's wrong?"

Before she can answer, the door swings open behind her, and I feel a wave of unease wash over me as I catch a glimpse of a tall figure in a dark coat, their presence imposing.

"Everything okay here?" Grant asks, sensing the shift in energy as he steps closer, his posture protective.

But before I can respond, Sarah's voice cuts through the tension, her eyes darting from me to the newcomer, confusion flooding her features. "You need to hear this, Julia. There's been an accident, and it's about..."

The stranger moves closer, his face half-shadowed, leaving me caught between the comfort of my candles and the rising storm of uncertainty. My heart pounds in my chest, an urgent thrum that matches the brewing chaos, and all I can think is that whatever is about to unfold could change everything.

Chapter 5: Tensions Rise

The doorbell chimed its delicate tune, breaking the stillness of my late afternoon solitude. I could feel the familiar flutter in my stomach as I set aside the bundle of herbs I had been preparing for the evening's ritual. The enticing aroma of sandalwood lingered in the air, mingling with the sweet, tangy scent of dried citrus peels, an unmistakable sign that the season of harvest was upon us. Each of my candles, crafted with care, held a flicker of the energy that thrummed beneath the surface of my being. With a gentle push, I opened the door, bracing myself for the sight of him.

Grant stood there, hands shoved into the pockets of his worn leather jacket, his tousled hair catching the golden sunlight that filtered through the trees. He flashed a grin, the kind that made my heart race and my knees weak. "I'm here for that candle," he said, a playful lilt in his voice that felt like a secret between us. "You know, the one for my 'friend.'"

"Of course," I replied, leaning against the doorframe, letting the warmth of the moment wash over me. "Is your friend particularly fond of rosemary and sage? Or should I go for something more... ethereal?"

"Ethereal sounds perfect." His gaze lingered on my face, and I felt the weight of it, a mix of admiration and intrigue. The tension that simmered between us was palpable, a current that threatened to pull me under if I let it.

As I rummaged through my supplies, I couldn't shake the feeling that the walls of my cozy shop were closing in, heavy with unspoken words and expectations. My heart quickened at the thought of the whispers swirling in the neighborhood, the way they slithered into my ears like unwanted vines. Grant wasn't just another visitor; he was a catalyst, a force of nature that upended my carefully constructed world. The witches, those wise and wily women, had their eyes on us, and I could almost hear their clucking tongues and the rustling of their shawls as they exchanged furtive glances.

"Are you still worried about the rumors?" Grant's voice pulled me from my thoughts, soft and probing, a stark contrast to the tension brewing beneath the surface. "I mean, they can't possibly think I'm some villain just because I've wandered into your candle shop."

"No, not a villain," I said, my tone teasing yet layered with truth. "More like the handsome stranger who makes my heart race and my magic surge."

He laughed, a deep, rumbling sound that sent a thrill through me. "Well, I'll take 'handsome stranger' any day over 'villain.' What do I need to do to earn a permanent spot in your shop?"

"Perhaps some charm and a dash of humility?" I quipped, trying to keep the atmosphere light, even as a part of me wondered if it was too late for that. "Or you could start by helping me with the harvest festival preparations. I could always use an extra pair of hands."

His brow arched with interest. "A festival, you say? Count me in. I'm great with crowds and can charm anyone with my dazzling personality."

"Is that what you call it?" I teased back, unable to hide my smile. I felt the magnetic pull between us strengthen, as if the universe conspired to bring our worlds closer together. "But be warned, it's a gathering of witches. You might want to keep your charm dialed down just a notch. You don't want to be hexed for stealing hearts."

"Hexed?" He leaned closer, eyes sparkling with mischief. "That sounds like a thrilling adventure. I'd be the hero who rescues you from your own kind."

"Or the fool who falls victim to a love spell," I shot back, enjoying our banter, the way it wrapped around us like a warm embrace. "Witches can be quite persuasive when it comes to matters of the heart."

ILLUMINATED BOUNDARIES

A shiver of excitement darted through me as our laughter echoed through the small space, the air thickening with possibilities. But just as the moment felt perfect, a sudden flicker in the overhead lights pulled me back to reality. I glanced up, annoyance prickling at the back of my mind. This wasn't the first time the lights had behaved oddly, but I dismissed it as a quirky old building with an unpredictable electrical system.

"Did you feel that?" I asked, shifting my attention back to Grant, who was watching me with an intensity that made my cheeks flush. The air felt charged, and I was acutely aware of every tiny movement, the way his fingers brushed against the candle jars, sending a tremor of energy through the room.

"Feel what?" His smile faded, concern creeping into his eyes. "Is something wrong?"

"Maybe not wrong, but..." I paused, searching for the right words. "I've noticed strange things happening when you're around. It's as if the magic here is alive, reacting to you."

He took a step closer, our proximity igniting a spark that danced between us. "What kind of strange?"

"Lights flickering, energy shifting, like the universe is trying to tell us something." I hesitated, knowing I was teetering on the edge of something significant. "I can't ignore it."

The moment hung between us, charged and electric, and I could see him processing my words, a hint of wonder mixed with unease shadowing his features. "Maybe it's a sign," he murmured, his voice barely above a whisper. "Or maybe it's just you and me, pulling at something we don't quite understand."

The air shifted again, heavier now, wrapping around us like a warm blanket. I felt a rush of fear and excitement, a heady mix that made my heart race. It was a dangerous line we were treading, one that could lead to either a beautiful revelation or a catastrophic fallout.

"Whatever it is," I said, my voice steady despite the storm brewing within, "I want to figure it out. Together."

The resolve in my words seemed to bridge the gap between our worlds, and I held my breath, wondering what we would uncover as we leaned into this unexpected journey.

The evening air wrapped around us, thick with anticipation, as I turned back to the candle-laden shelves, trying to regain my composure. Grant leaned against the counter, watching me with a gaze that felt both warm and probing. I tried to focus on selecting the right wick, my fingers dancing over the various scents, but the electric charge between us made concentration a challenge.

"Do you always make your candles with this much flair?" he asked, a teasing smile on his lips. "I mean, can't you just pop a few into the oven and call it a day?"

"Ah, yes, because nothing says 'witchcraft' like a batch of mass-produced vanilla candles," I shot back, amused. "No, each candle holds a piece of intention. They're not just for lighting; they're for casting spells, invoking emotions, creating ambiance. You're welcome to take one home, but be warned: they have a tendency to ignite feelings."

"Is that so?" he replied, the corner of his mouth twitching as he stepped closer, the warmth radiating from him almost tangible. "Maybe I should be careful about what I wish for then."

"Definitely," I said, my voice dropping an octave as I caught the intensity of his gaze. "You might end up stuck in a whirlwind of emotions that you didn't ask for."

"Sounds thrilling," he said, his playful tone matching the spark in his eyes. "But I think I can handle it. What's life without a little chaos?"

With a grin, I carefully selected a deep blue candle infused with lavender and chamomile, its rich aroma whispering of calm and serenity. "This one's perfect for someone who wants a little chaos but also needs to unwind. Just like me," I added with a wink. "You might be surprised at how much energy can be bottled in a simple wick."

"Surprised? I'm intrigued," he replied, his tone earnest now, the humor replaced by something deeper. "Do you believe in fate, then? That some forces push us together like this?"

I paused, the question hanging in the air like a delicate strand of spider silk, glimmering with potential yet fragile enough to break with the slightest breath. "I believe that some things are meant to be explored, at the very least," I replied carefully, feeling the weight of his inquiry. "But every choice we make shifts the course of that path. It's a delicate balance."

"I'm all for exploration," he said, stepping closer until the scent of sandalwood and cinnamon enveloped us. "Especially when it involves unexpected outcomes."

I smiled, the tension thickening as the space between us shrank. "What do you expect, then? A candle that grants wishes? An enchanted love potion?"

"Maybe just a bit of honest conversation without the fear of repercussions," he said, his voice lowering, almost conspiratorial. "It feels like there's something between us that's begging to be uncovered."

The air crackled with unspoken words, and I could feel the magic thrumming beneath my skin, urging me to let go of my reservations. But just as I opened my mouth to respond, the sudden darkness of the shop sent a jolt of panic through me. The lights flickered and died, plunging us into a shadowy cocoon.

"Great timing," I muttered, fumbling for my phone to use its flashlight. "Just as I was about to have a heart-to-heart."

"I think the universe just likes to keep us on our toes," Grant said, a hint of amusement in his voice as he reached for my hand in the darkness. His fingers intertwined with mine, and a rush of warmth surged through me, more potent than the lingering scent of the candles.

"Or perhaps it's sending us a message," I replied, my heart racing as I felt the energy pulsing between us. "Or reminding me that it's time to rethink my decision to let you in."

"Let me in? Or let me stay?" he asked, his voice low and steady. The way he held my gaze made my pulse race. "Because I have no intention of leaving, not when there's so much at stake."

The shadows seemed to swirl around us, and I could hear the faint echoes of whispers from outside, the neighborhood witches no doubt sensing the upheaval in the energy around me. "What do you mean by that?" I asked, trying to sound nonchalant, but the weight of his words hung heavy in the air.

"I mean that whatever magic is happening between us feels important. It's as if we're tapping into something ancient, something that transcends all the ordinary stuff," he said, his grip on my hand tightening ever so slightly. "I want to explore it, but it seems like it's more complicated than either of us expected."

With the darkness enveloping us, I felt both comforted and on edge. "It's complicated because it's real," I admitted, feeling the heat radiate from him. "And with that comes a whole host of consequences."

"Consequences can be fun," he countered, his voice teasing yet sincere. "They add flavor to life. And if we're in this together, I think we can navigate whatever comes our way."

"Are you suggesting a partnership?" I asked, amused, yet touched by the sincerity behind his words. "You do realize that witches have a tendency to drag unsuspecting souls into their chaos."

"I'm all about chaos," he replied, his tone playful again. "But maybe I'm naïve to think I could keep up with a witch's world."

"Naïve?" I laughed, the sound bright in the shadows. "More like optimistic. But I like that about you."

"Then let's be optimistic together." He paused, his expression growing serious. "Just promise me that you won't shut me out when things get overwhelming. I want to be here for you, for whatever comes."

I felt a swell of gratitude, a warmth blooming in my chest that pushed back against the shadows closing in around us. "If I promise that, you have to promise to be honest, no matter how hard it gets."

"Deal," he said, his thumb brushing over my knuckles in a gentle caress that made me shiver.

Just then, a burst of light flared to life, illuminating the shop in a warm glow, as if the universe had taken pity on our moment and restored the balance. The flickering overhead lights steadied, casting our shadows against the wall, a testament to the connection forming between us. I felt both exhilarated and terrified, the magic pulsating around us intensifying with each passing heartbeat.

"What now?" he asked, looking around the shop as if seeing it for the first time. "Shall we dive into the chaos together?"

"Only if you're prepared for what might come next," I replied, a spark of mischief lighting in my eyes.

"Chaos and all," he said, grinning widely, and I knew in that moment that whatever lay ahead, I wouldn't face it alone.

The air was thick with unspoken possibilities, and I could feel the gravity of the moment pulling us closer together. Grant stood a mere breath away, his warm gaze steady on mine, the faint flicker of candlelight dancing between us. I could see the desire in his eyes, a mirror reflecting my own longing, but there was something else lurking beneath the surface—an urgency that hinted at deeper connections and potential chaos waiting to unfold.

"Alright then," I said, my voice steady despite the whirlwind inside me. "Let's explore this chaos together. But I warn you, it comes with all the messiness of magic, and I can't predict what will happen."

"Messy can be fun," he replied, his smile disarming, eyes glinting with a hint of mischief. "Just think of it as an adventure."

With that, I felt a surge of adrenaline and a sense of reckless abandon wash over me. We were standing at the edge of something immense, and while every fiber of my being screamed caution, the thrill of possibility was intoxicating. "Okay, let's start with the harvest festival prep. It's a community thing, but there's always room for a new face—especially one with an eagerness for chaos."

"Lead the way, oh wise candle maker," he said, extending an arm as if he were my knight, ready to follow me into whatever unpredictable fate awaited.

I couldn't help but laugh, feeling lighter as I stepped into the cool evening air. Together, we walked through the bustling streets, the town alive with the anticipation of the festival. Lanterns swayed gently in the breeze, illuminating the sidewalks in warm hues, while the scent of roasted corn and cinnamon wafted through the air. It felt like a vibrant tapestry of color and sound, and in the midst of it all, I found myself reveling in Grant's presence.

"See? Not so scary out here," I said, nudging him playfully as we passed a stall selling homemade potpourri.

"Only if you can ignore the whispers," he replied, glancing sideways at a cluster of women eyeing us with unabashed curiosity.

"They're just protective. Witches can be a bit territorial, especially when it comes to outsiders," I explained, my voice low but tinged with humor. "But they'll warm up to you. Just keep that charming smile on."

"Charming, you say?" he teased, nudging me back. "I might be running out of charm soon, especially if I'm surrounded by powerful witches."

"You'll be fine," I assured him. "Just stay close to me. I'll be your shield."

With each step, the tension shifted, intertwining our fates in ways I couldn't yet comprehend. We reached a large community tent where vibrant fabrics billowed in the wind, and laughter mingled with the sounds of preparations. Here, families and friends were working together, tying garlands of dried flowers and hanging handmade ornaments that would light up the night sky.

"Ready to dive into the chaos?" I asked, glancing at Grant, who seemed a little awestruck by the spirited energy around us.

"Only if you promise to keep me from being hexed," he replied, his voice half-joking but with an edge of sincerity that tugged at my heart.

"I can't promise anything," I said, biting back a smile as I nudged him toward a table where pumpkins were being carved. "But let's give it a shot. We can start with these beauties."

As we approached the table, the familiar faces of my neighbors greeted us with knowing smiles. "Oh, look who we have here," Margaret, the eldest witch in the community, said with a wink, her eyes twinkling like stars. "Bringing an outsider to our sacred traditions, I see."

"Margaret, meet Grant," I said, trying to sound casual. "He's here to help with the festival."

"Help or hinder?" she shot back, her tone light but probing. "You never know with outsiders. They can sometimes bring more trouble than good."

"Hey now, I'm just a guy with a candle obsession," Grant interjected, raising his hands in mock surrender. "No trouble here."

Margaret arched an eyebrow, clearly not convinced. "Just remember, dear boy, the witches of this town have long memories. We don't take kindly to those who disrupt our magic."

"Thanks for the warning," he replied, his voice steady, though I could see the flicker of uncertainty in his eyes.

As the evening unfolded, we threw ourselves into the preparations, Grant throwing himself into the spirit of the festival with contagious enthusiasm. We carved pumpkins, crafted decorations, and exchanged stories with the locals, his laughter ringing out like music amid the soft murmur of the crowd. But even as the festivities brightened, I felt the undercurrent of unease lurking just beneath the surface.

As the sun dipped below the horizon, painting the sky in hues of orange and purple, I felt an unexpected twinge in my gut, a sense that something was shifting. The whispers I had felt before now echoed louder in my ears. I glanced at Grant, who was animatedly discussing the carving techniques with a small group, completely unaware of the tension thickening in the air.

"Are you okay?" he asked, suddenly turning to me, his brow furrowed with concern. "You look like you just swallowed a lemon."

"I'm fine," I replied, forcing a smile as I waved away his concern. "Just... feeling the energy of the night, you know?"

"Right," he said, skepticism lacing his voice. "Well, you know what they say: when in doubt, find a drink."

"Now you're speaking my language," I laughed, eager to shake off the creeping sense of dread. We wandered over to a nearby booth selling spiced cider, the warmth of the drink soothing against the chill of the evening.

As we toasted to our impromptu partnership in chaos, a sudden gust of wind swept through the festival, knocking over a nearby display of candles. The lights flickered once again, and the ground beneath us trembled. I exchanged a look with Grant, the air around us growing tense as if the universe had caught its breath.

"Did you feel that?" I asked, my heart racing, the magic within me resonating with an unsettling vibration.

"Yeah," he replied, his expression shifting from playful to serious. "What was that?"

Before I could answer, the festival lights dimmed entirely, plunging us into darkness once more. Gasps echoed around us, and a low hum of concern rippled through the crowd. I could feel the energy surging, wild and chaotic, sparking to life like a storm gathering in the distance.

"Stay close," I whispered to Grant, instinctively grasping his hand as we moved toward the edge of the crowd, seeking shelter from the impending chaos.

But then, just as suddenly as it had started, a brilliant flash of light illuminated the scene, a blinding glow erupting from the center of the festival. I squinted against the brightness, heart pounding as shadows danced wildly around us. The laughter and chatter turned to murmurs of alarm, and a collective sense of dread began to settle over the gathered crowd.

"What the hell is happening?" Grant's voice was barely above a whisper, fear mingling with fascination in his tone.

"I don't know, but we need to find out," I replied, adrenaline coursing through my veins. "This isn't just a power surge; it's something else—something dangerous."

As the light faded, revealing a swirling mass of energy, I knew we were standing at the precipice of something monumental, something that could change everything. In that moment, as the crowd gasped and murmured around us, I felt the ground shift beneath our feet, a surge of power urging me to act.

But before I could gather my thoughts, a chilling voice cut through the night, echoing ominously, "You've meddled in forces beyond your control. It's time to face the consequences."

The crowd fell silent, fear rippling through the throng as my heart dropped, and I turned to Grant, my pulse racing. Whatever was coming next, we were in it together—and there was no turning back.

Chapter 6: Into the Unknown

The air in the studio was thick with the sweet, earthy scent of lavender and beeswax, a combination that felt like a warm embrace on the cool autumn afternoon. I stood in the middle of my workshop, surrounded by shelves lined with jars of essential oils, fragments of dried flowers, and half-finished candles casting soft shadows against the walls. Sunlight filtered through the large windows, illuminating the delicate dance of dust motes in the air. It was a comforting haven, one I had meticulously crafted, each piece a testament to my attempts at balance in a world that seemed to delight in chaos.

Grant stepped in, his presence as buoyant as the crisp air outside. He brushed a hand through his hair, which caught the light just right, sending a spark of warmth through me that I quickly quelled. I didn't want to admit how much I enjoyed having him around, despite the string of calamities that seemed to accompany him like an unwelcome shadow. He flashed that easy smile of his, and I felt my heart race—not from anxiety but from a thrill I couldn't quite pin down.

"Wow," he said, glancing around the space, his eyes widening with curiosity. "This is incredible! You have a whole candle empire in here."

"Empire might be a stretch," I replied, attempting to sound nonchalant, but the pride slipped out despite my efforts. "It's more like a cozy little corner of chaos."

"Chaos is just order waiting to be discovered," he quipped, leaning against the table, fingers brushing over the various molds and tools. "What do you mean by 'little'?" He gestured toward the jars lining the shelves. "This looks like a serious operation."

I couldn't help but chuckle. "A serious operation for one person trying to avoid a serious life. That's me." I turned my back to him, pouring a mix of essential oils into a measuring cup, pretending I was focused on the task rather than his piercing gaze.

"Is that why you keep the world at arm's length?" he asked, his tone more serious now. "You can't deny there's something magnetic about you."

A blush crept up my cheeks, and I hated that he could see right through my carefully constructed walls. "Let's just say I have my reasons for wanting to keep things simple," I replied, trying to keep the conversation light, deflecting the intensity that had seeped into his voice.

As the mixture warmed on the stove, I reached for the lavender buds, allowing their calming scent to envelop me. Grant was still watching, his expression a mix of admiration and something more profound that sent my heart into a mini-jump. "I love the way you pour yourself into these candles. It's like you're creating little pieces of joy for people."

"Joy?" I raised an eyebrow, amused. "More like pieces of an obsessive ritual. You'd be surprised how therapeutic it can be to watch wax transform."

He stepped closer, his shoulder brushing against mine, and I felt a spark travel through the air. "I think it's beautiful. You take something so ordinary and make it extraordinary."

In that moment, I decided to share a piece of my world with him—an offering of vulnerability wrapped in warmth and sweet scents. "It's not just the wax and fragrance. Each candle holds a story, a part of me."

"Like a journal?" His curiosity piqued, his eyes lighting up.

"Something like that," I said, pouring the hot wax into a mold. "When I pour a candle, it's not just about the scent; it's about intention. Every blend I create has a purpose, a wish, or a memory attached to it."

"Give me an example," he pressed, leaning in closer, genuinely intrigued.

I hesitated, glancing at the flickering flame on the stove, feeling a weight of nostalgia. "Okay, there's this one I call 'Homecoming.' It's a blend of cedarwood and vanilla. It's meant to evoke the feeling of returning home after a long journey, that warm, comforting embrace."

"That sounds amazing." His enthusiasm was infectious, the way he leaned in, genuinely wanting to understand.

I let out a soft laugh, the tension in my shoulders easing just a bit. "It is, actually. I love how certain scents can transport you to different moments in your life."

"What about the scent of chaos?" he teased, his grin wide. "What's the candle for that?"

"Probably a combination of burnt toast and regret," I shot back, and he burst out laughing, a sound that warmed the very corners of the studio.

As we joked, I felt a connection thread itself between us, delicate yet strong, like the wick in the candle I was crafting. The atmosphere shifted, and for the first time, I felt a sense of comfort in his presence that I hadn't before—like perhaps I could share more, peel back another layer of my guarded heart.

"Are you ready for the secret?" I asked, suddenly serious, letting my fingers hover above the wax. Grant tilted his head, his expression shifting from playful to intent, like he sensed the gravity of what I was about to reveal.

"I'm all ears," he said, genuine interest replacing the light banter.

I took a deep breath, steadied myself, and decided to share not just the candles but the magic I infused into them. "These candles? They're not just for ambiance. They're vessels for intentions. I infuse them with energy—little bits of hope, dreams, and sometimes... I don't know, magic?"

His brows knitted together. "Magic? Like… witchcraft?"

"Not quite. More like connecting with the universe," I explained, feeling lighter with each word. "When I light a candle, I focus on what I want to manifest—whether it's healing, love, or even a simple wish for a good day. It's about channeling energy."

"Wait, so you're saying your candles have powers?" he asked, amusement dancing in his eyes.

"I know it sounds crazy," I admitted, feeling exposed. "But I believe there's something to it. The energy we put into the world matters."

"Crazy, huh?" He chuckled, crossing his arms, a teasing glint in his gaze. "So, if I burn a candle, does that mean I can make pizza appear?"

I rolled my eyes but couldn't suppress a smile. "If only it were that easy! But you'd probably burn it first. That's your chaos coming back to haunt us."

His laughter filled the studio again, and with it, the tension that had built over the last few weeks began to unravel. It felt good to share, to let him in even just a little, to trust that he wouldn't scoff or walk away. I had expected more skepticism, perhaps even judgment, but instead, he seemed genuinely captivated.

"Alright, I'm intrigued. What do I need to do to make a wish?" he asked, leaning closer, and I could feel the warmth radiating off him.

"First, you have to decide what you truly want," I said, meeting his gaze with a seriousness that belied the lighthearted nature of our conversation. "Then you light the candle and focus on that wish. The energy flows where attention goes."

Grant nodded, the humor fading from his face, replaced by a look of contemplation. "I think I could use some of that right about now."

"Careful what you wish for," I warned playfully, my heart racing. "You might end up with a pizza."

His smile faltered just a fraction, and for a heartbeat, I saw something deeper flicker in his eyes—a hint of vulnerability that matched the depth of the conversation. It was a fleeting moment, quickly masked by his usual bravado, but it struck a chord within me.

In that shared silence, the connection deepened, threading through the cracks of our banter and building something unexpected and profound. The tension crackled in the air, and I found myself wishing for more than just the perfect candle; I wanted to explore whatever this was blooming between us, even if it felt perilously close to unraveling the carefully woven fabric of my carefully guarded life.

As the last remnants of sunlight melted away, casting long shadows across the studio floor, I felt a palpable shift in the air, charged with an energy I couldn't quite name. The scent of lavender hung thick around us, weaving a tapestry of calm even as I navigated the undercurrents of uncertainty that Grant stirred within me. I turned back to the simmering pot, my heart racing with an unsettling mix of fear and exhilaration.

"You know," Grant said, leaning casually against the workbench, arms crossed, "if you keep this up, you'll have me believing I'm in the presence of an actual sorceress."

I laughed, shaking my head. "If only I had that kind of power. I'd conjure up a pizza and make my life a lot easier."

"Just the pizza?" he teased, stepping closer, a glimmer of mischief dancing in his eyes. "I would think you'd go for world peace or, at the very least, some good Wi-Fi."

"Honestly, Wi-Fi is overrated. I have my candles for good vibes, remember?" I poured the wax carefully into the molds, glancing at him through the steam rising from the pot. "I didn't ask you here for a comedy show, you know."

"I beg to differ." He moved around the table, his presence warm and unyielding, grounding me amid my swirling thoughts. "I think your life could use a little levity."

"It's not all bad," I said, choosing my words carefully. "But the world has a way of reminding me that lightness doesn't come easily."

"Tell me about it." His voice softened, and I caught a glimpse of the storm brewing behind his bright exterior. "Life can feel like a series of unfortunate events sometimes."

With a sudden surge of courage, I set aside the wax and faced him fully, determined to peel back my layers a little more. "I guess we both have our burdens. I tend to bury mine under wax and wicks."

He chuckled softly, but his expression turned serious. "Maybe it's time to let someone help you carry that weight."

The honesty in his voice ignited a warmth deep within me, igniting the desire to reach out, to pull him into my world even further. "Okay, but let's make a deal. You help me with my chaotic life, and I'll teach you how to make a candle."

"Deal," he replied, his enthusiasm infectious. "What's the first step?"

"First, we need to choose a scent. Something meaningful," I said, scanning the shelves, my heart racing as I pulled out a few jars filled with fragrant oils. "How about bergamot? It's uplifting, a little unexpected."

"Much like you," he said, a teasing smile breaking through.

"Flattery will get you everywhere," I shot back, unable to suppress the grin tugging at my lips. "And don't forget it."

As we worked together, blending the oils, our hands brushed occasionally, sending tiny electric shocks of awareness skittering up my arm. Each touch felt like an invitation to something deeper, something more than just candle-making.

"Okay, what now?" he asked, eyes glinting with playful challenge.

"Now, you get to pour the wax," I said, handing him the heavy pot, the weight of it oddly symbolic of the moment. "Just remember: pour slowly, with intention."

"Much like my dating life," he replied, rolling his eyes dramatically. "Slow and full of intention... and yet somehow messy."

I couldn't help but laugh, the sound echoing in the cozy space. "Well, you're getting the hang of it."

Grant focused intently on the task, and I couldn't help but admire the way he threw himself into every moment, body and soul. He poured the warm wax into the mold, a steady stream that gleamed like liquid gold in the dim light.

"Look at you! You're practically a natural," I said, clapping lightly.

"Watch out, world. I'm about to open my own candle shop," he quipped, a broad grin spreading across his face. "I can already see the sign: 'Grant's Candles of Chaos.'"

"Perfect. It'll be a hit!" I replied, unable to hold back a laugh. "You'd attract customers like moths to a flame—literally."

After the wax had settled, we stood together, gazing at the mold with shared pride. The laughter faded, replaced by a comfortable silence as we let the moment linger. I turned to face him, heart pounding in my chest. "Thanks for being here, Grant. I know it's not always easy."

"Trust me, this is far from easy," he said, his gaze steady and serious. "But I want to be here, for whatever that's worth."

"What if I told you that I have a tendency to mess up everything I touch?" I confessed, my voice barely above a whisper.

"I wouldn't believe you," he replied, stepping closer. "You're stronger than you think. I've seen it in the way you talk about your candles, how you make them. That's not just a hobby; it's a piece of your soul."

His words resonated deeply within me, a comforting balm on the rough edges of my insecurities. "I'm just afraid of getting too close to anyone," I admitted, vulnerability threading through my voice. "Every time I let someone in, the universe has a way of reminding me how messy life can be."

"Life is messy. That's the point," he replied, and I could hear the sincerity in his tone. "What matters is how we deal with it. You don't have to face it alone."

The weight of his words hung between us, heavy with promise and possibility. Just as I was about to respond, a loud crash echoed from the hallway, shattering the intimate moment. My heart dropped into my stomach, and instinctively, I reached for Grant's arm.

"What was that?" he asked, eyes wide, the playful spark gone.

I swallowed hard, my stomach twisting with dread. "Probably just my neighbor's endless collection of decorative knick-knacks."

"Or a sign that we should call it a night," he said, trying to lighten the mood, but I could hear the concern lacing his voice.

"No way. We can't let chaos win," I insisted, though my heart raced at the thought of what lay beyond the studio door. "We need to see what's going on."

"Okay, lead the way, fearless candle sorceress."

With a nod, I opened the door and stepped into the dimly lit hallway, Grant right behind me. The faint light flickered overhead, and I could feel the tension in the air, thick and oppressive. As we approached the source of the noise, I spotted a group of my neighbors gathered around a fallen bookshelf, books scattered like confetti on the floor.

"Oh, great," I muttered under my breath. "Another day, another disaster."

"Looks like the universe is really throwing you a party," Grant said, half-joking, but I could see the concern in his eyes.

"Let's help them," I suggested, moving forward, and to my surprise, he fell into step beside me, his unwavering presence a comfort against the chaos.

Together, we helped pick up the scattered books, the laughter of neighbors filling the hallway, lightening the mood despite the messy situation. As we worked, I felt a strange sense of camaraderie forming—not just among the neighbors but between Grant and me. Each shared smile, each moment of laughter reinforced the invisible thread that had started weaving us together.

After the chaos had settled and the bookshelf was righted, I turned to Grant, my heart fluttering as I caught his gaze. "See? Chaos can bring people together."

He smiled, the warmth of his expression melting away the tension that had built up in my chest. "You're right. Maybe it's not so bad after all."

In that moment, surrounded by laughter and camaraderie, I felt a shift within myself, a softening of my guarded heart. Perhaps I didn't need to be afraid of the messiness that life brought. Perhaps allowing someone in—chaotic or not—was worth the risk. As I glanced at Grant, I realized I was ready to step into the unknown with him, ready to face whatever came next, candle in hand.

The laughter from my neighbors slowly faded into the background, a distant melody that now felt oddly comforting. In the wake of the chaos, we returned to the studio, the sweet scent of lavender and beeswax enveloping us like a familiar blanket. The atmosphere shifted again, now punctuated by an air of intimacy that crackled with unspoken words.

As I set about cleaning up the remnants of our candle-making adventure, I could feel Grant watching me, his gaze heavy with a mix of curiosity and something deeper that made my heart race. The warmth of his presence was both a comfort and a challenge, as if I stood at the precipice of something new, terrifying yet exhilarating.

"Okay, so what's next in this candle-making saga?" he asked, his tone light but laced with genuine interest.

"Now we let this batch cool," I replied, gesturing toward the mold. "Then we can add the wicks and let them set. After that, we'll have a few candles ready for your magical powers."

"Great! I'm looking forward to my first candle—hopefully, it doesn't explode," he joked, the playful glint in his eye restoring a bit of normalcy to our evening.

"I'm starting to think you're a bad luck charm," I shot back, pretending to contemplate. "If my candles spontaneously combust, I'm blaming you."

He laughed, and I felt the tension of the earlier chaos dissolve further. "What if that's just part of my charm? It's a package deal, after all."

I rolled my eyes but couldn't hide my smile. "Just don't let it go to your head. We have to maintain some level of professionalism in this candle-making business."

"Ah, yes. Serious business." He moved closer, leaning against the table, arms crossed in mock contemplation. "So, what's the secret behind your candle-making? Besides all the 'magical' stuff?"

Taking a deep breath, I felt the weight of his gaze on me, urging me to share more. "It's about intention, really. When I pour the wax, I focus on what I want to achieve with that candle—what energy I'm putting into the world."

"Kind of like your own personal therapy session?" he suggested, tilting his head thoughtfully.

"Something like that. Each scent brings its own memory or emotion. It's... therapeutic."

"I can see that. What about this one?" He gestured to the mold filled with our freshly poured creation. "What's its purpose?"

"Ah, that's a blend of bergamot and lavender, meant to evoke a sense of calm and clarity. It's perfect for those hectic days when you need a little grounding," I explained, pride swelling in my chest.

"Seems fitting, considering our chaotic evening." He smirked, his eyes dancing with mischief.

"True. Though, if I'm being honest, I'm surprised you're not more freaked out by all this." I gestured around, taking in the shelves of jars and the warm glow of the studio. "You know, the whole 'magical' candle thing."

"Honestly? I'm not easily freaked out," he replied, shrugging. "I think it's kind of amazing. You've created your own little universe here."

"Thanks. It's my escape from reality."

"Not a bad place to hide," he said softly, a flicker of understanding passing between us.

Just then, the lights flickered ominously overhead, casting shadows that danced along the walls. I froze, heart pounding in my chest. "Is it just me, or is that a sign?"

He chuckled lightly, attempting to ease the tension. "You might be onto something. I can already hear the ghost of candle makers past warning us to turn back."

"Or maybe it's just the universe reminding us of our luck," I replied, trying to match his levity but feeling a wave of apprehension wash over me.

"Let's hope it doesn't come to that. What's the worst that could happen?" he asked, leaning back against the table with an air of defiance.

"Uh, have you met us?" I quipped, raising an eyebrow. "We seem to attract disaster like moths to a flame."

As if in response, the lights dimmed further, then flickered back to life, illuminating the studio with a sudden intensity. It felt almost like an electric jolt, and I took an involuntary step back, my heart racing. "Okay, that's new."

"Maybe the candles are fighting back!" he said, his grin widening. "Perhaps they sense my power."

"Your power?" I laughed, though I felt a shiver of uncertainty crawl up my spine. "I'd like to keep my candles intact, thank you very much."

"I think they'd prefer me over the chaos," he teased, but the underlying tension in his voice didn't escape me.

We shared a moment of quiet, our laughter fading as we both registered the pulse of energy in the air, a tangible force that seemed to vibrate between us. It was exhilarating and terrifying, as if the very fabric of reality had shifted, leaving us suspended in a bubble of possibility.

"Let's check on that wick," I suggested, moving to break the moment, trying to refocus on the task at hand.

"Sure thing," he said, but as he followed me, his expression turned serious. "What if there's something more to all this? The accidents, the chaos—maybe it's not just us."

I turned to him, surprised by the sudden weight of his words. "You think it's connected to me?"

"I don't know," he replied, his brow furrowing in thought. "But it feels like something is happening, like we're on the edge of something bigger. It's just... unusual."

The idea sent a chill down my spine. "Unusual" was a polite way of saying that every time he and I were together, something went wrong. I couldn't shake the feeling that I was somehow responsible.

"Hey," he said, stepping closer, eyes searching mine. "Whatever it is, we'll figure it out together. You don't have to face it alone."

"Right," I replied, though doubt clung to my words. "But what if it's too big?"

"Then we tackle it together, one candle at a time."

Just then, a loud bang resonated from the hallway, reverberating through the walls of the studio. Startled, we both turned, eyes wide. The door rattled violently, and my heart raced.

"What now?" I whispered, my voice barely audible.

"I have no idea, but it sounds like trouble," Grant replied, the humor draining from his expression as he instinctively moved closer to me.

"Should we check?"

"Of course. But let's not act like we're in a horror movie."

"Agreed. If anything jumps out at us, I'm throwing you in front," I shot back, trying to inject some levity back into the moment.

"Good to know where I stand."

Together, we approached the door, the unease between us thickening. I reached for the handle, my breath catching in my throat. Grant positioned himself slightly behind me, a protective presence that both comforted and unsettled me.

With a quick twist of the knob, I flung the door open, revealing a hallway shrouded in shadows. The flickering overhead lights barely illuminated the space, casting eerie silhouettes that danced along the walls. My heart pounded in my chest as I stepped forward, drawn by a magnetic pull of curiosity and fear.

As we moved into the hallway, the sound of shuffling footsteps echoed through the air, growing louder, more frantic. I glanced back at Grant, who met my gaze with a mix of determination and uncertainty.

"Do you hear that?" I whispered, the urgency in my voice rising.

"Yeah, and it doesn't sound friendly," he replied, tension radiating from him.

Before I could respond, the hallway plunged into darkness, the lights extinguishing with a finality that sent a jolt of fear coursing through me. The shadows swallowed us whole, and I felt Grant's hand find mine, grounding me in the encroaching panic.

"Stick together," he murmured, his grip firm around my fingers.

Suddenly, a loud crash echoed from the end of the hallway, followed by the unmistakable sound of something—someone—approaching. The air thickened with an ominous energy, and every instinct screamed for us to retreat. But before I could voice my fear, a figure emerged from the shadows, silhouetted against the faint light seeping through the studio door.

"Who's there?" I called out, my voice shaking, as I instinctively stepped closer to Grant.

And in that moment, as the figure stepped into the light, a realization washed over me, chilling my blood: it was someone I never expected to see again, someone whose presence would change everything.

Chapter 7: The Gathering Storm

The air crackled with electricity as I stepped into the coffee shop, the familiar aroma of roasted beans swirling around me like a warm embrace. The flickering lights overhead only added to the sense of disquiet that had settled in my chest, an unwelcome companion that I couldn't shake. I spotted Grant at our usual table, the one by the window that overlooked the bustling street, where people rushed by, blissfully unaware of the brewing storm in my life. His fingers danced across the laptop keyboard, and a small frown tugged at the corners of his mouth. I loved that frown, how it indicated he was deep in thought, perhaps pondering the mysteries of the universe—or, more likely, debugging the latest code for his latest project.

"Hey, you," I said, sliding into the chair across from him, trying to mask the tremor in my voice. "What's got you so serious?"

He looked up, his deep-set blue eyes lighting up as they met mine. "Just trying to figure out why the software keeps crashing. It's like it's possessed or something." His lips curled into a teasing smile, but the worry lingered in his gaze, echoing my own fears.

"Possessed? That's my specialty, you know." I tried to laugh, but the sound came out a little too strained. It felt as though the world was balancing on a tightrope above us, swaying precariously with each passing moment. "Let me guess, it's the ghosts in the machine?"

"Or maybe it's just faulty programming," he replied, smirking, but I could see the shadows of concern lurking beneath the surface of his wit. He gestured toward my untouched coffee, steam curling in delicate spirals, and I realized that I had hardly tasted it. "You're not drinking? That's a sure sign something's wrong."

I picked up the cup, the heat seeping into my palms. "It's not the coffee, Grant. It's—" I hesitated, unsure of how to voice the turmoil swirling in my mind. "Things have been... different lately."

"Different how?" His voice was low and steady, drawing me into a realm of safety even as chaos loomed outside.

"Strange occurrences. I mean, beyond the usual," I said, letting the words spill out. "The blackout downtown last week? I think it was my magic reacting to you. The moment we're apart, it feels like the city itself is alive, trying to communicate with me. But all it's doing is creating chaos."

His brow furrowed. "Chaos? Like what?"

"Like a burst pipe flooding the subway," I replied, rolling my eyes. "You know, typical witch problems." I leaned in closer, lowering my voice. "And then there are the other witches, those who work their magic in corporate offices and government buildings. They've started to take an interest in my little shop. They approach me with these veiled warnings wrapped in friendly advice. 'Control it,' they say, but control isn't the answer. I need to understand what's happening, and I suspect it has something to do with you."

Grant leaned back in his chair, his expression a mix of amusement and concern. "You think my coding is linked to your magic? That's a new one. I've had some wild ideas in my time, but this takes the cake."

I took a deep breath, letting the rich scent of coffee fill my lungs. "I know it sounds insane, but you have this way of making everything seem connected. Your algorithms—they dance to a rhythm that feels... familiar. Like they're intertwined with something bigger."

His gaze softened as he processed my words, and I could see the gears in his mind turning. "Alright, let's say there's something to this. How do we figure it out?"

"Together," I replied, feeling a surge of determination. "We dive into your code and see what it reveals. Maybe the answers lie within the lines of programming, and perhaps your magic has a role to play."

Grant's smile widened, a hint of mischief in his eyes. "Are you suggesting we engage in a little magic-infused tech troubleshooting?"

"Absolutely. It's the perfect blend of chaos and logic," I said, a laugh escaping my lips. The tension began to ease, the darkness outside momentarily forgotten. "Just promise me you won't try to hack me into your software system without permission."

"Only if you promise not to hex my coffee machine," he shot back, his voice light yet laced with an undercurrent of seriousness.

The playful banter was a necessary distraction, but the shadows remained. I could sense them lurking at the edges of our conversation, waiting for the right moment to creep back in. As I watched Grant type away, his fingers moving in a blur, I couldn't shake the feeling that the city was holding its breath, as if waiting for the storm to break.

"Do you think they're watching us?" I asked, my voice barely above a whisper.

"Who?" Grant looked up, curiosity etched across his features.

"The other witches," I clarified, leaning closer. "They feel different. More... organized. I've overheard whispers about something big coming, and I can't help but think it involves me. They want something from my shop, from my magic."

A flicker of concern passed across his face. "Then we need to be cautious. If they're as powerful as you think, we can't afford to underestimate them."

I nodded, the weight of his words settling heavily on my shoulders. "Agreed. But we can't live in fear either. We have to confront whatever this is, head-on."

He reached across the table, his hand covering mine. The warmth of his touch sent a wave of comfort through me, reminding me that I wasn't alone in this. "We'll figure it out together," he said, his voice steady and reassuring. "Just like always."

In that moment, I felt a flicker of hope ignite within me, a small flame against the encroaching darkness. Yet, the air was still charged with uncertainty, each moment a countdown to an unknown climax. Outside, the city continued its frenetic pace, oblivious to the gathering storm that loomed over us, but inside this little coffee shop, for just a moment, we were sheltered from the chaos—two unlikely allies standing at the precipice of something extraordinary.

The clatter of cups and the murmur of voices around us felt like a distant echo, fading into the background as I focused on Grant's hand, still resting over mine. His thumb traced small, absentminded circles on my skin, igniting sparks of warmth that curled around my anxieties like a comforting blanket. I couldn't help but wonder how long we could maintain this fragile truce with the chaos that loomed just outside our bubble.

"You know, if your magic is going haywire, I might be able to help," he said, a playful glint dancing in his eyes. "Just think of me as your personal tech support—without the annoying hold music."

"Oh, I don't know," I replied, raising an eyebrow. "If I take you up on that, I might find myself on the receiving end of some new kind of magic-induced glitch. What if you inadvertently turn my shop into a portal to another dimension?"

"Then I'll promise to visit regularly—assuming it's a fun dimension." He leaned closer, his voice dropping to a conspiratorial whisper. "Think of the Instagram possibilities."

I couldn't help but chuckle, the tension easing just a bit. But beneath the surface, the disquiet remained, gnawing at the edges of my resolve. "We should probably figure out how to harness this magic of mine before I inadvertently conjure something worse than an Instagram sensation. I'm not sure the world is ready for that level of chaos."

"Fair point," he said, his expression sobering. "How do you want to start?"

The question hung in the air, weighty and significant. I took a deep breath, the rich aroma of coffee mixed with the sharp scent of my unease. "What if we went through your recent code updates? Maybe there's something in there that mirrors what's happening to me—some kind of algorithm that's gone rogue."

He raised his eyebrows, intrigued. "Alright, let's do it. But I warn you, it might get technical. I mean, we're talking about lines of code that could make a coffee pot cry."

I laughed, but the laughter felt a little hollow. As we sat there, two friends teetering on the brink of discovery, the lights above us flickered again. The pulse of the city outside seemed to synchronize with the thrum of my heart. Whatever magic had slipped loose within me, it was awakening something in the world beyond our little corner of comfort.

After downing my lukewarm coffee, I watched as Grant pulled up a series of screens on his laptop. The glow illuminated his features, casting shadows that danced across his cheekbones. "Alright, let's see what kind of trouble your magic might be causing in my tech universe," he said, his fingers flying across the keyboard.

The lines of code unfurled before us, a sprawling tapestry of numbers and letters that felt almost like a spell in its own right. Each entry pulsed with a rhythm that resonated deep within me, echoing the strange tremors I had felt since the city began to conspire against us.

"Do you see anything unusual?" I asked, leaning closer, my curiosity piqued.

"Not yet, but give it time. Sometimes the oddities hide in plain sight." He smirked, the mischief glimmering in his eyes. "Like that time you tried to bake cookies and ended up summoning a rogue squirrel."

"Hey, in my defense, those cookies were meant to be enchanted! Who knew sugar could attract so many woodland creatures?" I shot back, feigning indignation.

He chuckled, but then his expression shifted, becoming more serious. "Alright, back to business. What if we check the logs for unusual activity? Something that might link back to your shop or those witches."

As he began typing again, I felt a shiver run down my spine. The witches—their veiled warnings echoed in my mind, an ominous reminder of the precarious balance I was trying to maintain. They hadn't just warned me about control; they'd hinted at something far more sinister. Something that suggested I was at the center of a storm that could engulf everything I held dear.

"Here we go," Grant said, his eyes narrowing at the screen. "There's something here—an anomaly. A spike in traffic to your shop's online platform just before each strange incident. It's almost like..."

"Like they're monitoring me," I finished, dread pooling in the pit of my stomach. "What does that even mean?"

"It means we need to dig deeper. If they're tracking your magic, they might have plans for it—plans that involve you and possibly... well, more than just your shop."

My heart raced as I processed his words. "What if they want to recruit me? Or worse, what if they intend to strip my magic away? It feels like they're surrounding me, waiting for the right moment to strike."

He met my gaze, the gravity of the situation evident in the way his jaw tightened. "Then we need to be prepared. If they're watching, we can't afford to let them see us sweat. We have to turn the tables."

The resolve in his voice made me feel emboldened. "So, we become the hunters instead of the hunted?"

"Exactly," he said, his smile returning, though it was more determined now. "But first, let's figure out how your magic operates in tandem with this code. Maybe we can find a way to shield you from their prying eyes."

I felt a flutter of hope at the prospect of taking control, but it was quickly overshadowed by the reality of the situation. I had never fully understood the depths of my abilities, and now it felt like I was being thrust into a battle without any preparation. The city's shadows seemed to thicken around us, a reminder that we were standing on the edge of something tumultuous.

"Okay, let's do this," I said, steeling myself. "But I want to make one thing clear: if things start to get too dicey, we pull back. I won't let myself be caught in the middle of a war I don't understand."

"Deal," Grant said, determination flaring in his eyes.

And so, we dove into the depths of code and magic, armed with little more than courage and an unwavering resolve. As the city continued to pulse around us, I couldn't shake the feeling that the storm was not just gathering; it was already at our doorstep, waiting to unleash its fury.

The moment we dove into Grant's code, I felt an electric pulse in the air, an urgency that drove us both deeper into the labyrinth of algorithms. I leaned closer, my fingers brushing against the cool metal of his laptop as we scrolled through lines of digital incantations. Each character seemed to hum with a strange energy, resonating with my own chaotic magic that swirled just beneath the surface.

"Okay, let's break this down," Grant said, his brow furrowed with concentration. "If your magic is reacting to these spikes in traffic, we might need to identify what triggers them. Is there a pattern?"

"Patterns are like weeds in a garden," I mused, tapping my chin thoughtfully. "They can be beautiful if you know how to cultivate them, but left unchecked, they can choke out everything else."

His eyes sparkled with intrigue. "I never thought I'd hear gardening advice in relation to coding. This is why I keep you around, you know."

"Just call me the magical gardener." I chuckled, but the lightness of our banter did little to ease the tightness in my chest. The weight of our discoveries hung over us like storm clouds ready to burst.

As Grant began analyzing the data, I felt the familiar tug of magic at the edges of my consciousness. It was as if the city itself was leaning in, eager to hear what we would uncover. But the thrill of discovery was tempered by a gnawing anxiety. "What if we find something we aren't prepared for?" I asked, my voice barely above a whisper.

"Then we deal with it," he said matter-of-factly, fingers poised over the keyboard. "Just like any other bug we encounter. You've faced tougher challenges, right?"

"Sure," I replied, trying to sound more confident than I felt. "Like that time I accidentally turned my ex's hair green during a breakup."

Grant burst into laughter, his rich voice breaking through the tension. "Now that's a solid comeback! If only you could turn your troubles into something as harmless as green hair."

"Trust me, I'd settle for that in a heartbeat." My laughter faded, replaced by a sense of urgency as I leaned in, watching the screen as if it held the key to my very existence. "What do you see?"

"Here's something interesting," he said, his tone shifting as he highlighted a series of dates. "The spikes coincide with your interactions with certain... figures in the witch community. Each one seems to correlate with an increase in online activity around your shop."

My stomach dropped. "They're monitoring me. I was right."

"Looks like it." Grant's fingers flew over the keyboard, pulling up additional data. "And there's a clear escalation. The last spike was a day before that blackout you mentioned."

"Are you telling me they might have caused it?" I felt a chill run down my spine. "What kind of influence do they have?"

"That's what we need to find out." He continued sifting through lines of code, the blue light illuminating his face, making him appear almost ethereal. "This could be an organized effort, targeting your shop specifically. They want something from you."

"Something I don't even know I have." My heart raced as I absorbed his words. The implications were vast and dark, and I couldn't shake the feeling that I was already too deep in the web they had spun.

Just then, the lights above us flickered again, more violently this time, as if responding to my growing unease. "We might want to wrap this up before—"

Before I could finish my sentence, the coffee shop's door burst open, a gust of wind swirling in, carrying the scent of rain and something else—something metallic, sharp. A figure stepped inside, drenched and shivering, and as their gaze swept across the room, my heart dropped. It was one of the witches who had approached me earlier, the one whose warnings had felt like a distant echo.

"Help," she gasped, her voice barely above a whisper. "You have to help me. They're coming."

Grant and I exchanged a look, the gravity of the moment sinking in. "Who's coming?" I demanded, trying to keep my voice steady.

"The others. The ones you don't understand," she said, her breath quickening as panic seeped into her words. "They know about your magic. They've been watching you for too long, and they're ready to take what's theirs."

"Isn't that just charming?" I quipped, attempting to keep the mood light even as dread coiled in my stomach. "What's their plan? A magic heist?"

"It's not a joke," she snapped, stepping closer, her eyes wide with fear. "You don't understand. This is bigger than your shop. They're planning something that could disrupt the balance of everything. And they're going to start with you."

Grant stood, moving protectively in front of me. "We're not afraid of threats. We'll deal with whatever it is together."

"Together, huh?" The witch shot a glance at him, her expression a mixture of skepticism and something darker. "You think it'll matter? They won't care who you are. They only care about power—and they won't stop until they have it."

The atmosphere shifted, thickening with a tension that was almost palpable. I could feel the shadows closing in around us, as if the very walls of the coffee shop were inching closer, urging us to make a choice.

"What do we do?" I asked, my voice steadying, determination pooling within me. "How can we prepare for this?"

"Don't trust anyone but each other," she warned, glancing nervously toward the door. "And keep your magic close. They'll try to exploit any weakness they can find."

"Great, advice I can take to heart," I muttered, my mind racing with possibilities. The reality was more daunting than I had ever imagined, and yet, amidst the chaos, a spark of defiance ignited within me.

"Let's not sit here waiting for them to come crashing in. If they want a fight, we'll give them one," Grant declared, resolve firm in his voice.

The witch took a step back, glancing anxiously at the door. "You don't understand what you're up against. They're everywhere. They could be anyone."

"I've dealt with chaos before," I asserted, my heart pounding fiercely. "I won't let them take control of my life. Not now, not ever."

As the wind howled outside, the lights flickered again, this time plunging us into darkness for a heartbeat that felt like an eternity. My magic surged, instinctively responding to the threat. When the lights returned, the witch was staring at me, her eyes wide.

"What did you just do?" she whispered, her voice trembling with a mix of fear and awe.

"I don't know," I admitted, glancing at Grant, whose expression mirrored my own bewilderment. "But I think we're about to find out just how far this rabbit hole goes."

Before I could say another word, the door burst open again, and a cold gust swept through the room, carrying with it a shadowy figure that seemed to ripple like smoke. My heart raced as I braced for whatever was about to unfold, knowing that the storm was no longer just gathering—it was here, and we were standing in its eye.

Chapter 8: Shattered Connections

The flickering lights cast a mosaic of shadows on the polished floor, their erratic dance echoing the tension that hung in the air like an impending storm. The launch event for Grant's latest project was a spectacle of innovation and ambition, filled with sleek white tables draped in silver cloth and screens showcasing the future of technology. Yet, despite the extravagance that surrounded us, my heart raced with an entirely different kind of adrenaline. I stood on the fringes of the crowd, the vibrant chatter of enthusiastic attendees swirling around me, but my focus was solely on him.

Grant was a vision against the backdrop of flashing cameras and eager reporters. His dark hair tousled just so, and that sharp jawline of his was set in determination as he spoke animatedly to a group of investors. I could almost see the invisible lines connecting him to his project, lines made of pure ambition and passion. But beneath that confident exterior, I sensed a crack—a fracture that threatened to widen with every passing moment. I had spent weeks trying to convince myself that my presence in his life was harmless, a fleeting distraction amidst his meteoric rise. Yet, as the room filled with anticipation and the air crackled with electricity, I felt the weight of my truth bearing down on me.

Just as Grant stepped away from the investors, a sudden hush enveloped the room. A low hum crescendoed into a sharp crack, and the lights sputtered ominously before plunging us into darkness. Gasps filled the air, accompanied by the frantic clicks of camera shutters in the pitch-blackness, eager to capture the moment that now felt like a prelude to chaos. Panic rippled through the crowd, and I could hear the faint whir of machines trying to compensate for the sudden loss of power. Then came the unsettling sound of equipment malfunctioning—a series of pops and fizzles, as if the very essence of technology had revolted against its own master.

In the brief chaos, I felt my heart drop. This was it. The unraveling of my carefully woven existence. I had always feared that my proximity to Grant would expose the very essence of my being, the glitches that had haunted me for years, but now it was happening in the most public way possible. My breath hitched as I instinctively stepped back, away from the tumultuous energy radiating from the center of the room. Grant was at the epicenter of it all, his expression morphing from confusion to frustration, and finally to a betrayal so palpable I could almost taste it.

When the lights flickered back to life, the flickering revealed a scene of disarray. Guests were scrambling, their voices rising in confusion and concern. Grant stood amidst the chaos, his eyes scanning the room until they locked onto mine. The world around us blurred as I felt every heartbeat echoing in the silence between us, the weight of unspoken words pressing down like a leaden cloak.

As he approached, his jaw tightened, and I braced myself for the confrontation I had both anticipated and dreaded. "What just happened?" he demanded, his voice low and edged with anger, slicing through the din of voices like a hot knife through butter.

I swallowed hard, suddenly aware of the eyes upon us—curious, judgmental, and hungry for gossip. "It was just a power surge," I replied, forcing a calmness into my tone that felt so fragile it might shatter if I breathed too hard. "These things happen."

"Don't give me that." He stepped closer, his intensity leaving little room for pretense. "You know something. This isn't the first time I've seen things glitch when you're around. Equipment fails, systems crash. I can't ignore it any longer."

My pulse quickened, not just from his words but from the realization that I was cornered. Grant's perceptive mind had caught on, weaving together the threads of my mysterious presence and the inexplicable occurrences that surrounded me. I could feel the walls closing in, the secrets I had so carefully guarded poised to spill out like a broken dam.

"Grant, I—"

"You what?" His voice rose, and a few heads turned our way, intrigue flickering in their gazes. "What, you think this is a game? Because it's not. You need to tell me what's going on. Now."

The urgency in his tone sparked something deep within me—a mix of fear and defiance. "And if I told you?" I shot back, my own voice rising in challenge. "What would it change? Would you be able to accept it, or would it just drive you away?"

For a moment, the crowd faded into a distant murmur, and it was just the two of us standing on that precipice. His gaze softened slightly, a flicker of vulnerability crossing his features, but it was quickly masked by a shield of frustration. "I can't stand not knowing. You're always right there, and yet it feels like I'm talking to a ghost. A part of me knows there's something more to you than just... the glitches."

In that moment, I saw the flicker of hope in his eyes, battling against the shadows of doubt. It was almost sweet, the way he was trying to pull me closer, even as he felt the distance between us stretching. "What if I'm not the one you want to know?" I countered, my heart pounding as I realized the stakes had never been higher. The truth felt like a double-edged sword, one that could slice through the fabric of our connection or bind us together in a way I'd never anticipated.

His expression hardened, but I caught the hint of desperation lurking beneath. "You're the one I want to know more than anyone else in this room, and I'm not about to let you walk away without answers."

The intensity of his gaze, a fusion of determination and desire, lit a spark in me, igniting the hope I had tried to extinguish. But the fear of revealing my secrets, of letting him see the chaos within me, loomed large. I took a shaky breath, my resolve wavering as I searched his eyes for any sign that he might understand. What if he didn't? What if this was the moment I lost him forever?

His gaze bore into mine, a kaleidoscope of emotions swirling in those dark depths. I could feel the pulse of the crowd around us, a distant murmur now, but the real storm raged in our shared space. The anticipation of confession hung heavy in the air, binding us together in a moment where vulnerability felt like a live wire, dangerous yet thrilling.

"Why do you keep dodging me?" Grant's voice was low, but the urgency was undeniable. "I've invested everything into this project, and I thought I could count on you to be in my corner. Instead, it feels like you're hiding some sort of... I don't know, a magic trick?" He gestured vaguely, frustration leaking through his polished exterior.

I couldn't help but let out a short, incredulous laugh, the sound surprising even me. "A magic trick? Is that how you see me?" The absurdity of it all broke through the tension, and for a fleeting moment, I caught the hint of a smile threatening to break the tension on his lips. It was enough to remind me that beneath his irritation lay the man I had come to adore—the one who could match my banter with a wit as sharp as his intellect.

"Maybe. Can you pull a rabbit out of a hat?" he shot back, a teasing glint in his eyes that lightened the moment, but I could see the seriousness lurking just beneath the surface. I took a deep breath, contemplating my next words carefully.

"Look, Grant, I can't tell you everything right now," I began, struggling against the instinct to retreat into the shadows of my own uncertainty. "It's complicated. You have to understand that this isn't just some whimsical secret."

"Complicated? That's an understatement. I need you to be straight with me. No more vague hints or half-truths." His gaze was unwavering, and I could feel the tide of tension swirling between us, pulling me in deeper.

"Fine," I relented, my heart racing as I squared my shoulders. "There's a reason things happen around me. It's not just bad luck, Grant. I... I don't control it."

The words hung in the air, and for a moment, the world fell silent, the chaos of the event fading into an almost dreamlike state. "What do you mean you don't control it?" he pressed, his voice barely above a whisper, as if he feared that raising it would shatter the fragile bubble we had created.

"I mean, it's like I'm a magnet for... things. Technology, electronics, you name it. If I'm around, things glitch, and I don't know why. I thought it was just me, some weird quirk, but it's becoming harder to ignore." My heart raced as I spoke, the truth spilling out like a dam breaking. "You must have seen it yourself. Your equipment, the glitches, the... failures. They happen when I'm near, and I don't know why."

He ran a hand through his hair, the frustration giving way to confusion. "So you're saying that you have some kind of—what, supernatural power? That's what you're telling me?"

"I don't know! I don't have answers!" I exclaimed, my voice rising with the swell of panic. "I just know that it's real, and it's affecting everything, including us." The words rushed out, the weight of my confession pressing down as the truth settled between us like an unwanted guest.

Grant stared at me, his expression a mixture of disbelief and awe. "And you didn't think to mention this earlier? You let me think it was all coincidence, that I was just imagining things?"

"I was trying to protect you!" I shot back, my defenses rising like a barrier. "I thought if I stayed away, it wouldn't interfere with your work, with your life. I didn't want to ruin this for you."

His eyes narrowed, the intensity sharpening once again. "So, you think that pushing me away is better than being honest? How does that even make sense?"

The challenge in his tone ignited a spark of rebellion within me. "Maybe it makes sense to someone who's been labeled a freak their entire life! I didn't want to be a burden!" The words spilled from my lips before I could stop them, and I felt my cheeks flush with shame.

"Burden?" His voice softened, and the anger drained from his expression, replaced with something akin to understanding. "You're not a burden. You're... you're the person I want by my side, but I can't fight a shadow, not when I don't even know what I'm dealing with."

His admission hung in the air, a lifeline thrown into turbulent waters, and I hesitated, my heart caught in a web of conflicting emotions. The thought of being with him, truly being with him, sent a warmth through me, but the fear of my truth—my reality—loomed larger than any desire I felt.

"I didn't want to be a liability," I confessed quietly, the vulnerability in my voice exposing the raw edges of my fear. "I didn't want you to see me as something broken."

"Broken?" he echoed, his tone incredulous. "You think I care about that? What I see in you is a brilliant mind, a heart that feels deeply, and someone who challenges me in ways I didn't think were possible. What does any of that have to do with glitches?"

The way he looked at me made my heart flutter, but it was tinged with a reality I couldn't ignore. "Grant, I'm not like everyone else. I can't promise you that I won't screw things up, that I won't put you at risk."

"And I can't promise you that my work will always be flawless, but I still show up every day, don't I?" He stepped closer, the intensity of his gaze leaving no room for retreat. "If you can be brave enough to tell me your truth, then I can be brave enough to help you face it. Together."

For a moment, the chaos around us melted away, the murmurs of the crowd fading into the background as the weight of his words settled over me like a warm blanket. The path forward was fraught with uncertainty, but the prospect of facing it with him was intoxicating, electrifying. I took a deep breath, feeling the air shift between us, filled with the promise of uncharted territory.

"Okay," I said finally, my voice steadier than I felt. "If we're doing this, then we're doing it right. No more secrets, no more hiding."

"Good," he said, relief washing over his features, but before we could delve deeper, a loud crack of thunder erupted outside, drawing our attention. The lights flickered again, but this time it was accompanied by the unmistakable roar of a storm brewing outside.

I glanced at Grant, the reality of the situation crashing down around us as the world spun wildly on its axis. "Looks like we're not the only ones facing a storm tonight," I murmured, a mix of dread and exhilaration coursing through me.

He laughed softly, the sound rich and warm, cutting through the tension like sunlight breaking through the clouds. "Well, if we can weather this one together, then I'd say we're off to a pretty good start."

And as the tempest raged outside, I felt a flicker of hope ignite within me—a fragile yet powerful light illuminating the unknown path ahead.

The storm outside surged in intensity, its booming echoes rattling the windows as if demanding our attention, but the real tempest raged between us. The air crackled with tension, thick and palpable, as the realization settled—our fragile connection had shifted irrevocably. With a determined glint in his eyes, Grant stepped closer, drawing me into the eye of this emotional hurricane.

"Let's get out of here," he said suddenly, a hint of urgency threading through his voice. "This isn't the place for a conversation like this."

"Are you suggesting we run away? Like, to where? The roof?" I replied, half-joking, the absurdity of the idea masking the anxiety swelling within me. The last thing I wanted was to confront my reality while standing under the shadows of glittering chandeliers and eavesdropping guests.

"Actually, I was thinking the fire escape, but we can use the roof if you're into that sort of thing," he countered, his lips curving into a playful smile. The lightness of his banter was a balm to my frayed nerves, but beneath it lay an urgency that pressed on my heart.

"Fine, let's go before someone decides to come check on us." I nodded, my pulse quickening not just from the impending discussion but from the thrill of defiance. Together, we slipped through the throngs of confused guests, weaving past the chaos of the event. The walls felt confining, closing in with the weight of the unspoken.

We made our way to the fire escape, its rusty metal ladder creaking ominously as we ascended. The gust of wind that greeted us on the roof was invigorating, a sharp contrast to the tension that had built in the room below. The skyline glimmered under the weight of the storm clouds, the city a tapestry of lights and shadows. I breathed in the cool air, feeling the chill seep into my bones, awakening senses dulled by the pressure of the evening.

"What's so special about being up here?" I asked, attempting to lighten the mood, though the gravity of our earlier conversation lingered like a specter.

"Freedom, maybe?" Grant replied, leaning against the low wall, his gaze fixed on the horizon. "Or perhaps it's just a good spot to look down at the chaos we just escaped. It's hard to think when you're surrounded by so many people."

"True, but I'd argue that chaos has its own allure," I mused, glancing at him. "Just look at us; we're like a walking soap opera right now."

He laughed, a rich sound that cut through the tension. "And yet here we are, trying to unravel a mystery that seems to be more tangled than my headphones after a long day."

"Now that's an impressive analogy," I smirked, grateful for the light-heartedness even as the storm within me raged on. "But let's get to the part where you want to know why I'm a freak of nature."

His smile faded, replaced by the seriousness of the moment. "Okay, let's lay it all on the table. You have a gift, or a curse, depending on how you look at it. It's something you haven't learned to control yet, but it doesn't define you. So why hide it?"

I turned to face him fully, feeling the weight of my own secrets pressing down like the clouds above. "Because I don't want to be defined by what I can't understand. It's terrifying, Grant. I've spent my whole life feeling like a misfit, and the last thing I wanted was for someone like you to see me as broken or... strange."

"Strange? Maybe. But that's what makes you interesting. I'm not looking for perfection; I'm looking for honesty." His gaze softened, and I felt the warmth radiating from him, drawing me closer.

"Honesty? You mean the kind where I tell you I might accidentally fry your brain if you get too close?"

"Exactly that," he replied, laughter dancing in his eyes. "Though I have to admit, I'm more worried about my heart being fried than my brain."

The air shifted, and a gust of wind swept across the rooftop, sending a shiver down my spine. I moved a little closer, drawn by both the chill of the wind and the warmth radiating from him. "Okay, here's the truth," I began, my voice steadying as I prepared to unearth the secrets I had buried deep. "I've never really understood my connection to technology. When I was a kid, things would just... malfunction around me. It was like I had a gravitational pull on electronic devices. I learned to avoid them—phones, computers, anything with a circuit board. The fewer things I touched, the better."

"Wow," Grant said, his tone serious now. "And you've been living with this all your life?"

"Pretty much. It made me feel like a walking hazard," I admitted, a hint of bitterness creeping into my voice. "So when I met you, I thought maybe I could be different. Maybe I could have a normal life, but I never imagined I would find someone who made me feel... accepted."

His expression softened, and I could see him processing my words, the realization of my struggle dawning upon him. "You don't need to hide from me, you know that, right? This doesn't change how I feel about you."

The warmth of his words flooded over me, igniting a flicker of hope in the shadowy corners of my heart. "You really mean that?"

"Of course I do. I've watched you navigate this mess, and it only makes me respect you more. You're not a freak; you're extraordinary," he said, his voice filled with sincerity.

I felt a mix of relief and trepidation wash over me, but before I could fully absorb the weight of his words, the clouds above burst open, releasing a torrential downpour. The rain pelted down in sheets, and the rooftop quickly transformed into a slippery canvas of chaos.

"Great timing!" I shouted over the din, laughter bubbling up despite the situation. "A little dramatic, don't you think?"

"Just nature's way of making our moment memorable," he quipped, stepping closer to shield me from the worst of the rain. "Let's get back inside before we both get drenched."

But as we turned to head back, a blinding flash of lightning illuminated the sky, and a deafening clap of thunder rumbled, vibrating through the air. In that instant, the ground beneath us trembled—a low, ominous vibration that sent a jolt of fear through me.

"What was that?" I gasped, gripping the ledge for support as the world seemed to shake.

"I don't know," Grant said, his eyes scanning the horizon, the light reflecting in his gaze. "It felt... different."

Before I could respond, the air crackled once more, and I felt an odd sensation in my chest, like static electricity dancing along my skin. I looked at him, and we shared a moment of understanding, a realization that whatever was happening, it was connected to me.

Then, just as quickly as it had begun, the tremor ceased, leaving a disconcerting silence in its wake. The rain fell steadily, but a heavy fog rolled in, obscuring our view of the city below.

"Let's go," Grant urged, but as he turned, I felt a powerful pull, as if the very air was charged with something more than just rain. A flicker of energy surged around me, and for a split second, I saw a vision—images of wires fraying, machines sparking, and a shadowy figure looming in the distance, watching us with intent.

"Wait!" I gasped, grasping his arm. "There's something else—something I need to tell you."

But just then, the ground trembled again, this time accompanied by a low growl of thunder that rumbled through the very bones of the building. My heart raced as I realized this was no ordinary storm; it felt like a warning.

"Julia!" Grant shouted, panic creeping into his voice as the shadows seemed to close in around us. "We need to get inside now!"

But it was too late. The fog thickened, and the ground shook once more, sending a shockwave of fear through me. I turned to him, my heart pounding, just as another flash of lightning illuminated the darkness, revealing the silhouette of that shadowy figure standing on the edge of the roof.

"Who are you?" I breathed, my voice barely a whisper.

And as the figure stepped closer, the world around us plunged into chaos, the storm roaring to life, and I realized that the true battle was just beginning.

Chapter 9: The Reckoning

The aftermath of the launch event unfurls like a tattered flag caught in a tempest. I stand at the threshold of my apartment, the scents of cinnamon and burnt coffee mingling in the air, a comforting yet chaotic backdrop to the storm brewing outside. The bustling streets of Brooklyn, once a canvas of vibrant colors and eclectic sounds, have transformed into a battleground of whispers. Gossip drips from the lips of my neighbors, each word sharp enough to slice through the dense fog of uncertainty that clings to me like the summer humidity.

As I pour a cup of what I optimistically refer to as coffee, my hands tremble slightly, not from caffeine but from the electric anticipation of what's to come. The mug, adorned with a cheeky saying about the necessity of caffeine in a world gone mad, seems to mock me as I take a sip. The taste is bitter, much like the reality I'm grappling with. Every swirl of steam rising from the cup carries with it the ghosts of my decisions, the uninvited consequences of a single night where glamour and magic collided in a spectacular burst of color and chaos.

Outside my window, the city pulses with life, its heartbeat quickening as if it senses the turmoil within me. The chatter of voices filters in, punctuated by the occasional honk of a taxi or the rhythmic clatter of heels on the pavement. Yet beneath that familiar symphony lies a darker undercurrent, the whispers of the corporate witches growing louder, more insistent. They've caught a whiff of my power, and like sharks sensing blood in the water, they circle, waiting for the moment I show weakness.

I draw a deep breath, grounding myself against the chaos. The walls around me feel less like a sanctuary and more like a cage. The magic I once wielded with such ease now thrums within me, restless and wild, as if it knows I am on the precipice of a decision that could shatter the very foundation of my existence. It pushes against my boundaries, demanding release, demanding recognition, and yet I hesitate. What if I unleash it and lose control? What if I become the very thing I've feared?

Just then, a knock on the door sends a jolt through me, breaking my reverie. The sound echoes in the silence, insistent and heavy. I glance at the clock—far too early for friendly visits, and certainly too early for corporate witches. Heart racing, I wipe my palms on my jeans and step toward the door, each footfall a reminder of the stakes I'm navigating.

I fling the door open to reveal Grant, standing there like a beacon of calm amid my storm. His dark hair tousled, a hint of stubble lining his jaw, he looks like he's just stepped off a magazine cover dedicated to effortlessly cool New Yorkers. But the shadows under his eyes tell a different story. "We need to talk," he says, his voice low, tinged with urgency.

"Talk? Or do you mean another one of your spontaneous escapades?" I shoot back, my sarcasm a feeble shield against the anxiety clawing at my insides. I can't deny the spark of familiarity that ignites between us, an unspoken connection that has deepened since that chaotic night. But this isn't the time for flirting or nostalgia; the stakes are too high.

"Can I come in?" His eyes flicker to the hallway, as if anticipating an audience. I nod reluctantly and step aside, feeling the weight of our past settling around us like an old quilt—familiar yet fraying at the seams.

Once inside, he leans against the door, his posture relaxed but his expression intense. "It's about the launch event. There's been fallout—serious fallout. The witches are mobilizing, and they want you."

"Me?" I laugh, but it comes out hollow, a brittle sound that doesn't quite mask my fear. "I'm just a girl trying to make a living here, Grant. They can't just... decide to want me. It's not like I'm some rare magical artifact."

His gaze sharpens, the warmth in his eyes replaced by something colder, more resolute. "You're more than just a girl. You have power, and they know it. You were the one who sparked that energy at the event, and they want to harness it."

I swallow hard, the implications of his words settling in the pit of my stomach like a stone. The magic that had once felt like a playful companion now loomed over me like a specter, threatening to consume me whole. "What do they want with me?" I whisper, the fear lacing my voice more palpable than ever.

"To control you. To use you for their own purposes. You're a conduit for something bigger, and they'll stop at nothing to exploit it." He steps closer, his breath mingling with mine in the stillness of the room. "We need to figure this out. Together."

Together. The word hangs between us, heavy with the weight of what it could mean. A part of me craves that bond, that alliance forged in the fires of chaos, but another part recoils at the thought. I can't drag him into this mess; he deserves better than the turmoil I've unleashed.

"Grant, you don't have to—"

"I'm not leaving you to deal with this alone." His voice is firm, cutting through my hesitations like a blade. "You think I'd let the witches sink their claws into you while I stand idly by? Not a chance."

A rush of warmth spreads through me, wrapping around my heart like a silken ribbon. In this moment, amidst the swirling storm of uncertainty, I realize that perhaps I don't have to face this reckoning alone. The choice that looms on the horizon feels less daunting with him by my side, even if it means diving into the abyss together.

"I'm scared," I admit, the vulnerability spilling from my lips, surprising both of us.

"Good," he replies, a smirk dancing at the corners of his mouth. "It means you're still human. Embrace it, and let's figure out how to turn the tide. Together."

In the face of looming darkness, I find strength in his words. The city outside continues its relentless rhythm, but in this moment, time seems to stand still as we prepare to confront the wild, untamed magic that binds us both.

The coffee pot gurgles its last breath, an almost mournful sound, as I pour the dregs into a chipped mug that has seen better days. I stand at my kitchen counter, an island of chaos amid the turbulent sea of my thoughts. The flickering fluorescent light above casts an unforgiving glare, illuminating the scattered papers—bills, notes, and remnants of half-formed spells that have turned into dust bunnies beneath my couch. Each of them represents a choice I've made or a path I've avoided, and right now, I'm overwhelmed by the multitude of decisions waiting to be faced.

Grant leans against the wall, arms crossed, a silent sentinel amidst my internal storm. His presence is both grounding and unsettling; he exudes an air of confidence that makes my heart race, but I can't ignore the gnawing worry that hangs between us. What if my choices put him in harm's way?

"I'm not going to disappear on you, you know," he says, breaking the silence. His voice carries a hint of amusement, but there's a seriousness lurking beneath. "You're acting like I'm going to vanish into thin air if things get dicey."

"Maybe I just want to be the one who vanishes," I shoot back, attempting to mask my vulnerability with bravado. "A nice beach, some sun, and a cocktail that doesn't involve magic sound pretty appealing right now."

"Ah yes, because running away has always been your strong suit," he quips, a knowing smile playing on his lips. "Remember last summer when you tried to escape to the Hamptons? You ended up back in the city the next day because you couldn't resist the lure of your favorite taco truck."

A smile tugs at the corners of my mouth, and for a brief moment, the tension in the room eases. The taco truck was a good memory, one of those tiny joys that make the chaos of life bearable. "Okay, fine, you got me there," I concede. "But this isn't a taco truck situation, Grant. We're dealing with witches who are probably conjuring my demise as we speak."

"Then let's be the ones conjuring something better." His tone shifts, the playful banter giving way to something more earnest. "You have power, Emma. Power that could reshape everything."

I narrow my eyes, skepticism creeping in. "And what if I can't control it? What if I end up like one of those cautionary tales you hear about on the subway?" I shudder at the thought of being consumed by my magic, becoming a cautionary legend whispered about in hushed tones. "You've seen how it reacts when I get flustered. It's like a wild stallion that thinks it's a unicorn."

He steps closer, his gaze steady and unyielding. "That's exactly why you need to embrace it. Tame the wild stallion, ride it, and turn it into something spectacular."

The gravity of his words settles on me like a heavy cloak, both comforting and constricting. I take a deep breath, letting the warmth of his presence seep into my skin, urging me to step beyond my fears. "And if I fail?"

"Then we'll deal with it. Together."

As the words hang in the air, the weight of our situation seems to shift, and I feel the first flicker of hope igniting in the pit of my stomach. Just then, a sharp knock on the door startles us both, slicing through the tension like a hot knife through butter. My heart races as I exchange a quick glance with Grant, the unspoken question lingering between us: Who could it be now?

Before I can voice my concerns, he strides toward the door, a protective energy radiating from him. "Let me handle this," he says, his tone leaving no room for argument. He opens the door, and my heart sinks.

Standing there, arms crossed and a smug smile plastered on her face, is Miriam, one of the corporate witches who had made her presence known at the launch event. She's draped in a sleek, dark trench coat that complements her raven hair and striking features, looking every bit the formidable force that she is.

"Good morning, Emma," she says, her voice dripping with saccharine sweetness that makes my skin crawl. "I hope I'm not interrupting anything important."

"Oh, just planning world domination, you know, the usual," I reply, my voice laced with sarcasm as I shoot a glance at Grant, who is still standing protectively in front of me.

Miriam's smile widens, but it doesn't reach her eyes. "Charming as always. I'm here to discuss a very important matter regarding your recent... escapade."

"Isn't it customary to send a text or something before dropping by uninvited?" I counter, crossing my arms defiantly.

"Perhaps, but urgency calls for direct action." Her gaze sweeps past me, assessing the state of my apartment with a critical eye. "You seem a bit... frazzled. Magic running wild? I can help with that."

"I'm sure you can," I say, sarcasm lacing my words again. "But I'm not interested in your kind of help."

"Is that so?" Her eyes glint with something sharper, something dangerous. "You see, my dear Emma, your magic is far too potent to be left untamed. You don't truly understand what you're capable of, but I do. And I assure you, I can help you channel it. For a price, of course."

"I'm not for sale," I retort, the words spilling from my lips with a defiance that surprises even me. Grant stands beside me, an unwavering presence, and I feel emboldened.

Miriam's expression hardens, a flicker of irritation flashing across her face. "Think carefully before you dismiss this offer. The witches are mobilizing, and soon you'll find yourself backed into a corner. Power doesn't wait for anyone, least of all you."

Her words hang heavily in the air, each one a dagger aimed directly at my heart. Fear coils around me, and I sense Grant's hand brush against mine, a subtle reminder that I'm not alone in this. "You don't know what you're asking for," I say, my voice steady despite the tremor of uncertainty beneath.

"I know exactly what I'm asking for. And the question is, do you want to be the master of your destiny, or do you want to be a pawn in someone else's game?"

The ultimatum sits between us, charged with tension and the weight of impending choices. Grant shifts beside me, his presence a steadying force against the whirlwind of thoughts spinning in my mind. I can feel the heat of the magic inside me, restless and eager, reacting to the challenge laid before me.

In that moment, the air crackles with possibility. The decision looms large, and though fear tugs at my insides, I can't ignore the flicker of excitement sparking to life. There is power within me—wild, untamed power. The question now isn't whether to embrace it, but how. As I meet Miriam's challenging gaze, I realize the reckoning is not just about magic; it's about choosing who I will become in this chaotic dance of fate.

The tension in the air thickens, each heartbeat echoing like a drumroll as I face Miriam, the embodiment of everything I've been trying to avoid. Grant's steady presence beside me provides a fragile comfort, yet my heart races with uncertainty. The light filtering through the window glints off Miriam's dark trench coat, casting a shadow that seems to stretch ominously across the room.

"I'm not interested in playing your games," I say, forcing my voice to remain even. "I won't be part of your power-hungry machinations."

Miriam tilts her head, a sardonic smile playing on her lips. "You misunderstand me, dear. This isn't a game; this is survival. You may see yourself as some innocent bystander, but the world you've stepped into is far more dangerous than you realize. The witches are gathering, and they will not hesitate to use force if necessary."

A chill runs down my spine at the thought of a coven converging, their intentions clouded in mystery and malice. I glance at Grant, whose jaw is set, eyes narrowed in determination. "And you think I can just stroll into that chaos, magic at my fingertips, and be the hero?"

Miriam takes a step closer, her voice dropping to a conspiratorial whisper. "Not a hero, Emma. A queen. You're on the verge of a great awakening, and you need guidance to harness it. I could be that guide."

I hold her gaze, my stomach churning with a mix of temptation and revulsion. The allure of power flickers like a flame, drawing me closer even as I want to step back. "And what's your price?"

Her smile widens, revealing a hint of sharp teeth beneath. "It's simple. I want your allegiance. Your loyalty to the coven. In return, I will teach you to control your magic. Imagine what you could accomplish—what we could accomplish—together."

A soft laugh escapes me, tinged with disbelief. "So, I get to play the pawn in your power struggle, and in exchange, I become your personal sorceress? Sounds like a fantastic deal."

"Think of it as an investment," she replies, her voice smooth as silk. "You don't have to trust me now, but when the time comes, you'll realize that aligning with us is your best chance of survival."

"Survival, huh?" I echo, sarcasm lacing my words as I cross my arms defensively. "What's your version of survival? Spilling my secrets to the highest bidder? I'd rather take my chances with the witches outside than risk becoming your little puppet."

Miriam's expression hardens, the veneer of charm slipping away like the last light of dusk. "You are making a grave mistake, Emma. Your magic is a beacon, and those who see it will come for you. They won't be as lenient as I am."

"Lenient?" I scoff, disbelief washing over me. "You're the one standing in my living room, trying to manipulate me into joining your coven. How's that for 'lenient'?"

Grant steps forward, cutting through the tension. "You need to leave," he states, voice firm but low, the kind of tone that would make a lesser witch quail in her heels. "We're not interested in your offers or your threats."

Miriam's eyes flash, a predator sensing that the hunt may be slipping through her fingers. "You'll regret this, both of you. The world is shifting, and when it does, I hope you're not caught on the wrong side."

With that, she turns on her heel, gliding out of my apartment as if she were made of shadows, leaving behind a suffocating silence that seems to echo her warning. I exhale, a rush of relief mingled with apprehension flooding through me. "That was fun," I murmur, attempting to lighten the atmosphere.

Grant chuckles, the tension easing slightly. "Yes, because nothing says 'great day' like being threatened by a corporate witch."

"Do you think she'll actually come after us?" I ask, my voice wavering as the gravity of her words sinks in.

"Possibly," he replies, his brow furrowing. "But we'll be ready. We can't let fear dictate our next moves. We need to find a way to harness your magic, not just for self-defense, but to take back control."

"Control," I echo, the word tasting foreign on my tongue. "You make it sound so simple. Just channel the wild magic inside me like I'm flipping a switch."

"Maybe not simple," he concedes, "but it's a start. We need to understand what you're capable of. If we can draw on your strength, we can face whatever comes next."

I nod, though my mind races with the implications of that statement. What if I could control my magic? What if I could be the queen Miriam mentioned, wielding power instead of cowering beneath it? But the thought also sends a shiver of fear down my spine. What would it mean for me to embrace that identity?

"First things first, we need a plan," I say, attempting to refocus. "A safe place to practice and learn how to wield this magic without, you know, accidentally blowing something up."

"Agreed," Grant replies, his tone turning serious again. "We should find someone who can help—someone knowledgeable about the arcane arts."

"Do you have anyone in mind?" I ask, my heart racing at the thought of reaching out to another witch. The very idea makes my skin prickle, but I know it's necessary.

"There's a woman I've heard whispers about. They say she's powerful and has a way of teaching those who seek her guidance." He hesitates, searching my eyes for a response. "But she's not easy to find. And some say she's... eccentric."

"Eccentric?" I repeat, a mixture of dread and curiosity swirling within me. "Define 'eccentric'—are we talking oddball neighbor with garden gnomes or more like 'witch of the woods'?"

"More the latter," he says, a smile breaking through. "She's rumored to live on the outskirts of Brooklyn, a little cottage nestled among the trees. It's like stepping into a fairytale, but there are stories that she doesn't take kindly to uninvited guests."

"I suppose that makes two of us," I mutter, half-joking.

"Don't worry. I'll handle the introductions." He brushes a hand through his hair, revealing a spark of determination that makes me believe he can do it. "Just remember, whatever she's like, we'll face it together."

As we prepare to venture into the unknown, I can feel the weight of Miriam's words lurking at the edges of my consciousness. The world outside feels different now, charged with an energy I can't quite place, as if it's holding its breath, waiting for something to happen.

We step out into the bustling Brooklyn streets, where the familiar cacophony feels like an entirely different world. The air is alive with possibilities, and a flicker of excitement ignites within me, pushing me forward. But as we walk, a sudden chill wraps around me, a warning against the impending storm.

Then, as if summoned by my very thoughts, a shadow flits past, cloaked in darkness. I glance around, but the streets remain bustling and bright. Just when I think my mind is playing tricks on me, a sharp scream pierces the air—a sound filled with sheer terror.

I turn, my heart racing as the reality of the moment slams into me. There, in the distance, a figure stands shrouded in darkness, pointing directly at me. Panic floods my senses as the world around me sharpens into focus, the hustle of the city fading into a hushed silence.

"Emma!" Grant's voice pulls me back, but it's too late; the reckoning has begun, and I can no longer ignore the storm brewing on the horizon. The figure lifts a hand, and in that instant, I realize this is only the beginning.

Chapter 10: Fractured Light

The late afternoon sun spills through the window, drenching my studio in a warm, golden glow that dances playfully on the walls. It's a deceptive light, one that invites tranquility, yet I can't shake the feeling that something sinister lurks just beyond my line of sight. My workbench, cluttered with an assortment of waxes and fragrances, is both my sanctuary and my prison. Each candle I craft is a small act of defiance against the whispering winds of doubt that swirl around me, promising that nothing will ever be the same again.

As I melt the beeswax, the rich, sweet scent envelops me, wrapping around my senses like a comforting blanket. I pour the molten mixture into molds, watching it take shape—this is where I find solace, amidst the flickering flames and the soothing aroma of lavender and sandalwood. Each candle I create is imbued with intention, infused with the hopes and dreams I wish to manifest. I envision the evenings they will light, the shadows they will cast, and the warmth they will bring to cold, dark corners. But with each passing hour, I feel the weight of the witches' warnings pressing heavier on my shoulders, as if they are trying to pull me back into the shadows from which I've only just begun to emerge.

The clang of the doorbell jolts me from my thoughts. It's a sound I've come to dread, for it means another interruption in my fragile peace. I wipe my hands on my apron, the fabric stained with splashes of color from my latest batch of candles, and make my way to the door, my heart quickening with anticipation. I brace myself for another visit from one of the local witches, their faces often cloaked in mysterious intentions.

When I pull open the door, the unexpected sight of Grant sends my heart into a tailspin. He stands there, a hesitant smile playing on his lips, his dark hair tousled as if he's just come from a wild chase. His eyes, usually so steady, flicker with an emotion I can't quite place. I momentarily forget the tension that has built between us, the unspoken words that hang like storm clouds in the air.

"Hey," he says, the single syllable packed with layers of meaning.

"Hey," I reply, my voice steadier than I feel. I'm acutely aware of the chasm that separates us, a distance filled with things left unsaid, doubts festering in the silence.

"Can I come in?" He shifts on his feet, a nervous energy crackling between us.

I step aside, allowing him to enter, the air crackling with unacknowledged tension. The moment he crosses the threshold, I feel a familiar sense of home mixed with an unsettling anxiety. He pauses, taking in the sight of my studio, cluttered yet vibrant, a chaotic symphony of creativity that feels utterly me.

"It smells amazing in here," he says, a hint of nostalgia in his tone. "Like honey and dreams."

I can't help but smile at the compliment, even as I feel a pang of longing for the camaraderie we once shared. "Just trying to create some light," I say, gesturing toward the candle molds scattered across the table.

He moves closer, his fingers grazing the edge of a mold, and I feel the warmth of his presence wash over me. "Are you still working on that new scent?"

"Yeah," I reply, my voice wavering slightly. "It's a blend of jasmine and something earthy. I thought it might ground me, you know?"

He nods, the understanding in his gaze softening the harsh edges of our reality. "I think you're already pretty grounded. But this—" he waves his hand around the studio, "this is like... a magical cocoon."

A flicker of joy dances in my chest, but it's quickly doused by the shadow of our recent estrangement. "Thanks, I guess. But even cocooned creatures have to emerge eventually."

His smile falters, and for a moment, the air thickens with unspoken truths. "What if I told you that you're not alone in this?"

I study him, searching for any sign of the playful banter that once flowed so easily between us. "What do you mean?"

"Those witches..." He hesitates, and I can sense the weight of his next words, like a stone held just below the surface of a tranquil lake. "They're not just here for you. They're trying to keep an eye on things, on the balance of it all."

I scoff lightly, my heart racing. "As if I need their help. I can handle my own magic, thanks."

"But can you?" He leans in closer, his voice dropping to a conspiratorial whisper. "What happened with the last candle? The one you tried to create for the festival?"

The mention of that disaster brings a flood of shame, heat rushing to my cheeks. "That was an accident. I miscalculated the ingredients."

"An accident that caused a bit of a scene," he reminds me gently, his brow furrowed with concern. "And now, they're here, lurking, making sure you're not going to blow us all up."

The jest fails to bring levity; instead, it pricks at my unease. "I'm not some novice witch who can't handle her craft, Grant. I'm—"

"Exactly, you're a talented witch, but talent doesn't always mean control." His voice is low, his eyes earnest, piercing through my bravado. "You need to be careful. The energy here is stronger than it seems. I've seen things—"

"Things? What things?" My voice sharpens, a mixture of fear and curiosity.

"Things that can fracture light, break the very fabric of our reality," he replies, his gaze intense and unwavering. "Things that can pull you under."

I shiver at his words, a sense of foreboding washing over me. "And what makes you think I won't just rise above it?"

"Because," he says, a teasing smile playing on his lips despite the seriousness of our conversation, "I'm worried you'll accidentally become a candle version of a supernova. You light up the room but leave everything around you in ashes."

A laugh bubbles up, unexpected and relieved, cutting through the tension that had threatened to consume us. "So, what's the plan? You're going to keep me from blowing up the neighborhood with my 'supernova' magic?"

He takes a step back, the air between us charged with possibilities. "Why not? After all, it's about time we team up again."

And just like that, the weight of isolation begins to lift, as if the universe itself is shifting back into alignment, one candle at a time.

The familiar scent of melting wax and fragrant oils envelops me as I step back into my sanctuary. The air is thick with a promise, yet it hangs heavy, as though it knows secrets I haven't yet unearthed. Grant's presence lingers in the space between us, a reminder of the connection we once shared—a connection that now feels as fragile as the delicate wick I'm about to thread through a fresh candle mold.

"Can we try a new blend?" he asks, his eyes sparkling with the mischief I've missed. "Something with a little more... flair?"

"Flair? Are you suggesting I make candles that sparkle and sing?" I chuckle, rolling my eyes but already considering the possibilities.

"Maybe just a hint of danger." He leans against the workbench, arms crossed, and I can't help but admire how his casual posture belies a sense of purpose. "You know, to keep the locals on their toes."

"Right, because the last thing I want is for my candles to be associated with spontaneous combustion." I give him a playful nudge, relishing the ease that comes with our banter.

"Hey, if they combust, they'll make a great story at the next coven meeting," he retorts, a twinkle in his eye. "The Candle Witch Strikes Back."

I can't help but laugh, the sound echoing warmly in the space. It's a sound that feels foreign after weeks of solitude, yet familiar enough to stitch some comfort back into my heart. "Well, if you're volunteering to be my safety officer, I might consider it."

"Safety officer? I like the sound of that. It has a nice ring to it, don't you think?" He grins, and for a moment, it feels as if the shadows that had clouded my heart have been lifted, revealing the vibrant colors of our shared history.

"So, what's the first order of business?" I ask, moving to gather my supplies.

"I was thinking," he says, his voice dipping lower as if we're about to embark on a grand adventure, "what if we created a candle for the upcoming harvest festival? Something that encapsulates all the magic of the season."

I pause, considering the idea. The harvest festival has always been a vibrant celebration of the community, a time when the streets are filled with laughter, food, and the earthy scent of autumn. "You mean like a harvest-scented candle?"

"Exactly!" His enthusiasm is contagious. "We could blend the essence of pumpkins, cinnamon, and maybe a hint of something floral, like chrysanthemums. It would be the perfect addition to any celebration."

"Floral? In a harvest candle?" I raise an eyebrow, teasingly skeptical. "Are we making a dessert or a centerpiece?"

"Why not both?" He flashes a boyish grin, and I feel the warmth of our easy connection rekindle in a way I thought was lost. "Imagine it: the comforting scent of spiced pumpkin pie mixed with the crispness of falling leaves, all wrapped in a floral embrace."

I roll my eyes, but I can't help smiling at his enthusiasm. "Alright, let's do it. But I'm calling it 'Autumn's Embrace'—that sounds more poetic and less like we're inviting a food fight."

"Deal!" He claps his hands together, a spark of energy igniting the room. "Now, let's get to work."

As we gather the ingredients, our hands brush occasionally, sending tiny shocks of electricity up my arm. I try to ignore the flutter in my stomach, the memories of our previous connection bubbling up like the wax melting in the pot.

"I missed this," he says suddenly, his tone more serious as he pours a vivid orange wax into a bowl. "I missed us, you know?"

The vulnerability in his words catches me off guard, and I turn to face him, unsure of how to respond. "Me too. It's just…" I hesitate, searching for the right words. "Things have been different since…"

"Since the incident?" he finishes for me, his expression somber.

"Yeah." I sigh, the weight of the past crashing over me like a cold wave. "I don't want to keep having these heavy conversations when all I want is to light candles and feel normal again."

He nods, his brow furrowing in thought. "I get it. But sometimes, addressing the chaos is part of finding that normalcy. We can't just pretend everything's fine."

"Fine. But it has to be in small doses," I say, a playful glint returning to my eye. "For every serious topic, we make a ridiculous candle."

"Now that's a challenge I'm willing to take," he replies, the spark of our banter reigniting. "How about a 'Candle of Unfathomable Regret' for all those heavy moments?"

I can't help but laugh. "Perfect. It could be scented like burnt toast and tears."

We both dissolve into laughter, the tension breaking like a wave against the shore. With renewed energy, we dive into our task, measuring and mixing, the studio becoming a sanctuary of creativity and collaboration. As we blend the ingredients, I find myself more attuned to the rhythms of his movements—how he delicately measures out the cinnamon, how he pours the wax with the confidence of someone who has always belonged here, in this space, with me.

"Hey, what about a dash of clove?" he suggests, peering at the array of spices before us.

"Clove? Bold choice, Mr. Safety Officer." I mockingly adjust my imaginary glasses, adopting a tone of faux seriousness. "What's next? A sprinkle of nutmeg to really spice things up?"

"Why not?" He winks, the charm radiating from him like a beacon. "Let's live a little dangerously."

"Alright, but if anyone asks, we're going for a comforting 'autumn vibe,' not a 'kitchen explosion.'"

As we continue, I find myself feeling lighter, the weight of our earlier conversation lingering but fading into the background. The intimacy of our collaboration fills the studio, the space becoming a canvas painted with laughter and lingering glances. I can see the passion and determination in Grant's eyes, a fire that mirrors my own, igniting an unspoken understanding that we are navigating this unpredictable path together.

With each candle we craft, it feels as though we are sculpting not just wax but also the very essence of our connection. The air thickens with unspoken words, layered with history and potential, and as I glance at him, I can't help but wonder what it would mean to truly embrace this new chapter, to weave our lives together in a way that honors both the past and the unpredictable future ahead.

The rhythm of our candle-making grows more familiar as we work side by side, the harmony between us resonating in ways I hadn't anticipated. Grant moves with a confidence that is both reassuring and energizing. It's remarkable how the simple act of pouring molten wax can feel like a form of alchemy, transforming not just ingredients, but the very essence of our shared moments. As the spicy scent of cinnamon and clove fills the room, I catch glimpses of the old Grant, the one who laughed without reservation, the one who could lighten the heaviest of days with a single quip.

"Okay, but if we're doing this, we need to give our masterpiece a proper backstory," he declares, glancing sideways at me with a conspiratorial grin. "How about a tragic tale of lost love that somehow finds its way back during the harvest festival?"

"Lost love?" I arch an eyebrow, amused. "Are you drawing from personal experience?"

"Touché," he replies, his smirk widening. "But think of it this way: our candle could be a beacon of hope for the heartbroken souls who wander too close to the bonfire."

I laugh, a sound that feels like a soft balm over the frayed edges of my heart. "You're really going for the melodrama, aren't you? What's next? A ballad sung by a wandering minstrel?"

"Only if it's accompanied by a heartfelt lute," he says with a mock-seriousness, and we both dissolve into laughter again.

Yet, beneath our banter lies an undercurrent of something deeper, something that flickers just out of reach. I turn my attention back to the mixing bowl, stirring with purpose as I contemplate our creation. The colors swirl together, each hue blending into the next, creating a vibrant tapestry that reflects our mood, our connection.

"Alright, my poetic partner," I say, bringing the conversation back to the task at hand. "What about the label? It needs a catchy name, something that captures the essence of our tragic romance theme."

"'Fleeting Flames of Autumn Love'?" he suggests, grinning like a schoolboy.

I roll my eyes, half-laughing. "That's a bit much, don't you think? How about something simpler? 'Autumn's Embrace' covers the seasonal aspect without diving too deep into the angsty abyss of love."

"Autumn's Embrace it is," he concedes with mock solemnity. "A candle to warm the hearts and souls, or at least distract them from their impending doom."

With a shared sense of purpose, we pour the fragrant mixture into the molds, the rich amber liquid gliding smoothly, filling the shapes that will soon transform into our aromatic creations. As the candles set, the sun dips lower in the sky, casting a warm glow that dances across the walls like spirits of the season coming to life.

"Have you ever thought about what it would be like to make a candle that actually captured a memory?" Grant asks, his tone suddenly pensive, as if he's wading into deeper waters.

"Like a memory candle?" I consider, intrigued. "What would that even smell like?"

"Exactly! Think about it: you could capture the scent of your grandmother's kitchen or the first time you walked through a field of wildflowers. Each wick would hold a story."

A sense of nostalgia washes over me, stirring memories I hadn't thought of in ages. "My grandmother's kitchen smelled like fresh bread and vanilla. It was a haven."

His gaze softens, and I can see him imagining it, too. "We could create a line of memory candles. Not just scents but experiences."

"And what would your experience be?" I ask, a teasing lilt in my voice.

"Definitely something adventurous, like the smell of the ocean mixed with bonfire smoke—no, wait! The scent of freshly baked cookies with the sound of laughter drifting through the air." His enthusiasm is palpable, and I find myself wishing for more moments like this, where creativity and camaraderie blend effortlessly.

As we finish pouring the last of the wax, I hear the unmistakable sound of voices drifting in from the street below. The annual harvest festival is in full swing, a vibrant celebration of the community that fills the air with laughter, music, and the tantalizing aroma of spiced cider. I can't help but feel a pang of longing, an ache for connection and celebration that feels just out of reach.

"Should we take our creations to the festival?" I suggest, my heart racing at the thought of sharing our work with the world.

"Absolutely! But only if we don't create a stampede with our alluring scents," he quips, winking.

I smile, my heart fluttering at the prospect of stepping back into the world, of engaging with the community that feels both familiar and intimidating. "What if they think we're just two eccentric candle makers?"

"Let them think it," he replies, his confidence infectious. "As long as they're drawn in by the smell and the story, who cares what they think?"

With that, we grab our newly crafted candles, carefully balancing them as we step outside into the crisp autumn air. The streets are alive with color—pumpkins line doorsteps, twinkling lights hang from trees, and laughter dances on the breeze. I take a deep breath, the scent of cinnamon and apples mingling with the earthy aroma of fallen leaves, grounding me.

We weave through the crowd, Grant's arm brushing against mine, the contact sending sparks of familiarity and warmth through me. "So, what's the plan?" he asks, glancing around as if searching for inspiration.

"Let's find a good spot to set up. Maybe by the main square where people gather for the festivities?"

"Great idea," he replies, and we begin to make our way toward the heart of the celebration. As we stroll, I feel the weight of expectation settle on my shoulders, a mix of excitement and anxiety. What if they don't like our candles? What if they think we're just two people playing at witchcraft?

"Relax," Grant says, sensing my apprehension. "It's about having fun and sharing what we love. You know, spreading light."

His words wrap around me like a warm embrace, and I nod, pushing my worries aside as we reach the bustling square. It's a kaleidoscope of joy—children darting between stalls, vendors shouting their wares, and musicians strumming cheerful tunes.

We find a corner to set up our small display, placing our candles on a rustic table adorned with fall leaves and tiny gourds. The flickering flames of our creations dance in the twilight, casting warm shadows that pull people in like moths to a flame.

As night descends, the candles glow more brightly, each one holding the promise of autumn memories and shared stories. I watch as people approach, drawn by the warm scents, their faces lighting up with curiosity and delight. The festival feels alive, an extension of the magic we've created together.

"Look at them!" I say, unable to hide my excitement. "They're loving it!"

"Of course they are," he replies, a grin breaking across his face. "You've poured your heart into these, and that's what they're responding to."

Just then, a shadow moves in the periphery of my vision. I turn to see a woman, cloaked in dark fabric, approaching us with a purposeful stride. The laughter and music fade into the background as she stops before our table, her eyes scanning the candles with an intensity that sends a shiver down my spine.

"Interesting wares you have," she says, her voice low and rich like the earth itself.

I exchange a glance with Grant, unease creeping in as the festival atmosphere shifts around us.

"Uh, thank you!" I manage, forcing a smile. "They're all handmade."

"Handmade indeed," she replies, her gaze piercing through me. "But it is the intentions behind them that truly matter."

"What do you mean?" I ask, my heart quickening.

Her lips curl into a knowing smile, the kind that promises secrets better left untold. "Beware, little candle maker. Sometimes, the light you create can draw forth shadows."

Before I can respond, she turns on her heel and disappears into the crowd, leaving behind an unsettling silence that wraps around us like a fog.

"What was that about?" Grant asks, concern etching his features.

"I—I don't know," I stammer, the weight of her words hanging heavy in the air. "But I have a feeling we're about to find out."

As the festival continues around us, a sense of foreboding settles deep in my bones. The flickering candles cast playful shadows, but I can't shake the feeling that something sinister lurks just beyond the flickering glow. The magic of the evening feels tainted, a reminder that while light can illuminate, it can also reveal the darkness waiting in the corners.

Chapter 11: The Witching Hour

My sleep is plagued by restless dreams, visions of darkened skies over the Brooklyn Bridge and waves of energy rippling through the city. Each night unfolds like a twisted carnival, with shadows flitting at the edges of my mind, never fully forming, yet insistent enough to drag me from the depths of slumber. This particular evening, as I drift between wakefulness and the murky embrace of sleep, I hear whispers calling my name. The sound is soft, almost tender, yet the urgency beneath it prickles my skin. I rise from my bed, drawn to the window, where the city sprawls like a living, breathing entity, vibrant even in the darkness. The skyline glitters like scattered diamonds, and for a moment, I'm entranced, as if the entire world outside is alive, waiting for something to unfold.

The air outside is electric, charged with anticipation, making the hairs on my arms stand at attention. I step into the cool night, my bare feet sinking into the concrete, the chill seeping into my bones. The streets are empty, but they hum with a life of their own, as if the very ground beneath me knows secrets I have yet to uncover. I wander, my feet guided by an instinct I can't quite understand, past the flickering streetlights and shadows that loom larger than life.

As I cross the threshold of an alley, a gust of wind brushes against me, swirling leaves and debris, and I can't shake the feeling that I'm being watched. My heart quickens, a steady thrum echoing in the quiet night. I find myself on a rooftop overlooking the East River, where the moonlight dances on the water, casting a silver sheen over the dark expanse. It's here that I stumble upon a circle of witches gathered, their silhouettes barely discernible in the moonlight, a tapestry of shadow and mystique.

They stand in a loose formation, their voices weaving in and out of the night air, enchanting and chaotic. I feel drawn to them, a moth to the flame, though a whisper of caution tugs at my mind.

"You shouldn't be here," one of them murmurs, her voice like honey dipped in dark mischief. She steps forward, revealing a mane of wild curls and eyes that flicker with a light all their own. "But perhaps you were meant to find us."

"Meant to find you? What are you all doing up here?" I ask, the bravado of my words tinged with disbelief. The witches share a knowing glance, an unspoken language that seems to ripple between them. "The balance of the city is shifting," the one with the wild curls explains, her tone suddenly grave. "We've felt it, felt the threads of fate pulling taut. If we don't act soon, everything you hold dear will be swept away."

My stomach sinks at her words. "What do you mean? What's happening?" I struggle to process the weight of her revelation, my mind racing with images of my life—the café where I work, my tiny apartment filled with books, and the friendships that color my days. The thought of losing it all is a chilling prospect, and I refuse to let fear take root in my heart.

"There's a force at play, something ancient and dark," another witch interjects, her voice like a winter wind, sharp and cold. "It stirs in the depths of the city, and it hungers."

The gravity of their words clings to me, suffocating yet invigorating. "But how can I help? What do you need from me?" I feel a flicker of resolve igniting within, a spark that refuses to be snuffed out.

The first witch tilts her head, studying me with a penetrating gaze. "You possess a light, a potential that resonates with the very heart of this city. But you must learn to harness it, to wield it against the darkness encroaching upon us."

My pulse quickens at the thought. "What does that even mean? I don't know anything about magic or whatever this is." I wave a hand toward the circle, the flickering shadows and whispered incantations swirling around us. "I'm just an ordinary girl."

"Ordinary?" she scoffs, a mischievous smile breaking across her face. "Ordinary is an illusion, darling. All it takes is a spark." She gestures to the others, who nod in agreement, their expressions shifting from solemn to spirited. "We can guide you, teach you the ways of our craft. But you must be willing to embrace it."

The prospect both excites and terrifies me. What do I really know about witches? Growing up, they were always painted as sinister figures, lurking in the woods, chanting spells under the cover of night. But these women, standing together beneath the full moon, radiate a power that feels more like a dance than a threat.

I take a deep breath, inhaling the scent of the river and the distant notes of city life. "I'm in," I declare, surprising myself with the conviction in my voice. "Tell me what to do."

As they begin to instruct me, the words wash over me like a tide, invigorating and overwhelming. The sky above shifts, dark clouds creeping in as if drawn to our gathering. I can feel the energy crackling, pulsing around us like a living thing, and for the first time, I understand that I'm standing at the precipice of something monumental, a choice that could alter the course of my life forever. The air thickens with magic, and I know this is just the beginning.

As the witches begin their incantations, their voices intertwine like threads of silk, delicate yet firm, weaving a tapestry of magic that envelops me. Each syllable reverberates in my bones, and I can feel the energy coiling around us, tightening like a noose of anticipation. I watch as they move, fluid and graceful, their gestures choreographed in a way that speaks of long hours spent mastering their craft. My heart races with exhilaration, a heady mix of fear and thrill.

"First, you must ground yourself," the wild-haired witch instructs, her tone softening. "Feel the earth beneath your feet. Let it anchor you." I close my eyes, willing my breath to slow, and focus on the rough texture of the rooftop underfoot, the way the cool air dances around my skin.

"Okay, I'm grounded," I declare, opening my eyes with a hint of bravado, despite the tremor in my voice.

"More like you're just standing there, looking cute," another witch quips, her dark hair cascading over her shoulders like a waterfall. "But we'll take it."

"Cute? I'll have you know I'm also incredibly brave," I shoot back, a smile creeping across my face.

"Bravery is just a costume we wear to hide our terror," she replies, her eyes sparkling with mischief. "But let's see if you can conjure something real."

The air shifts again, and I sense the potency of their magic surging around me, an undercurrent that tingles against my skin. "What do you want me to conjure?" I ask, half-joking, my heart racing with the idea that maybe, just maybe, I could summon something extraordinary.

"Start with a feeling," the wild-haired witch suggests, her voice turning serious. "What do you want most in this moment?"

I hesitate, the question unfolding in my mind like a blooming flower. "To understand all of this. To feel... connected." I gesture to the skyline, the moon reflecting on the water like a path leading me somewhere unknown. "Everything feels so chaotic. I want to know how to navigate it."

The witches exchange knowing glances, and the air thickens with unspoken words. "That's a powerful wish," the wild-haired one muses, and suddenly, a gust of wind sweeps through, rustling our clothing and sending a chill down my spine. "Focus on that, let it fill you."

As I close my eyes again, I feel warmth bloom in my chest, a vibrant light pulsing in rhythm with my heartbeat. I envision the city, not just as a collection of buildings and streets but as a living organism, each person a vital cell within its body. The thought ignites something deep within me, and I project that feeling outward, letting it swirl around me, seeking connection.

The witches begin to chant, their voices rising in intensity, the vibrations threading through the air. I feel something shift within me, like a door opening to a hidden chamber, revealing not just the power of my desire but the interconnectedness of everything around us. My heart races as I catch glimpses of faces flickering through my mind—friends, strangers, and memories I had almost forgotten. Each one radiates a warmth, and for a moment, I can see the city as a tapestry, vibrant and alive.

"Keep going," the dark-haired witch encourages, her eyes gleaming. "Let it out."

"I want to protect it," I breathe, barely aware of my own voice. "I want to protect my city, my home."

Suddenly, the ground beneath me trembles, a soft rumble that reverberates through my body, urging me to look down. The earth seems to pulse in response to my words, and I gasp as a shimmering light begins to rise from the rooftop, swirling in brilliant hues of gold and green. The witches step back, their expressions shifting from anticipation to awe.

"Do you see?" the wild-haired witch whispers, her voice trembling with excitement. "You're creating it!"

I blink, hardly able to believe it. The colors swirl around us like ribbons, weaving a cocoon of light. My heart swells with joy, and a sense of power surges through me, overwhelming yet exhilarating. "I didn't know I could do this," I whisper, feeling more alive than I ever have.

But the moment is fleeting. A sharp crack slices through the air, and the brilliant light flickers violently, dimming in an instant. My heart drops as shadows loom larger at the edges of our circle. The witches share worried glances, and I feel the magic quivering around us, uncertain and vulnerable.

"What was that?" I ask, my voice edged with panic.

"There's something else," the wild-haired witch says, her gaze darting toward the horizon. "An imbalance. We need to contain it."

Before I can process her words, a figure emerges from the shadows, a dark silhouette against the fading light. My pulse quickens, fear coiling around my heart. "Who are you?" I demand, my voice steadier than I feel.

The figure steps forward, revealing a man cloaked in shadows, his features obscured but his presence undeniable. "You've stirred the waters, little witch," he says, his voice smooth and dangerous, like silk wrapped around a blade. "And now, you must face the consequences."

An unsettling chill races down my spine. "What do you want?" I challenge, defiance flaring within me.

He smirks, a flicker of amusement in his dark eyes. "To restore balance. You've tapped into forces you don't yet understand."

"Perhaps you should enlighten me," I shoot back, my bravado masking the trembling uncertainty beneath.

"Enlightenment has its price," he replies cryptically, the shadows around him swirling like tendrils of smoke. "And you may not be ready to pay it."

Before I can respond, the witches huddle closer, their voices rising in a flurry of incantations, trying to reclaim the energy that is threatening to spiral out of control. I stand there, caught in a web of magic and danger, knowing that the moment has transformed from exhilarating to perilous in the blink of an eye. The city I longed to protect suddenly feels like a battleground, and I'm just beginning to realize that the fight has only just begun.

The air crackles with tension, the weight of the figure before me suffocating and charged, as if every breath I take is an invitation to danger. The witches huddle closer together, their faces drawn with concern, and I can feel the pulse of their magic thrumming in the space between us. I can't back down; something has shifted, and I've found myself in the middle of a storm, both thrilling and terrifying.

"Why should I trust you?" I challenge the shadowy figure, my voice firm despite the quickened rhythm of my heart. "You just materialized out of nowhere, and now you're talking about balance like it's a game."

He steps forward, the moonlight catching the edges of his face, revealing a chiseled jaw and eyes that glimmer with a dangerous allure. "Trust is a luxury you can't afford right now," he replies, a wry smile curving his lips. "But know this: what you've awakened tonight has the potential to bring forth a reckoning, and not all of it will be pleasant."

"Thanks for the vote of confidence," I retort, crossing my arms defiantly. "So what is it you want from me? If this is my fault, I'd like to know how to fix it. I'm not about to let some shadowy disaster take everything from me."

He arches an eyebrow, clearly intrigued by my spirit. "Spunk, I like that," he muses, though his eyes darken with something that feels almost predatory. "But recklessness is dangerous. You're on the edge of a precipice, and one wrong step could plunge you into darkness. You want to protect your city, yet you toy with forces beyond your comprehension."

"Then explain it to me!" I demand, my frustration boiling over. "I'm not just going to stand here while you speak in riddles. I deserve to know what I'm dealing with."

His expression softens, just a fraction, and for a fleeting moment, I sense a connection—a hint of understanding that pulls at my chest. "You're brave, but bravery without knowledge is a fool's errand," he says quietly. "There are ancient forces, buried under the weight of this city, that feed on fear and chaos. You've inadvertently stirred them. But it's not too late. You can still learn."

"I'll learn," I assert, determination flooding my veins. "But I need your help. All of this," I gesture to the flickering lights of the city below, the dark water of the East River shimmering under the moonlight, "it matters to me."

"Very well," he concedes, his voice low and smooth, yet there's an undertone of warning. "But you must tread carefully. The deeper you delve, the more perilous the path becomes."

"Great, just what I wanted to hear," I mutter sarcastically, though the truth is I'm both terrified and exhilarated. "So, where do we start?"

"First, you must harness your emotions," he replies, his gaze piercing through me. "Your magic is tied to how you feel. Fear can suffocate it, but so can anger or desperation. You need to channel your energy into something productive."

The witches shift, and the wild-haired one speaks up, her voice filled with urgency. "He's right. We can help you with that, but you must commit to this, body and soul. It won't be easy."

"I'm ready," I promise, feeling the weight of their collective gaze. The energy of the moment feels monumental, and I can't help but want to grasp it tightly.

The shadowy figure nods, a flicker of approval in his eyes. "Let's begin with a simple exercise. Focus on something you love. Allow that emotion to swell within you, and when you feel it strongly enough, project it outward. You'll see how it interacts with the magic surrounding us."

I take a deep breath, closing my eyes and centering myself. Instantly, images flood my mind—my tiny apartment filled with mismatched furniture, the scent of coffee wafting through the air, laughter with friends echoing around me. I latch onto the memory of a rainy day spent curled up with a good book, the world outside forgotten.

As I conjure that warmth, I feel a glow begin to build in my chest, a soft pulse that radiates warmth and safety. "Okay, I can do this," I whisper, though I can't shake the underlying fear that perhaps I can't.

"Let it out," the dark figure encourages, his tone a mix of urgency and fascination. "Project it."

I visualize the golden light flowing from me, wrapping around the witches and the figure, illuminating the rooftop in a soft glow. When I open my eyes, I'm startled by the sight. The light is vibrant, alive, as if it has its own consciousness, swirling and weaving through the air like a ribbon.

"Good," the wild-haired witch praises, her eyes bright with excitement. "But can you maintain it?"

I concentrate harder, willing the light to remain, but as I do, I feel the ground tremble beneath us, the energy shifting dramatically. The shadows deepen, and suddenly, the air feels charged with an uninvited menace.

"What's happening?" I gasp, my concentration faltering as panic wells within me.

The shadowy figure's expression tightens, a flicker of concern crossing his face. "We've drawn attention," he warns, eyes darting toward the edges of the rooftop. "We need to stabilize this before it spirals."

Before I can ask what he means, an explosive gust of wind bursts through, snatching the golden light from my grasp. The light flickers and wanes, and I feel a chilling presence surge around us, overwhelming in its intensity.

The witches shout incantations, their voices rising in a frantic melody as they try to regain control, but the shadows surge forth, twisting and contorting as if alive. A voice echoes from the darkness, low and reverberating, sending chills cascading down my spine. "You think you can summon the light and not face the darkness that comes with it?"

"What are you?" I manage to stammer, feeling the cold seep into my bones. The very essence of fear wraps around me, thick and suffocating.

"I am the reckoning," the voice responds, and in that instant, the shadows coalesce into a figure that looms large and foreboding, a silhouette against the moonlight. Its eyes glow like embers, and as I take a step back, my heart thrumming wildly in my chest, I realize that this battle is far from over.

In that moment, the world tilts, the fragile balance I had hoped to restore threatening to shatter. The city beneath us holds its breath, and I know I have only just begun to understand the depths of the magic at play—and the dangers that come with it.

Chapter 12: An Unexpected Ally

The moon hung low, casting a silvery sheen over the bustling streets of downtown, where the sounds of laughter and hurried footsteps mingled with the distant honk of horns and the clattering of heels on pavement. I found myself in a quiet corner café, its dimly lit interior inviting and warm, an escape from the frenetic energy outside. As I stirred my chamomile tea, the steam swirling in delicate tendrils, I felt a wave of uncertainty wash over me. Grant was back in my life, and the weight of that realization pressed against my chest like a thick fog.

His arrival had come unannounced, as if he were a phantom conjured by my chaotic thoughts. One moment, I was diligently crafting the latest batch of my hand-poured candles—each one infused with fragrant oils and a hint of the magic that lingered just beneath the surface of my everyday existence. The next, there he was, leaning against the doorframe of my workshop, his silhouette sharp against the evening light, exuding an air of confidence that felt both familiar and unsettling. The smile that spread across his face was the same one that had ignited a spark in my heart all those months ago, but this time, there was an edge to it, a layer of something unspoken that left me wary yet intrigued.

"Mind if I join you?" he had asked, his voice a smooth drawl that wrapped around me like a warm blanket, igniting the memories of our past. I nodded, unable to find my voice, as he settled across from me. "I've been thinking about that project I mentioned," he continued, his gaze intense, searching mine for answers. "It's something big—something that could change everything, but I need your help."

I instinctively straightened in my chair, the cozy ambiance of the café fading into a backdrop of uncertainty. "What kind of project?" I asked, feigning nonchalance as I cradled my mug, the warmth seeping into my palms. I knew he was different now, a man shaped by his ambitions, but a part of me still yearned for the boy who had once shared dreams and secrets beneath the stars.

"Top-secret," he said with a smirk that hinted at mischief. "I'm not supposed to talk about it, but I think your candles could hold the key to solving a problem we've encountered." The way he leaned in, the gravity of his words, pulled me closer to the edge of intrigue. "I wouldn't come to you if I didn't believe in your talent. Your craftsmanship is... extraordinary."

There was a pause, a heartbeat suspended in the air as I processed his words. The idea of my candles being used for something significant was intoxicating, yet a nagging apprehension pulled at my gut. The last time I had let my magic out into the world, it had spiraled beyond my control. "Grant, I don't know if I'm the right person for this," I admitted, the honesty trembling on my lips. "My abilities... they're unpredictable."

"Exactly," he countered, his eyes gleaming with an intensity that made my heart race. "That unpredictability is what we need. There's a spark in what you create, something that defies logic. I can't explain it all now, but believe me, we're facing a challenge that requires a little bit of the unexpected."

The air between us crackled, and I could feel the pull of possibility—a thread woven between our lives, connecting the past with the present. I could hear the whispers of my intuition urging me to tread carefully, yet the glimmer of hope in Grant's eyes was hard to resist. We had shared too much history, too many moments steeped in laughter and unspoken words, for me to simply turn away.

"We can meet after hours," he suggested, his tone shifting to one of quiet determination. "No one will be around to judge or interfere. Just you and me, and this project that could change everything."

Against the backdrop of the café, where laughter and conversation danced like the flickering candle flames I cherished, I found myself nodding. It felt like a step into the unknown, a venture into a world where our shared history could blossom anew. "Okay, I'm in," I said, my voice steady even as my heart fluttered with uncertainty. "But we'll need to be cautious. I don't want to unleash anything I can't control."

Grant's smile widened, a flash of triumph that sent warmth blooming in my chest. "We'll figure it out together. I promise."

And just like that, a partnership was forged in the depths of uncertainty. The city hummed outside, but within that small café, we were cocooned in a bubble of potential. As we discussed the logistics, the world around us faded into insignificance. My mind raced with ideas and possibilities, each more vibrant than the last. We sketched out plans on napkins, laughter mingling with serious deliberation, as I felt a flicker of my old self returning.

It wasn't just the prospect of collaborating that sparked joy within me; it was the way Grant looked at me, like I was a treasure he was eager to uncover. The subtle glances and fleeting touches ignited memories of warmth, of late-night talks under the stars and the dreams we had spun together like a web of wonder.

Yet, a part of me hesitated, the remnants of doubt swirling in my mind. This could be a chance for redemption, a way to reclaim the magic I had nearly lost, but it could also unravel everything I held dear. As we wrapped up our meeting, I felt the weight of expectation settle over my shoulders, mingling with an electric thrill that I couldn't shake. This was more than just a project; it was a leap of faith, an unexpected path leading into the heart of the unknown, and for better or worse, I was ready to embrace it.

The first meeting after our fateful conversation had settled into an uneasy rhythm, a blend of anticipation and trepidation that wove through my days. I found myself glancing at my phone, half-hoping for a message from Grant, as the glow of the city lights cast an enchanting glow over the skyline. Our clandestine rendezvous would happen in the quiet of my workshop, where the smell of beeswax and lavender lingered, a sanctuary where time seemed to fold in on itself. Each flicker of the flame as I lit the candles felt like a promise—warmth and light battling the shadows that encroached at the edges of my world.

When Grant arrived, he carried with him a sense of urgency, his presence commanding attention. "We've got a problem," he said, his tone grave, and I felt a shiver race down my spine. "The tech team is stuck. They need something that can bridge the gap between data and intuition, and I think your candles can do just that."

"Bridge the gap? You're not talking about lighting up a room, are you?" I quipped, attempting to lighten the tension as I gestured for him to sit at my workbench. "Because, while I appreciate a good ambiance, I'm not sure I can save the world with a lavender scent."

His chuckle was genuine, cutting through the anxiety like a knife. "You'd be surprised at the power of ambiance. The right scent can enhance cognitive function, trigger memories—"

"Great, but how do we turn that into code?" I leaned back, crossing my arms, trying to mask my excitement with skepticism. "It sounds a little...unorthodox."

"Exactly!" he exclaimed, his enthusiasm infectious. "We need to think outside the box. Imagine combining data algorithms with sensory experiences. Your candles could hold the key to unlocking that connection, creating an environment where intuition and analysis meet."

As he spoke, his hands animatedly slicing through the air, I could see the wheels turning in his mind. There was an energy in the air, a spark of inspiration igniting ideas in both of us. The prospect of using my creations in such an innovative way sent a thrill through me, making my heart race. I had always known there was something special about my candles; they weren't just wax and wicks; they were imbued with a piece of my soul.

"What's the catch?" I asked, narrowing my eyes. "There's always a catch."

"Maybe not a catch, but there are risks," he admitted, his gaze turning serious. "The tech team is skeptical. They need proof that this approach can work before they'll invest resources. That's where you come in."

I bit my lip, the taste of uncertainty souring the thrill that had blossomed moments ago. "You mean I have to perform some kind of demonstration? In front of people who live and breathe binary code?"

"Essentially," he replied, his eyes glinting with mischief. "But think of it this way: this is your chance to showcase your talent on a larger stage, to prove that your work is more than just pretty candles. You could change how they think about the intersection of technology and creativity."

"Change how they think?" I echoed, my heart racing with the prospect, even as a whisper of doubt flickered in the back of my mind. "What if they laugh? What if it doesn't work?"

"Then we laugh too," he replied, a lopsided grin breaking across his face. "But I have a feeling they'll be impressed. I know I am."

As I watched him, that familiar warmth spread through me again, the connection rekindling like the glow of a flame in the dark. Maybe this was a way for me to reclaim the magic I had nearly lost, to redefine what it meant to blend the mundane with the extraordinary. "Okay, I'll do it," I said, my voice steadier than I felt. "But only if you promise to stand by me. I'm not going to face a panel of techies alone."

His expression softened, and the playfulness melted into something deeper, something almost vulnerable. "I wouldn't dream of leaving you to fend for yourself. We're in this together."

Our evenings became a flurry of creativity and collaboration. We worked side by side, sketching out ideas and testing scents that could evoke specific emotions or memories. Each time I dipped my fingers into the warm wax, I felt like I was melding a piece of myself into something greater. It was exhilarating and terrifying, the kind of rush that made my heart race as I danced on the edge of the familiar and the unknown.

One night, as we mixed essential oils, I found myself teasing him about his perfectionist tendencies. "You know, if you keep sniffing that bottle like it's the answer to all our problems, I might just have to start charging you for therapy."

"Trust me," he replied with a smirk, "my problems are far beyond what any candle can fix." He then set the bottle down, leaning closer, the scent of cedarwood enveloping us like a cloak. "But I'm willing to explore a new path, especially if it involves collaboration with you."

My laughter rang through the workshop, mingling with the faint sound of traffic outside. In that moment, it felt like the world outside had faded, leaving just the two of us in our little sanctuary, where dreams flickered like candle flames. Yet, beneath the laughter lay an undercurrent of tension, a reminder that our venture could unravel in unexpected ways.

One late evening, as the city lights shimmered like stars through the workshop window, I noticed Grant's brow furrowed in thought, a storm brewing behind his eyes. "What's on your mind?" I asked, instinctively reaching out to place a hand on his arm.

He hesitated, looking torn between the desire to share and the urge to protect. "I've been thinking about how the team will react when they see the candles. There's a lot at stake here, and I don't want you to get hurt if it doesn't go as planned."

"Thanks for the vote of confidence," I replied, half-joking, though his concern struck a chord within me. "But if it fails, it's not the end of the world. I've faced rejection before. This isn't my first rodeo."

His gaze intensified, and the air between us thickened with unspoken words. "It's different now. We're creating something unique together. You mean something to me beyond just this project."

My heart raced at his admission, a rush of warmth spreading through me, mingling with the lingering threads of doubt. This connection we shared was palpable, a fabric woven with moments of laughter, shared fears, and an underlying current of longing. But with each passing day, I couldn't shake the feeling that we were standing at a precipice, teetering between possibility and peril.

As we leaned closer, the world outside faded, replaced by the quiet intimacy of the workshop, where every flickering candle illuminated our hopes and fears. There, in that fragile space, I realized that whatever happened next, we were forging a path that was uniquely ours, and the unexpected twists were what made the journey all the more thrilling.

The days turned into a blur of candle-making and late-night brainstorming sessions, where the lines between work and companionship began to blur in the warm, flickering light of my workshop. I could feel the anticipation building as our demo day loomed closer. The air was thick with a heady mix of lavender and excitement, each candle we crafted infused with a purpose that felt almost tangible.

"Have you thought about the pitch?" Grant asked one evening, leaning against the counter, his eyes locked on mine, searching for reassurance. He had become an unexpected anchor, a presence that soothed the storm brewing within me.

"Not exactly," I replied, a playful smile dancing on my lips. "I'm still trying to decide if I should wear a lab coat or a witch's hat."

"Please, not the hat. We want to be taken seriously here," he quipped, his laughter a melody that lightened the atmosphere. "But seriously, we should focus on how these candles can enhance cognitive function. If we can convince them to look beyond their spreadsheets and see the potential in our ideas, we might just change the game."

I rolled my eyes playfully. "So, my candles will become the new coffee for the tech world? Just imagine: 'Need to code? Light a candle!'"

"Hey, don't knock it until you've tried it." He stepped closer, the warmth radiating off him mingling with the candlelight. "But in all seriousness, if we can frame this around experience and emotion, we might capture their attention."

As we discussed the finer points of our pitch, a sense of confidence began to take root within me, mingling with the nervous fluttering of uncertainty. It was exhilarating, but I couldn't shake the feeling that the stakes were higher than just winning over a few skeptical techies. This was my chance to reclaim a part of myself that had been lost for too long.

The evening of the presentation arrived with an electric buzz in the air. I dressed carefully, choosing a simple black dress that flowed like the shadows in my workshop, paired with a bold red lipstick that felt like a shield against the nerves fluttering in my stomach. Grant showed up a little earlier than expected, his shirt crisp, a hint of cologne adding to the heady atmosphere.

"Look at you, ready to take the world by storm," he said, his gaze sweeping over me. "I might be the one who's nervous now."

"Don't worry, I'll just cast a spell if things go sideways," I replied, flashing a grin to mask my own anxiety.

He chuckled, but his eyes betrayed a glimmer of concern. "Let's keep the spellcasting to a minimum. We want them to see the magic in the candles, not in any paranormal activity."

We arrived at the tech hub, an imposing structure of glass and steel, its sterile walls a stark contrast to the warmth we'd created in my workshop. The atmosphere inside was electric, the low hum of conversations and the rapid tapping of keyboards echoing through the hall. As we walked into the presentation room, my stomach twisted with anticipation.

"Remember, breathe," Grant murmured as we took our places at the front. "You've got this."

The panelists were seated before us, their expressions ranging from skeptical to mildly intrigued. I took a moment to absorb the ambiance—the sterile lighting, the sleek tables, the cold metal of the microphones. As I stood before them, I felt the weight of my dreams pressing against my chest, a mix of excitement and apprehension swirling within me.

"Thank you for having us," I began, my voice steady as I introduced our project. With each word, I felt the warmth of my candles flickering in my mind, their potential illuminating the path ahead. Grant stood beside me, his confidence radiating, and I could feel the familiar rhythm of our collaboration flowing between us.

As we began demonstrating how each candle scent corresponded to specific cognitive functions, I could see the expressions of the panelists shifting. They leaned in, their interest piqued as the flickering flames danced in tandem with my words. I spoke about how certain fragrances could stimulate memory recall while others encouraged focus and creativity. The atmosphere grew electric, and I could sense the shift in energy, the way our ideas were starting to take root.

Halfway through our pitch, however, I noticed a shadow flickering at the edge of my peripheral vision. One of the panelists, a tall woman with a sharp bob and even sharper features, had a look of skepticism plastered on her face, her arms crossed tightly against her chest. She interjected, her tone laced with condescension. "You really believe that a candle can influence someone's ability to process data? We're in the tech industry, not a holistic spa."

The room held its breath, the tension palpable. I felt Grant's presence shift beside me, ready to defend our work, but I knew I had to handle this. "Actually," I countered, my heart racing, "scientific studies have shown that certain scents can significantly affect mood and cognitive function. It's not just about the flame; it's about creating an environment that fosters creativity and collaboration."

"Sure," she replied with a roll of her eyes, "but can you guarantee results? You're asking us to invest in something that sounds... well, a bit whimsical."

"Whimsical can be effective," I shot back, surprising myself with my boldness. "But if you're looking for guarantees, you might want to reconsider your career choice. Innovation isn't built on guarantees; it's built on taking risks and exploring new ideas."

A murmur of surprise rippled through the room, and I could feel the energy shifting, like a gust of wind stirring the air. Grant shot me an encouraging look, and I knew we had to push forward.

"Let's demonstrate," he suggested, turning to me, his eyes alight with mischief. "How about we light a candle?"

I glanced at the panelists, their expressions a mix of disbelief and curiosity. With a nod, I reached for the lavender candle we had crafted, its soothing scent ready to fill the air. As I lit the wick, the flame flickered to life, casting soft shadows on the walls. Almost immediately, the scent enveloped the room, weaving its way into the corners, wrapping around the panelists like an embrace.

"Close your eyes," I instructed, a spark of intuition guiding my words. "Breathe deeply and focus on the scent. Let it wash over you."

As they complied, I could feel the energy shift again, the atmosphere thickening with anticipation. It was a gamble, a leap of faith that could either make or break our pitch. Moments passed, each heartbeat thundering in my ears as the tension coiled tighter.

Then, one by one, their expressions began to soften. The woman who had been so skeptical opened her eyes, a flicker of surprise crossing her features. "That's... actually calming," she admitted, her voice softer than before.

Encouraged, I pressed on, "Now, imagine harnessing this effect in a workplace setting. The potential for increased productivity and creativity is not only possible; it's measurable."

Just as I felt the tide turning in our favor, the lights flickered. The sudden change caught everyone off guard, and for a brief moment, panic skated across the room like a winter chill. But I was no stranger to unexpected twists. I turned to Grant, ready to reassure him that we could manage whatever hiccup came our way.

However, as I looked toward him, I noticed the shadow behind his eyes—a flicker of something darker. It was a brief flash, but it sent a jolt of unease through me. Before I could ask what was wrong, the lights dimmed further, plunging us into near darkness, the candles' flickering flames suddenly the only source of light.

"Is this part of the presentation?" a voice called out, tension threading through the air as whispers began to ripple among the panelists.

"No! This shouldn't be happening!" I exclaimed, my heart racing as the room seemed to grow colder, the atmosphere thickening with an energy that felt almost alive.

And then, in the depths of that encroaching darkness, I caught a glimpse of something unexpected—a shadow darting at the edge of my vision, moving with a speed and intent that sent chills down my spine. I turned to Grant, a question poised on my lips, but before I could speak, the candle flames flickered violently, casting eerie shapes on the walls.

The door slammed open, the sound echoing through the room, and my breath caught in my throat. A figure stood silhouetted in the doorway, the details obscured by the shadows, but the presence was unmistakable—a wave of unease swept through me as I realized that whatever this was, it was far beyond just a simple tech presentation.

"Grant!" I shouted, panic rising as the figure stepped closer, and the flickering light revealed a face I never expected to see. A face that threatened to unravel everything I thought I knew.

Chapter 13: Glitches in the Code

The fluorescent lights flickered overhead as I leaned closer to the screen, the soft hum of the computer blending with the rhythmic tapping of Grant's fingers against the keyboard. Each keystroke felt like a spell, a delicate incantation that summoned something neither of us fully grasped. My heart raced as I watched the lines of code swirl into a frenzied dance, intertwining with the remnants of my magic lingering in the air like the sweet scent of lilacs in spring. It was intoxicating and terrifying, a heady mix that left my senses heightened.

"Did you see that?" Grant's voice broke through my reverie, sharp and excited. His brow furrowed, deepening the lines of concentration etched into his face, giving him an intensity that made it hard to look away. "The glitch—it's not just a malfunction. It's almost... alive." He turned to me, his eyes alight with curiosity and something deeper, something I dared not label.

I swallowed hard, feeling the weight of the revelation settle between us like a heavy fog. "Alive?" I echoed, searching for the right words. "Or perhaps it's just reacting to my magic. You know how unpredictable these things can be." The truth was more complex than I dared admit. Every time I conjured a spell, the air shimmered, and the digital world responded with echoes of my intent, like a mirror reflecting my innermost thoughts. It was exhilarating and frightening, and I was beginning to wonder if we were tampering with forces better left undisturbed.

He shook his head, the frustration palpable. "You're too modest. Magic or not, this code is bending in ways I've never seen before. It's like it wants something." His gaze held mine, searching for a deeper understanding, or perhaps for confirmation of his growing theory.

The words hung in the air between us, thick with tension. "Wants something?" I mused, rolling the thought over in my mind like a crystal ball in the palm of my hand. The idea that our collaboration was awakening a dormant consciousness in the code felt absurd, yet undeniable. I could feel it too, a subtle energy thrumming beneath my skin, beckoning me to explore the uncharted territory of our combined skills.

"Maybe we should take a break," I suggested, my voice a soft whisper against the backdrop of clacking keys. "Step back and reassess. This might not be what we think it is." A part of me, the rational part, clung to the notion of safety, while another part yearned for the thrill of discovery. The latter won out, as it always did.

Grant leaned back in his chair, rubbing his temples. "A break? We've hardly made any progress. If anything, we're on the brink of something extraordinary." His passion was palpable, a palpable heat radiating from him that made my pulse quicken. I admired his determination, even as I feared what it might lead to.

"Extraordinary or catastrophic?" I countered, a playful smirk tugging at the corners of my mouth. "Remember what happened last time we pushed too hard? I still can't explain the talking cat incident." I couldn't help but chuckle, the memory of that chaos offering a brief reprieve from the tension mounting in the room.

He laughed, a rich sound that reverberated through the air, lighting up the dim office like the dawn breaking through the night. "Fair point. But how often do we get the chance to explore the intersection of magic and technology? We're standing on the precipice of something revolutionary!" His eyes sparkled with enthusiasm, igniting a flicker of my own excitement.

I leaned closer, our hands brushing as I pointed to the screen. "Okay, let's explore it, then. But we need to set some boundaries." I could feel the warmth of his skin against mine, an electric connection that sent shivers down my spine. "What happens if we cross them? If we lose control?"

Grant's expression shifted, a shadow flickering across his face. "We won't. I promise." His voice was low and steady, but there was an undercurrent of uncertainty that I couldn't ignore. "But we need to try. Together."

Together. The word resonated within me, weaving itself into the very fabric of the moment. I couldn't help but feel that we were embarking on something far more profound than simply merging magic and code; we were delving into the depths of trust, collaboration, and perhaps even a connection that stretched beyond the confines of our individual worlds.

With a determined nod, I straightened up, feeling a newfound resolve. "Alright, then. Let's see what this glitch can tell us."

As we leaned over the keyboard together, our fingers danced above the keys, intertwining like a symphony of light and sound. The screen flickered once more, an iridescent pulse echoing through the room. Suddenly, a cascade of colorful sigils burst forth from the code, swirling around us like a whirlwind of neon stardust. My heart raced as I recognized the symbols—they were the same ones I used in my spells, ancient and powerful.

"What in the world..." Grant breathed, his eyes wide as he watched the display in awe.

"Exactly," I murmured, my voice barely a whisper. "It's responding to us. To our combined energy."

As I reached out to touch the vibrant symbols floating in the air, a jolt of energy surged through me, a fusion of magic and technology that ignited every nerve ending. It felt as if the very essence of our collaboration was manifesting before our eyes, and I realized with a mix of exhilaration and trepidation that we had opened a door to an unknown realm.

"What do we do now?" Grant asked, his voice laced with a mixture of excitement and apprehension.

"Now," I said, my heart pounding, "we figure out what it wants."

The pulsating sigils hung in the air, vibrant and alive, casting a kaleidoscope of colors that reflected off the walls like a dance of fireflies at dusk. My heart thudded in my chest, each beat echoing the rhythm of uncertainty and thrill that surged through the room. Grant's breath quickened beside me, and I could feel his gaze locked on the swirling patterns, his intrigue palpable. It was as if we had stumbled upon a forgotten language, one that beckoned us to decipher its secrets.

"Are we supposed to do something with it?" Grant asked, his voice barely above a whisper, as if the very act of speaking might shatter the delicate spell woven around us. I glanced sideways at him, noticing how the soft glow of the screen illuminated his features, accentuating the determination etched into his brow. He looked like a scholar caught in the grips of discovery, a spark of genius dancing in his hazel eyes.

"Honestly? I'm not sure," I replied, a playful grin breaking through my anxiety. "Last time I tried to interact with magic like this, I ended up turning my cat purple for a week. And he was not amused."

Grant chuckled, shaking his head. "What is it with you and your pets? You'd think they'd come with a warning label."

I shot him a mock glare, my lips curling into a smile. "Oh, please. It's not my fault that Felix can't handle a little excitement. Just ask him about the time I tried to give him a bath."

His laughter filled the room, but it was short-lived as our attention snapped back to the vibrant patterns swirling around us. "Focus, Miss Catastrophe," he said, adopting a mock-serious tone that made my stomach flip. "We need to figure out how to harness this."

"Right, harnessing chaos. Just what every aspiring sorceress dreams of," I quipped, rolling my eyes while my pulse thrummed with adrenaline. "Okay, let's see if we can control it."

Tentatively, I raised my hand toward the sigils, fingers tingling with the familiar hum of magic, and whispered the incantation that resonated deep within my core. The air crackled around us, a tangible energy igniting with every syllable. The symbols reacted instantly, shifting and swirling in response to my words. They formed intricate shapes, weaving together like vines in a hidden garden, until they settled into a single, clear symbol that pulsed like a heartbeat.

"That's... new," Grant murmured, eyes wide as he leaned closer. "What does it mean?"

I squinted, trying to recall the ancient text that had woven itself into my memory during late-night study sessions, poring over dusty tomes by candlelight. "It's a sigil for connection. A bond between realms." My breath caught in my throat. "But I've never seen it manifest like this."

"Could it mean our magic is intertwining with the code? That we're creating something unique?" His enthusiasm was infectious, and I found myself swept up in his excitement, a thrill racing through me.

"Possibly. But it also means we're treading into dangerous territory," I cautioned, my heart thrumming in time with the sigils. "If the magic takes on a life of its own, who knows what could happen?"

"Maybe it's meant to," he suggested, his tone shifting from excitement to something more serious. "What if this is the breakthrough we've been searching for? A way to merge our worlds?"

Before I could respond, the sigil shimmered brighter, sending a wave of energy that enveloped us, wrapping us in a cocoon of warmth. I gasped as the room seemed to expand, the walls fading away to reveal an endless expanse of vibrant light and color. It felt like stepping into a dreamscape, one where possibilities were as limitless as the stars above.

"Is this—are we in some kind of trance?" Grant's voice trembled, both awe and fear lacing his words. I turned to him, the intensity of his gaze making my heart race.

"Not a trance. More like an overlap," I replied, my voice steady despite the exhilarating chaos swirling around us. "It's like the magic and code are merging, creating a new reality. But we need to remain grounded."

"Grounded. Right." He took a deep breath, his fingers curling into fists as he focused on the sigils. "Let's see if we can steer this."

Together, we began to channel our energy into the sigil, directing our thoughts and intentions like arrows aimed at a target. The colors around us shifted in response, bending to our will as the patterns morphed into familiar shapes—circuit boards, algorithmic strings, and finally, something that resembled a portal.

"What the hell?" I breathed, staring at the gateway forming before us, a shimmering door that flickered like a mirage. "Are we really thinking about stepping through that?"

"We won't know until we try," Grant said, his voice tinged with a reckless excitement that sent a thrill down my spine.

"Easy for you to say. You're not the one who'll have to deal with the consequences if we end up in some parallel universe where cats rule the world," I shot back, half-joking, though a sliver of panic knotted in my stomach.

"Look," he said, stepping closer to the portal, "this is the chance to explore something groundbreaking. We could unlock secrets we never dreamed possible."

His determination was both infuriating and irresistible, a magnet drawing me closer to the edge of the unknown. With a deep breath, I leaned in, peering into the swirling depths of the portal, a tempest of colors and shapes swirling within. It beckoned to me, whispering promises of discovery and danger, tempting me to take that leap of faith.

"Fine, but if I end up as a cosmic guinea pig, I'm haunting you for the rest of eternity," I retorted, my heart pounding in my chest.

Grant grinned, a boyish charm lighting up his face, and without further ado, he took my hand, giving it a reassuring squeeze. "Then let's make this a ride worth haunting."

As we stepped through the portal, the world dissolved around us, and I braced for impact, the rush of wind and light enveloping us in a whirlwind of possibility. The moment felt suspended in time, a delicious blend of fear and exhilaration. And in that instant, I knew our lives were about to change in ways we could never have imagined.

The moment we crossed the threshold, the world around us erupted in a dazzling symphony of colors and sounds that felt both alien and familiar. It was like stepping into a painting come to life, each brushstroke imbued with a heartbeat of its own. The air was thick with possibility, a tangible energy that made my skin tingle and my breath catch in my throat. I glanced at Grant, whose eyes sparkled with wonder, reflecting the chaotic beauty that surrounded us.

"Welcome to our brave new world," he quipped, a hint of mischief dancing in his voice as he looked around. "Just try not to trip over the magic."

"Ha! It's not the magic I'm worried about," I shot back, struggling to keep my footing on the shifting ground that felt less like earth and more like liquid light. "It's whatever wants to eat us for dinner."

He laughed, but there was a seriousness in his eyes that made my stomach twist. "No one said discovery was easy," he said, his tone shifting slightly. "But we're in this together, remember?"

"Together," I echoed, the word hanging between us like a promise. My heart swelled with warmth, though a shadow of doubt flickered at the edge of my mind. What exactly had we unleashed by stepping into this vibrant chaos?

As we ventured further, the kaleidoscope of colors began to coalesce into more defined shapes—towers of crystalline structures reached for a swirling sky, while streams of data pulsed like rivers through the air, glimmering with electric energy. I felt a pull, an irresistible urge to reach out and touch the vibrant streams that flowed around us. It was intoxicating, the essence of magic and technology intertwined in a way that ignited my very core.

"Do you think the sigils can help us communicate with this place?" I asked, curiosity sparking in my voice.

"Maybe," Grant replied, a thoughtful frown crossing his face. "But we need to be careful. It's easy to get lost in a place like this." He glanced around, his brow furrowed as if he sensed something I didn't.

As if to prove his point, the ground beneath us trembled, sending ripples of energy coursing through the air. The once gentle streams of light shifted, twisting and coiling like serpents. I felt a jolt of fear as a shadow darted in the corner of my eye, a flicker of movement that sent chills down my spine.

"Grant, did you see that?" I whispered, my heart racing.

"What?" He turned sharply, his eyes scanning our surroundings. "What did you see?"

"Something moved. Over there." I pointed into the vibrant chaos, my pulse quickening. The atmosphere felt charged, as if the very essence of the place was awakening to our presence, and not all of it was welcoming.

We stepped cautiously toward the shifting shadows, uncertainty prickling at my skin. The vibrant energy swirled around us, thickening the air like fog. I could sense the magic pulsating, a heartbeat of its own that resonated with mine. It was both exhilarating and disconcerting, and I could feel the line between fear and fascination blurring dangerously.

"Whatever it is, it's not happy we're here," Grant murmured, his voice low and tense.

A loud crack echoed through the air, like thunder striking in the midst of a clear sky. The ground trembled more violently, and I stumbled, grabbing hold of Grant's arm to steady myself.

"Stay close," he said, his grip tightening around my wrist.

I nodded, my heart pounding in rhythm with the chaos around us. Just as I began to feel anchored by his presence, a figure emerged from the swirling colors. It was a silhouette at first, cloaked in shadows, but then it stepped into the light—a being of pure energy, shimmering with a brilliance that made my heart race.

"Who dares trespass in the realm of the Code?" the figure boomed, its voice resonating with power and authority, sending a shiver down my spine. The air crackled around us as if the very atmosphere reacted to its presence.

"Uh, just two curious souls," I stammered, forcing a grin that felt more like a grimace. "We didn't mean to intrude. We were just... exploring."

The figure regarded us with an intensity that made me feel exposed, as if it could see into the very depths of my being. "Exploring?" it repeated, a hint of skepticism lacing its tone. "You tread on sacred ground, where magic and technology intertwine. Your intentions must be pure, or the consequences will be dire."

Grant stepped forward, a look of determination on his face. "We're here to understand. To learn. We didn't come to disrupt anything."

"Understand?" The figure's voice boomed, shaking the very essence of the air around us. "Understanding does not come without sacrifice. The Code demands balance. You must be prepared for what lies ahead."

"What do you mean by 'sacrifice'?" I asked, my voice shaking slightly. The weight of the figure's words hung in the air like a storm cloud, threatening to unleash chaos at any moment.

"Every choice has a cost," it intoned, the energy swirling around it growing more volatile. "You cannot wield the power of the Code without losing something dear."

I glanced at Grant, his expression a mix of determination and uncertainty. The world around us seemed to pulse with a dark intensity, the vibrant colors dimming as the figure's words sank in.

"Is there any way to navigate this without... sacrificing?" I ventured, my heart racing.

The figure's gaze hardened, and I could feel the weight of its judgment pressing down on me. "Only if your resolve is unwavering. Only if your hearts are true."

As the last word echoed through the air, the ground trembled again, this time more violently, and a crack appeared beneath our feet, splitting the ground like a fissure in reality.

"Grant!" I shouted, panic surging through me as I felt the earth give way beneath us. We were tumbling, spiraling downwards into the depths of the unknown, the vibrant chaos above fading away into darkness.

"Hold on!" he shouted, reaching for me as the abyss swallowed us whole.

In that moment, as we fell into the void, I realized we had crossed a threshold from which there might be no return, the weight of our choices pressing down on us like the darkness that surrounded us. And as the last light flickered from our grasp, I couldn't shake the feeling that we were on the brink of something monumental, teetering between salvation and oblivion.

Chapter 14: Unraveled Truths

The fluorescent lights buzzed overhead, casting a sterile glow over the conference room. I perched on the edge of my chair, fingers tapping nervously against the smooth surface of the polished mahogany table. The air felt thick, suffused with the mingling scents of expensive cologne and the artificial freshness of industrial-grade air freshener. Each inhale carried the weight of the corporate witches' presence, an uninvited chill that crept into my bones. They were here again, their perfectly tailored suits draped over their frames like armor, their smiles sharp enough to cut glass.

The leader of the trio, Marissa, leaned forward, her lips curling into a smile that didn't quite reach her eyes. "You're a talented girl, Miranda," she began, her tone syrupy sweet. "Everyone around here knows it. But talent, as you well know, is often wasted when it lacks direction. What's the point of being gifted if you're not wielding that gift to its full potential?"

I resisted the urge to roll my eyes. If only she knew how much direction I was already juggling. There was Grant's project, the intricacies of which danced in my mind like a swarm of fireflies, each flickering thought a testament to the hours we'd spent mapping out the future of our company. Yet here I was, caught in a trap spun by these predatory women who thrived on the weaknesses of others. I could almost hear the snap of their web closing in on me.

Marissa continued, her voice laced with that same insidious sweetness. "You've been helping Grant with his project, haven't you? We find that kind of collaboration... intriguing." She emphasized the last word, and a shiver skittered down my spine. "You understand what we're proposing, don't you? Join us, become part of something larger than yourself, and you'll never have to look over your shoulder again."

Part of me screamed to reject their offer, to stand firm in my loyalty to Grant. I could picture him now, sitting in his office, pouring over the designs we'd painstakingly created together. His brow furrowed in concentration, lips twisting into that charming smile whenever he'd glance up to catch my eye. I couldn't betray him. Not now. Not after everything we had built. Yet the glint in Marissa's eyes told me she was not merely offering a partnership; she was presenting an ultimatum wrapped in silk.

"Imagine it, Miranda," chimed in Tara, another member of the witchy triumvirate, her voice lilting as if she were serenading me with a death sentence. "A seat at the table, access to resources, and protection from the very people who would seek to undermine you. The world is full of those who'd be more than happy to tear you down, but with us, you could soar."

It was enticing, their vision, a heady cocktail of ambition and fear. I could see it: a secure future, a powerful position, the chance to silence the nagging voices of doubt that gnawed at me like rats in a pantry. But it came at a price I wasn't willing to pay. "I'll think about it," I found myself saying, the words spilling out before I could stop them.

Marissa's smile widened, revealing the predatory glint of satisfaction in her eyes. "You're a smart girl, Miranda. Take your time. We'll expect an answer soon. After all, we wouldn't want any... accidents to happen."

As they departed, the heaviness of their visit lingered like a noxious cloud. The conference room felt colder, and I shivered involuntarily, as if their threats had seeped into the very walls. I stood up, my legs shaky as I navigated the minefield of my emotions. I needed a plan, a way to protect Grant and our project without succumbing to the seductive power these women offered.

Stumbling out of the meeting room, I fought back a wave of nausea. I wasn't about to let their threats dictate my choices. But how could I fight back when the stakes were so high? I needed to find a way to warn Grant without revealing too much.

Just as I was about to step into the elevator, my phone buzzed in my pocket. The screen lit up with a message from Grant. "Can you come to my office? I need your input on something." The urgency in his words sent a rush of warmth through me, but it was quickly overshadowed by the looming dread of what I had just faced.

I took a deep breath, steeling myself as I made my way down the corridor. With each step, I crafted a version of reality in my mind—a reality where I could keep Grant safe while devising a way to escape the witches' snare. I pictured our conversations, the laughter that had flowed so freely between us, and how that laughter made the corporate world feel a little less suffocating.

As I entered his office, the familiar scent of fresh coffee and paper filled my senses, soothing my frayed nerves momentarily. Grant looked up, a frown creasing his forehead, concern etched into his features. "You look pale," he said, his voice a low rumble that sent a thrill through me. "Is everything okay?"

I forced a smile, trying to mask the turmoil swirling inside me. "Just a little meeting with some of the higher-ups. Nothing I can't handle."

"Good," he said, but the scrutiny in his gaze suggested he wasn't buying my facade. I sat across from him, the weight of my secret pressing down like a heavy cloak.

"I've been thinking about the project," I began, my heart racing. "There are a few changes we could implement to improve our presentation."

He nodded, his attention sharpening as he leaned forward, and I realized then how much I didn't want to drag him into the darkness I'd been thrust into. The stakes had never felt higher, and I was caught in a web of lies that could ensnare us both if I wasn't careful.

The moments ticked by, each second stretching like taffy, as I shared my ideas, weaving our dreams into tangible plans. But in the back of my mind, the witches' ultimatum lurked like a shadow, whispering that I was running out of time. The choice was clear: surrender my integrity or risk everything for a future that felt increasingly uncertain. And as I met Grant's hopeful gaze, I knew I had to fight.

The sun dipped low on the horizon, casting long shadows through the glass walls of Grant's office. The city buzzed beneath us, alive with its evening rhythm, yet the warmth of that bustling life felt distant as I sat there, grappling with the tension that clung to my skin like static. Grant's gaze held mine, the depth of his concern etched across his features, and I felt a mix of gratitude and guilt. Gratitude for his unwavering support and guilt for the secrets I now bore.

"Are you sure everything's okay?" he pressed, his brow furrowing as he leaned back in his chair, fingers steepled in thought. "You've been off lately."

I swallowed hard, my mind racing to construct a plausible narrative. "It's just work stress. You know how it is," I replied, injecting a casualness into my tone that I didn't quite feel. "Deadlines are creeping up, and I've got a million things to juggle. I'm sure you can relate."

He chuckled, a low, melodic sound that sent a thrill through me. "Oh, absolutely. I once tried to juggle three projects at once. Spoiler alert: I dropped all of them and ended up having to work through the weekend."

I laughed along with him, the sound feeling forced yet comforting. "Well, I promise I won't drop anything crucial. Just a few ideas to toss around, and I think we'll be on our way to something great."

Grant leaned forward, resting his elbows on the table, the tension easing from his shoulders. "Let's hear it, then. What are you thinking?"

As I laid out my suggestions for the project, I watched the way his eyes lit up with every detail. It was intoxicating to see him animated, his passion for our work palpable in the air. But the thrill of collaboration couldn't mask the gnawing worry in my chest. I had to protect him, and the project, from the corporate witches who sought to ensnare us both.

"So, if we pivot the marketing strategy to focus on sustainability, we can appeal to a wider audience," I suggested, watching his brow furrow in concentration. "Think about it: eco-friendly practices, local sourcing—"

"—It's brilliant," he interrupted, a grin breaking across his face. "That angle would resonate with our target demographic. It's fresh, it's timely. I love it."

I basked in his praise, the compliment igniting a spark of hope in me, but just as quickly, that hope dimmed. Every word exchanged felt like a precious moment taken from the future we might lose if the witches succeeded in their machinations.

"Do you think we could make it work?" he asked, his enthusiasm infectious.

"Absolutely," I said, my voice stronger than I felt. "We just need to fine-tune our presentation for the next meeting. I can handle the slides, and I know a few tricks to make the data pop."

"Perfect. You handle the slides, and I'll focus on the pitch." His eyes locked onto mine, the connection between us pulsing with unspoken understanding. "We make a hell of a team, don't we?"

"More like a dynamic duo," I replied, injecting a playful note into my voice. "We'll have everyone convinced we're the next big thing since—well, since whatever that thing was."

He chuckled, shaking his head. "Let's just hope it's not a fad. I prefer our success to be a little more... timeless."

A warmth settled in my chest, an echo of the connection we had forged in this demanding world. But as the evening wore on, the shadows grew longer, reminding me of the threats looming just outside our bubble. I could feel the pressure building like a storm cloud, a tension that swirled around us, suffocating and relentless.

"Hey," Grant said suddenly, his expression shifting. "You okay? You seem a little... distant."

I masked my unease with a smile, but inside, I was scrambling. How could I keep him safe when I was already entwined in danger? "I'm just thinking ahead. We have a lot to accomplish, and I want to ensure we're ready for anything."

"Good thinking," he said, his tone easing again. "Just remember, we're in this together. Whatever happens, I'm here for you."

His words wrapped around me like a warm blanket, but the thought of dragging him into my chaos was unbearable. "Thanks, Grant. It means a lot."

As the meeting came to a close, the weight of our shared ambitions settled heavily on my shoulders. I gathered my notes, forcing a smile as I looked up to meet his gaze. "Let's tackle this tomorrow. I'll have the slides ready by morning."

"Can't wait," he replied, a playful glimmer in his eye. "And hey, don't be a stranger. Come by later? We could order some dinner. I make a mean reservation."

I laughed lightly, but the truth was, I was torn. I wanted nothing more than to share a quiet evening with him, perhaps to distract myself from the storm brewing outside. But I also needed to figure out how to confront the witches, to safeguard our project without bringing him into the fray. "I'll see what I can do. My schedule's pretty packed, but I'll try."

"Try hard," he teased, his eyes narrowing playfully. "I'll hold you to it."

The door clicked shut behind me as I stepped into the corridor, my heart pounding with conflicting emotions. The encounter with the witches echoed in my mind, a dark symphony that played over and over. They knew too much; they were dangerous and, worse yet, persuasive. As I made my way to my desk, I resolved to devise a plan—one that didn't involve betrayal but rather a clever maneuvering of information.

The evening air felt electric as I pulled my coat tighter around my shoulders, each step taking me away from the safe haven of Grant's office and deeper into the uncertainties that lay ahead. I passed by familiar faces, exchanging nods and smiles, but inside, I was spiraling.

I needed help. Someone who could understand the gravity of my situation without getting caught in the crossfire. Tasha, my closest confidante, popped into my mind. A fierce strategist and a friend who could read between the lines, she would know how to navigate this treacherous terrain.

I texted her quickly, my fingers moving with urgency: "Can we meet? It's urgent."

The reply was almost immediate: "On my way. You okay?"

I felt a flicker of relief. Tasha had always been my anchor, the one person I could count on to offer clear-headed advice in a swirling sea of chaos. I waited anxiously in the lobby, scanning the glass doors for her familiar figure.

When she walked in, her vibrant energy filled the space, the way her long curls bounced with each step a reminder that chaos could also be beautiful. "What's going on?" she asked, her voice low but laced with concern.

I pulled her aside, weaving through the lobby's hustle, my heart racing as I explained everything—the ultimatum, the threats, the project with Grant. Tasha listened intently, her expression shifting from concern to determination.

"Okay, we need a plan," she said firmly. "You can't let them pull you into their web. They're after power, and they see you as a key to that. But you're smarter than that."

I nodded, grateful for her unwavering belief in me. "I just don't know how to protect Grant without dragging him into this mess."

"Leave that to me," she replied, a mischievous glint in her eye. "Let's devise a way to keep you both under the radar. You're not in this alone."

With Tasha at my side, I finally felt the weight of the witches' threats begin to lift. We would confront the darkness together, armed with wit and strategy, ready to unravel the tangled threads of deception that bound us.

The café bustled around us, a comforting hum of chatter and clinking coffee cups, yet I felt as though I were encased in a glass bubble, watching the world move while I stood still. Tasha and I settled into a corner booth, the leather seats worn and inviting, but I couldn't shake the tension coiling in my stomach. She stirred her coffee absentmindedly, her brow furrowed in thought as I recounted the details of my encounter with the witches.

"So, they think they can just waltz in here and threaten you?" Tasha's voice held a sharp edge, her fierce spirit shining through. "That's ridiculous. Who do they think they are?"

"Corporate overlords, apparently," I replied, a bitter laugh escaping my lips. "I'm just a pawn in their game, and they're making it clear they want to control the board."

"You are so much more than a pawn," she shot back, her green eyes blazing. "They're threatened by your talent and by the work you're doing with Grant. It's not just a project; it's your future. We need to turn the tables on them."

I leaned back, contemplating her words, the bitterness of the coffee lingering on my tongue. "How do we do that? They have the leverage. If they expose me, it's not just my reputation at stake. It's Grant's work, everything we've built together."

"Then let's come up with a strategy that keeps both of you safe while pulling their teeth," Tasha suggested, her enthusiasm rising. "They think they're the big bad wolves, but what if we turn them into the sheep?"

The thought was exhilarating. "You mean play them at their own game?"

"Exactly. We need to sow a little chaos of our own." She leaned in closer, lowering her voice as if sharing a secret. "What if we leak some misinformation? Something juicy enough to make them panic? That could buy us time."

I couldn't help but smile at the idea, the thrill of rebellion washing over me. "You're a genius, you know that?"

"I'm a genius who likes a good challenge," she quipped, raising her mug in a mock toast. "Let's brainstorm. What would really shake them up?"

We dove into the planning, our conversation crackling with energy as we bounced ideas off each other like we were kids again, plotting how to get back at the bullies on the playground. Tasha suggested I plant a rumor about Grant's project having a secret investor, someone influential, to make the witches sweat. I nodded, catching the momentum. The idea of turning the tables ignited a flicker of hope within me.

"Maybe we could stage a little misdirection," I said, excitement bubbling. "What if I act like I'm seriously considering their offer? They'd never see it coming."

"Perfect! You'll be the perfect double agent," she grinned, and for a moment, the heaviness in my chest lifted. "And when they let their guard down, we strike. We keep them focused on you while we work behind the scenes."

"Right! While they're busy trying to reel me in, we'll find a way to expose their plans."

The ideas flowed freely, each one more audacious than the last, and for a while, I lost myself in the thrill of it all. This was the spark I needed, a way to regain control. Yet as the plan took shape, a nagging doubt tugged at the back of my mind. Would it work?

Tasha's phone buzzed, and she glanced at it, her expression shifting. "I have to take this. It's work," she said, sliding out of the booth. "But don't lose that momentum. Keep thinking!"

I nodded, but as I watched her walk away, the weight of the situation pressed down on me again. I tapped my fingers against the table, thoughts racing. My mind was a labyrinth of worry, but it was also a beacon of resolve.

After Tasha returned, we wrapped up our meeting with a renewed sense of purpose. I knew what I had to do. I needed to keep my facade intact while simultaneously plotting our course of action. But the thought of lying to Grant nagged at me. I needed to protect him, but the burden of deception felt like a chain around my neck.

As I stepped back into the cool evening air, my mind whirred with thoughts of our plan. I headed toward my apartment, the city lights flickering like stars, casting shadows that danced in the corners of my vision. I couldn't shake the feeling that the witches were always one step ahead, lurking just out of sight.

When I reached my building, I hesitated at the entrance. I took a deep breath, reminding myself of the stakes. Grant had to remain oblivious to the threats looming over us, and that meant I needed to keep everything under wraps until our plan took flight.

Inside, the elevator ride felt interminable, each floor ticking away like a countdown. My mind wandered to Grant, his laughter, the way he made even the most mundane tasks feel significant. What would he think if he knew the web I was weaving behind his back? The idea of involving him in the turmoil made my stomach twist with anxiety.

Finally, the elevator dinged, and I stepped into my apartment. The familiar clutter greeted me, a comforting chaos that reminded me of all the hours spent working late, chasing dreams and deadlines. I tossed my bag onto the couch, flopping down beside it, exhaustion creeping in.

But just as I was about to unwind, my phone buzzed again. Glancing down, I saw an unfamiliar number flashing on the screen. My heart skipped. I answered cautiously, "Hello?"

"Miranda, it's Marissa."

The chill in her voice sent a shiver down my spine, her tone as smooth as silk yet edged with steel. "We need to talk."

"About what?" I replied, trying to keep my voice steady, the threat of her presence hanging heavy in the air.

"Your little project with Grant. It seems we might have a bit of a misunderstanding."

Every instinct screamed to hang up, but I held my ground. "I don't think there's anything to discuss. I'm quite busy."

"Busy? Oh, I think you'll want to clear your schedule," she purred. "Let's meet. I have some information that may interest you."

My stomach twisted at her words. "What kind of information?"

"Let's just say it involves Grant's future—and yours."

The line went dead, and I stood frozen, the realization crashing over me like a wave. The witches weren't just waiting for me to slip up; they were already playing their cards, and I was the centerpiece of their game. My breath quickened, the walls closing in, leaving me with a gnawing sense of dread.

The plan that had felt so empowering now seemed precarious, teetering on the edge of disaster. I needed to act fast, but would I be able to outsmart them before they made their next move? The stakes had never been higher, and I was running out of time.

Chapter 15: The Breaking Point

Everything comes crashing down the night Grant confronts me with the truth I've been trying to avoid. He stands there, framed by the flickering lights of the half-lit room, eyes narrowed and mouth set in a thin line of disbelief. The air between us crackles with unspoken words, a tension so thick it feels as if the very walls are holding their breath. I can see him piecing it all together, the missing puzzle pieces of my life—my obsession with candles that flicker to life at my command, the strange glitches that haunt our quiet moments, the uncanny way the world bends around me when my emotions run high.

"Is this some kind of joke?" His voice is low, almost a whisper, yet it pierces the stillness like a knife. I want to reach out, to reassure him, but I feel frozen, rooted to the spot as fear coils around my heart. The last thing I want is to push him further away, but the truth looms like a dark cloud. "This isn't what it looks like," I say, my voice trembling despite my best efforts to sound steady. I'm a master of control when it comes to my abilities, but tonight, I feel like a marionette with frayed strings, a puppet on the verge of collapse.

"Then what is it?" His eyes search mine, seeking the truth beneath layers of lies and half-truths. In that moment, I realize just how vulnerable I've made myself by allowing him into my world. I can feel the words teetering on the tip of my tongue, but they refuse to come out. The weight of my secrets hangs heavily in the air, a suffocating fog that clouds my thoughts.

"I—I've been trying to figure it out," I stammer, my heart racing as I grasp for the right words. "There are things I can do, things that shouldn't be possible." My gaze drops to the floor, unable to meet his piercing stare. "But it doesn't change who I am. I'm still me."

"Still you?" he echoes, incredulity etched into his features. "What does that even mean? You've kept this from me, all of it.

Do you have any idea what I'm feeling right now?" His voice rises, echoing off the walls, each word a dagger, each syllable a reminder of the walls I've built around myself.

I open my mouth to respond, to explain how I've fought to keep my abilities under wraps, how I've tried to carve out a normal life in a world where 'normal' feels like a distant memory. But before I can gather my thoughts, a wave of emotion crashes over me, a storm of fear, regret, and desperation that bubbles to the surface. As I reach for him, something inside me snaps—an electric surge of power erupts from my core, wild and untamed. The glass in the windows explodes outward with a shattering crash, showering the room in a glittering rain of fragments.

"Grant!" I scream, but the sound is lost in the chaos as darkness envelops us, the power surging like a living thing. I watch in horror as he stumbles back, his face a mask of shock and betrayal, his breath hitching as he takes in the scene around us. The silence that follows is deafening, heavy with the weight of my mistake.

I've crossed a line I can't uncross. My heart pounds in my chest, a frantic drumbeat echoing in the stillness. I don't know what I've done—only that I can feel the remnants of my power dancing on the edges of my fingertips, begging to be unleashed once more. But all I can think about is Grant, the look on his face, the way his trust is slipping through my fingers like sand.

"What are you?" he asks, his voice trembling, laced with fear that twists like a knife in my gut. The question lingers in the air, heavy and suffocating. It's the same question I've asked myself countless times, a riddle with no easy answer.

"I'm just..." I pause, my voice barely a whisper. "I'm just trying to figure it all out." But as I speak, I can see the distance growing between us, a chasm carved by secrets and misunderstandings. It feels like I'm losing him all over again, and the thought sends a wave of panic coursing through me.

He takes a step back, eyes wide with disbelief, and I feel the world tilt on its axis. "You can't just throw things around like that! What if you hurt someone?" The accusation stings, a lash of truth that cuts deeper than I'd like to admit.

"I didn't mean to! I just—" But my words falter, caught in the web of chaos I've woven. I take a deep breath, my chest tight with despair. "I'm scared, Grant. Scared of what I can do, scared of what I might become."

His expression softens for a brief moment, but then he shakes his head, the tension between us snapping like a taut string. "I can't do this," he murmurs, turning away, his back a solid wall of rejection. The finality of his words echoes in the hollow space of the room, drowning out the whispers of the night.

"Wait!" I cry, desperation clawing at my throat as I reach out, my fingers brushing against the cold, shattered glass on the floor. "Don't go. Please, let me explain."

But he doesn't turn back. Each step he takes toward the door feels like a small earthquake, shaking the foundation of everything we've built. As the door clicks shut behind him, a crushing silence envelops me, and I realize I've lost something precious, something that may never return. The darkness swirls around me, thick and suffocating, and for the first time, I feel utterly alone in a world that suddenly feels vast and empty.

The silence left in the wake of Grant's departure was a living thing, heavy and oppressive. I stood in the dim room, the shards of glass glimmering like fallen stars at my feet, their sharp edges reflecting the flickering candlelight that had once felt so comforting. The air was thick with the scent of burnt wick and an undertone of something more—fear, perhaps, or the remnants of the chaos I had unwittingly unleashed. Each breath felt like a chore, the weight of my secrets pressing down on my chest, constricting like a vise.

I had always known there would be a reckoning. I had just hoped it wouldn't arrive on a night when my heart was already teetering on the edge of despair. My fingertips tingled with residual energy, a reminder of the power I had tried so hard to control. I glanced at the broken window, where a gentle breeze swept through, carrying away the last remnants of warmth and comfort.

"Nice job, genius," I muttered to myself, kicking a piece of glass across the floor. It clinked softly, a bitter echo of my crumbling resolve. What had I been thinking? I had walked a tightrope for so long, carefully balancing my truth against the façade of normalcy. And in a single moment of panic, I had shattered everything.

I sank into a chair, the wood cool beneath me, grounding me in the aftermath of my emotional storm. The candle flames danced wildly, as if mocking my turmoil, and I closed my eyes, willing them to steady. When I opened them again, I was met by the reflection in the darkened window. My own eyes stared back, wide and disheveled, the weight of my choices etched into the lines of my face.

"Get a grip," I whispered, taking a deep breath to quell the rising tide of tears. I couldn't let myself drown in self-pity; there was too much at stake. I had built a life around the notion of safety and control, only to let it slip through my fingers in a moment of vulnerability. With Grant gone, the walls of my carefully curated existence began to feel like a prison, closing in on me with relentless pressure.

I stood and paced the room, my thoughts racing like wild horses. Was there any way to salvage this? Could I reach out, explain myself? The thought made my stomach churn. What would I even say? "Oh, by the way, the bizarre occurrences you've noticed? Totally normal for me—let's just pretend they don't exist."

The absurdity of it all made me chuckle bitterly, but the laughter faded, leaving only a hollow echo in its wake. In that moment of vulnerability, I felt the weight of the world pressing down, the realization that my secrets were no longer just mine. They had bled into the lives of others, dragging them into a chaos I had fought to contain.

As I moved toward the kitchen, seeking refuge in the mundane act of making tea, I caught sight of a faint glow from my candle collection. They had always been my solace, my escape, each one infused with my energy, a tether to a world I could almost control. I hesitated, my hand hovering above the matchbox, a sudden urge washing over me to set the room aglow once more. But the thought of another explosion, another fracturing of trust, sent me stumbling back.

I was spiraling, losing myself to the dark thoughts that lurked at the edges of my mind. I needed to find a way to reclaim the pieces of myself I had lost, starting with confronting the reality of my situation. I grabbed my phone, its screen casting a faint light in the encroaching darkness, and stared at Grant's contact. Should I send a message? A simple apology?

Just as my finger hovered over the screen, a sharp knock at the door jolted me from my reverie. My heart raced as I turned, uncertainty flooding my senses. Who could it be at this hour? The last person I wanted to see was Grant, but a flicker of hope ignited at the thought of him returning, ready to listen. I opened the door cautiously, bracing myself for confrontation.

Instead, I was met by a figure wrapped in shadows, the dim light of the hallway barely illuminating a familiar face. It was Leah, my best friend and the only person outside of Grant who knew the full extent of my struggles. Her wide eyes were filled with concern, and a myriad of emotions surged through me at the sight of her.

"Hey, I saw the lights flickering and heard the glass shatter. What's going on?" Her voice was steady, but I could sense the undercurrent of worry threaded through her words.

"I—" My voice faltered. What could I possibly say to explain the unraveling of everything? "I messed up, Leah. Big time."

She stepped inside, her presence warm and grounding. "Talk to me."

As I sank back into the chair, the weight of my emotions spilled forth, a torrent of words that tumbled out like an unleashed dam. I recounted the confrontation with Grant, the burst of power, the broken glass—how it had felt as though I was losing control of not just my abilities but my life. Leah listened, her eyes widening in disbelief at the mention of my powers, but she didn't interrupt. She let me unravel until the last remnants of my turmoil faded into silence.

"Wow," she finally breathed, her brow furrowed as she processed what I had just revealed. "That's... intense. But you have to understand, you're not alone in this. You never have been."

I looked up at her, the warmth of her words wrapping around me like a much-needed embrace. "But what if Grant can't understand? What if he walks away for good?"

"Then he doesn't deserve you," she replied firmly, her voice a steady anchor amidst my swirling fears. "You have to be honest, not just with him, but with yourself. You can't hide who you are. It's too exhausting."

Leah's conviction ignited something within me—a spark of determination that had been dormant since the night had begun. Perhaps it was time to embrace my truth fully, to step out from behind the shadows I had cast around my heart. I took a deep breath, the air feeling lighter, more buoyant, as I realized that honesty was the first step toward reclaiming my power—not just the kind that surged through my fingertips, but the power that came from being my true self.

"Okay," I said, my voice steadying with resolve. "You're right. I need to talk to him."

"Good," she nodded, a hint of a smile creeping onto her lips. "Let's get you ready. You're going to knock his socks off."

In that moment, I felt a flicker of hope ignite within me, the shadows receding as I prepared to face the unknown. Together, we would find a way through this tangled mess, and perhaps, just perhaps, I could reclaim the pieces of my heart that I had almost lost.

The tension between us lingered long after Grant had slammed the door behind him, a taut wire ready to snap at the slightest provocation. Leah's presence offered a small balm to my frayed nerves, her unwavering gaze steadying me as I gathered my thoughts. "You're going to need a game plan," she said, her voice infused with determination that clashed beautifully with the tumult in my heart. "We can't just wing it. Grant's not the kind of guy who'll take to cryptic messages and vague explanations."

I nodded, feeling the heaviness of uncertainty settle on my shoulders. "You're right. I can't just spill everything at once. He's not ready for that." The very notion made my stomach twist. What if he rejected me? What if the chaos of my life drove him away for good?

"Okay, let's break this down," Leah urged, her eyes sparkling with the thrill of planning. "What's the most important thing you want him to understand?"

I hesitated, turning the question over in my mind like a delicate piece of porcelain. "That I'm still me. I'm not just this... this power." The weight of the truth felt like a stone in my throat. "I've kept it hidden because I thought it would keep everyone safe, but now..."

"Now it's all out in the open," Leah interjected, her expression shifting from concern to fierce resolve. "You need to show him who you really are, the good and the messy. That's what love is, right? Embracing the whole package, even the freaky bits."

Her words struck a chord, resonating in the depths of my uncertainty. I was done hiding, done tiptoeing around the truth like it was a sleeping giant. "You're right," I said, a newfound confidence rising within me. "It's time to be honest—not just with him, but with myself."

"Good. Now, how about we give you a little pep talk? A bit of charm to help soften the blow?" She flashed a mischievous grin that was both comforting and invigorating. "Maybe a tiny spell or two?"

I rolled my eyes but couldn't help the smile creeping onto my face. "You know spells don't work like that. I can't just wave a wand and make everything okay."

"Wouldn't that be nice?" Leah quipped, her laughter ringing through the stillness. "Imagine how easy life would be! No messy breakups, no awkward conversations, just 'abracadabra, let's fall in love.'"

As much as I appreciated her humor, the reality of what lay ahead gnawed at me. The clock ticked ominously, reminding me that time was slipping away. "Okay, I need to get my thoughts straight before I face him. Can you help me practice?"

"Absolutely. Let's role-play," she said, clapping her hands together as if she were gearing up for a theatrical performance. "I'll be Grant. Hit me with your best shot."

We started the back-and-forth, Leah's impression of Grant surprisingly spot-on, complete with his concerned furrowed brow and those piercing blue eyes that had always made my heart skip. Each exchange felt more real, the stakes rising with every practiced word, every carefully crafted argument. I navigated through the labyrinth of my emotions, trying to find a way to convey everything I needed him to understand without overwhelming him.

After what felt like an eternity of rehearsing, Leah leaned back, a satisfied smile dancing on her lips. "That was brilliant! You're going to knock his socks off."

"Or completely scare him away," I shot back, nerves curling in my stomach.

"Not if you stay focused," Leah reassured me. "You've got this. Remember, it's not just about him. You're claiming your truth, too."

I took a deep breath, steeling myself for what lay ahead. "Okay, let's do this."

We stepped outside into the crisp night air, the sky sprinkled with stars, a twinkling reminder of how vast the universe felt compared to my personal turmoil. With every step toward Grant's apartment, I could feel the energy shifting around me, a palpable hum of anticipation mingled with anxiety. My heart pounded like a war drum in my chest, urging me forward even as doubt tried to creep in.

Arriving at his doorstep, I hesitated, my hand hovering over the doorbell. This was it. I had to embrace my truth, to fight for the connection that had flickered like a candle, dimmed but not extinguished.

Before I could second-guess myself, I pressed the button. The sound echoed through the quiet hallway, a sharp note that resonated deep within me. I could hear the soft shuffle of footsteps approaching, each one drawing closer to the brink of an uncertain reunion. My heart raced as the door swung open to reveal Grant, his expression a mixture of confusion and guarded hope.

"Hey," I managed, my voice steady despite the whirlwind of emotions swirling inside.

"Hey." His tone was cautious, as if testing the waters before diving in.

"I—" The words caught in my throat, the weight of everything threatening to crush me. I could feel Leah's presence behind me, a comforting anchor even in the midst of my chaos. "I need to talk."

He stepped aside, and I entered the familiar space that now felt foreign, heavy with unspoken words and broken trust. The room was dimly lit, shadows flickering along the walls, creating an atmosphere thick with tension.

"Look, I know things got... out of hand," I began, my voice faltering slightly. "But I'm not here to make excuses. I just need you to understand why I've kept everything hidden."

"Do you?" he asked, his brow furrowed. "Because it feels like you've been lying to me."

"I wasn't lying! I was trying to protect you," I replied, a note of desperation creeping into my voice. "There are things I can do, things I don't fully understand myself. And I thought if I kept them hidden, it would keep you safe."

"You thought lying would keep me safe?" His voice sharpened, the edge of betrayal slicing through the air between us.

"No! I didn't mean to lie—"

"Then what do you mean?"

"Grant, just give me a chance to explain," I pleaded, desperation clawing at my insides.

He ran a hand through his hair, the frustration radiating off him like heat from a flame. "I need more than just explanations. I need to know what I'm dealing with."

"Okay," I said, grounding myself, preparing to bare my soul. "I've always felt different, like I was meant for something beyond the ordinary. My abilities—"

Just then, an eerie sound interrupted us. It began as a low hum, vibrating through the very foundation of the room. I could feel it deep within my bones, an unsettling energy that twisted the air around us.

"What is that?" Grant asked, eyes darting toward the windows.

"I don't know," I admitted, the unease spiraling into panic. "It's never happened before."

The hum intensified, resonating with a palpable force that made the hairs on my arms stand on end. Shadows flickered ominously along the walls, and as I turned to look, I saw the candles on the table begin to flicker violently, their flames bending in unnatural directions.

"Something's wrong," Grant said, taking a step back.

"No, wait—" I reached for him, but the room trembled as if caught in the grip of a powerful storm. My heart raced, fear washing over me as the ground shook beneath our feet.

And then, with a deafening roar, the power surged, ripping through the air and plunging us both into chaos.

The lights flickered and died, leaving us engulfed in darkness, and I could feel something deep within me awakening, something I had never been ready to confront. A sudden, visceral dread coursed through me as I realized that whatever was happening was far beyond anything I had anticipated.

With a flicker of the candles casting ghostly shadows against the walls, I heard Grant's voice, shaky but clear, "What have you done?"

And just like that, the world I had been so careful to maintain shattered once more, leaving only uncertainty in its wake.

Chapter 16: Ashes and Embers

The days stretch on, each one blurring into the next like paint smeared across an unfinished canvas. My magic feels like a storm trapped inside a glass jar, rattling with the weight of its own existence, ready to shatter the fragile boundaries that contain it. I stand at the window, watching the rain dribble down the panes like tears. The sky outside is a dull, leaden gray, reflecting my mood. I can't escape the feeling that the city itself has turned against me, the cobblestones slick with rain and secrets, whispering about the choices I've made and the chaos that swirls just beneath the surface.

There's a tension in the air, thick enough to cut. I've never felt so isolated, even among my own kind. The other witches, once my friends, now regard me with a mixture of pity and fear, their murmurs blending with the wind that howls through the alleyways. I can sense their unease, like a weight pressing down on my shoulders. Every time I step into the common area, their laughter stops, the atmosphere shifting as if I've walked into a room filled with smoke. I force a smile, but it feels like a mask slipping from my face, revealing the turmoil beneath.

My heart races as I catch my reflection in the window—my own eyes seem to glimmer with an unnatural light, flickering like the candle flames that once brought me peace. I can hardly recognize myself anymore, and the knowledge sends a chill racing down my spine. It's as if the power within me has taken on a life of its own, one I can no longer control. It coils and writhes, a wild beast clawing for freedom, and I am terrified it might break loose at any moment.

The rain picks up, hammering against the glass in a furious rhythm, and I turn away from the window. Perhaps it's time to confront this beast instead of cowering in its shadow. I head toward my small altar in the corner of the room, cluttered with trinkets and remnants of past rituals. A forgotten crystal glimmers under the fading light, and I reach for it, feeling its energy pulse against my fingertips. I've always believed that crystals can help center my magic, but tonight it feels more like a tease, promising calm while hiding the storm within.

As I close my eyes, I can almost hear the whispers of my ancestors urging me to harness the chaos, to bend it to my will instead of letting it consume me. I focus, taking a deep breath, but the moment I try to pull the energy into myself, it slips away like water through my fingers. Panic wells up, a tightening knot in my chest. Just as I'm about to let it go, a sharp knock jolts me from my reverie. The sound echoes through the room, a reminder that I'm not alone in this struggle, even if the world feels like it has turned its back on me.

I open the door cautiously, half-expecting to find another witch looking at me with suspicion. Instead, it's Rowan, a fellow witch whose presence is as grounding as the earth itself. Her long auburn hair is damp from the rain, framing a face that usually carries a warm, welcoming smile. Tonight, however, concern etches lines around her eyes. "You've been avoiding us," she says, her voice steady, but I can hear the underlying tremor of worry.

"I'm not avoiding anyone," I retort, a little too sharply. My irritation flares like the magic within me, volatile and uncontained. I can feel the air between us shift, charged and heavy, as Rowan's brow furrows.

"You can't keep pushing us away. We want to help you, but you have to let us in," she says, stepping closer. The sincerity in her eyes catches me off guard. The truth is, I'm scared—scared of what I might become, scared of hurting those I love. But I'm equally terrified of being alone.

"I don't need help," I manage to say, but the words feel hollow, even to me. I can hear the thrum of my power, wild and unpredictable, urging me to either embrace it or unleash it in a way that could hurt those around me.

Rowan crosses her arms, a gesture that usually signifies her unyielding support but tonight feels more like a barrier. "You can't control this on your own. None of us can. You're stronger with us, but you have to be willing to trust."

Her words hang in the air like an uninvited guest, demanding attention. I want to argue, to shove her away, but the truth of her statement clings to my thoughts. I realize, deep down, that I crave the comfort of connection, the knowledge that I am not alone in this battle against my own powers. I take a breath, steadying myself as the storm within me roils.

"What if I hurt you?" The admission spills from my lips, raw and unguarded. It's a fear I've harbored, one that gnaws at me like a hungry animal. Rowan takes a step closer, her expression softening, the fierce strength of her spirit shining through.

"Then we'll face it together. You're not alone, and you don't have to bear this burden by yourself," she says, and for a moment, I see the truth in her eyes, the bond we share as witches, as friends. My walls begin to crumble, piece by piece, and the warmth of her reassurance seeps into my heart.

In that moment, the rain outside quiets, as if the world is holding its breath, waiting for me to make a choice. I can feel the energy thrumming in the air, urging me to embrace this connection. I nod, tentative but resolute, ready to step into the unknown, where shadows and light intertwine, and the chaos might just lead me to a power greater than I ever imagined.

The soft patter of the rain outside continues to serve as a backdrop to my spiraling thoughts, a symphony of chaos and tranquility playing in a delicate balance. Rowan stands before me, her presence a reassuring anchor amidst the tempest brewing inside. I finally allow a deep breath to settle within me, the air thick with an unspoken promise of camaraderie. "Okay, let's do this," I say, the words tinged with a blend of resolve and vulnerability. The shift in my tone doesn't escape her notice; she nods, the corners of her mouth lifting into a tentative smile.

"Good. We'll start with grounding exercises. I know it sounds cliché, but they work," she says, her voice warm and inviting. I can't help but chuckle, the tension easing slightly. "Cliché? Please, save that for the witches' book club. I'm more of a 'breathe in the chaos, breathe out the calm' kind of girl."

Rowan rolls her eyes, but there's an underlying affection in the gesture. "Chaos, huh? That explains the current state of your hair." I reach up, fingers raking through my unruly locks, which have taken on a mind of their own in the midst of this emotional storm. "Hey, it's called 'creative expression.'"

With that, we settle into a rhythm, finding a quiet space on the floor of my cluttered living room, scattered with remnants of spells past. I close my eyes, letting the comforting scents of sandalwood and sage wrap around me like a blanket. "Just breathe," Rowan prompts, her voice steady and rhythmic, cutting through the noise in my mind.

The room begins to feel smaller, the walls creeping in as I try to find that elusive calm. The energy within me buzzes, a live wire threatening to snap at any moment. I picture the storm inside—wild and chaotic—but as I focus, it begins to take shape, each bolt of energy a part of me, a force I can harness instead of fear. The power crackles under my skin, and I take a deep breath, feeling it course through me like electricity.

"Breathe, remember?" Rowan nudges me gently. "You're doing great." I can hear the pride in her voice, and it warms me. "You'd think I'd remember the basics of breathing, but clearly, I'm a work in progress."

Laughter bubbles between us, breaking the tension that has wrapped around us like a vine. As we delve deeper into our meditation, I feel the chaos begin to ebb, my magic settling like a calm sea after a storm. There's an undeniable strength in having Rowan here, a reminder that I don't have to navigate this turbulent landscape alone.

After what feels like an eternity of quiet reflection, I open my eyes. The room comes into focus, brighter somehow, as if the shadows have retreated. "So, what's next? Should we summon a unicorn or maybe just order pizza?" I ask, a playful glimmer in my eye. Rowan laughs, the sound infectious, and I bask in the warmth of our connection.

"We could use some pizza after that," she agrees. "But first, we need to test that new grounding you've got going." The prospect of channeling my magic feels less daunting with her by my side. I rise to my feet, the energy within me a gentle hum now, rather than a violent thrumming.

We gather our materials—some crystals, a few herbs, and an assortment of candles. It feels surreal, almost ceremonial, as we set up the small table at the center of the room. I can't shake the sensation that something big is about to unfold, like the quiet before an exhilarating rollercoaster drop. "Alright, what are we doing exactly?" I ask, a hint of uncertainty creeping into my voice.

"We're going to create a small circle," Rowan explains, her hands deftly arranging the crystals in a perfect pattern. "This will help you channel your magic more effectively. You've got all this power, but we need to direct it. Think of it as...aiming a powerful water hose instead of just letting it spray everywhere."

I snort at the imagery, but her analogy resonates. "So, I'm the hose, and my magic is the water? Got it." I chuckle, but there's a serious undertone to the exercise. The weight of expectation hangs in the air, a tangible thing I can almost reach out and touch.

Once the circle is formed, we sit down opposite each other, our knees barely touching. "Ready?" she asks, her eyes locking onto mine, bright with determination. "Ready as I'll ever be," I reply, my heart racing with a mix of excitement and trepidation.

Rowan nods, and we begin to chant softly, the words rolling off our tongues like a familiar melody. The air shifts, electric and alive, as the crystals begin to glow faintly, pulsing in time with my heartbeat. I can feel my magic responding, the chaotic energy within me swirling and coiling like smoke, ready to be unleashed.

"Focus on what you want to achieve," Rowan instructs, her voice steady. "Imagine your magic weaving through the circle, binding it to you." I close my eyes, envisioning the power, the energy like a thread of light, wrapping around me, binding me to the earth beneath us.

The moment stretches, the air thickening, and then, suddenly, I feel it—a surge of warmth radiating from the center of the circle, a wave that crashes over me and wraps around my heart like a comforting embrace. I gasp, the sensation both exhilarating and terrifying. My magic, no longer a beast I fear, feels like an extension of myself, an ally in this chaotic world.

But just as I begin to embrace this newfound connection, a loud crash echoes from the other room, shattering the tranquility like glass falling from a great height. My heart skips, the spell faltering as I jerk my eyes open. Rowan's expression shifts, worry dancing across her features. "What was that?" she breathes, her voice laced with concern.

"Not a clue," I reply, adrenaline pumping through my veins as I scramble to my feet. The energy from our circle flickers, threatening to dissipate into nothingness. "Stay here, I'll check it out," I say, half-heartedly attempting to sound brave. The last thing I want is to face whatever danger lurks beyond our small sanctuary, but something primal urges me forward.

I inch toward the door, my heart pounding like a drum, every instinct screaming for me to retreat. The stillness of the apartment feels like a fragile illusion, one that could shatter at any moment. As

I push the door open, I'm met with the sight of shattered glass and scattered remnants of my world, the shadows creeping in as if ready to claim me once again. The chaos of the night is far from over, and with it comes the lingering question of what lies beyond the storm I've only begun to face.

I step into the wreckage of my living room, heart racing as shards of glass glimmer like fallen stars scattered across the hardwood floor. A decorative vase that once held dried lavender now lies in pieces, a poignant reminder of how quickly things can spiral out of control. The pungent scent of broken ceramic mingles with the lingering aroma of sage, and for a fleeting moment, the chaos feels surreal, almost dreamlike. But the reality hits hard as I glance around, looking for the source of the disturbance.

"Rowan!" I call out, the sound of my voice breaking the thick silence. Anxiety coils in my gut as I feel my magic flicker uneasily in response to the tension. I brace myself for anything—a rogue spirit, a misplaced charm gone awry—but nothing prepares me for what I find.

Rowan stands at the threshold of my kitchen, her eyes wide and apprehensive. She's holding a delivery box, the lid flung open to reveal a half-eaten pizza. "Well, this is new," she deadpans, her tone a mixture of disbelief and humor that almost makes me laugh amidst the chaos.

"You have to be kidding me. Did the pizza try to break in?" I reply, a mix of relief and irritation flooding through me. "I was expecting a ghost, not a late-night snack."

"It might as well be a ghost. I ordered it an hour ago, and they just tossed it through your window." She gestures to the mess, her eyes narrowing as she steps carefully over the debris. "You've got to start being more careful. At this rate, the city will sue you for property damage."

"Right, because that's the main concern here," I scoff, kneeling to pick up the larger pieces of the vase. "First, I lose control of my magic; now my decor is staging a rebellion."

"Decor doesn't stand a chance against the forces of chaos," she says, the lightness in her tone drawing a smile from me despite the circumstances. "But really, what was that?" She glances over her shoulder, still half-expecting some paranormal activity to follow.

"Honestly? I have no idea," I admit, glancing around as unease prickles at the back of my mind. "This place is supposed to be a safe haven, not a scene from a horror film."

"Speaking of horror films, did you forget that there's a full moon tonight?" she asks, raising an eyebrow knowingly. "You know how that affects the energy around here."

I can feel the truth of her words settle in my bones. The full moon is a beacon for heightened emotions and unpredictable magic, something I should have factored into my plans. "Fantastic. Just what I need—an unpredictable full moon on top of everything else," I groan, feeling the weight of the evening settle on my shoulders like a heavy cloak.

Rowan reaches over to help me gather the broken pieces, her fingers deftly maneuvering the glass as if she's done this a thousand times. "Okay, let's clean this up before something else happens. Then, we can regroup and figure out what to do next. Maybe we can harness some of that moon magic to help you regain control."

As we work side by side, the air hums with an unspoken energy, an intimacy that feels comforting in the face of the chaos. We share quick, sidelong glances, each of us keenly aware of the heavy load we carry—my magic, her concern, the city alive with its own mysteries. "You know," I begin, carefully placing a piece of broken ceramic into the box, "I never thought I'd find myself relying on a pizza to save me from a meltdown. It's definitely not in the rulebook for witchcraft."

"Witchcraft rulebook?" she muses, her eyes twinkling with mischief. "You must have skipped the chapter on culinary rescue. Clearly, pizza is the magic elixir we all need."

We laugh, but the sound feels distant, as if the universe is playing a cruel joke. Just then, a tremor runs through the floor, a subtle vibration that makes my skin prickle. I freeze, my heart racing anew. "Did you feel that?" I ask, my voice dropping to a whisper.

Rowan looks at me, her smile fading. "Feel what?"

"The floor... it felt alive, like it was shifting," I murmur, unease creeping back in. The magic within me flares, responding to something deeper and more primal. It's as if the very foundation of our reality is trembling under the weight of what is to come.

Before Rowan can respond, the lights flicker overhead, dimming to a ghostly glow before they plunge us into darkness. The sudden absence of light wraps around us like a shroud, leaving only the faint illumination of the streetlamps filtering through the window.

"Great, just what we need," I say, sarcasm tinged with fear. "If it's not the pizza, it's the power. What's next? The fridge attacks?"

Rowan moves closer, her eyes scanning the room. "Stay calm. We just need to find the flashlight," she says, her voice steady despite the palpable tension.

With a quick flicker of movement, I push aside the scattered papers on the kitchen table, my fingers brushing against something cold and metallic. "Found it!" I exclaim, holding the flashlight aloft like a beacon.

The beam cuts through the darkness, illuminating the chaos we've been trying to contain. Just then, another tremor ripples through the floor, this time stronger, almost like the pulse of a heartbeat. My breath catches in my throat. "This isn't normal, is it?" I whisper, dread pooling in my stomach.

Rowan's expression hardens. "No, it's not. We need to figure out what's going on."

The floor vibrates again, and I can hear a distant rumble, a sound like thunder but deeper, resonating through the very walls of my sanctuary. "What if it's an earthquake?" I suggest, trying to reason with the wild panic rising within me.

"Not an earthquake," she replies, her voice laced with urgency. "Earthquakes don't behave like this. Something is awakening."

The implications of her words settle over us like a heavy fog, the air charged with an energy I can't quite grasp. As we stand in the dim light, the vibrations intensify, and I can feel the magic surging within me, twisting and writhing as if it senses the disturbance.

Suddenly, the floorboards beneath us crack, a sharp sound like the snapping of a twig echoing through the room. I leap back instinctively, the flashlight beam shaking wildly as I try to catch my breath. "This is not happening," I murmur, fear clawing at my throat.

Rowan steps back, her eyes wide with horror. "We have to get out of here," she urges, her voice firm. "Now."

But before we can move, the wall behind me shudders violently, a deep growl resonating from the depths of the earth itself. A fissure opens up, splintering the wood and sending a chill racing down my spine.

The world tilts, and in that moment, I know we're standing on the brink of something dark and powerful, something that has been waiting for the right moment to rise. The flashlight flickers, and in the darkness, I see it—a shadow, shifting and swirling just beyond the crack. It pulses with an ancient energy, hungry and ready to consume everything in its path.

"Get back!" I scream, but the words barely leave my mouth before the shadow lunges, a fierce, swirling mass of darkness that threatens to pull us into the abyss. In that moment, my magic surges in response, instinctively racing to protect us, but I can feel it teetering on the edge of chaos, ready to unleash either salvation or destruction. The air crackles with uncertainty, and as the darkness swallows the light, I brace myself for whatever is about to happen next.

Chapter 17: Secrets of the Ancestors

The air was thick with the scent of sage and something sweet, almost like burnt sugar, as I stepped into the dimly lit shop. A faded sign swung lazily above the entrance, its letters barely legible, hinting at the secrets held within. Shelves crowded with dusty tomes and peculiar artifacts jutted out in every direction, forming narrow passageways that invited the curious and the brave. I had heard whispers of The Oracle in hushed tones at local cafés, her name an incantation of its own, tinged with both reverence and a healthy dose of fear.

With each step, the wooden floor creaked beneath my feet, a soft symphony of age echoing through the cramped space. Cobwebs draped like lace curtains in the corners, and a few jars containing curious specimens—dried herbs, shimmering liquids, and what looked suspiciously like a finger bone—sat like guardians of hidden knowledge. The faint flicker of candles cast dancing shadows, their light flickering against the walls as if they were conspiring with the darkness.

I was here, driven by a desperation that gnawed at my insides. The thrill of seeking out a piece of my past intertwined with a nagging fear of what I might uncover. My heart raced as I approached a heavy oak counter, where The Oracle stood, her silver hair cascading down her back like a waterfall of moonlight. She was a vision, draped in layers of flowing fabric, adorned with charms that jingled softly with each movement. Her eyes, deep-set and wise, twinkled with the mischief of countless secrets.

"Ah, you must be the seeker," she croaked, her voice resonating like the crackling of firewood in a hearth. "Your energy crackles like static, begging for release." I felt my cheeks flush under her keen gaze. There was no escaping the truth of my quest, nor the peculiar familiarity I felt in her presence.

"I need answers," I admitted, my voice barely above a whisper. "About my family... my heritage." The words tumbled out, heavy with years of buried questions. The Oracle leaned in, her expression shifting from curiosity to something more profound, as if she could see the very fabric of my being laid bare before her.

"Ah, the lineage of the ancients runs through your veins," she said, nodding slowly, as if contemplating the weight of the words. "You carry the echoes of those who walked before you, powerful witches whose whispers shaped the very essence of this city. They were feared, revered, and ultimately forgotten. But their magic remains, hidden like the jewels in a treasure chest." She motioned for me to sit, and I sank into a chair that seemed to sigh beneath my weight.

"Your power," she continued, her eyes narrowing, "is unlike any I've seen in a long while. It disrupts the natural order, bends the rules of reality. But it comes with a price." The flickering candlelight highlighted the sharp angles of her face, and I felt a shiver crawl down my spine. "Many have tried to wield it, and few have succeeded without losing themselves in the process."

"What does that mean?" I asked, my voice trembling slightly. "Am I destined for something... terrible?"

The Oracle chuckled, a sound like dry leaves rustling in a wind that had long since died. "Destiny is a fickle mistress, dear one. You were never meant to be ordinary. You hold within you the potential for greatness, but also the weight of darkness. Choose wisely." Her words hung in the air, thick and heavy, resonating deep within me.

As she spoke, images flooded my mind—visions of powerful women in flowing robes, standing against storms of energy, their eyes glowing with a fierce light. They were my ancestors, I realized, each one of them a part of the tapestry that was my life. I could feel their strength vibrating in my bones, a melody sung through generations, powerful and haunting.

"Tell me about them," I urged, desperate to connect the dots. "What happened to my family?"

The Oracle leaned back, fingers steepled beneath her chin, and the shadows danced across her face. "Long ago, they harnessed magic that was both a gift and a curse. They fought against the very forces of nature, sought to rewrite the rules of existence. But such power attracts attention, and not all who gaze upon it do so with good intentions." She paused, letting the weight of her words settle like dust in the air.

"They became pariahs, hunted for their abilities. In their fear, they hid, created barriers between themselves and the world, until eventually, they faded into the very fabric of society. But you, my dear, you are their legacy. And the world is calling for you to awaken that legacy."

A flicker of fear stirred within me, coiling tightly around my heart. "What if I don't want it?" I blurted, a wave of rebellion rising to the surface. "What if I want to be ordinary?"

"Ah," she said, her voice low and musical, "that is the trick, isn't it? To be ordinary in a world that demands extraordinary. The choice is yours, but remember—power, once awakened, cannot be easily silenced." Her eyes held mine, unyielding, challenging.

I left the shop that day with a heart heavy with anticipation and dread, the weight of my ancestry clinging to me like a shroud. As I stepped back into the bustle of Brooklyn, the city thrumming with life, I felt the undercurrents of magic swirling around me, a pulse just beneath the surface. The Oracle's words echoed in my mind, a mantra that urged me to confront the truth of who I was and what I could become.

But the choice remained, tantalizingly out of reach, like a high-hanging fruit that beckoned but threatened to fall into chaos if plucked too soon. And as the vibrant colors of the city blurred around me, I realized I was on the precipice of a journey that would not only reveal the secrets of my ancestors but also test the very limits of my soul.

The city buzzed around me as I made my way down the crowded streets, a chaotic tapestry of life threading through the spaces between my thoughts. The Oracle's words echoed in my mind like an incantation, swirling and tumbling through the day. I felt a peculiar combination of exhilaration and trepidation, as if I were teetering on the edge of a precipice, where one wrong step could send me spiraling into the unknown.

As I turned a corner, the clamor of the city faded slightly, replaced by the rhythmic clatter of a nearby café where the scent of fresh espresso and baked goods wafted enticingly into the air. I could hardly resist the lure of warmth and comfort. Sliding into a small table by the window, I ordered a cappuccino, the barista flashing me a knowing smile as he recognized the look of someone wrestling with deep thoughts. I could almost hear my mind brewing alongside the coffee.

The smooth surface of the frothy drink mirrored the tumult within me. I glanced outside, watching the world bustle by, each face carrying its own story, its own burdens. My thoughts drifted back to the Oracle, her vivid descriptions of the past weaving through my imagination like a spell. I sipped my drink, the warmth spreading through me, comforting yet insufficient to banish the chill of uncertainty.

"Lost in thought, or just pretending to be mysterious?" A voice broke through my reverie, playful and teasing. I looked up to find a tall figure leaning against the counter, a smirk playing at the corners of his mouth. He had tousled dark hair and bright green eyes that sparkled with mischief.

"Maybe a little of both," I replied, a grin creeping onto my face despite myself. "It's hard to maintain an air of intrigue when your brain feels like a blender on high speed."

"Ah, the conundrum of life," he declared dramatically, swooping into the seat opposite mine. "I'm Liam, your friendly neighborhood philosopher-slash-barista. So, what's stirring in that pretty little head of yours?"

I couldn't help but chuckle. "You must be quite the observer to deduce my inner turmoil from a mere cappuccino order."

He raised an eyebrow, his smirk widening. "You'd be surprised what a good barista can tell. Plus, you look like someone who just encountered a truth that might change everything. It's written all over your face."

"Okay, you got me," I admitted, feeling an odd sense of camaraderie with this stranger. "I just spoke with someone who claims to know about my family's magical history. It's a lot to process."

His eyes widened, interest piqued. "Magical history? Now that's intriguing. Spill the beans!"

I found myself sharing my encounter with The Oracle, my words spilling out in a torrent of excitement and fear. As I recounted the tales of my ancestors and the weight of expectation resting upon me, Liam listened intently, his expression shifting from amusement to genuine concern.

"Sounds like you've got a lot on your plate. But you know, having power is only half the battle. It's what you do with it that counts," he said, leaning forward. "You could become a force for good, or—"

"Or a disaster waiting to happen?" I interjected, my heart racing at the thought. "Exactly. That's what has me so rattled. I don't want to be responsible for something terrible."

His gaze softened, and he leaned back, folding his arms with a thoughtful look. "Maybe you should look at it differently. Think of it as an opportunity. You could break the cycle of fear and create something new. Make your own path."

The weight of his words hung between us, heavy yet somehow liberating. I couldn't help but admire his perspective, which was refreshingly optimistic. "You make it sound so easy," I said with a half-laugh. "Just casually redefine my destiny over a cup of coffee."

"Hey, I'm not saying it'll be easy. But you're not alone. The moment you step into the unknown is when the real magic happens." He smiled, and the warmth of it settled around me like a favorite blanket.

Just then, the café door swung open, and a gust of wind swept in, carrying with it an unexpected chill. I turned to see a figure standing in the doorway, silhouetted against the bright sunlight outside. My breath caught in my throat. The figure was familiar, though it took me a moment to register why. It was a man from my past, a shadow I had hoped would remain buried.

"Max," I whispered, half in shock, half in disbelief. He stepped inside, the jingle of the door breaking the momentary tension. Our eyes met, and for a fleeting second, the air crackled with an electric tension, memories rushing back like a tide that refused to recede.

"Fancy meeting you here," he said, his voice smooth but laced with an undercurrent of something more. He scanned the café, his gaze landing on me before he approached. "Thought you had vanished into thin air."

"And you've returned from your mysterious absence," I shot back, unable to suppress the sharpness in my tone.

Liam, sensing the shift in atmosphere, cleared his throat and slowly slid his chair back. "I'll just... uh, get back to work," he muttered, shooting me a quick, reassuring smile before retreating to the counter.

"Nice guy," Max said, leaning against the table, his presence suddenly feeling all too close. "I didn't know you were into the whole... coffee-shop philosopher thing."

"Unlike you, I don't have the luxury of disappearing whenever things get complicated," I snapped, anger and hurt bubbling to the surface.

"Complicated?" he echoed, an eyebrow raised, as if my life were nothing more than an intriguing riddle. "You don't know the half of it."

"Then enlighten me." I folded my arms, daring him to share the secrets that had kept him away.

A silence hung between us, heavy and charged. The cacophony of the café faded into the background as we stood on the precipice of an uncharted conversation, the history between us a tapestry woven with threads of both love and betrayal.

Finally, he sighed, running a hand through his hair, revealing a vulnerability I hadn't expected. "I came back because... things are shifting. There are forces at play, things you don't know about yet. I didn't want to involve you, but it seems like fate has other plans."

My heart raced, the tension twisting my stomach into knots. "What do you mean? Are you involved in this?"

"Let's just say I've been on a journey of my own. And it might be intertwined with yours in ways we can't yet understand." His gaze held mine, a storm of emotions flickering in his eyes.

This was no longer just about my ancestry or the Oracle's prophecy. This was about secrets, connections, and the fragile strands that wove our lives together.

Max's eyes held a storm of emotions that I struggled to decipher. The café, once a warm cocoon of comfort, now felt like a battleground where past wounds were laid bare, and new tensions were set to ignite. "What kind of forces?" I demanded, leaning forward, my heart thudding in my chest as I scanned his face for any hint of deception.

He ran a hand through his hair, a gesture that always seemed to reveal his uncertainty. "The kind that doesn't care about the personal lives of individuals. There are those who seek the power your ancestors once wielded, and they're starting to take an interest in you." His voice lowered, urgency threading through his words like a lifeline thrown into turbulent waters.

"I'm just trying to figure out who I am," I protested, frustration bubbling to the surface. "I didn't ask for any of this! I don't want to be part of some ancient battle for power."

"You don't get to choose that," he replied sharply, his intensity piercing through my defiance. "Your lineage is more than just a footnote in history. It's alive, and it has implications that stretch far beyond what either of us can imagine."

I leaned back, my mind racing. The weight of his words pressed down on me, and the reality of my situation began to crystallize. "So, what do I do now? Just sit back and wait for some shadowy figures to come knocking at my door?"

Max shook his head, frustration flickering in his eyes. "No, you need to be proactive. We have to find out what they want. If they're looking for you, it's not just about power. There's something more at stake, something they believe you can unlock."

The café was growing increasingly stifling, the air charged with a mix of anxiety and intrigue. I could feel the eyes of the barista darting my way, curious about the drama unfolding at our table. Outside, the city continued its dance, oblivious to the tumult brewing within me.

"I'm not ready for this," I confessed, my voice barely above a whisper. "What if I can't handle whatever it is they want from me?"

Max leaned closer, the warmth of his presence a stark contrast to the chill creeping down my spine. "You're stronger than you think. And you won't have to face it alone." He hesitated, as if weighing his next words carefully. "I'll help you."

The offer lingered between us, heavy with unspoken promises and shared histories. But doubts gnawed at me like shadows creeping along the walls. "Why now? Where have you been all this time?" I pressed, my voice laced with skepticism. "Why should I trust you?"

"Because I never stopped caring," he replied, sincerity lacing his tone. "I made mistakes, and I thought staying away would protect you. But clearly, I was wrong. You're in this, whether you want to be or not."

I felt the walls of my carefully constructed world beginning to crumble, the cracks wide enough to let doubt seep through. Just as I opened my mouth to respond, a loud crash echoed through the café, drawing every eye toward the entrance. The door swung open, a gust of wind slamming it against the wall, and in strode a figure draped in black, their face obscured beneath a hood.

A silence fell over the room, a thick tension wrapping itself around us. The newcomer surveyed the café, eyes glinting like shards of glass. The atmosphere shifted, charged with an electric fear that sent a shiver down my spine. My heart raced as the figure took a step forward, and in that moment, it felt as if time had frozen.

"What do you want?" I managed to croak, my voice barely above a whisper. The weight of the Oracle's warnings swirled in my mind, mixing with the urgency of the present moment.

The hooded figure chuckled, a low sound that reverberated through the stillness, slicing through the tension like a knife. "I seek what is mine," they declared, their voice a low growl that felt like a threat wrapped in silk. "The power that flows through your veins belongs to my order, and you have something we need."

Max stood up, positioning himself protectively in front of me. "You're not taking her anywhere," he snapped, his bravado a fragile barrier against the dark presence looming before us.

"Foolish boy," the figure said, disdain lacing their voice. "You think you can protect her? You have no idea what you're up against." The tension thickened, and I felt my heart hammering against my ribcage, the instinct to flee battling with the need to stand my ground.

"What does that even mean?" I asked, my voice rising slightly in defiance. "I won't let you dictate my life!"

A sardonic smile spread across the figure's face, and they stepped closer, pulling back the hood to reveal sharp features framed by dark hair. Their eyes glinted with an unsettling light, a mixture of fascination and malice. "You think you have a choice? You're just a pawn in a much larger game."

As the words left their lips, the atmosphere in the café shifted. I could feel the air crackling with energy, thick and suffocating. Max took a step forward, ready to confront this intruder, but I reached out and grasped his arm, my instincts screaming at me to tread carefully.

"What game?" I pressed, needing to understand. "What do you want from me?"

The figure leaned in, their voice a whisper now, intimate and insidious. "The blood that courses through you is the key to unlocking an ancient power. But you must choose a side, and the clock is ticking."

Panic surged within me, clawing at the edges of my resolve. I wanted to retreat, to flee back into the comforting chaos of the city outside, but I was rooted to the spot, caught in this web of fate that felt both exhilarating and terrifying.

The hooded figure straightened, casting one last glance around the café. "You'll need to decide quickly. The night is long, and our patience is short." With that, they turned, sweeping out of the café like a shadow retreating into darkness, leaving the air charged with the promise of chaos.

"What just happened?" I gasped, my breath catching in my throat as the weight of uncertainty settled upon me once again.

Max's expression mirrored my shock, disbelief etched into his features. "I don't know, but we can't ignore this. Whatever they want, it's only the beginning."

As the café returned to its normal rhythm, the patrons murmured in confusion, but all I could focus on was the pulse of fear racing through my veins. In that moment, I understood that my life had irrevocably changed. The choices before me shimmered with uncertainty, and I was standing on the threshold of a path I had never intended to walk.

And just as the reality of my newfound power settled over me, a ringing from my phone jolted me from my thoughts. I glanced at the screen, my heart plummeting as a name flashed before me—one I never expected to see again.

Chapter 18: A Dangerous Bargain

The air was thick with tension as I stepped into the dimly lit room, the walls adorned with ominous symbols and the scent of incense hanging like a shroud. Flickering candles cast shadows that danced and twirled, reminiscent of spirits caught in an eternal waltz. The corporate witches, draped in tailored black robes that exuded both authority and malice, gathered around a polished table, their eyes glinting with curiosity and caution. I could almost feel the crackle of their power buzzing in the atmosphere, a stark reminder of what I was up against.

"Is this the part where you beg for our help?" one of them sneered, her voice silky but sharp, slicing through the tension like a knife. It was Amara, the most notorious among them, known for her silver tongue and her penchant for manipulation. I had always been wary of her; she had an uncanny ability to turn words into weapons, to ensnare her opponents in a web of their own making.

"Not quite," I replied, forcing my voice to steady, though my heart raced like a trapped bird. "I'm here to propose a different arrangement." The words spilled out before I could second-guess myself. It was a gamble, one that could either forge an unlikely alliance or land me in deeper trouble than I already faced.

Their expressions shifted, surprise flickering momentarily in their eyes before they masked it with calculated indifference. I could almost hear the gears turning in their heads, weighing the benefits of my proposition against the risks.

"What could you possibly offer us that we don't already possess?" another witch, clad in a deep emerald robe, interjected, her skepticism evident.

I took a breath, channeling every ounce of courage I had. "An alliance. A temporary truce to stabilize the chaos that's been unleashed. You know as well as I do that the magic is spiraling out of control. If we don't act swiftly, it won't just threaten my world; it will threaten yours too."

Silence enveloped the room, a thick blanket of contemplation. I could almost hear the collective heartbeat of the witches, each pulse resonating with power and intrigue. They were assessing me, dissecting my every word, and I stood at the precipice of potential disaster or unexpected collaboration.

Finally, Amara leaned back in her chair, her fingers steepled under her chin, her gaze piercing. "And what do you propose we do in this alliance?"

I could feel the heat rising in my cheeks, the weight of my proposal pressing down like a tangible force. "We pool our resources. You have the knowledge and the influence; I have access to the remnants of the magic, the raw energy flowing through the city. Together, we can harness it, redirect it before it consumes us all."

One of the witches scoffed, the sound echoing in the otherwise quiet room. "You think we'd trust you, after everything that's happened? Your precious city is teetering on the brink of disaster, and you waltz in here expecting us to play nice?"

"Trust is a luxury we can't afford," I shot back, surprising even myself with the intensity of my words. "This isn't about trust; it's about survival. If I wanted to undermine you, I would have done it already. But I'm here instead, offering a way forward."

Their expressions softened slightly, the tension shifting from hostility to curiosity. I felt the ground beneath me shifting, the potential for a fragile understanding blossoming. But I knew better than to get ahead of myself.

After what felt like an eternity, Amara nodded slowly, a wicked smile creeping across her lips. "Very well, let's entertain this notion. But know this: if you cross us, it won't just be your magic at stake. You'll lose far more than you can imagine."

A chill ran down my spine, but I held her gaze, unwilling to show weakness. "Understood. Just as long as Grant remains untouched, we have a deal."

The moment I said his name, I could see their interest piqued. Grant, with his charming smile and a heart that beat too fiercely for this world, was the one thing that made me vulnerable, the one thing I refused to let them tarnish.

"Consider it done," Amara replied, a glint of mischief in her eyes. "For now."

As I left their lair, the weight of the bargain settled heavily on my shoulders. I had danced with fire, and while I hoped to emerge unscathed, I knew that the flames could just as easily consume me. The city felt different as I stepped back into the night, the air charged with an electrifying mix of hope and dread.

I couldn't shake the feeling that I had only scratched the surface of something far more sinister than I could ever understand. The whispers of power curled around me, tempting and threatening all at once. I had bought us time, but the battle ahead loomed larger than life itself.

In the distance, the lights of the city flickered like stars, beautiful yet distant, each one a reminder of what was at stake. Grant was out there, blissfully unaware of the storm brewing beneath the surface. I had to protect him, to shield him from the consequences of my choices. But as the magic surged and the stakes escalated, I couldn't shake the feeling that I was no longer the one in control.

Suddenly, the weight of my decision hit me like a wave, and I found myself longing for the simplicity of yesterday—when my biggest worry had been whether to order takeout or try my hand at cooking. Now, I was entrenched in a dangerous game where every move counted, and the players were more treacherous than I had ever anticipated.

With resolve blooming within me, I forged ahead, ready to face the consequences of my actions. Each step echoed with the pulse of the city's magic, each heartbeat a reminder that I was entwined in a narrative far grander than my own. I would fight tooth and nail to protect what mattered most, even if it meant standing shoulder to shoulder with those I had once deemed enemies. The night was young, and the battle for balance had only just begun.

The moon hung low in the sky, casting a silvery glow over the streets as I made my way back to my apartment. Each step felt heavy, laden with the weight of the deal I had struck. I had danced dangerously close to the flames, but the thought of Grant kept me grounded. The city was alive with the hum of magic, a cacophony of chaos that thrummed beneath my feet like a restless heartbeat.

As I approached my building, the familiar creak of the front door seemed to sigh in relief. Inside, the scent of cinnamon and apples lingered, remnants of my earlier attempt at baking, a futile exercise in domesticity that had ended with me covered in flour and a half-baked pie abandoned on the counter. I dropped my keys on the table and leaned against the cool surface, trying to shake off the anxiety that clung to me like a second skin.

Moments later, the soft padding of paws echoed down the hall. My cat, Whiskers, appeared as if summoned, her gray fur gleaming under the overhead light. She strutted toward me with an air of nonchalance, tail high, as if she sensed my unease. I bent down to scratch her head, finding solace in the rhythmic purring that filled the room.

"Looks like I've just made a deal with the devil," I murmured, feeling the ridiculousness of my situation wash over me. "And I didn't even get a snack out of it."

Whiskers blinked lazily, unimpressed by my melodrama, and I couldn't help but chuckle. "You're right; I should be focusing on the important things—like preventing an apocalypse instead of wallowing in self-pity."

The reality of my newfound alliance settled heavily on my shoulders. I had crossed an invisible line, and while I held my ground, uncertainty lingered like a shadow, ever-present and impossible to ignore. I grabbed a glass of water, gulping it down, feeling the coolness ease the tension coiling within me.

My phone buzzed insistently on the table, pulling my attention away from my spiraling thoughts. It was a message from Grant. A simple "Hey, how's it going?" yet it made my heart flutter. Just seeing his name lit a spark of warmth that fought against the chill of the night.

I typed back quickly, "Just made a bargain with some witches. Typical Tuesday, right?"

I didn't have to wait long for his response. "You always seem to find trouble. Do I need to come rescue you?"

A smile crept onto my face as I thought of his earnest concern. "Only if you promise to bring snacks. Negotiations can be exhausting."

He replied with a string of laughing emojis, which made me grin wider. There was something about our banter that eased the tension knotting my stomach, reminding me of the world outside of magic and mayhem. "I'll be over in a bit. Stay put, hero."

Hero. The term swirled in my mind, but I brushed it off. I didn't feel like a hero; I felt like a girl stumbling through a storm, desperately hoping she wouldn't get swept away. Yet, somehow, the thought of him coming over filled me with a warmth I hadn't anticipated.

After a few hurried minutes of straightening up, I set the half-finished pie on the table and lit a couple of candles. The flickering flames cast dancing shadows on the walls, creating a cozy ambiance that contradicted the turmoil within me. I poured another glass of water, and the sound of footsteps approaching made my heart race.

Grant stepped inside, his presence filling the room with an easy charm that always disarmed me. His tousled hair caught the light just right, and that smile—oh, that smile—could melt the iciest of hearts. "You weren't kidding about the trouble, were you?"

"Maybe a little drama is good for the soul," I replied, trying to sound casual. "You know, spice things up."

He raised an eyebrow, skepticism dancing across his features. "Spice? Or are we talking full-on chili pepper chaos?"

"Let's go with chaos for now." I gestured to the table, trying to shift the focus. "Would you like to sample my latest culinary disaster?"

As he moved to the table, I felt the warmth of his presence seep into the room, a stark contrast to the cold shadows that loomed in my mind. He picked up the pie, inspecting it with an exaggerated seriousness. "This looks...interesting."

I laughed, watching him try to suppress a grin. "Interesting is a good word for it."

With a playful roll of his eyes, he cut himself a generous slice. "Well, if I perish from food poisoning, I'll make sure to haunt you."

"Deal! You can stay and keep me company in the afterlife," I teased, unable to resist the playful banter.

As we dug into the pie, I found comfort in the ease of our conversation, the weight of the world outside momentarily fading. Grant shared stories from his day, his laughter echoing through the small space, wrapping around me like a warm blanket. The worries and threats that loomed over us faded into the background, leaving only the sound of his voice and the warmth of shared moments.

Yet, as I savored the familiar rhythms of our connection, a nagging thought crept into my mind. The witches were now a part of my life, and I couldn't hide that from him forever. I glanced at

Grant, his features illuminated by the flickering candlelight, and felt a twinge of guilt.

"Grant, there's something I need to tell you," I began, my heart thumping against my ribcage.

He paused mid-bite, concern flickering in his eyes. "You're starting to sound serious. Is everything okay?"

The weight of my secret pressed against me, a pressure that felt both suffocating and necessary. "I made a deal with the witches."

His brow furrowed, and for a moment, I feared I'd crossed a line too far. "The corporate ones? Why would you do that?"

"Because they know the city's magic better than anyone. I thought if we work together, we might stabilize everything before it gets worse. But—"

"But?" he prompted, leaning forward, genuine worry etched across his features.

"But I also made it clear that they can't touch you. I won't let them threaten you."

Silence stretched between us, thick and heavy. I held my breath, hoping he'd understand the gravity of the situation. After a moment, he sighed, running a hand through his hair, his expression a mix of admiration and frustration.

"Why do you always feel the need to protect me? I can take care of myself, you know."

"I know you can," I replied, my voice barely above a whisper. "But I care too much to let anything happen to you."

His gaze softened, the tension in the air shifting slightly. "And I care about you. That's why I worry."

Our eyes locked, and in that moment, the world outside faded entirely. I felt a flicker of hope, a glimmer of something deeper between us, and I was reminded that even amidst chaos, there could be moments of peace—if only for a breath. But just as quickly as the warmth spread, an icy reminder slithered back into my mind:

the witches were lurking, and the deal I had made was far from foolproof.

A soft knock at the door shattered our moment, and I cursed under my breath. "Who could that be?"

"More witches?" he joked, but I could see the tension creeping back into his expression.

I shrugged, trying to shake off the unease, and moved to open the door. The moment I swung it wide, the atmosphere shifted, the magic in the air thickening with a palpable tension. There stood a figure, cloaked in shadow, a haunting presence that sent a chill racing down my spine.

"Did someone say witches?" the figure purred, their voice smooth as silk yet laced with an undercurrent of danger. The realization hit me like a punch to the gut—this was not the end; this was merely the beginning of a far more complicated game, one where the stakes had just been raised.

The figure at my door stepped forward, their silhouette sharp against the glow of the hall light, the shadows wrapping around them like an intimate cloak. I barely had time to register their presence before they moved into the room, exuding an aura that felt both unsettling and magnetic. Their eyes, gleaming with an otherworldly intensity, swept over Grant and me, sizing up the situation with a predatory curiosity.

"Who invited you?" I snapped, my voice sharper than I intended, catching myself in a tangle of confusion and irritation.

"Invitations are so passé, darling," the stranger said, their voice smooth, dripping with a languid charm. "I go where I please."

Grant shifted beside me, instinctively stepping closer, his posture tense. "And what is it you want?"

The stranger tilted their head, amusement dancing in their eyes. "Oh, I'm just here to discuss your little deal with the corporate witches."

My heart sank. "You know about that?"

"Sweetheart, in my line of work, knowledge is currency. And I happen to be quite rich," they replied, flashing a smile that revealed teeth just a touch too sharp to be entirely comforting.

The room felt suddenly smaller, the air thickening with an invisible pressure. I glanced at Grant, who looked as if he were ready to either throw a punch or bolt for the door. "Look, we're not interested in whatever game you're playing," I said, trying to keep my voice steady despite the unease curling in my stomach.

"Oh, but you should be," they purred, stepping closer, the shadows clinging to them as if they were a living thing. "You see, those witches are not known for their loyalty, and they certainly don't appreciate being outmaneuvered. I'd hate for something unfortunate to happen to you or your charming friend here."

"Charming, huh?" Grant muttered, crossing his arms as if to protect himself from the palpable threat.

"Don't let his good looks fool you; he can be quite dangerous." I shot Grant a look, silently pleading him to keep his cool.

The figure chuckled softly, eyes sparkling with mischief. "I like the dynamics here. Very tense. Very entertaining. But I assure you, I'm not here to cause a ruckus—at least not yet."

"Then what do you want?" I pressed, trying to cut through the haze of intimidation that surrounded them. "If you're not here to threaten us, then state your business."

Their smile widened, and for a moment, I thought I saw something lurking beneath the surface—a flicker of a darker intention. "I want to offer you a proposition. One that would make your current deal with the witches look like a child's game."

My instincts screamed at me to refuse, but curiosity gnawed at me like a persistent itch. "What kind of proposition?"

"An alliance, of sorts," they said, tapping a long finger thoughtfully against their lips. "You want to stabilize the chaos, yes? I can help you with that."

I glanced at Grant, who was watching the stranger with wary eyes, his mouth set in a firm line. "And what's the catch?" I asked, my heart racing.

"Ah, you're so astute," the figure said, genuine admiration lacing their tone. "Let's say you and I could work together to harness the magic flooding your lovely city. I'd offer guidance, resources, and a little bit of my own... flair. In exchange, all I require is a tiny favor. Something innocuous, really."

A chill shot down my spine, and my instincts screamed that this was too good to be true. "What kind of favor?"

"Just a little piece of your soul," they said casually, as if discussing the weather. "Nothing too dramatic. Just a fragment. You'll hardly notice it's gone."

Grant's expression turned incredulous. "Are you serious? That's your big offer?"

"Why, yes! You see, I thrive on magic, and you, my dear, are teeming with potential." They turned to me, their gaze piercing into mine, as if trying to dissect my very essence. "Imagine what you could achieve with my help. The power, the control. You'd be able to protect your dear friend and your city. And I assure you, the fragment I desire will not hinder you in the slightest."

I felt like I was teetering on the edge of a cliff, my mind racing as I processed their words. The allure of power whispered sweetly in my ear, tempting me to take the plunge. But in the depths of my gut, a deep unease coiled. "And what if I refuse?"

The figure leaned closer, their voice dropping to a conspiratorial whisper. "Oh, sweetheart, refusal isn't an option. You're already entangled in this web. The witches will turn on you when it suits them, and I'm afraid your charming little bargain won't hold against their wrath."

"Let me guess; you'd swoop in to save the day?" Grant's tone dripped with sarcasm, though I could hear the tension in his voice.

"Precisely!" The stranger straightened, a triumphant glint in their eye. "You catch on quickly. We could be an unstoppable force, you and I. Think of it as a partnership. You gain the power to control the magic, and I get my piece of the puzzle. Everyone wins."

As they spoke, the gravity of their proposition weighed heavily on me. A sliver of my own ambition stirred within me, battling against the instinct to recoil from their dark charm. I could almost envision it—a world where I had control, where I could protect Grant and my city without fear. But at what cost?

"I need time to think about this," I finally said, my voice steady despite the maelstrom of thoughts swirling in my head.

"Time is not a luxury you have, darling," they replied, their demeanor shifting slightly, the charm slipping to reveal something sharper underneath. "But I'll grant you a small reprieve. However, if you choose to entertain the thought of declining... well, let's just say the consequences won't be pleasant."

With that, they stepped back, the shadows coiling tighter around them as if waiting for their master's command. "Consider your options wisely. I'll be in touch."

And just like that, they were gone, leaving an echo of danger and uncertainty in their wake. I turned to Grant, his brow furrowed, eyes wide with concern. "What just happened?"

"I think we've attracted something far worse than the witches," I said, the reality settling in like a heavy fog.

"Are you seriously considering it?" His voice was incredulous, disbelief coloring every word.

"No! I mean—" My heart raced as I struggled to find the right words. "I don't know! It's tempting. They're offering what I need to protect you, to save the city. But it feels wrong."

"Because it is wrong! Don't you see? This is exactly what they want—to play on your insecurities, your fears. You can't trust them."

"I know that!" I snapped, frustration boiling over. "But what if it's our only chance?"

He stepped closer, lowering his voice. "There has to be another way. You're stronger than this. Don't let them manipulate you."

As his words sank in, I felt the heavy weight of uncertainty push down on me again. Could I navigate this dangerous web alone? Would I lose everything trying to play their game?

Suddenly, my phone buzzed again, the screen lighting up with a notification. I glanced at it, and my heart dropped—the message was from one of the corporate witches.

"Tonight's magic is growing stronger. We expect to see you soon."

Panic surged within me, and I met Grant's gaze, fear pooling in my stomach. "We need to go. Now."

But as I turned to grab my jacket, the lights flickered, casting erratic shadows that danced on the walls. The air grew thick, the magic vibrating with an intensity that made my skin prickle.

And then, with a deafening crack, the door slammed shut, sealing us inside. I whipped around to face Grant, his expression mirroring my own growing dread.

"What the hell is happening?" he exclaimed, backing away from the door as if it were a live wire.

A low growl reverberated from the darkness beyond the door, a sound that sent a jolt of fear straight through me. "I think we might have company," I whispered, the realization settling like a weight in my chest.

Before I could react, the door burst open with a force that sent me stumbling backward, and a figure emerged from the shadows, their features obscured but their intent unmistakable.

"Time's up," they hissed, stepping into the flickering light, revealing the unmistakable insignia of the witches tattooed on their wrist. "We've come to collect."

A rush of adrenaline surged through me, and in that moment, I understood that this battle was far from over. The stakes had just escalated, and I was about to discover exactly how deep the darkness ran.

Chapter 19: Crossing the Threshold

The air in my apartment was thick with tension, a silence punctuated only by the low hum of my laptop, the glow illuminating the chaos of my life. I stood at the edge of the room, a witness to the remnants of what once felt like order: books stacked in precarious towers, remnants of half-finished projects strewn across the table, and a single mug that had become my makeshift companion, its contents long cold. This was my sanctuary, a chaotic little world where magic and technology often collided, but today it felt more like a battlefield.

The sun dipped low on the horizon, casting a golden hue over everything. I was perched on the precipice of my decision, fingers hovering above the keyboard, heart thudding in rhythm with my thoughts. Grant. I had avoided him like a stubborn shadow, the memories of our last encounter still fresh in my mind. His disappointment had felt like a physical blow, but now, I needed him more than ever. The fragile alliance I had forged with the other coven was as tentative as a spider's web, glistening in the morning dew but easily shattered by the slightest breeze.

I took a deep breath, the scent of coffee mingling with the lingering smell of incense, and typed out a message. It was a strange combination of vulnerability and defiance, an invitation to step back into the whirlwind of our past. "Grant," I wrote, the name feeling heavy on my tongue. "I need your help."

It took an eternity for his reply to flash across my screen, the little dots dancing in my chest like fireflies. Finally, "I'm listening." A simple phrase, but it felt like an invitation to a deeper conversation, a portal to possibilities I had never dared to explore.

In the dim light, I leaned closer to my laptop, typing furiously as I laid bare the chaos threatening to consume us. I described the magic spiraling out of control, the corporate witches prowling like predators, their hunger for power palpable in the city's underbelly. Each word felt like a confession, a stripping away of my defenses. I had been so afraid to show him the mess I had become, but here I was, opening the door to the parts of my life that had always been shrouded in secrecy.

His response came quickly, as if he had been waiting on the edge of his own turmoil. "Meet me at The Circuit. We'll talk."

The Circuit. The name conjured a rush of memories. It was a sleek, modern café nestled between a tech startup and a boutique selling crystals—an odd juxtaposition that perfectly encapsulated our world. We had spent countless hours there, mapping out our dreams, our futures, and the balance of magic and technology that danced in the air around us. It was the last place I had expected to feel comfort, yet somehow, it was the only place I could picture myself right now.

As I stepped outside, the evening air was cool against my skin, a welcome contrast to the suffocating atmosphere of my apartment. The city buzzed with life, the streets illuminated by a patchwork of neon signs and the laughter of late-night revelers. My heart raced, each beat matching the rhythm of my footsteps. I could almost taste the exhilaration and uncertainty mixing in my mouth like a heady cocktail.

When I arrived, Grant was already there, his silhouette framed by the café's soft glow. He was leaning against the wall, arms crossed, looking both imposing and oddly vulnerable. The sight of him sent a flood of emotions crashing over me—relief, nostalgia, and the pang of regret.

"Hey," I said, approaching him with cautious optimism.

"Hey." His gaze flickered to mine, the tension between us thickening like the steam rising from the coffee bar inside.

We stepped into the café together, the familiar smell of roasted beans and the gentle hum of conversation wrapping around us like a warm blanket. I ordered a latte, my usual choice, while Grant opted for something darker, more intense—a reflection of his current mood, perhaps. As we settled into a booth in the corner, I felt the weight of our history pressing down on us, the unspoken words hanging in the air like a delicate web.

"I've been thinking," I began, my voice steady despite the storm brewing inside me. "About everything that's happened. I know I messed up, and I can't change the past. But I need you to understand that I didn't choose this."

"Neither did I," he shot back, his voice low but fierce. "I didn't choose to get tangled up in your world, and I certainly didn't choose to be dragged into this mess."

"Then let's untangle it together," I urged, desperation creeping into my tone. "I need your technology, your insights. The corporate witches are more dangerous than you know. They've turned our city into a chessboard, and the stakes are higher than ever."

He studied me for a moment, his eyes narrowing as if trying to decipher the truth behind my words. "What do you suggest? We just throw ourselves into the fray with no plan?"

"Sometimes, the best plans come from improvisation," I replied, my voice laced with determination. "We know each other well enough to predict our moves. We can combine our strengths, Grant. You with your tech and me with my magic."

He leaned back, his expression softening, if only slightly. "I'm not saying it's a bad idea, but trust isn't built overnight. You can't just expect me to jump back into the fire after everything."

"I know," I said, swallowing hard. "But I'm here, and I'm willing to try."

The tension between us shifted, morphing from antagonism into something that felt almost like collaboration. He nodded slowly, the unyielding lines of his jaw softening just a bit. "All right. We'll see where this goes. But I'm not promising anything."

As we began to hash out our strategy, weaving together the strands of his technology with my magic, a sense of relief washed over me. The weight on my shoulders lightened, replaced by the exhilarating thrill of potential. In that dimly lit café, amidst the flickering shadows of our shared past, we crossed the threshold into a new chapter, one that promised both danger and hope. Together, we would unravel the connections threatening our city, step by step, as we ventured into the unknown.

The clinking of cups and the soft murmur of conversations enveloped us like a warm embrace as Grant and I plotted our strategy. The café's dim lights flickered above, casting a cozy glow that belied the brewing storm outside. I watched him as he leaned over the small table, his brow furrowed in concentration, the shadows playing across his sharp features. There was a tension in the air, a current of electricity that crackled between us, making the mundane feel like a pivotal moment.

"Okay, let's break this down," he said, tapping his fingers against the table, a rhythmic beat that seemed to echo my racing heart. "We need to identify the key players in this corporate witch mess you're dealing with. Who's at the top?"

I took a deep breath, recalling the cryptic whispers I'd heard in the darker corners of the city—rumors that danced like phantoms, both elusive and tangible. "The main one is a woman named Selene. She's ruthless, with a knack for exploiting vulnerabilities, both in people and systems. She has her fingers in every tech pie around here, and her magic is just as insidious. It's like she's weaving a net that's slowly tightening around the city."

Grant's expression hardened as he absorbed the information. "And you think she knows about our... collaboration?"

"She must," I replied, leaning closer, urgency fueling my words. "The coven I reached out to is a rival of hers. If she finds out we're working together, she won't hesitate to take us down. It's not just about magic anymore; she's playing a long game, and we need to be a step ahead."

"Then we need to disrupt her plans," he said, determination lacing his voice. "We should find a way to leverage your magic with my technology to turn the tables."

I nodded, feeling a swell of hope. "What if we create a digital barrier? Something to shield my spells while I investigate further into her operations. We can set up traps, magical beacons that alert us whenever she makes a move."

"Not a bad idea," he conceded, a hint of admiration glinting in his eyes. "But we need to be careful. Magic and technology don't always play well together. I can integrate some firewalls, but if your spells go haywire, it could backfire."

"I'll be careful," I assured him, though my stomach churned at the thought of unleashing wild magic. "And if we manage to disrupt her plans, it could throw her off balance. Make her think twice before she strikes."

Grant glanced around the café, his eyes darting to the other patrons, ensuring we weren't drawing attention. "We need a safe space to work—somewhere we can really dig into this without worrying about being overheard."

"The old warehouse on Third Street," I suggested, excitement bubbling within me. "It's secluded, and I've warded it against prying eyes. We can set up our base there."

"Then it's settled. Let's get to work," he said, pushing back from the table with a sense of purpose that reignited the fire in my chest.

As we left the café, the cool night air hit us like a refreshing splash of water. I felt invigorated, the weight of uncertainty slowly lifting as the thrill of planning overtook me. Our destination loomed ahead, a forgotten relic of the city's industrial past, where dust and shadows mingled with whispers of lost magic.

The warehouse creaked under the weight of history, the iron door groaning as we pushed it open. Inside, the space was vast, echoing our footsteps against the concrete floor. Broken windows allowed slivers of moonlight to pierce through, illuminating the corners that had long been left untouched. I closed my eyes, sensing the lingering energy within the walls, a tapestry of memories begging to be woven anew.

"Home sweet home," I quipped, stepping further inside and gesturing for Grant to follow. "A little rough around the edges, but it's got character."

He chuckled, shaking his head. "Character? This place looks like it's one step away from a horror movie."

"True, but it's perfect for what we need. No distractions, just us and our plans."

We set to work, transforming the warehouse into our makeshift command center. As we organized the space, I couldn't help but steal glances at Grant. There was something magnetic about his presence, a mix of intellect and determination that drew me in. He moved with purpose, every action deliberate, as if he were assembling the pieces of a puzzle only he could see.

"Okay, let's see what we're up against," he said, pulling out his laptop and setting it on a dusty table. I conjured a small flame, the flickering light illuminating our makeshift workspace. The contrast of the warm glow against the cool blue of his screen was oddly comforting, a reminder that both magic and technology had their places in this world.

As Grant began to type, his fingers flying over the keys with precision, I closed my eyes and focused on my own magic. I summoned a spark of energy, intertwining it with my will. A shimmering shield formed in the air between us, a delicate barrier that felt as tangible as the wood beneath my fingertips. "This will protect us from unwanted eyes," I explained, glancing at him. "Let's see what Selene is hiding."

He looked up, a mixture of awe and skepticism etched across his features. "You make it sound so easy."

"Easier than you think," I replied, confidence radiating from me as I tapped into my magic. "It's about intention, about belief. Once you understand that, it all becomes a part of the dance."

"Let's dance, then," he said, a smirk playing at the corner of his lips. "Just try not to step on my toes."

We dove into the work, the atmosphere charged with a combination of urgency and unspoken camaraderie. Hours slipped away, the world outside fading as we immersed ourselves in the shadows of Selene's operations. Each click of the mouse and whispered incantation drew us closer to the heart of the web she had spun, unveiling layers of deception that wrapped around the city like a sinister fog.

"Here," Grant said, his voice low but excited as he pointed to the screen. "She's been siphoning energy from the city's grid. It's all connected—her power is rooted in technology. If we can disrupt this flow..."

I felt a thrill course through me. "We could cut her off at the source. But how do we do it without drawing her attention?"

"Distraction," he said, a glimmer of mischief in his eyes. "Create a diversion while we pull the plug. Something flashy enough to make her look away."

I grinned, the possibilities swirling in my mind. "I know just the thing."

We began to plan, laughter and excitement mingling as we spun our ideas into reality. The night stretched on, the warehouse filled with our voices as we navigated the delicate balance between magic and technology. In that moment, under the watchful gaze of the moon, I felt something shift—a connection deepening between us, as intertwined as the strands of fate that had brought us together.

We were no longer just two individuals navigating our own worlds; we were allies, bound by a shared purpose. And as the clock ticked away, I couldn't shake the feeling that we were on the brink of something extraordinary, a dangerous game that could change everything.

As the night deepened, our plans coalesced like threads woven into a tapestry of defiance and determination. The glow of Grant's laptop cast flickering shadows across the warehouse walls, where remnants of the past whispered secrets to us. Our makeshift command center transformed with every moment spent there, the energy crackling like static in the air. Ideas sparked between us, igniting a fire that chased away the encroaching darkness, both literally and metaphorically.

"Okay, so we've got the basics down. Distraction on the night of the tech conference," Grant said, his fingers flying over the keyboard, creating a digital storm. "We can use a mix of your magic and my tech to make it look like the whole place is experiencing a major blackout."

"Perfect. It'll be chaos, and Selene won't know what hit her," I replied, my mind racing. "I can throw a few illusions into the mix to make it even more convincing. Shadows dancing, lights flickering. It'll be like a scene out of a movie."

"A horror movie, maybe," he quipped, shooting me a teasing glance. "Just don't summon any ghosts while you're at it. I'm not ready to face the undead today."

I laughed, the sound bubbling up from somewhere deep within me, a sound that felt foreign yet welcomed. "I promise to keep the ghosts at bay. Just the occasional ghoul, perhaps."

The banter flowed easily between us, a rhythm forming in the chaos of our planning. There was a thrill in our shared energy, a camaraderie that crackled like electricity. The earlier tension had shifted, replaced by a mutual understanding that we were in this together, navigating the storm side by side.

As we mapped out the logistics, I felt a flicker of anxiety. "What if we fail?" I asked, the weight of the question lingering in the air like an unwelcome guest. "What if Selene anticipates our move?"

Grant paused, his fingers stilled on the keyboard, and for a moment, the light in his eyes dimmed. "Then we adapt," he said, his tone serious but resolute. "We've got each other. Whatever happens, we'll figure it out."

The sincerity in his voice wrapped around me, grounding me in the moment. It was a reminder that, despite the chaos outside, we had forged a connection strong enough to withstand the tempest that loomed ahead.

Just as the atmosphere began to settle, the ground beneath us trembled. A low rumble, deep and menacing, vibrated through the concrete floor, sending a shiver up my spine. Grant's eyes widened as he exchanged a glance with me, both of us momentarily frozen in disbelief.

"What was that?" he asked, his voice barely above a whisper.

"I don't know," I replied, unease creeping into my chest. I reached out, my senses tingling as I tried to decipher the source of the disturbance. The air crackled with an unfamiliar energy, as if the very fabric of reality was shifting around us.

We moved toward the large bay door, the metal frame creaking ominously as I placed my hand on it. A pulse of energy coursed through me, a warning that something was terribly wrong. "We need to get out of here," I said, urgency threading my words.

"Wait—let me grab my laptop!" Grant called out, but I shook my head.

"Leave it. We can't risk being trapped." My instincts screamed at me to move, to escape whatever was brewing beyond the walls of our sanctuary.

As we sprinted toward the exit, the ground heaved again, this time more violently. Dust rained down from the ceiling, swirling in the air like tiny specters. I glanced back at the laptop, the flickering screen a beacon of our efforts, but there was no time to think.

With a final push, we flung the door open, stepping out into the night. The city outside was in disarray, the streets illuminated by an eerie glow, as if a fire had ignited somewhere nearby. The distant sounds of chaos filled the air—siren wails, shouts, and the unmistakable crack of energy sparking.

"What the hell is going on?" Grant asked, his voice a mix of awe and dread as he took in the scene before us.

I squinted into the distance, where shadows flickered like living entities, twisting and writhing. "I think Selene knows we're onto her," I said, fear threading through my voice. "She's not just playing defense anymore; she's striking first."

"Look!" Grant pointed down the street, where a figure emerged from the darkness, moving with a grace that was both beautiful and terrifying. Long hair flowed behind her like a dark waterfall, and her eyes glinted with an otherworldly light, radiating power.

"It's Selene," I whispered, a chill creeping down my spine. "And she's not alone."

Behind her, a group of shadowy figures appeared, cloaked in the same darkness that seemed to swirl around Selene. Their presence filled the night with a palpable tension, a reminder that we were standing at the edge of a precipice, teetering on the brink of disaster.

"Grant, we need to—" I started, but before I could finish my thought, Selene raised her arms, and a wave of energy surged toward us.

Instinct kicked in, and I shoved Grant aside, summoning my own magic in a desperate attempt to shield us from the oncoming blast. My heart raced as I conjured a barrier of light, the shimmering wall barely holding against the force that crashed into it.

"Hold on!" I yelled, pushing against the surge of energy, feeling the strain in my bones as I fought to maintain the barrier. "We need to retreat!"

"Back to the warehouse?" he shouted, but I could see the uncertainty in his eyes.

"No!" I replied, gritting my teeth. "We can't go back there. It's compromised. We have to find a way to outmaneuver her."

Just as I spoke, the barrier began to crack, tendrils of darkness creeping through like vines threatening to strangle us. Selene laughed, a sound both chilling and mocking, echoing through the chaos. "You think you can escape? This city belongs to me!"

With a surge of adrenaline, I summoned all the energy I could muster, focusing on the light within me. "We're not done yet!" I shouted, pushing against the darkness with everything I had.

In that moment of desperation, I glimpsed a path through the chaos, a narrow alley that seemed to beckon with the promise of escape. "Grant! Over there!" I pointed, feeling the connection between us strengthen as we locked eyes, an unspoken understanding passing between us.

"Let's go!" he yelled, and together we bolted toward the alley, dodging the tendrils of darkness that lashed out like angry serpents.

But just as we reached the entrance, I felt a sharp pain slice through my side—a sudden, blinding pain that forced me to my knees. I glanced down to see a glimmering shard embedded in my flesh, a piece of Selene's magic designed to disrupt mine.

"Zara!" Grant's voice rang out, panic surging through him as he turned back to help me.

"No!" I gasped, the world around me dimming as I struggled to keep my focus. "Keep moving! I'll... I'll be right behind you!"

The darkness around me swirled, pulling me deeper into its grasp. I could see Grant hesitating, torn between staying with me and running for safety. "Go!" I shouted, desperation lacing my words. "You have to warn the others!"

With a pained expression, he turned and sprinted down the alley, the sound of his footsteps fading into the night. I was left alone, the weight of the darkness pressing down on me, the sharp shard in my side pulsating with an insidious energy.

As I struggled to regain my footing, I could hear Selene's laughter echoing through the alley, a cruel reminder that this fight was far from over. The darkness coiled around me like a serpent, tightening its grip, and I knew in that moment that I was teetering on the edge of an abyss, facing a choice that could change everything.

With a deep breath, I gathered what remained of my strength, ready to face whatever was coming. But the shadows were closing in, and I felt the world slipping away, uncertainty threatening to swallow me whole. In that final heartbeat, I realized that the battle had only just begun, and I had to find a way to rise above the darkness before it consumed me entirely.

Chapter 20: The Heart of the City

The air thickens as we descend deeper, the flickering light of our flashlights casting ghostly shadows against the crumbling brick walls. Each step echoes like a whispered secret, hinting at the stories woven into the very fabric of this forsaken place. I can almost hear the city breathing beneath us, an ancient entity that has seen more than I ever could. It stirs a sense of reverence within me, coupled with a gnawing apprehension. Grant's footsteps shuffle behind me, his presence a solid reminder that I am not alone in this descent into the unknown, even if our intentions often clash.

"Isn't it romantic?" Grant quips, his voice a smooth drawl that belies the tension in his posture. He sweeps his arm toward the tunnel, as if it were a gallery showcasing lost artifacts of the city. "Just us, a couple of urban explorers, delving into the shadows of Brooklyn. You know, just a casual Tuesday."

"More like a fatal error," I mutter, clutching my flashlight tighter. "If we don't find that Nexus, we might end up as urban legends ourselves—two fools who ventured too deep into the city's heart and never returned."

The tunnel narrows, and I feel an involuntary shiver dance down my spine. I can almost picture it—the headlines: "Two Adventurers Disappear in NYC Subway: A Modern Tale of Hubris." I push the thought aside. We have to focus. The Nexus, a rumored source of unparalleled power, is somewhere down here. If we can harness its energy, we might just tilt the balance in our favor, shifting the tides of the escalating war between the corporate witches and the tech entities vying for control.

The flickering lights above us sputter as we pass beneath a rusty old sign, its paint peeling and barely legible. "West 4th Street Station," it reads, a forgotten relic of a time when this tunnel pulsed with life. Now, it languishes in silence, a witness to decades of neglect. A rush of adrenaline courses through me—here, in this space, the stories of every commuter who once rushed through could collide with our own.

"Can you feel that?" Grant's voice pulls me from my reverie. I turn to see a strange gleam in his eyes, as if he is attuned to something I can't quite grasp. "It's like the walls are whispering."

"More like they're groaning," I reply, attempting to inject humor into the moment, though my heart races with unease. We push further, and the atmosphere shifts palpably. The air grows thick with an almost electric charge, a sensation that crackles along my skin like static. Shadows seem to shift, and for a moment, I could swear I saw something dart just beyond the beam of my flashlight.

"Did you see that?" I ask, glancing back at Grant, who's now scanning the walls with a focused intensity. His demeanor shifts, the casual bravado replaced by a seriousness that sends a shiver down my spine.

"Just the remnants of the city's magic," he replies, though his voice lacks conviction. "It can feel... alive in places like this. Just breathe through it."

As if to test his words, I take a deep breath, filling my lungs with the stale air tinged with rust and something vaguely sweet, like damp earth. It's a strange contrast to the tension swirling in my chest. I glance down the tunnel, where it curves out of sight. "Let's keep moving."

We press on, the darkness closing in around us. Every now and then, I catch glimpses of faded murals on the walls—vivid colors that tell tales of a city once alive with culture, now reduced to remnants of itself. I run my fingers over one, the brushstrokes rough against my skin. The art depicts a time when this space was vibrant, a cacophony of laughter and voices, not the echo of solitude we now navigate.

Suddenly, we stumble into a larger chamber, a cavernous expanse that feels like the belly of the city. Graffiti blankets the walls, each tag a testament to the artists who came here to make their mark, to leave behind a piece of themselves in this forgotten sanctuary. In the center, an enormous pipe juts out from the ground, covered in vines and shimmering with an otherworldly glow. This has to be it—the Nexus.

I can feel the energy thrumming beneath my feet, a pulse that resonates with the very essence of the city. "This is it," I breathe, the words slipping from my lips before I can reconsider.

"Is it?" Grant's voice drops to a whisper, his eyes narrowing as he steps closer to the glowing pipe. "Are you sure?"

The moment hangs heavy between us, charged with possibility and dread. "It has to be," I insist, moving toward the light, though every instinct screams for caution.

As I approach, a sudden rush of wind swirls through the chamber, swirling dust and debris like a tempest. The glow intensifies, casting our shadows long against the walls. I can feel the energy beckoning me, urging me to reach out. My heart pounds in my chest, echoing the city's rhythm.

"Wait!" Grant's voice cuts through the chaos, but I am already lost in the moment, captivated by the power emanating from the Nexus. My hand reaches out, trembling slightly, yearning to touch the surface of the pipe, to unlock the secrets it promises.

And then, everything shifts.

The ground trembles beneath us, and with a deafening roar, the walls around us begin to shake. Cracks spiderweb across the chamber, the very essence of the city protesting against our intrusion. I pull my hand back as if stung, panic surging through me. "What did I do?"

"Nothing good," Grant mutters, his eyes wide as the ceiling begins to shed dust and debris like a dying star. "We need to get out of here!"

But before we can react, the Nexus unleashes a blinding light, enveloping us both. My vision blurs, and the world around us spins, reality warping as if we're being pulled into a different dimension. I grasp for something—anything—to ground myself, but all I can feel is the energy coursing through me, wild and untamed.

"Hang on!" Grant shouts, and the last thing I remember before the light swallows us whole is the sound of our hearts beating in unison—a frantic rhythm that echoes in the depths of Brooklyn's forgotten soul.

The light envelops us, a searing brightness that pulls at the very threads of my existence. For a heartbeat, there's nothing but an overwhelming silence, the kind that settles deep in your bones, as if the world has momentarily paused to catch its breath. Then, with a dizzying whirl, the light shatters like glass, scattering into a kaleidoscope of color and sound.

I find myself sprawled on a rough, uneven surface, the air sharp and cool against my skin. It takes a moment for my vision to clear, and when it does, I'm greeted by an astonishing sight. We're no longer in the subterranean tunnels of Brooklyn. Instead, I'm surrounded by a vast landscape that pulses with life, the very essence of magic spilling from the ground like fresh rainwater soaking into parched earth.

"Did we die?" Grant groans, pushing himself up next to me. His expression is a mix of bewilderment and awe, his usually composed demeanor shaken. "I think I preferred the subway."

I push myself into a sitting position, taking in the vibrant hues that surround us—emerald greens, sapphire blues, and rich golds weave together in a tapestry of unimaginable beauty. Trees stretch toward a cerulean sky, their trunks swirling with patterns that pulse like the heartbeat of the city we left behind.

"Welcome to... wherever this is," I say, my voice tinged with disbelief. "If this is heaven, I'm not sure I want to meet my maker."

Grant chuckles, brushing dirt off his jacket. "If this is heaven, I'm expecting a margarita bar and at least one pool boy."

I can't help but laugh, the sound bright against the backdrop of this surreal landscape. "If I find a pool boy, I'm definitely claiming him for myself."

As we stand, the ground beneath us feels alive, vibrating softly as if acknowledging our presence. I step forward, drawn to a glimmering stream that winds its way through the landscape like a liquid sapphire. It sparkles under the sunlight, beckoning me closer.

"Careful," Grant warns, his voice more serious now. "This could be an illusion or worse—a trap."

"Or a really nice vacation," I counter, my curiosity piqued. "But you're right; we should be cautious. Still, it's breathtaking. I've never seen anything like it."

The stream winds around rocks that shimmer with a light of their own, casting prismatic reflections that dance on the surrounding flora. I take a tentative step toward it, the urge to touch the cool water nearly overpowering.

"Don't lose your head, okay?" Grant cautions, following closely behind. "This place might be a paradise, but we're still on a quest, remember?"

"Right, the Nexus." The weight of our mission rushes back, grounding me. "We need to find a way to access its power before it's too late."

As if answering my unspoken thoughts, the air shifts, carrying a whisper that sounds almost like laughter. I glance at Grant, who raises an eyebrow, mirroring my apprehension. "Did you hear that?"

"Yeah, and I'm not sure whether to be terrified or intrigued," he replies, scanning our surroundings.

Suddenly, a figure emerges from behind the trees, graceful and ethereal. She glides toward us, her long hair flowing like liquid silver, and her skin shimmering in the soft light. Dressed in flowing garments that ripple with colors reflecting the vibrant environment, she resembles something straight from a fairytale.

"Welcome, travelers," she says, her voice melodic, wrapping around us like a warm embrace. "You seek the Nexus, do you not?"

"How did you know that?" I ask, my heart racing with both excitement and trepidation.

"The land knows its seekers," she replies, a knowing smile gracing her lips. "But beware, for the power you seek is not without its dangers. It demands sacrifice and courage, the likes of which you may not possess."

"Courage? Sacrifice?" Grant scoffs lightly. "We've dealt with worse."

"Have you?" She raises an eyebrow, and in that moment, the atmosphere thickens with a tension that sends a shiver down my spine. "To command the Nexus is to understand the balance of your desires and the cost of your ambitions. What are you willing to risk?"

I exchange a glance with Grant, his expression serious now. The weight of her words hangs between us, heavy with implications. "We're prepared to do what it takes," I say, trying to project confidence even as my heart races.

The woman tilts her head, studying us. "Then follow me, but tread carefully. The path to the Nexus is fraught with trials that will test your resolve."

As she turns, leading us deeper into this vibrant realm, I feel a mix of exhilaration and fear. Every step seems to thrum with energy, as if the ground itself is alive, urging us to continue. The trees bend slightly as we pass, their leaves whispering secrets I long to understand.

"What do you think she meant by trials?" Grant murmurs, falling into step beside me.

"Something tells me it won't involve a friendly game of charades," I reply dryly, my mind racing with possibilities. "I can't shake the feeling that this is just the beginning. We're standing on the edge of something vast and unpredictable."

"Great, just what I needed. More uncertainty," he quips, though I can see the excitement flickering in his eyes, echoing my own. "Let's just hope we're not competing with some mystical creatures for a magic crystal or something. I'm not sure I'd fare well against a dragon."

"I'd take a dragon over corporate witches any day," I counter, laughter bubbling up inside me. "At least dragons have a clear motivation—like hoarding treasure or eating knights. Corporate witches are just... well, corporate."

Grant rolls his eyes, but the corner of his mouth twitches in a suppressed grin. "True enough. Just keep your wits about you, and maybe we'll leave this place with both our lives and whatever power the Nexus holds."

As we venture further into the enchanting wilderness, the landscape begins to shift again. The trees thicken, their trunks twisting into shapes that feel both inviting and menacing. An inexplicable tension hangs in the air, a promise of challenges ahead that makes my pulse quicken.

I look at Grant, and despite the uncertainty, a spark of determination ignites within me. We're in this together, and whatever awaits us in the depths of this magical realm, we will face it side by side. The city above may have held its breath, but down here, in the heart of this vibrant world, I feel alive, ready to embrace whatever twists lie ahead.

The trees close in around us, their twisting limbs reaching like fingers through the mist that hangs lazily in the air. Sunlight filters through the leaves, creating a mosaic of dappled light that dances across the forest floor, illuminating patches of vibrant moss and delicate flowers that seem to pulse with energy. There's a beauty here that feels almost overwhelming, and yet, it's tinged with an undercurrent of danger that keeps me on edge.

"Are you sure we should be following her?" I murmur to Grant, glancing back at the ethereal woman ahead of us. Her figure flows through the trees like a whisper, seemingly at one with the vibrant surroundings. "I mean, what if she's luring us into a trap?"

Grant shrugs, his eyes narrowed as he observes our guide. "It's either that or we turn back and risk facing whatever waits for us in the tunnels. Besides, what do you have against a little adventure? You've always been one for a good thrill."

"Adventure? Yes. Death trap? Not so much," I retort, though a flicker of excitement flares within me. There's something undeniably magnetic about this place, about the possibilities it holds. I can feel the weight of the Nexus's power thrumming beneath the surface, almost like a siren's call.

As we weave through the lush undergrowth, the woman leads us to a clearing where the ground rises gently, revealing a shimmering pool at its center. The water glows with an iridescent light, swirling colors that shift and flow like liquid gemstones.

"This is the heart of the realm," she says, her voice echoing softly in the stillness. "To access the Nexus, you must immerse yourselves in the waters. But heed this warning: what you seek will come with a price."

Grant glances at me, his brow furrowing. "You mean to tell me we're supposed to jump in there? Just like that?"

"Looks like it's either a swim or bust," I reply, peering into the pool's depths. "But what kind of price? Because 'price' can mean a lot of things."

She smiles, a cryptic expression that sends another shiver down my spine. "The waters reveal truths, desires, and fears. You will face what lies within you. Only then can you grasp the power of the Nexus."

"Great," Grant mutters, his voice laced with sarcasm. "Nothing like a little soul-searching with your swim. Just what I needed on my to-do list."

"We'll have to face whatever it is together," I reassure him, though my heart thuds with uncertainty. "That's how we've made it this far, right?"

He nods, though the tension in his jaw tells me he's far from convinced.

Without further ado, I step closer to the edge of the pool, the air thick with anticipation. The water ripples, sending shimmering patterns cascading across its surface. I take a deep breath and plunge my hand into the cool depths. The sensation is electric, a jolt that shoots up my arm and sparks a thousand tiny fireworks of awareness.

"Do it, Grant!" I call back, urging him to follow my lead. "It's now or never!"

With a resigned sigh, he steps up beside me, his hesitation palpable. "You're really going to make me do this, aren't you?"

"Absolutely," I grin. "No backing out now!"

As if in response to our determination, the water begins to bubble and swirl, a vortex forming in the center. I glance at Grant, who looks more determined than ever, and together we plunge into the pool. The moment we break the surface, everything changes.

Colors explode around us, vibrant and overwhelming, each hue laced with emotions I can barely comprehend. The world warps, and I'm yanked into a whirlwind of memories and visions. I find myself standing in a bustling Brooklyn street, the air thick with laughter and music. I see myself as a child, holding hands with my mother, her smile radiant as she twirls me around.

"Mom!" I gasp, reaching for the shimmering apparition. But as my fingers stretch toward her, she fades like mist.

I'm thrust into another memory, this time darker. Shadows loom over me, whispers clawing at the edges of my mind. "You're not good enough," they taunt, each voice a reminder of the insecurities I've battled. "You'll never succeed."

"No!" I scream, fighting against the tide of doubt. "I refuse to accept that!"

The shadows swirl around me, threatening to drown me in despair. But just as I feel the weight of their darkness closing in, a bright light breaks through, illuminating my path. I see Grant, his face determined, as he fights his own battles within the depths of the pool.

"Don't let them win!" he shouts, his voice cutting through the chaos. "You're stronger than this!"

His words ignite a fire within me, a fierce determination that pushes back against the shadows. I stand tall against the weight of my fears, and with a fierce scream, I surge forward, breaking free from their grasp. The light engulfs me, lifting me higher, guiding me through the storm of my past.

As the chaos subsides, I find myself back in the clearing, gasping for air, drenched and trembling. Grant emerges beside me, equally shaken but alive with a newfound energy.

"Did we just have a mystical therapy session?" he breathes, looking incredulous.

"Seems like it," I laugh breathlessly, but there's a note of seriousness that underpins my words. "I think we faced our fears. But I don't know if that's enough to claim the Nexus's power."

The woman stands before us again, her expression inscrutable. "You have taken the first step, but the true test awaits. The Nexus requires a choice—a sacrifice that reflects your heart's desire."

"What kind of choice?" I ask, anxiety creeping into my chest.

She gestures toward the pool, where the water glows even brighter, swirling with vibrant energy. "Only you can decide what you are willing to give up to gain the power you seek. What would you sacrifice to change your fate?"

Grant and I exchange uncertain glances. What could we possibly give up? What mattered most to us?

Before I can voice my thoughts, the ground beneath us trembles violently. The once tranquil pool now roils with dark energy, twisting into a menacing whirlpool.

"What's happening?" I shout over the growing noise, panic rising within me.

"The balance is shifting!" the woman cries, her voice rising above the chaos. "You must act quickly!"

As the pull of the whirlpool grows stronger, I feel a sharp tug at my core—a reminder of everything I hold dear, of every choice I've made. The decision looms before me like a precipice, and I'm teetering on the edge, unsure of how far I'm willing to fall.

In that moment, an image flashes before my eyes: my mother's laughter, Grant's unwavering support, the life I've built despite the darkness. All of it is intertwined, a web of love and sacrifice.

"Together," I shout, my voice resolute. "We make this choice together!"

But just as the words leave my mouth, a thunderous crack echoes through the clearing, and the ground shatters beneath us. The whirlpool swallows everything in its wake, dragging us down into the abyss, leaving nothing but the echoes of our desperate cries as the darkness closes in around us.

Chapter 21: Descent into Darkness

The subway tunnel envelops us, transforming the familiar clatter of the city above into a muffled hum, a mere whisper against the vibrant pulse of the underground. The air is thick with an almost palpable energy, a sensation that tingles at the nape of my neck and sends shivers down my spine. As I step carefully on the cracked concrete, the coolness seeps through my sneakers, anchoring me to this strange new reality. Above us, the world may be racing on, but here, time feels suspended, as if we've crossed an invisible threshold into a realm where the ordinary blurs with the extraordinary.

The walls, once sterile gray, are now a canvas of chaotic beauty, splattered with graffiti that seems to writhe and shift in the shadows. Intricate designs swirl together, forming symbols that whisper secrets of ancient magic. They glow with an ethereal light, each flicker casting an otherworldly luminescence that dances across our faces. I catch a glimpse of my reflection in one particularly vibrant piece, my wide eyes shimmering with curiosity and trepidation. It's a reminder that I am not just an observer in this realm; I am a part of it, a tiny thread in the grand tapestry of a story far greater than my own.

"Do you feel that?" I ask, my voice barely above a whisper. Grant, a few paces ahead, pauses and turns to me, a faint smirk tugging at the corner of his lips. He's always had that way of lighting up the dark corners of my mind, a beacon of reassurance amidst the chaos.

"Feel what? The tingling sensation of impending doom?" His teasing tone is like a balm, even if it is laced with a hint of seriousness. "Yeah, I feel it too. This place isn't just a shortcut; it's a warning."

With a quick glance around, I take a deep breath, the air thick and sweet with the scent of damp earth and something else—something spicy and electric that sets my heart racing. It's intoxicating, a blend of danger and allure that pulls me deeper into the unknown. I take a step forward, drawn in by an invisible thread that feels almost like fate. With every step, the walls seem to close in, the air thickening with an ancient energy that vibrates through my bones. I can't help but wonder what lies ahead, what secrets this underground labyrinth holds.

As we venture deeper, the remnants of spells long forgotten float through the air like whispers. I can almost hear the echoes of incantations, the sighs of sorcery woven into the very fabric of the tunnel. It's mesmerizing, like watching the tail end of a shooting star, brilliant yet fleeting. I can't help but reach out, my fingers brushing against the cool stone, feeling the magic pulse beneath my touch. It's as if the tunnel is alive, breathing in rhythm with our own heartbeats.

But then, the atmosphere shifts, and a palpable tension clings to the air. A sudden rush of wind sweeps through the tunnel, carrying with it the scent of ozone, and I freeze. It's that instinctive, primal fear—the kind that tells you something is very wrong. My heart thunders in my chest as I exchange a quick glance with Grant. His expression darkens, and I can see the wheels turning in his mind, weighing our next move.

"Stay close," he murmurs, his voice low and steady, a contrast to the chaos swirling around us. I can't tell if it's meant to reassure me or to remind himself that we're in this together. Either way, it works.

Just then, without warning, the ground beneath us shudders, a deep rumble echoing through the tunnel like the growl of a slumbering beast. I stumble, a surge of panic gripping my insides as the earth cracks open, revealing a gaping chasm that seems to extend into the abyss itself. My heart races, and in that split second, the world blurs, colors swirling in a dizzying dance. Grant's hand shoots out, catching my arm just in time, anchoring me back from the brink.

"Easy there," he says, his voice a firm tether amidst the chaos. "This isn't the time for a dive into the underworld."

I laugh nervously, the sound echoing strangely against the stone walls. "Right, I prefer to keep my limbs intact." My heart is still racing, but his presence calms me, like a lighthouse guiding me through a storm.

We move cautiously, navigating around the chasm, the ground beneath our feet shifting and trembling as if protesting our intrusion. The deeper we venture, the more tangible the magic becomes, crackling in the air around us like static electricity. I can feel it tugging at my senses, enticing and overwhelming all at once. It's intoxicating, and yet I can't shake the feeling of danger lurking just beyond the veil.

As we press on, the atmosphere thickens, swirling with anticipation and something darker. A distant sound reaches us—a low, resonant growl that sends a shiver down my spine. I glance at Grant, whose eyes are narrowed, scanning the shadows. "We need to keep moving," he says, urgency creeping into his tone.

Just as I turn to follow him, a figure emerges from the darkness, cloaked in shadow, their presence both commanding and foreboding. My breath catches in my throat as I take in the stranger's silhouette, an air of power radiating from them. "You shouldn't be here," they say, their voice smooth like silk but with an edge that cuts through the air.

My heart races as I step closer to Grant, instinctively seeking his strength. The tension hangs thick, a charged silence that begs for a spark. It's a moment pregnant with possibility, where fear intertwines with excitement, and I can't help but feel that everything I've ever known is about to change.

The figure before us stands resolute, a shadow cloaked in mystery, the dim light barely illuminating their features. I can make out high cheekbones and a sharp jaw, the kind of face that could have been carved from marble, timeless and imposing. Yet it's the eyes—piercing and otherworldly—that hold my gaze. They flicker with an unsettling intelligence, as if this stranger knows more about me than I do about myself.

"Who are you?" Grant's voice slices through the tense atmosphere, steady yet laced with a subtle edge. There's a hint of protectiveness, an unspoken promise that he won't let anything happen to me.

The stranger tilts their head slightly, a sardonic smile curling their lips. "You ask who I am, but perhaps you should be more concerned with where you are." They take a step forward, the shadows swirling around them like a cloak, each movement fluid and graceful, reminiscent of a dancer caught in a dream. "This place is a crossroads, a sanctuary for those who tread the line between the mundane and the arcane."

"Sounds delightful," I mutter under my breath, unable to mask the sarcasm. I steal a glance at Grant, who shoots me a warning look, his expression taut.

Ignoring my comment, the stranger continues, "You've wandered into territory that is not yours, and the magic here does not take kindly to trespassers."

I feel the weight of their words settle over me, heavy and suffocating. It's one thing to feel the thrill of adventure, but quite another to recognize the perilous stakes involved. The air hums with a tension that feels almost sentient, as if the very walls are holding their breath, waiting for something to snap.

"We didn't mean to intrude," Grant replies, his tone softer now, a hint of diplomacy lacing his words. "We're looking for answers."

The stranger arches an eyebrow, curiosity sparking in those enigmatic eyes. "Answers are easy to find, but they often come at a price." They pause, letting the words linger in the air like a tantalizing promise. "What you seek could lead to revelations that may shatter your understanding of reality."

"Great. Just what I wanted to hear." I can't help the eye roll, though my heart races at the thought of unearthing truths I might not be ready for. "But honestly, it sounds like a standard Tuesday for us."

The stranger chuckles softly, the sound rich and layered, as if they're finding humor in a private joke. "You certainly have a flair for understatement." Their gaze flicks to me, and I can't shake the feeling that they're peeling back my layers, uncovering the vulnerabilities I keep hidden.

"What's your name?" I ask, feeling a surge of boldness.

"Names hold power, dear one. I am known by many, but in this moment, you may call me Vale."

"Vale," I repeat, testing the name on my tongue. "So you're like a... guardian of the tunnel? The keeper of secrets?"

"More like a reluctant guide," Vale replies with a wry smile, the corners of their lips quirking upward. "And you, little flame, have a fire that is both intriguing and reckless."

"Thank you, I think?" I manage, flustered by the intensity of their gaze. "What can I say? I like to keep things spicy."

A flicker of amusement dances in Vale's eyes, but the moment is brief, overshadowed by the pressing danger lurking in the air. "Your humor will serve you well, but you must tread carefully. There are forces here that do not appreciate jesters."

"Jesters? Oh, great. I thought I signed up for an epic adventure, not a comedy club."

Grant shifts beside me, a low growl of frustration escaping his lips. "Enough with the banter. We're here to find answers. Just tell us what we need to do."

Vale's expression turns serious, and I sense the weight of their knowledge bearing down on us. "Very well. There is a spell hidden within these tunnels, one that binds the magic to this place. It has been fractured, weakened over time. If you wish to uncover the truth you seek, you must first mend what has been broken."

I look at Grant, who nods, determination etched on his face. "And how do we do that?"

Vale steps aside, gesturing toward a narrow passageway shrouded in darkness. "Follow the path where the runes glow brightest. But beware—the magic that resides here is capricious. It may lead you to your desires, or it may expose your worst fears."

"Just another day in the life," I quip, although my stomach twists at the thought of facing my own shadows.

"Stay close," Grant urges, his voice low as we step into the passage. The atmosphere shifts again, the air growing thick with anticipation, almost charged with electricity.

As we walk, the glow from the walls intensifies, illuminating symbols that pulse like a heartbeat. I can't help but reach out, fingers grazing the surface of the stone, feeling the energy surge beneath my touch. It's a sensation both exhilarating and unnerving, as if the magic is alive and aware of our presence.

"I can't believe we're doing this," I whisper, half in awe, half in disbelief. "One minute we're having coffee, and the next, we're in a magical labyrinth."

"Welcome to my life," Grant replies, a smirk dancing across his lips. "Who knew our coffee dates would lead to shadowy tunnels and ancient spells?"

I laugh, the sound echoing through the passage, but it's a fleeting moment of levity. As we venture deeper, the shadows seem to grow heavier, the whispers of the past becoming more insistent. I can feel the magic thrumming in the air, a symphony of possibilities that both entices and terrifies me.

Just then, a low growl reverberates through the tunnel, echoing off the walls and vibrating in my bones. My heart races as I turn to Grant, who has gone rigid, tension radiating from him like a warning beacon.

"Did you hear that?" I ask, my voice trembling slightly.

"Yeah, and I don't think it's just the echoes playing tricks."

Before I can respond, a figure darts from the shadows—a blur of motion that leaves a chill in its wake. I barely have time to react before it lunges toward us, and instinct kicks in. I grab Grant's arm, pulling him back just as the creature—a twisted, snarling entity of shadow and fury—swings its claws through the space where we stood a moment before.

"Run!" Grant shouts, his voice cutting through the chaos, and we take off down the passage, the creature's growls reverberating behind us. Adrenaline surges through my veins as we race into the unknown, the weight of magic and danger pressing against us with every step.

We sprint through the twisting passage, heartbeats synchronizing with the pounding footsteps of the shadowy creature behind us. The air crackles with a frantic energy, wrapping around us like a storm, each breath an effort against the rising panic. I can feel the darkness closing in, its breath heavy on my neck as we weave through the maze of flickering lights and pulsating runes.

"Why is it always the dark, creepy tunnels?" I huff, my legs burning from the exertion. "Couldn't we have stumbled upon a sunny beach instead?"

"Sunny beaches don't usually come with magic," Grant fires back, glancing over his shoulder. His eyes are wide, filled with determination but also that familiar spark of mischief. "Besides, you know how I feel about sunburn."

"Right, who needs SPF when you have shadowy entities trying to eat your face?" I laugh breathlessly, even as the fear coils tighter around my chest. My laughter is a thin veneer over the terror, a way to keep the darkness at bay—at least until we can escape.

The creature's growl reverberates through the tunnel, its hunger palpable as it closes the distance between us. I can feel it in the marrow of my bones, a cold wave of dread that threatens to consume me whole. I push myself to run faster, the adrenaline kicking in, but the corridor feels like it stretches on forever.

"Turn here!" Grant shouts, his voice cutting through the chaos as he veers sharply to the right. I follow without question, instinct guiding me as we plunge into a narrower passageway, the walls closing in like a protective cocoon.

The atmosphere shifts, the air growing thick with a heady mix of magic and fear. The graffiti on the walls seems to shift and writhe in the dim light, the symbols morphing into grotesque faces that leer at us, their mouths twisting into silent screams.

"What is this place?" I gasp, trying to make sense of the madness around us.

"The crossroads Vale mentioned," Grant replies, urgency lacing his tone. "It's a hub of magic, but it's also a battleground."

"A battleground?" I echo, my stomach dropping at the implications. "Great, just what we needed—a magical war zone."

Just then, we stumble into a larger chamber, the space opening up around us like the maw of a great beast. The ceiling soars high above, lost in shadow, while the walls are adorned with intricate carvings that seem to pulse with life. In the center of the room stands a massive stone pedestal, its surface covered in an array of symbols that glow like embers in the dark.

"Look!" I point, my pulse quickening at the sight. "That has to be what Vale meant!"

Grant nods, his expression a mix of hope and anxiety. "We need to get to it. If we can restore the spell, maybe we can push back whatever is chasing us."

As we rush toward the pedestal, the growling intensifies, the creature lurking just beyond the entrance, its presence a suffocating weight in the air. I can almost feel its predatory gaze boring into my back.

"What do we do?" I ask, panic rising like bile in my throat. "How do we restore a spell?"

Grant skims the surface of the pedestal, tracing the glowing runes with his fingers, a frown creasing his brow. "It looks like there are slots for something...maybe these symbols represent ingredients? Or tokens?"

"I knew I should have brought a snack," I quip, trying to keep the fear at bay. "What are we supposed to offer? A piece of my soul?"

"Tempting, but let's keep that as a last resort." He shoots me a brief smile before refocusing on the pedestal. "We need to find out what these symbols mean."

Suddenly, the air shimmers, a surge of energy erupting from the pedestal. The room shakes, and the walls seem to lean in, as if the very stones are straining to hear our conversation. "We don't have time for a history lesson!" I shout, the growl of the creature echoing ominously behind us.

"Right," he agrees, his voice firm. "Let's see if we can activate this thing."

Grant places both hands on the pedestal, and the symbols flare to life, glowing brighter, casting an eerie light around us. The runes flicker in response to his touch, and I feel the energy shifting in the room, a current of magic swirling through the air.

"Something's happening," I murmur, eyes wide as the energy builds, crackling with potential. The creature's growl grows louder, reverberating through the chamber, a terrifying reminder of our impending doom.

The symbols around the pedestal glow like a constellation of stars, each one pulsing in time with my racing heart. I lean closer, trying to decipher their meanings, when a voice suddenly fills the air, rich and deep, resonating like a forgotten melody.

"To mend what has been broken, you must offer what is lost," it intones, echoing through the chamber. "Only then shall the balance be restored."

"What does that mean?" I ask, bewildered, my heart pounding in my chest.

"I don't know!" Grant replies, frustration spilling into his voice. "But we have to figure it out fast."

Just then, the shadows ripple, and the creature bursts into the chamber, a mass of claws and teeth, eyes glinting with predatory hunger. The moment freezes, the air thick with anticipation, as it lunges toward us, its growl morphing into a primal roar that shakes the very foundation of the tunnel.

"Now would be a good time for answers!" I scream, instinctively grabbing Grant's arm as we back away from the pedestal. The magic around us flares wildly, lighting the shadows with blinding brilliance.

"Look!" Grant shouts, pointing to a glowing symbol at the pedestal's edge. "It's missing something!"

I squint, recognizing the shape—an ancient rune that resembles a heart. "Do you think we need—"

"Something we've lost!" He finishes my thought, his eyes wide. "But what?"

The creature lunges again, and instinctively, I push Grant aside, taking a step forward, ready to confront the darkness that threatens to consume us both. "I'll figure it out!" I declare, my voice steadying in the face of fear.

Just as the creature reaches for me, I feel a rush of warmth, a connection sparking between us—a moment of clarity in the chaos. "What have I lost?" I whisper, and the answer floods over me, clear as day.

In that instant, I realize that it's not just a token; it's a piece of myself. A memory, a part of my soul that I must reclaim to restore balance.

"Grant, I know what to do!" I shout, my voice rising above the cacophony as I focus on the energy swirling around me.

But before I can act, the creature lunges once more, and the darkness closes in, threatening to pull me into its suffocating embrace. The world spins, and the pedestal begins to hum, a low resonance vibrating through the ground.

"Don't you dare!" Grant yells, desperation coloring his tone.

In that moment, I'm faced with a choice—to confront my fear and sacrifice what I thought was lost, or succumb to the darkness that waits just beyond the reach of the light. The choice hangs heavy in the air, a question that demands an answer.

As the creature's claws graze my skin, I reach out, ready to give what is necessary, feeling the world slip away into the abyss. The light flares, illuminating the chamber in a blinding white, and with it, the line between magic and reality blurs, teetering on the edge of salvation or destruction.

Chapter 22: The Source of Power

The air buzzes with an electric charge, crackling like the heart of a storm. As I step into the cavernous space, the remnants of the tunnel behind me fade away, swallowed by shadows that cling to the walls like secrets. I'm enveloped by a swirling blend of old magic and lost technology, a scene that seems plucked from a fever dream. The nexus ahead, a pulsating mass of vibrant hues, radiates an aura that feels alive—almost sentient. It thrums in my chest, syncopating with the rhythm of my heart, and I can't shake the feeling that it knows me, just as I long to know it.

The corporate witches around me, clad in their pristine black robes, chant their incantations with a practiced precision. Their voices harmonize like a well-rehearsed choir, but beneath the surface, I sense their unease. The way their brows furrow and their lips twitch tells a different story—this is no ordinary disruption. Their rituals attempt to smooth over the chaos, to tame what seems both a creature and a curse. But as I step closer, the energy swells, a rogue wave crashing against the shore of their spells, defying their every effort.

I can see it clearly now—thick cables snake through the debris, intertwining with shards of crystal that glimmer in the low light, remnants of some long-forgotten enchantment. This isn't merely a malfunctioning power source; it's a volatile marriage of old magic and the remnants of an industrial age, a juxtaposition of nature and machinery that feels like the heartbeat of the city itself. With every pulse, I can feel my own magic responding, almost as if it were a long-lost twin, yearning for recognition.

"Back away from it!" one of the witches shouts, her voice laced with authority and a hint of panic, as if I'm not already aware of the danger. I catch a glimpse of her narrowed eyes, filled with the fear of losing control over the very thing we've come to confront. "It's too powerful!"

I hesitate for a heartbeat, but curiosity tugs at my essence. The voices of the past echo softly in my mind, urging me to break free of the binds that have been set by those who came before. What if I could do what they couldn't? What if, instead of subduing this energy, I could learn from it?

"I can handle it," I assert, my voice steady despite the tumultuous magic swirling around me. The witches turn their gazes to me, a blend of disbelief and desperation etched across their faces. I step forward, feeling the heat radiating from the nexus, a fiery pulse that resonates with my own energy.

"Don't be reckless!" another witch warns, her fingers trembling as she gestures wildly. "You have no idea what you're dealing with!"

"Exactly," I reply, a smirk playing on my lips as I cross the final distance. "And that's the whole point."

The moment my fingers brush the surface of the nexus, an electric shock races up my arm, and I gasp, caught between exhilaration and trepidation. The energy envelops me, pulling me in, and I'm flooded with visions that cascade like a waterfall, vibrant and chaotic. Brooklyn unfurls before me—a tapestry woven with stories of resilience, of witches gathering under the moonlight, of struggles and triumphs, all stitched together by the magic that weaves through the city streets.

The voices grow louder, whispering incantations that twist around my consciousness, coaxing me to listen, to learn. I see faces—older witches with silver hair and weathered hands, their eyes shimmering with wisdom. They beckon me, offering glimpses of their lives, their histories intertwining with my own. I can feel their hope, their fears, their yearning for a world where magic and technology could coexist in harmony.

But just as quickly, the visions twist, dark shadows creeping into the light, the echoes of despair and failure mingling with the triumphs. I see the old magic being snuffed out, the rise of cold machinery in its place, the tension building until it shatters into chaos. It's a warning, a reminder of what happens when ambition overreaches, when power is misused.

"Stop! You're going too deep!" one of the witches shouts, pulling at my arm, but I shake her off, determined to embrace the chaos. This isn't just a source of power; it's a legacy, and I'm not ready to let it slip away.

With a fierce resolve, I reach deeper, letting my own magic intertwine with the energy around me. It's a dance—a chaotic waltz of light and shadow, a test of will and connection. I draw on the strength of the witches who came before, channeling their wisdom while grounding myself in my own identity. I am not just a bystander in this tale; I am a player, and I refuse to let this nexus be tamed by fear.

Suddenly, a surge of energy erupts, a shockwave that sends me staggering back, but I stand my ground. I feel the chaos within me, an explosive potential waiting to be unleashed, and as I gather my breath, I glance at the witches, their expressions a mix of awe and disbelief.

"Join me," I call out, my voice cutting through the tumult like a beacon in the night. "This is ours to shape, not to fear. Together, we can find the balance."

Their hesitation is palpable, but the flicker of hope ignites in their eyes. Slowly, they inch closer, drawn by the promise of unity, the allure of creating something greater than any of us could achieve alone. And in that moment, with the nexus pulsating like a heartbeat around us, I realize that power isn't just something to wield; it's a tapestry of connections, a web of shared histories and dreams waiting to be woven into reality.

The air crackles with anticipation, the very fabric of reality warping around us as I stand before the nexus, a chaotic entity that feels like a pulsating heart at the center of the universe. Tendrils of energy snake outwards, weaving through the remnants of machinery and the gathered witches, their faces illuminated by the glow of the ever-shifting light. I can sense their skepticism simmering beneath their well-rehearsed chants. It's as if I've burst into a carefully orchestrated performance, and I'm either the unexpected star or the hapless interloper who might ruin the show.

"Do you even know what you're doing?" one of them snaps, her tone sharp enough to cut through the tension. Her dark hair whips around her face, framing eyes that shimmer like glass. "This isn't just a light show; it's dangerous!"

I chuckle softly, relishing the thrill of the moment. "I was born in Brooklyn, sweetheart. Dangerous is practically my middle name." With a flick of my wrist, I conjure a flicker of energy, a delicate stream of lavender light that dances at my fingertips. The air hums with my magic, and I feel the disbelief radiating from them, as palpable as the electricity in the air.

"Stop playing around!" she insists, but there's a flicker of curiosity in her eyes. "You have no idea what kind of forces you're meddling with."

"Or perhaps I do," I retort, stepping closer to the nexus. "This is a conversation we should be having, not a battle." The moment my words spill into the atmosphere, the nexus responds, the colors shifting and swirling with a vibrancy that takes my breath away. It's as if the very essence of Brooklyn is whispering to me, urging me to dive deeper into the chaos.

As I delve into the energy, I can feel it responding to me, a living thing that recognizes my intent. I draw on the memories swirling within—visions of long-gone witches, their laughter and tears intertwined with the very essence of this city. It's an intoxicating rush, and suddenly, the cacophony of their chants fades into the background, leaving only the sound of my heartbeat reverberating through the air.

"You think you can just waltz in here and charm the chaos?" another witch interjects, her arms crossed, skepticism etched across her face. "You're not a corporate witch. You don't know our ways."

"And that's precisely the point," I shoot back, a grin spreading across my face. "Sometimes, it takes someone from the outside to see the bigger picture. You're so focused on control that you're missing the beauty in this mess."

At that moment, a jolt of energy arcs between us, a sudden flash that crackles with potential. I realize I've struck a nerve, igniting something within her that longs to break free from the rigidity of their traditions. She hesitates, her defenses wavering, and I see a flicker of recognition pass through her eyes—a shared understanding of the desire for more than just stability.

"Fine, show us what you've got," she challenges, but there's an underlying excitement in her voice, as if she's eager to see what unfolds when I step into the storm rather than shying away from it.

With renewed vigor, I plunge deeper into the nexus, intertwining my magic with its chaotic pulse. It's like diving into a turbulent ocean, where every wave is a memory, every current a story begging to be told. The brilliance of the colors grows richer, swirling into vibrant shades of turquoise and emerald, and I let myself be swept along, riding the waves of energy as I find my footing.

Suddenly, the air shifts. A gust of wind rushes through the cavern, carrying with it echoes of laughter, of camaraderie long forgotten. I glimpse fleeting images—young witches learning their craft under the watchful gaze of their mentors, their hands weaving spells in the air, their faces lit with joy. But then the images shift again, darkening into moments of conflict: chaos, confusion, and betrayal. I see a rift growing, a schism between tradition and innovation, and I feel the weight of their choices pressing down on me.

"Stop it!" I shout, breaking the spell of silence that hangs heavy in the air. "This isn't just a historical reenactment; it's a lesson! You're afraid of this power because you're afraid of what it could mean."

The witches exchange uneasy glances, the truth of my words hanging like a storm cloud. "You don't understand!" one of them insists, frustration evident in her voice. "If we lose control here, we could lose everything. This isn't just a matter of magic; it's about the safety of the entire city."

"And what is safety without freedom?" I counter, a fire igniting within me. "You can't cage this energy, not without suffocating what makes us who we are. The city thrives on chaos—it's alive, and it will fight back if we ignore it!"

I draw a deep breath, grounding myself in the tumultuous energy swirling around me. "We can work together. We can forge a new path that honors the past while embracing the future." I extend my hands toward the witches, inviting them into the dance rather than demanding their surrender.

One by one, they begin to step forward, uncertainty etched across their features. As they close the distance, I can feel the energy shift again, like the tremor before an earthquake, filled with potential. I lock eyes with the dark-haired witch who challenged me, and she nods, a silent acknowledgment of the leap we're about to take together.

"Okay, let's do this," she finally relents, and with a collective breath, we form a circle around the nexus, a fragile but potent connection sparking to life.

"On three?" I suggest, a playful grin creeping onto my face.

"More like on five," she shoots back, a glimmer of humor breaking through her seriousness.

"Fine, fine," I chuckle, buoyed by the sudden levity. "One, two—"

"Wait! Is anyone even counting?!" another witch exclaims, her voice breaking the tension.

"Three!" I shout, laughter spilling from my lips as I let the magic flow through me, igniting the air around us.

Together, we unleash a wave of energy, a chaotic torrent that melds our intentions and hopes, forging a bond between our disparate magics. The nexus erupts, colors exploding into a magnificent display that lights up the cavern like a thousand fireflies dancing in unison.

It feels as if the very essence of Brooklyn is rising around us, merging past and present, tradition and innovation into a beautiful tapestry of light. I can feel the city breathing, its heart resonating with ours as we embrace the power we've unlocked together.

For a moment, it feels as if time stands still, as if the chaos has found its rhythm, and I can't help but think that maybe, just maybe, we're all exactly where we're meant to be.

The explosion of energy envelops us, a vibrant storm that crackles with potential. It feels like an awakening, as if the very spirit of Brooklyn, with all its grit and glory, has risen to join us in our endeavor. My heart races in sync with the swirling light, and as I glance around, I see the witches finally letting go of their rigid fears, their eyes sparkling with determination. This is not just a moment of collective magic; it's a revolution in the making.

"Okay, what's next?" the dark-haired witch asks, brushing her hair back from her face, her expression one of exhilaration mixed with uncertainty. "Because I've never done anything like this before."

"Just trust your instincts," I reply, my voice steady, fueled by adrenaline. "We're not here to control this energy; we're here to dance with it."

"Great, I always wanted to be a magical dance partner," she quips, a teasing smile breaking through her seriousness. It's a welcome breath of levity in the charged atmosphere, and I can't help but chuckle.

With a collective breath, we synchronize our movements, drawing on our unique energies while allowing the nexus to guide us. I can feel the pulsing magic merging with ours, a brilliant spectrum of colors shimmering like a kaleidoscope caught in the wind. The energy becomes a song, its rhythm urging us to match its tempo, to lose ourselves in the notes of chaos and creation.

"What if we summon something unexpected?" one of the other witches whispers, a note of caution slipping into her voice.

"Unexpected is my middle name," I reply, a mischievous glint in my eyes. "Let's invite the wild into our little soirée."

As if responding to my challenge, the energy around us shifts, and I feel a strange tugging sensation, as if we're on the brink of something monumental. A cascade of images washes over me—of ancient rites performed under the full moon, of laughter echoing through forgotten alleyways, of hope igniting the darkest corners of the city. The nexus thrums with this collective history, and I can feel it reaching for something beyond our understanding.

"Don't fight it," I urge, watching as the witches' initial hesitations begin to melt away. They lean into the energy, allowing themselves to become conduits for its power. As our magic entwines, the chaos settles into an intricate pattern, revealing a design we hadn't anticipated.

But just as the atmosphere begins to hum with harmony, a jarring sound slices through our connection—a mechanical screech, followed by a sudden flicker of darkness. The colors dim, and the nexus begins to pulse erratically, like a heartbeat struggling to stabilize.

"What the hell was that?" the dark-haired witch exclaims, her expression shifting from joy to panic.

"Something's off," I murmur, my heart pounding in my chest. I can sense the energy fraying at the edges, unraveling like an old sweater that someone's hastily tugged on. "We need to tighten our focus."

"We can't just pull it back! It's alive!" another witch interjects, her voice rising in pitch. "What if we lose control?"

"Then we'll just have to be extraordinary," I reply, trying to mask the growing unease settling in my gut. "Whatever happens, we're in this together."

With newfound determination, we shift our energy, weaving a net of light and intention around the nexus. As we do, I catch sight of the old machinery that surrounds us—long-dormant gears and rusted pipes that seem to hum with anticipation. The nexus roars like a tempest, and suddenly, a violent pulse surges outward, knocking us off our feet.

The world tilts, and I grasp desperately for anything to anchor myself. The witches tumble around me, and I can hear their panicked breaths mingling with the rising wind. "Hold on!" I shout, straining to regain my balance as the ground beneath us seems to shake with a life of its own.

"Are you sure you know what you're doing?" the dark-haired witch yells, her voice laced with both fear and admiration.

"More or less!" I shout back, gripping the energy like a lifeline. I can feel the chaos intensifying, wrapping around us like tendrils of smoke. In that moment, I see a flicker of something in the corner of my vision—an apparition, a shadowy figure forming just at the edge of the nexus.

"Look!" I point, my voice barely breaking through the cacophony. The figure is vague at first, just a swirl of energy and memories, but as it solidifies, I realize it's an embodiment of the very magic we've been invoking.

"Who are you?" I demand, my heart racing. "What do you want?"

Its eyes lock onto mine, swirling with ancient wisdom and unfathomable sadness. "I am the keeper of the balance," it whispers, the voice echoing through the chaos like a haunting melody. "You tread a fine line between creation and destruction. Choose wisely."

"Choose?" I echo, bewildered. "What do you mean choose?"

With a slow, deliberate motion, the apparition extends a hand towards the nexus, and I watch as the energy fractures into two distinct paths—one shimmering with potential and the other dark and ominous, swirling like a storm about to break.

"Choose!" it commands again, a thunderous urgency behind the words. "What you decide now will shape the fate of your city."

Panic rises within me, a visceral jolt of fear at the weight of the choice laid before us. I glance at the witches, their faces a mixture of determination and terror, and I realize we are standing at the precipice of something monumental. I take a deep breath, my heart racing, my magic swirling around me like a tempest.

But before I can voice my decision, the ground beneath us begins to crack, fissures splitting the earth, and the very essence of the city trembles as if sensing our impending choice. The dark path surges with ferocity, and I feel the pull of its allure, the promise of power that whispers to my most primal instincts.

"Make your choice!" the apparition booms, its voice resonating through the chaos, echoing the urgency in my chest.

And in that moment, as the energy surges and the shadows creep closer, I realize I am not just fighting for my magic or for the city; I'm fighting for the very essence of who I am. My heart beats wildly, and as I stand teetering on the edge, the world around me begins to dissolve into darkness, the nexus quaking with a terrible power that seems determined to swallow us whole.

Time stretches, and as the shadows swirl and beckon, I can feel my pulse racing, my breath caught in my throat, poised to make a choice that could change everything.

Chapter 23: A Dangerous Sacrifice

The air hung thick with tension, a palpable energy that seemed to vibrate against my skin as I stood at the edge of the forest, where the trees twisted and turned like dark sentinels guarding secrets I was only beginning to understand. Shadows danced under the canopy, weaving an intricate tapestry of light and dark that mimicked the chaos inside me. I could feel it—the nexus, that mysterious rift in reality that had been growing ever since I had stumbled upon its hidden depths. It beckoned to me, a siren song of power and despair, whispering promises of greatness mingled with the threat of annihilation.

Behind me, the corporate witches huddled in a tight circle, their faces pale and drawn, yet their eyes glimmered with the flickering light of the candles I had infused with my magic. They had come to me seeking guidance, the supposed prodigy of our generation, but now they looked to me with desperation etched into their features. I was supposed to have the answers, but standing there, I felt more like a lost child than a sorceress.

"Is this really the best we can do?" My voice wavered, more a statement of disbelief than a question. "Candles? How do we expect these little lights to hold back a force like that?"

One of the witches, a stern woman named Aveline with silver-streaked hair pulled back into a tight bun, shot me a look that could curdle milk. "It's not just about the candles, Elara. They are a conduit for your magic. You've seen how they reacted when you first lit them."

I remembered the surge, the way the flames had danced wildly, licking the air as if hungry for more than mere wax. My heart raced at the memory. "Yes, but they won't be enough. It feels... it feels like it wants something more."

"It?" Aveline arched an eyebrow, skepticism written all over her. "Are we talking about the nexus or your magical ego?"

I bristled at her tone but held my tongue. The truth was, the nexus had become an entity of its own—an overwhelming force that seemed to feed off our fears and desires, turning them against us. I could feel its pulse, a dark thrum beneath my skin, and I had no doubt it would not rest until it claimed its due.

"You're right." The voice that broke the silence was soft but filled with a quiet strength. It was Mirella, the youngest among us, her wide eyes glistening with a mixture of determination and fear. "It wants something from us. A sacrifice, perhaps."

A heavy silence settled over the group as her words sank in, the weight of their implications suffocating. Sacrifice. The word rolled off my tongue like a bitter pill, and I felt the collective tension rise, an electric current that coursed through the air.

"What kind of sacrifice?" I asked, though I suspected I already knew the answer.

"Your magic," Aveline said bluntly. "You could use the energy of the candles to stabilize the nexus, but it would only be a temporary fix. To truly contain it, you'd have to give up a part of yourself."

The suggestion hit me like a punch to the gut. The thought of losing my magic—my very essence—felt like a slow burn igniting within me, a combination of fear and rage. The magic was not just power; it was identity, a lifelong companion that had shaped every aspect of my existence. To sacrifice it would be akin to losing a limb, a part of my soul that had always been intertwined with who I was.

"I can't," I gasped, clutching my chest as if that would somehow shield me from the impending reality. "I won't."

"Think about what's at stake," Aveline pressed, her voice almost soothing yet laced with urgency. "If we don't act now, the nexus will consume everything—our homes, our lives, everything we've built. You have to be willing to pay the price."

Her words were like a knife twisting in my gut, and the image of my world collapsing around me clawed at my heart. I thought of the laughter of my friends, the warm embrace of my family, and the whispers of the trees in the forest—my sanctuary.

A vision flickered through my mind, a fleeting image of the nexus swallowing it all, leaving nothing but emptiness in its wake. I felt the pull again, stronger this time, a magnetic force coaxing me toward the abyss. The idea of losing my magic was terrifying, yes, but losing everything else was unthinkable.

"I need to think," I muttered, stepping back, seeking the safety of distance. I turned my back on the witches, moving further into the depths of the forest. Each step felt heavier, a battle waged against the despair clawing at my insides.

As I ventured deeper, the air turned cool, the fragrance of damp earth and moss wrapping around me like an embrace. The world around me felt alive, pulsating with energy, and I breathed deeply, searching for clarity. The trees loomed like ancient guardians, their whispers mingling with the rustling leaves, urging me to listen—to heed the call of my own heart.

Then it struck me, a realization as sharp as a blade. The magic wasn't just a part of me; it was my connection to the world, a thread that wove together my existence and the lives around me. Sacrificing it would mean severing that bond. But if I didn't act, wouldn't I lose everything I cherished anyway? The paradox tightened around me, a knot that felt impossible to untangle.

"Damn it," I whispered to the shadows, my voice filled with resolve. "I will not let this destroy us. I will find a way."

With renewed determination, I turned back toward the witches, ready to confront the decision looming over me like a dark cloud. As I walked, the whispering trees seemed to cheer me on, their leaves rustling like applause. My heart pounded with the weight of my choice, but deep down, I understood that whatever the sacrifice, I would face it with courage. The true essence of my magic had always been rooted in love and connection, and as long as I held onto that, perhaps there was still a glimmer of hope.

The atmosphere shifted as I returned to the group, a mixture of fear and resolve coursing through me like a current. The flickering candlelight illuminated the faces of the corporate witches, casting shadows that danced like restless spirits. They looked up, their expressions a kaleidoscope of hope and desperation, their gazes searching for reassurance from me. I felt their weight, the burden of their expectations pressing down like the heavy branches of the trees around us.

"I've made my decision," I declared, forcing the words out even as my throat tightened. "We need to use the candles, but not just the energy they hold. I'll need to give them something more—my magic. It's the only way to stabilize the nexus properly."

Aveline's eyes widened, and for a moment, disbelief hung between us like an unsaid spell. "You can't be serious. That's—"

"—insane?" I interjected, the edge in my voice sharper than I intended. "I know. But think of the alternative. If we don't act now, we risk losing everything." The thought of the nexus devouring our world ignited a fire in my gut.

Mirella stepped forward, her brow furrowed. "But what will you have left? Your magic is part of you. It's—"

"Everything, I know." I sighed, letting the truth settle heavily in the air between us. "But if I don't try, I'll lose everything anyway. It's better to make a choice than to let fate decide for us."

The witches exchanged glances, a silent conversation unfolding in the space between their breaths. Aveline finally nodded, albeit reluctantly. "We will support you, Elara. But we need to be careful. The nexus is unpredictable, and it will not hesitate to take more than you intend to give."

"Like a bad date," I quipped, attempting to lighten the mood despite the seriousness of the situation. "It may look inviting at first, but it will leave you questioning your life choices."

Aveline's lips twitched, and for a moment, the weight of despair lifted. "Let's hope it doesn't come to that. We can't afford to make mistakes."

With our resolve solidified, we arranged the candles in a circle, their waxy forms standing tall like sentinels awaiting their fate. I felt the familiar warmth of my magic coursing through me, a heady mix of power and fear. Each candle flickered as if in response to my thoughts, and I realized this was no ordinary ritual; it would take every ounce of my strength to guide the energy effectively.

Taking a deep breath, I placed my hands over the candles, feeling their heat radiate against my palms. "Let's begin," I said, my voice steady despite the storm brewing inside. As I closed my eyes, the world around me faded, replaced by a kaleidoscope of colors swirling in my mind—a dance of magic that pulsed in rhythm with my heartbeat.

A sudden chill rushed through me, and I opened my eyes to see the nexus shimmering in the distance, a dark rift pulsating with malevolence. "It's time," I murmured, channeling my magic toward the candles. The flames responded, growing taller, twisting into elegant spirals that filled the air with a sweet, smoky scent.

As the energy surged through me, I felt the familiar thrill of power, a sensation that had always been intoxicating. But beneath that rush was an undercurrent of dread; I was standing on the precipice of something monumental, a cliff that threatened to swallow me whole.

"Focus, Elara," Aveline urged, her voice a steady anchor amidst the tempest. "Channel your magic into the candles. Let them absorb it."

I nodded, drawing on my strength. My breath quickened, and with each exhale, I poured my essence into the flickering flames. The candles absorbed my magic like a sponge, growing brighter as the air around us hummed with energy. It was exhilarating yet terrifying, the sensation of relinquishing a part of myself to something larger than I could comprehend.

"Now, Elara, you need to bind it," Mirella instructed, her eyes wide with intensity. "Use your will to contain the energy."

I concentrated, envisioning the energy weaving around the nexus like a protective barrier, but with every pulse of magic I released, I felt a piece of myself slipping away. A weight settled in my chest, heavy and unyielding. The fear of losing my magic intertwined with the desperation to save my world, creating a tension that left me gasping for breath.

Just as I felt the last remnants of my essence beginning to dissolve into the flames, the ground shook violently, sending tremors through my body. The nexus roared in response, a guttural sound that vibrated through the very marrow of my bones. "It's fighting back!" I shouted, panic rising like bile in my throat.

"Hold it steady!" Aveline commanded, her voice sharp with urgency. "You're almost there!"

I gritted my teeth, willing my magic to hold firm. As the candles flared brighter, I focused all my energy on the barrier, feeling the pull of the nexus as it attempted to reclaim what I was trying to contain. A surge of fear clawed at my insides, threatening to unravel me entirely.

In that moment of chaos, a flash of doubt flickered through my mind. What if this was all for nothing? What if I sacrificed my magic only to see it fail?

"Trust yourself, Elara!" Mirella's voice sliced through my uncertainty, fierce and resolute. "You're stronger than you know."

The words ignited something within me, a spark that pushed back against the encroaching darkness. I let out a roar, a primal sound that echoed through the clearing as I tightened my grip on the energy swirling around me. With renewed determination, I poured every last shred of my will into the barrier, visualizing the nexus being contained, held at bay by the strength of my sacrifice.

As the flames erupted in a dazzling display, I felt a final rush of magic surge through me, spiraling out into the world, intertwining with the candles and weaving a net that wrapped around the nexus. For a fleeting moment, everything hung in the balance—a dance of light against shadow, hope against despair.

Then, with a thunderous roar, the nexus began to recede, the dark energy collapsing inward as the barrier held strong. I could feel my magic waning, slipping away like grains of sand through my fingers. As the last vestiges of my essence flowed into the candles, a searing pain shot through me, and I stumbled back, breathless.

The candles flickered violently before settling into a steady glow, casting a warm light that illuminated the clearing. The nexus had been contained, but I felt an emptiness where my magic once pulsed, a hollow ache that gnawed at my core.

A silence fell, heavy with the weight of our shared victory, but I could sense the shift within me—an unsettling void that would never truly be filled. I had sacrificed a part of myself for the greater good, but at what cost? As I leaned against a tree for support, I glanced at the witches, their faces a mixture of relief and concern.

"Did it work?" I managed to ask, my voice barely above a whisper.

Aveline stepped forward, her eyes searching mine. "For now. But the price you paid... it will change you, Elara."

"I know," I replied, the reality settling in like a heavy cloak. "But it was worth it."

In that moment, amidst the shadows and flickering lights, I realized that while my magic was an integral part of who I was, it had never defined me entirely. I would find a way to reclaim my strength, to rise from the ashes of my sacrifice. The road ahead would be uncertain, but I was determined to forge my own path, with or without the magic that had once been my lifeblood.

The glow of the candles flickered like stars in the dusk, casting a warm embrace around me as I leaned against the ancient tree, still trembling from the aftermath of my sacrifice. The witches were all gathered, their expressions reflecting the fragile line we'd walked between triumph and despair. I felt like a deflated balloon, floating in a world where my essence had been plucked, leaving behind only the remnants of what once made me whole.

"Is it over?" Mirella asked, her voice soft but edged with an anxiety that felt like static in the air.

I took a breath, letting the sweet scent of melting wax fill my lungs. "For now," I replied, my voice hoarse. "But I can't shake the feeling that the nexus will find a way to return. It's not finished with us."

Aveline, ever the pragmatist, looked at me with a furrowed brow. "You're not wrong. Magic like that doesn't simply disappear. It lingers, waiting for a chance to reemerge."

"Great," I said, rolling my eyes despite the seriousness of the moment. "So we've effectively bought ourselves a ticket to the next magic apocalypse."

Laughter broke the tension, a bright spark in the somber air. "You do have a way of making disaster sound charming," Aveline replied, a hint of admiration in her tone.

"It's a gift," I quipped, but the truth hung heavy in my chest. I might have retained my sense of humor, but the hollow space where my magic had been felt insatiable, like a relentless void that demanded to be filled.

As the shadows lengthened, we began to gather our supplies, the remnants of the ritual. I could feel the weight of the evening's events pressing down, heavy like the humid air before a storm. Just when I thought we were about to disperse, a gust of wind whipped through the clearing, sending leaves swirling into the air like confetti at a celebration. It wasn't the gentle breeze of dusk; this felt charged, alive with energy.

"Did anyone else feel that?" Mirella asked, her eyes wide, darting around as if the very air might reveal a hidden threat.

"It's not just you," I replied, my instincts on high alert. "It feels like something's coming."

Suddenly, the candles flared, brightening unnaturally, casting long shadows that danced across the ground. The light pulsed rhythmically, as if in sync with a heartbeat, an echo of the dark force we had just contained.

"Step back!" Aveline commanded, her authoritative tone cutting through the tension.

We retreated a few steps, our eyes fixed on the now flickering flames, which began to sway as though caught in an invisible wind. I could feel a familiar energy thrumming beneath the surface, a beckoning sensation that tugged at my very being.

"What's happening?" Mirella breathed, fear etched in every line of her face.

I swallowed hard, trying to piece together the puzzle that was rapidly shifting before us. "I think the nexus is fighting back. It's trying to break free."

As if in response to my words, a crackling sound erupted from the ground, and fissures began to spiderweb through the earth around us. The air grew thick with tension, and I sensed the nexus coiling beneath us, a serpent waiting to strike.

"Do you think the candles are unstable?" Aveline shot a worried glance my way.

"It's not the candles," I said, feeling the tension in my chest tighten further. "It's me. The magic I gave up—it's still connected to the nexus somehow."

The realization hit like a punch. My sacrifice hadn't merely contained the nexus; it had bonded me to it in a way I hadn't anticipated. "We need to do something. Now."

Mirella's eyes were wild with panic. "What do you want us to do? If it's connected to you, it could mean—"

"Don't say it!" I snapped, but the truth loomed, dark and undeniable.

A sudden burst of energy shot through the clearing, making the ground tremble beneath our feet. The candles erupted, flames licking at the air as they formed an arc around me. I felt the pulse of the nexus thrumming through my veins, a siren call demanding I answer.

"Fight it!" Aveline shouted, her voice rising above the chaos. "You can't let it take you again!"

But I could feel it, the dark tendrils of the nexus wrapping around my mind, coaxing me into its embrace. Images flashed before me—memories of magic, power, and a world where I felt invincible. It promised everything I'd sacrificed, an alluring whisper that brushed against my consciousness, tempting me to surrender.

"No!" I cried, shaking my head violently. "I won't go back!"

With a desperate surge, I focused on the bond I still felt with the witches, the shared strength that had brought us together. "You have to help me!" I yelled, reaching out for them, my voice cracking with urgency. "We need to create a counterbalance. I can't do this alone!"

Aveline moved first, stepping closer to me, her expression fierce and determined. "We'll help you, Elara. We'll fight this together!"

Mirella joined her, taking my hand in hers, grounding me. "We can't let it win. Remember what you've fought for!"

I took a deep breath, feeling the warmth of their hands against mine. Together, we closed our eyes and focused, pooling our collective energy, amplifying the flickering flames of the candles. The light swelled, growing brighter, casting the shadows deeper as we stood united against the darkness that threatened to consume us.

As our magic intertwined, I felt a surge of power flooding through me, stronger than before. The nexus, sensing the shift, writhed beneath the earth, a feral beast clawing to break free. The ground shook violently, and I could hear the distant rumble of thunder, nature's angry response to the chaos we had unleashed.

"Push against it!" Aveline shouted, her voice firm and commanding.

With one last burst of will, I unleashed everything I had, channeling my strength into the flames, desperate to hold the darkness at bay. The candles erupted in a dazzling display of light, illuminating the clearing as if a thousand suns had risen at once.

But just as victory felt within reach, a deafening roar pierced the air, shaking the very foundations of our reality. The nexus surged upward, a shadowy mass twisting and coiling, and for an agonizing moment, I lost my grip on the magic that held it back.

"Stay with me!" Aveline shouted, her eyes fierce as she anchored herself to me.

But then, a violent shockwave ripped through the air, and everything spun into chaos. The world blurred around us, colors and sounds melding into a cacophony of noise, until the very ground beneath me vanished. I grasped at the air, desperate to hold onto something—anything—but the darkness swallowed me whole.

And then, nothing.

Chapter 24: Threads of Fate

The air crackled with tension, a palpable hum that vibrated through my bones as I took a step forward, ready to embrace the chaos that surrounded us. Shadows danced across the ancient stone walls of the chamber, their flickering forms twisting like tendrils of smoke in the dim light. I could feel the pulse of magic thrumming through the ground beneath my feet, a reminder of the power that lay dormant and the burden that had become mine to bear.

Grant's presence was a steady anchor in this storm. He was not just a brilliant mind with a penchant for all things technological; he had a way of standing tall, his shoulders squared against the weight of uncertainty. I had watched him grapple with the impossible, his brow furrowed in concentration as he found ways to merge the digital and the mystical. Today, that determination shone brighter than ever, his eyes a fierce blue that mirrored the depths of the ocean, ready to dive into whatever lay beneath.

"Let's do this," he said, his voice a low rumble that somehow managed to pierce through my doubts. There was an undeniable confidence in him, a spark of something that ignited a fire in my own chest. I couldn't help but nod, though my heart raced at the thought of combining our powers, blending my magic with his technology. It was a leap into the unknown, an uncharted territory that could lead to salvation or destruction.

As we began the ritual, the room around us seemed to breathe, the air thickening with the scent of earth and ancient stone. I closed my eyes, allowing myself to sink into the rhythm of the energy that flowed between us. The flickering candles cast a warm glow, illuminating the intricate symbols etched into the ground—a language older than time itself. Each line pulsed with potential, whispering secrets of power and connection.

With a steady breath, I reached for the magic within me, feeling it swirl like a tempest. I envisioned the threads of energy weaving through the room, intertwining with the technology Grant had so meticulously prepared. His devices, sleek and shimmering, sat poised on a nearby altar, each one a beacon of hope in our dark hour. The idea of binding the ethereal with the mechanical was as terrifying as it was exhilarating, but I was willing to risk everything.

"Ready?" Grant asked, his voice a thread of calm in the storm brewing inside me.

"More than ready," I replied, forcing a smile despite the anxiety twisting in my gut. The truth was, I was terrified—not just of what we were about to attempt, but of how much I had come to rely on him. This was more than a partnership; it felt like we were fusing our very essences together.

As I reached out, I could feel the warmth of his hand clasping mine, our fingers interlocking in a gesture that felt profoundly intimate. Together, we drew on the energy flowing through the room, channeling it into the devices that hummed softly, their lights pulsing in time with the rising tide of our magic. I felt the weight of his gaze, steady and unwavering, and it anchored me as I began to weave the spell.

"Focus on the connection," he urged, and his voice wrapped around me like a protective cloak. "Imagine the energy flowing seamlessly between us, like threads in a tapestry."

With each word, I felt the tendrils of magic respond, drawing nearer, weaving into the digital ether he commanded. It was an intoxicating sensation, the way our powers melded together, creating something entirely new. I envisioned the threads shimmering, a kaleidoscope of colors bursting to life as we worked in tandem.

But just as the energy began to stabilize, a dark shadow flickered at the edges of my vision. A chill crept through the air, wrapping around us like a shroud. My heart lurched, the sudden shift sending shockwaves through our connection.

"Did you feel that?" I gasped, glancing at Grant, whose expression shifted from focused determination to immediate concern.

"Yeah," he said, his brow furrowing. "It's like something... or someone is trying to disrupt us."

The temperature in the room plummeted, and I felt the magic recoil, as if sensing a threat. The delicate threads we had woven began to fray, snapping under the pressure of the encroaching darkness. My instincts screamed at me to retreat, to protect what we had forged, but there was no time.

"Keep going!" Grant shouted, his voice fierce, a lifeline amidst the chaos. "We can't let them break through!"

I gritted my teeth, forcing the magic to respond to my will. It fought back, a wild stallion unwilling to be tamed, but I clung to the connection we had built, pouring my energy into it. I envisioned the threads tightening, reinforcing the boundaries we had established.

With a desperate surge, I pushed forward, feeling the magic respond, coiling around us like a protective barrier. And then, just as I thought we might regain control, a figure materialized from the shadows—a silhouette that seemed to draw the very light from the room.

"Enough!" The voice was smooth as silk, laced with malice. "You think you can defy me?"

My heart raced as I recognized the voice, a chilling echo from my past. The darkness around the figure shimmered, revealing a face I had hoped never to see again. A smirk curled on his lips, confidence radiating from him as he stepped forward, the very embodiment of danger.

"Is this the best you can do?" he taunted, and I felt my resolve falter. The energy surged around us, chaotic and unstable, like a wild storm raging at sea. Grant's grip tightened, and I could see the determination etched into his features, a stark contrast to the dread pooling in my stomach.

"Together," he urged, his voice cutting through the fear. "We can't let him win."

A rush of adrenaline flooded my veins, igniting a fire I had thought extinguished. With renewed vigor, I met Grant's gaze, and in that moment, I understood—we were stronger together, a force of nature that could withstand any storm.

The tension in the air thickened like fog, wrapping around us as Grant and I fought to stabilize the fraying threads of our ritual. His presence was a reassuring weight beside me, and I clung to it like a lifebuoy in a storm-tossed sea. The dark figure loomed before us, its shadow a shroud that threatened to swallow the light we had painstakingly created. I could feel the pulse of magic echoing through the room, thrumming with urgency, as though it, too, recognized the peril we faced.

"Who invited the dark cloud?" I muttered under my breath, attempting to inject a bit of humor into the dire situation. It was a feeble attempt, and I could feel Grant's sideways glance of disapproval. He was focused, but I appreciated his effort to keep the tension from strangling us entirely.

The figure stepped forward, its smirk widening, a malevolent gleam in its eyes that sent a shiver racing down my spine. "You really think you can succeed where others have failed?" The voice was smooth, like satin laced with poison. "You're nothing but children playing with toys."

"Maybe we're just a couple of kids who know how to throw a party," Grant shot back, his tone sharp but laced with that familiar bravado that had first drawn me to him. I admired how he could wield sarcasm like a sword, cutting through the heaviness of the moment.

"Cute," the figure replied, a mocking tilt to its head. "But this isn't a game, and I am not here for entertainment."

I could feel the magic swirling around us, a tempest of energy that wanted to break free, and I knew we had to act quickly. The creature before us was more than a mere obstacle; it was a dark well of power, and it thrived on fear and chaos. The air grew heavy with anticipation, thick enough to slice through, and as my heart raced, I focused on the glowing symbols beneath my feet.

"Grant," I whispered urgently, "we need to channel the energy into something more substantial. We can't let him disrupt the flow."

His brow furrowed with concentration, the gears in his mind whirring furiously. "Right. We'll create a barrier. Something to keep him out while we solidify our connection."

With a nod, we settled into a rhythm, our breaths synchronized as we pulled on the threads of energy, weaving them together like strands of silk. I could feel the warmth of Grant's hand in mine, a steady pulse that countered the icy dread creeping in from the dark figure. The glowing symbols beneath us flared brighter, lighting up the room with a kaleidoscope of colors that danced like fireflies.

"Come on, magic," I murmured, coaxing it like a stubborn child. "You've done great things before. Don't fail me now."

The energy surged, pushing against the encroaching shadow, and I could sense the change in the atmosphere. The darkness wavered, momentarily faltering as if taken aback by the sheer force of our combined will. Grant's eyes locked onto mine, a silent agreement passing between us, and I felt a jolt of determination igniting my core.

"Let's show him what we've got," he said, his voice a steady anchor amidst the rising storm.

With a powerful thrust of energy, we directed our magic toward the figure, a brilliant arc of light that spiraled outward. The shadow recoiled, its smirk faltering as the light crashed against it like a wave, pushing it back into the recesses of the chamber. But even as I celebrated the small victory, I could feel the ground trembling beneath us, as if the very stones were groaning in protest.

The figure's voice rose above the chaos, a chilling laugh that sent a jolt of fear through me. "You think that will stop me? I thrive on chaos! Your little display of magic is nothing but a flicker in the dark."

"No, it's a spotlight," I shot back, gritting my teeth as I focused harder, willing the magic to bend to our will. "And we're about to turn it up."

I concentrated on the barrier we were forming, visualizing it as a shield, a brilliant wall of light that would protect us from the encroaching shadow. I could feel the energy pooling, surging with every heartbeat, and I could sense Grant mirroring my intentions. Together, we could create something formidable.

As we directed the energy, I felt a shift—a tremor beneath our feet that sent a ripple of dread through me. The ground seemed to quake as if responding to the figure's taunts, and I struggled to keep the barrier intact. "Grant!" I shouted, panic rising in my chest. "It's like the earth is fighting back!"

"Then we fight harder!" he called, his voice a rallying cry in the storm. He tightened his grip on my hand, and in that moment, our connection became a conduit of power, our energies entwining and amplifying each other.

With renewed fervor, we thrust the barrier forward, feeling it solidify around us like a cocoon. The dark figure screeched, the sound piercing through the air like glass shattering, and I couldn't help but smirk at the look of confusion that crossed its face. The magic coursing through us felt alive, a roaring river of energy that surged and swelled with purpose.

"I think we've just hit a nerve," I said, my heart racing as I reveled in our small triumph.

"Don't get cocky," Grant replied, his tone light but his eyes serious. "We're not out of the woods yet."

Before I could respond, the figure unleashed a wave of darkness, a tangible force that slammed against our barrier, testing its strength. The impact reverberated through my bones, a jolt that made me stagger. I could see the glow of our shield flickering, the threads of energy trembling under the strain.

"Hold it together!" Grant shouted, determination etched across his face. "We can't let him break through!"

I took a deep breath, steadying myself as I leaned into the magic, pouring every ounce of strength I had into reinforcing our shield. The energy crackled around us, and I felt the heat rising, the colors blending into a vibrant tapestry that pulsed with life.

In that moment, I understood the stakes—this was not just a battle against a dark entity but a fight for our very souls. The thought sent a shiver down my spine, but with Grant by my side, I felt an unyielding resolve swell within me. We could do this. Together.

The energy crackled around us, a symphony of chaos harmonizing with the rhythm of our hearts. As we stood together, our hands entwined, I could feel the surge of magic coursing through me, alive and vibrant. It pulsed in time with the flickering lights of Grant's devices, each beep and whir a reminder of the precarious balance we were trying to maintain against the dark figure's relentless advance.

"Is it just me, or does he look a little annoyed?" I quipped, trying to lighten the mood as the shadowy form struggled against the barrier we had formed. The creature's features twisted into a mask of fury, its eyes glinting like shards of glass, but the tension in the air was thick enough to cut.

"Annoyed might be an understatement," Grant replied, a hint of a grin breaking through the intensity of the moment. "I think we've officially entered the 'unleash the beast' phase."

We shared a brief, charged look, a moment of solidarity amidst the impending doom. Together, we were an unstoppable force, and the electricity in the air wrapped around us like a cloak, infusing me with determination. I squeezed Grant's hand, drawing strength from our connection as I focused on the magic swirling around us, molding it into a barrier that felt like a second skin.

The dark figure lunged forward, and I braced myself for the impact. The barrier shimmered as the force collided with it, a sound like thunder echoing in the chamber. I could feel the magic within me responding to the threat, ready to retaliate, but I had to keep my wits about me.

"Grant, on three!" I called, summoning every ounce of will I could muster. "One... two... three!"

We pushed forward together, our energies intertwining and amplifying each other's power. The barrier flared bright, and for a moment, the darkness hesitated, a flicker of uncertainty crossing its twisted features.

"Nice work, kid," Grant said, a satisfied smile creeping onto his face. "Now let's give him a taste of his own medicine."

"Medicine? More like a cocktail of fury and retribution," I retorted, feeling the adrenaline rush through my veins. With every heartbeat, I channeled the energy into the barrier, envisioning it as a wave crashing against the shadow, sending it reeling back into the depths of the chamber.

As I intensified the spell, the air thickened with power, and I felt the ground shake beneath us, a primal force reacting to our call. "We need to anchor this!" I shouted over the din. "I can feel it trying to pull us under!"

"On it!" Grant replied, quickly recalibrating his devices, his fingers dancing over the screens with a deftness that left me in awe. He was a maestro orchestrating a symphony of chaos and control, and I could only hope that our combined efforts would be enough.

The shadow snarled, and suddenly, a blast of darkness surged forth, splintering the barrier with an unholy scream. My heart raced as I watched our hard-won shield flicker like a dying flame. "Grant!" I shouted, panic clawing at my throat. "It's breaking!"

"Hold on!" he barked, his determination a steady drumbeat in the chaos. "We can do this! Trust in the connection!"

In that moment, I closed my eyes, letting the magic envelop me, filling every fiber of my being. I envisioned the threads weaving together, forming a tapestry of resilience and strength. My fear morphed into anger, a fierce resolve to protect what we had created.

With a deep breath, I thrust my arms outward, directing the energy like a conductor guiding an orchestra. "Together!" I called, our voices blending into one powerful command. The energy surged again, reinforcing the barrier with renewed vigor, pushing back against the encroaching darkness.

The figure writhed, its form twisting in an angry dance, but I could see the flicker of uncertainty returning. "This is not the end!" it hissed, the voice dripping with venom. "You think you can escape your fate? I am the shadow that walks beside you, the darkness that cannot be cast away!"

"Sounds more like a bad romance novel than a threat," I retorted, trying to keep the moment light even as I felt the strain of our struggle. "I'm pretty sure I'm the heroine here, and you're just the villain with a tragic backstory."

Grant chuckled softly, the sound a balm against the tension. "Well, if we're in a novel, I'd say this is the part where the heroine triumphs against the odds."

"Then let's make sure we don't get canceled in the next chapter," I shot back, channeling our magic with every ounce of strength. The air shimmered around us as we pressed forward, pushing against the figure with everything we had.

But just as victory seemed within our grasp, the ground beneath us shattered, sending a shockwave that knocked us off our feet. I gasped as the barrier cracked, the energy spilling out like water from a broken dam.

"Grant!" I screamed, reaching for him as we tumbled to the ground, the world spinning around me. The figure loomed above us, its laughter a chilling echo in the chaos. "You think you can defeat me? You are merely delaying the inevitable."

My heart raced as I scrambled to regain my footing, desperately trying to channel the last remnants of energy. But the darkness closed in, wrapping around us like a suffocating fog. I felt the weight of despair creeping into my chest, the feeling that we were running out of time.

"Not yet!" Grant shouted, scrambling beside me. "We've come too far to give up now! Think of what's at stake!"

I closed my eyes, fighting to summon the last flickers of our magic, feeling the bond between us pulse like a heartbeat. With a deep breath, I opened my eyes, steeling myself against the encroaching darkness. "We'll find a way," I said, my voice steady despite the panic swirling within me.

And then, as if in answer to my resolve, a bright light erupted from the very ground beneath us, a blinding flash that pushed back against the shadows. It surged upward, illuminating the room in a brilliant glow, and I realized that the magic was not just ours to wield—it belonged to the very essence of the nexus we stood upon.

But just as hope began to flicker, the figure lunged forward, its shadowy hand reaching for us, a dark claw poised to strike. In that terrifying instant, everything shifted, and I knew we were standing at the precipice of something monumental.

With a heart full of determination, I screamed, "Together!" But even as the words left my lips, I felt a powerful force yank me backward, the world spinning away, plunging us into darkness as the figure's laughter echoed in my ears.

The last thing I saw was Grant's eyes wide with disbelief before the light vanished, leaving nothing but the oppressive blackness that threatened to swallow us whole.

Chapter 25: The Calm Before the Storm

The city glimmered under the wash of moonlight, its vibrant hues muted into a palette of silvery shadows. As we strolled through the empty streets, the cobblestones glistened with dew, reflecting the scattered streetlamps like little stars fallen from the sky. The air was heavy with the scent of damp earth and lingering jasmine, an intoxicating blend that played tricks on my senses. It felt surreal to walk here, side by side with Grant, the ghostly quiet interrupted only by the distant hum of traffic. He didn't speak, and neither did I, as if uttering words would shatter the fragile peace that enveloped us.

With every step, I could feel the magic beneath the surface of the world, an electric pulse that thrummed in the depths of my veins. It was as if the city itself were alive, its heart beating in rhythm with my own. The aftermath of our battle still lingered in the air—a heady mix of adrenaline and uncertainty. I wanted to believe that we had turned a corner, that the corporate witches had retreated for good, but the hollowness inside me whispered that our troubles were far from over.

Grant's hand was warm on mine, a grounding presence amidst the turmoil swirling within. The way his fingers intertwined with mine felt reassuring yet electrifying, a tether that pulled me back to the moment. I glanced at him, his profile illuminated by the soft glow of the streetlights, the sharp angles of his jaw casting shadows that danced across his skin. His eyes, always so expressive, held a flicker of concern, a mirror to my own unease. "You okay?" he finally asked, his voice low and smooth, like velvet.

I nodded, forcing a smile that felt more like a mask than genuine reassurance. "Just thinking about... everything."

He stopped walking, turning to face me fully. "You're worried, aren't you?" The directness in his gaze disarmed me, and I could only shrug, a noncommittal gesture that somehow conveyed the depth of my apprehension.

"I can't shake the feeling that we've only seen the tip of the iceberg," I admitted, looking away. It was easier to focus on the cobblestones, each one a world of its own, than to meet the intensity of his gaze. "I mean, we just stabilized the nexus, but what if it was just a distraction? What if they're plotting something worse?"

His thumb brushed over my knuckles, a tender gesture that sent a surge of warmth through me. "Whatever it is, we'll face it together," he promised, his voice firm yet laced with an undeniable softness. "You're not alone in this."

The sincerity of his words wrapped around me like a warm blanket, but I still felt that cold knot in my stomach. The corporate witches had always played a long game, weaving their machinations through the fabric of our lives like the intricate patterns of a spider's web. I could almost hear the whispers of their schemes echoing through the alleys, plotting and scheming, hidden in the shadows.

As we resumed our walk, the silence returned, more pronounced this time. It was heavy, thick with unsaid words and unvoiced fears. I glanced at the flickering lights overhead, shadows playing tricks on my mind, and for a brief moment, I imagined the world around us dissolving into chaos. But then, in the distance, the soft murmur of laughter broke through the quiet, drawing my attention to a small café spilling light onto the pavement. Its warm glow contrasted sharply with the cold night, inviting and alive.

"Should we?" I asked, motioning toward the café. The thought of hot cocoa and the comforting buzz of people felt like a lifeline, a distraction from the tumult brewing beneath the surface.

Grant's smile was infectious, breaking the tension that had settled between us. "Absolutely. I could use some sugar to fuel my late-night heroics."

As we crossed the street, the gentle jingle of the doorbell announced our arrival, and the cozy warmth enveloped us like an embrace. The scent of freshly brewed coffee and baked pastries hung in the air, wrapping around me, momentarily easing the weight in my chest. We found a small table tucked in the corner, away from the lively chatter, where I could steal glances at him without fear of being caught in the intensity of our shared gaze.

"So, tell me," he said, leaning forward, his elbows resting on the table. "What's your ideal escape from all this craziness?"

I paused, allowing the question to linger in the air as I pondered my answer. The truth was, I craved a world where magic was just a distant whisper, a world where I could sip my cocoa in peace without the ever-present dread of dark forces looming just outside the door. "I'd say a cottage in the woods, maybe with a view of a lake," I began, weaving my dream into words. "A place where the biggest concern is whether to roast marshmallows or make s'mores. What about you?"

He chuckled, the sound rich and warm. "I think I'd go for a high-rise apartment with a city view. You know, to watch the chaos unfold while I sip my coffee in my pajamas. A little ironic, don't you think?"

I laughed, the sound bright and genuine, breaking the tension that had clung to us like mist. "I can see it now: you, with your fuzzy slippers, analyzing the city's crime rate from your perch."

"Exactly," he said, his grin wide. "But what I really want is a cozy spot to escape to with you. Somewhere we can let our guards down."

The intimacy of his words sent a flutter through me, igniting something deep within. It was a tantalizing prospect, one that hinted at more than just a shared fantasy. But just as I was about to reply, a cold gust swept through the café, extinguishing the laughter and chatter like a candle snuffed out in the dark.

My heart raced, a familiar sense of foreboding creeping back in. I exchanged a glance with Grant, who had gone pale, his brow furrowed in concentration. Something was off, an unspoken tension that hung heavily in the air, like the calm before the storm. The laughter faded, replaced by an unsettling silence that made my skin prickle.

And then, just like that, the door swung open, and the night outside rushed in, carrying with it a chill that made the hairs on the back of my neck stand on end. The moment felt suspended in time, and I could sense that whatever was waiting beyond that threshold was about to change everything once more.

The door swung open with an eerie creak, and the ambiance of the café shifted dramatically, the warmth and laughter fading as a cold draft swept through the room. A figure stood silhouetted against the night, their presence strikingly out of place amid the cozy glow of the café. It was a woman, her features obscured by the shadows that clung to her like a second skin. She had an air of undeniable confidence, each step forward echoing with purpose, yet something about her made the air feel charged, as if the very atmosphere crackled with tension.

Grant stiffened beside me, our momentary reprieve evaporating in an instant. I instinctively leaned closer to him, searching his expression for reassurance, but all I found was a flicker of wariness in his eyes. The patrons around us fell silent, eyes darting toward the newcomer, curiosity laced with apprehension. I could feel my heart pounding in my chest, each beat drumming a warning that this was no ordinary interruption.

"Anyone missing a little magic?" the woman called, her voice smooth yet edged with mischief. She stepped into the light, revealing a cascade of dark hair that framed her sharp cheekbones, and her eyes glinted with an intensity that was both captivating and unsettling. There was something about her presence, something that hinted at danger wrapped in charm, and it sent a shiver down my spine.

"I think we're all good here, thanks," I managed to say, trying to sound nonchalant while my instincts screamed at me to run. Grant squeezed my hand tighter, a silent reminder that we were in this together, whatever this was.

The woman's lips curled into a smile that felt more like a challenge than an invitation. "Oh, but I think you'll want to hear what I have to say." She leaned against the counter, crossing her arms as she surveyed the room, her gaze finally settling on us. "You two have been quite the topic of conversation. Word travels fast in a city like this, especially when witches are involved."

"Who are you?" Grant asked, his voice steady but tinged with an underlying tension. He stood protectively in front of me, a barrier between the unknown and our fragile sense of security.

"Call me Lila," she replied, her tone casual, as if she were discussing the weather rather than the implications of her presence. "I come bearing tidings of a storm on the horizon. You see, stabilizing the nexus was only the first step. There are those who won't let this slide, who will fight to reclaim their power."

I could feel the weight of her words settling in the pit of my stomach. "What do you mean? We've done everything we can to push back against them."

Lila chuckled softly, a sound that seemed to dance mockingly around the room. "You think that's enough? There are layers to this city, layers of magic and ambition. The corporate witches are just the surface; there are deeper currents at play. And they won't stop until they get what they want."

"Great," I muttered under my breath, glancing at Grant. "Just when I thought we could catch our breath."

"Tell us what we need to do," Grant interjected, his voice steady but his eyes betrayed a flicker of doubt. "If there's a storm coming, we need to prepare."

Lila's smile widened, revealing an unsettling gleam in her eye. "I admire your eagerness, but it's not that simple. The forces at work here are not easily thwarted. You'll need more than determination. You'll need allies, and you'll need to dig into the past—the history that shaped this city, the very foundation of its magic."

"History?" I echoed, feeling a surge of uncertainty. "What kind of history?"

"The kind that's buried," she replied, leaning closer, her voice dropping to a conspiratorial whisper. "The tales of those who came before, those who wielded power in ways you can barely fathom. You'll need to unearth the secrets of the Nexus Council, and trust me, they're not all pretty."

The mention of the Nexus Council sent a chill down my spine. They were legendary figures, shrouded in myth and whispers, said to have shaped the very fabric of our world. The idea of delving into their stories felt daunting, as though we would be peeling back layers of time that were best left undisturbed.

"Where do we start?" Grant asked, his voice firm, pulling me back to the present. The urgency in his tone sparked a flicker of determination within me.

"Follow the signs," Lila instructed, her gaze piercing as if she could see into my very soul. "The city speaks in symbols—old graffiti, forgotten paths, places where magic lingers. You'll know when you find it. But heed my warning: not all who seek the truth will survive it."

With that, she straightened, brushing her hands against her skirt as if shaking off the weight of her own words. "I've said my piece. Do with it what you will, but remember—magic is a double-edged sword. It can save you, or it can destroy you. Choose wisely."

Before I could respond, she turned on her heel and sauntered toward the door, her presence dissipating into the shadows like a wisp of smoke. The café was left in stunned silence, the chatter of before replaced by a heavy air of anticipation and dread.

"What just happened?" I breathed, turning to Grant, who looked equally bewildered.

He shook his head, eyes narrowed in thought. "I don't know, but we can't ignore this. We need to find out more about the Nexus Council, and fast."

The urgency of his words ignited a fire within me. "Right. We need to hit the books. The library might have old archives or records."

"Or we could visit some of the older folks around town," Grant suggested, his eyes lighting up with an idea. "You know, the ones who've lived here forever. They might have stories."

"Great plan, but where do we start?"

"We'll figure it out together," he said, determination shining in his eyes.

As we gathered our things, the atmosphere shifted again, the initial tension giving way to a shared purpose. I felt a new resolve settling over me, a sense of camaraderie with Grant that transcended the chaos surrounding us.

But as we stepped out into the cool night air, a flicker of doubt gnawed at the edges of my mind. Lila's warning echoed like a haunting refrain, leaving me to wonder just how deep the darkness ran and whether we had the strength to face it. The city whispered around us, its secrets swirling in the wind, and I couldn't shake the feeling that we were just beginning to uncover the truth—a truth that might change everything.

The chill of the night air wrapped around us like a shroud as we stepped outside, each breath a visible puff of warmth in the otherwise still atmosphere. The streetlights cast long shadows, stretching like fingers reaching toward the unknown, and I couldn't shake the sense that we were being watched. Grant walked beside me, his presence a comforting weight, but the tension crackling between us felt tangible, a shared apprehension that threatened to bubble over.

"Do you think she was right?" I asked, glancing sideways at him, my heart racing with the implications of Lila's cryptic warning. "About the council? The history?"

"Right or wrong, we need to find out," he replied, his voice steady but laced with an urgency that mirrored my own. "We've faced worse, haven't we?"

I chuckled lightly, the sound breaking the tension for a fleeting moment. "Oh sure, let's just pile on another layer of madness. It's not like we've had enough already."

Grant smirked, that familiar twinkle of mischief igniting in his eyes. "Hey, it builds character. Think of it as an extreme sport."

"Extreme sport? Right, because I've always wanted to put my life on the line for a history lesson."

"Ah, but it's not just any history lesson. It's a magical one!" he teased, giving my hand a reassuring squeeze.

Our banter was cut short as we turned onto a narrow side street, dimly lit and lined with ancient brick buildings that seemed to huddle together, sharing secrets of their own. The air felt charged, and a low hum of energy pulsed beneath my skin, intensifying with each step. I paused, tilting my head as I noticed something on the wall beside me—an old mural, faded but unmistakably intricate, depicting a swirling pattern that looked eerily similar to the nexus symbol.

"Look at this," I whispered, my finger brushing against the rough texture of the paint. The colors were muted, yet there was an undeniable vibrancy, as if the mural had been infused with magic long ago.

"Nice find," Grant said, stepping closer to examine it. "What do you think it means?"

I squinted at the images, tracing the lines with my eyes. "It could be a map, or a warning. It's hard to tell."

Just then, a flicker of movement caught my attention from the corner of my eye. I turned sharply, my heart leaping into my throat as I spotted a figure lingering in the shadows. A man, tall and cloaked in darkness, stood just beyond the streetlamp's glow, watching us with an intensity that sent chills racing down my spine.

"Um, Grant?" I said quietly, my voice barely above a whisper. "I think we might have company."

Before he could respond, the figure stepped forward, revealing a face I hadn't expected to see—a face from the past. It was Marcus, an old acquaintance from the magical underground, known for his sharp wit and even sharper alliances. His reputation had always been a double-edged sword, a mixture of charm and danger that left many on edge.

"Fancy meeting you here," he said, his voice smooth as silk, laced with a hint of mockery. "Didn't expect to see you two in this neck of the woods."

"Marcus," I replied cautiously, my instincts telling me to tread lightly. "What are you doing here?"

He shrugged, a nonchalant gesture that felt rehearsed. "Oh, just passing through. I heard whispers about the nexus stabilizing, thought I'd see how the new powers are faring." His eyes sparkled with mischief, a predator's gleam that sent a shiver down my spine. "You know how it is—always good to keep an eye on the competition."

"Competition?" Grant interjected, stepping forward. "We're not here for a contest, Marcus. We're trying to figure out what's happening in this city."

"Ah, the ever-noble quest," he said, an exaggerated sigh escaping his lips. "But what if I told you that you're chasing shadows? That your search for truth might lead you right into a trap?"

"Are you trying to warn us or scare us?" I shot back, annoyance bubbling beneath my calm facade. "We can handle ourselves."

"Can you? Or are you just pretending?" Marcus tilted his head, the smirk on his lips deepening. "Lila was right about one thing—you'll need allies, and you might want to consider the company you keep."

"Is that a threat?" Grant's voice was low, a dangerous edge cutting through the playful banter.

"Oh, not at all." Marcus leaned closer, his eyes gleaming. "Just a friendly suggestion. You see, the Nexus Council has its eyes on you. And they're not the forgiving type."

My stomach twisted at his words. "What do you know about them?"

"Enough to know that they've been waiting for someone like you to stir the pot." His voice dropped, becoming almost conspiratorial. "They've been monitoring the energy fluctuations, the disturbance you've caused. And they're not pleased."

"Then we'll deal with it," I declared, a sudden surge of defiance rising within me. "We've faced down witches and dark magic; we're not afraid of a council."

"Ah, bravery is admirable, but it can be quite foolish." Marcus straightened, the playful demeanor slipping away to reveal a steely resolve. "Just remember, not everyone you meet will have your best interests at heart. Watch your back. You'll need to find the truth before they find you."

With that, he turned and disappeared into the shadows, leaving us reeling in the aftermath of his unsettling presence. I felt the weight of his warning linger in the air, a reminder that the danger wasn't just external; it was lurking within the very threads of our world.

"What just happened?" Grant breathed, his eyes wide with the lingering shock of our encounter.

"I think we just got a crash course in magical politics," I replied, my heart racing. "And it doesn't feel good."

We stood there, the night wrapping around us like a dark cloak, and I realized just how precarious our position had become. The storm Lila had spoken of was closing in, and I could feel its winds stirring, threatening to engulf us in chaos. As the shadows deepened, the energy in the air shifted once more, and I knew we were at the precipice of something monumental.

But before I could voice my thoughts, a low rumble echoed through the night, vibrating beneath our feet, a sound so deep and primal that it sent a thrill of dread coursing through my veins. The earth trembled, and the lights flickered overhead, illuminating the street with a flickering uncertainty.

"We need to get to safety," Grant urged, urgency lining his voice.

Just as we turned to flee, a brilliant flash lit up the sky, illuminating the cityscape in a blinding glow. My breath caught as I caught a glimpse of something soaring above—something dark and menacing, casting a shadow over the street like a harbinger of doom.

"Julia, run!" Grant shouted, pulling me along, but my feet felt rooted to the ground, my heart pounding in my ears.

In that moment, as the air crackled with energy and the city held its breath, I knew the calm before the storm had shattered. We were no longer just players in a game; we were the center of a brewing tempest, and the world as we knew it was about to change forever.

Chapter 26: Echoes of the Past

The air buzzed with an unusual vibrancy as I strolled through the cobbled streets of Bellwether. The sun, a reluctant artist, splashed hues of amber and gold against the weathered facades, casting shadows that danced like phantoms in the afternoon light. I was on a mission, though my destination was an undefined blur in my mind—a whisper of adventure pulling me toward the forgotten corners of the city. Each step resonated with the low thrum of magic that seemed to pulse beneath the surface, an undercurrent of energy both exhilarating and unnerving.

As I wandered, the familiar strains of laughter and conversation floated on the air, merging seamlessly with the melody of distant music spilling from a nearby café. It was a cacophony that soothed rather than irritated, a reminder that life, even in its chaotic form, carried on around me. I passed a street performer, a woman with wild curls and a voice that echoed through the alleyways, enchanting passersby with a ballad about lost loves and unfulfilled dreams. I stopped for a moment, entranced, caught in the spell of her performance. There was something about her—a spark of connection that whispered of shared experiences and unvoiced fears.

"Hey, love!" she called out, her eyes glinting with mischief as she caught me staring. "You look like someone who could use a song or two. Care to join?"

I laughed, the sound bubbling up unexpectedly, breaking the tension I didn't realize had settled in my chest. "As long as it's not a ballad of doom. I'm not in the mood for heartbreak today."

She grinned, her lips curving with the kind of warmth that makes you feel seen. "No doom here, only the sweet serenade of life's absurdity. Come on, you're among friends."

With a playful nudge, I joined her, losing myself in the lyrics as they wove a tale that echoed my own thoughts and dreams. For those few moments, the world around me melted away, and I felt an exhilarating sense of belonging, as if I were part of something larger than myself. Yet as the song faded, a gentle reminder brushed against my consciousness—the pull of the past, the weight of unfulfilled promises and forgotten dreams, beckoning me to explore the deeper layers of my existence.

The city had its secrets, I knew. Each corner held stories begging to be unearthed, and as I walked away from the café, I could almost hear the echoes of those narratives whispering through the leaves overhead. My feet moved instinctively toward a side street I had never noticed before, its entrance framed by curling ivy and an ornate iron gate that looked like it had been forgotten by time. There was an allure about it, a sense of mystery that sparked my curiosity like kindling to a flame.

Pushing the gate open, I stepped into a narrow pathway lined with the remnants of history—weathered bricks and moss-covered stones leading to an old brownstone, its once-bright paint now dulled by the passage of years. The house loomed like a guardian of secrets, its windows clouded and reflective, holding the faintest traces of life once lived. The scent of damp earth and blooming wildflowers wafted through the air, mingling with the tang of something electric—a promise of magic just beyond reach.

Inside, the atmosphere thickened with history. Dust motes danced in the slanted sunlight filtering through the cracks in the walls. My heart raced as I approached a small table tucked into the corner, cluttered with faded photographs and yellowed letters. But it was the journal that drew my attention, its leather cover cracked and worn, as though it had absorbed the whispers of time itself.

I lifted it gently, as if it might crumble to dust under my touch, and opened it. The ink inside swirled like smoke, forming elegant script that told the tale of a witch from a bygone era. Her words danced across the pages, weaving spells of a different kind—a magic rooted in the earth, entwined with the very fabric of life itself. She wrote of a world where power flowed like water, shaping destinies and intertwining souls. I could feel her energy surging through the ink, a palpable connection bridging the gap between past and present.

As I read, I was drawn deeper into her narrative—stories of love and loss, of battles fought and won, of a magic that thrived on the fringes of reality. It was both a caution and an invitation, an echo of her longing to pass on what she had learned, a legacy that felt intimately entwined with my own burgeoning abilities. I traced my fingers over the pages, absorbing the weight of her words, the sense of urgency that pulsed through her prose. This was not merely a relic; it was a call to action, a challenge to embrace the full extent of my potential.

I had spent so long feeling like a misfit, like my magic was a wildflower trying to blossom in the cracks of a busy pavement. But here, in this forgotten brownstone, I began to see the truth: my power was not an aberration but a continuation of a lineage steeped in resilience and strength. With each turn of the page, I felt the pieces of myself rearranging, like the scattered fragments of a broken mirror slowly finding their way back together.

Outside, the city buzzed with life, unaware of the shift taking place within me. But I could feel it—an electric thrill coursing through my veins as I realized the significance of this moment. I was not merely a spectator in this world; I was an integral part of its tapestry, woven together with those who had come before me, each thread vibrant and alive.

The sun dipped lower in the sky, casting a golden glow over the pages of the journal. I felt a sense of urgency, a need to uncover more, to dive deeper into the echoes of the past. With newfound determination, I closed the journal and tucked it under my arm. This was only the beginning, a spark igniting within me, urging me to explore not just the magic that had been left behind but the magic that lay dormant within myself, waiting to be unleashed.

The sun dipped lower, casting elongated shadows that danced across the worn floorboards as I stepped back into the bustling rhythm of the city. My heart was a wild drum in my chest, fueled by the echoes of the journal's words still swirling in my mind. I clutched it tightly against my side, as if it were a lifeline tethering me to a world I was just beginning to understand. Outside, the streets had transformed; the golden light painted everything with a warm glow, and I could feel the pulse of life buzzing around me, more vibrant than ever.

"Hey, time traveler!" A voice sliced through the murmurs of the crowd, pulling me from my reverie. It was Ben, a local barista with a knack for mixing coffee and banter in equal measure. His unruly curls caught the light like a halo, and his eyes sparkled with mischief as he leaned against the entrance of the café where we often crossed paths. "Did you finally discover the secrets of the universe, or just another dusty old book?"

I chuckled, the energy of the day swelling inside me. "A little of both, actually. You wouldn't believe the stories I found. They're practically begging to be told."

"Ah, the allure of dusty pages! I bet they're not half as intriguing as the one about the barista who can brew the best caramel macchiato in town," he quipped, his grin widening.

"Now that's a legend worth investigating," I shot back, my playful tone matching his. "Perhaps you could give me a private tasting session to unveil your secrets."

"Careful, or I might just charge you admission," he said with a wink, pushing himself off the wall and stepping closer. "But I'm all in if it means I get to hear more about this 'magical' journal of yours. What's the scoop?"

The warmth radiating from his presence felt comforting, like the first sip of coffee on a brisk morning. Yet, a part of me hesitated. The journal was a treasure I had unearthed alone, a piece of my unfolding journey that felt too intimate to share just yet. But something in his gaze urged me to let him in. "It's a tale of power and history, of witches who've walked these streets long before us. It feels... connected, you know?"

"Connected how?" Ben's curiosity was piqued, and I could see the gears turning behind his bright eyes.

"Like I'm part of a lineage that has thrived here—people who had to navigate their own challenges while embracing their magic. It's inspiring, but also a little terrifying." I met his gaze, searching for understanding. "Imagine discovering you're part of something much bigger than yourself."

His expression softened, and he nodded as if grasping the weight of my words. "That sounds incredible, actually. Like you're piecing together a puzzle that could reveal a whole new world." He paused, his brow furrowing slightly. "But if this journal holds so much power, do you feel ready to embrace it?"

"Embrace it?" I echoed, the word hanging heavy in the air. "That's the crux, isn't it? It's a lot to take on. What if I'm not enough?"

"Look at it this way," he replied, his voice steady. "Every great story has its conflicts, right? Heroes who don't feel heroic until they confront their fears. You're on that path, whether you realize it or not."

His words settled over me, a blanket of reassurance. I could almost feel the tendrils of magic from the journal intertwining with my own insecurities, coaxing me toward courage. "You might be onto something," I conceded, a smile creeping onto my lips. "Maybe I just need to lean into this chaos."

"Then lean away! But maybe not too far—there's a fine line between 'leaning in' and face-planting into a pile of chaos." He winked, his playful tone cutting through the weight of the moment, and I couldn't help but laugh.

As the sun sank lower, painting the horizon in shades of lavender and deepening blue, I felt a spark of determination igniting within me. "You know what? I'm going to delve deeper into this journal tonight. There's something waiting for me there, something I need to uncover."

"Want some company?" Ben asked, a hopeful glint in his eye.

"Only if you promise to keep the coffee flowing," I teased, my heart warming at the thought of sharing this journey with him. "And maybe a snack or two. I can't unravel magic on an empty stomach."

"Deal. Just don't blame me when you're too wired to sleep," he shot back, a playful grin spreading across his face.

With a playful shove, I headed toward my apartment, the journal under my arm and the promise of a magical evening awaiting me. I felt the buzz of excitement as I made my way home, my thoughts racing through possibilities. What other secrets would the journal unveil? And what kind of magic had those words woven into the fabric of my destiny?

Once inside, I settled into my favorite reading nook, a cozy spot by the window where the soft glow of a lamp bathed the room in warm light. I cracked open the journal again, its scent of aged paper and ink filling the air. The words seemed to shimmer with an energy of their own, urging me to dive deeper.

I lost myself in the stories of the witch who had written them. She spoke of rituals performed under the full moon, spells cast to protect the city, and the intricacies of magic intertwined with love and heartbreak. Each tale pulled me further into her world, and I began to see parallels between her life and my own. Her struggles mirrored my own fears, and her triumphs filled me with hope.

Then, as I flipped through the pages, a loose sheet fell out, fluttering to the ground like a feather. I picked it up, heart racing as I realized it was a sketch. It depicted a gathering of witches around a fire, their faces illuminated by flickering flames. But at the center of the image stood a figure—a woman whose features were strikingly familiar. I squinted at the drawing, my breath catching in my throat as I recognized the resemblance.

It was me.

The implications hit me like a tidal wave, sending ripples of shock coursing through my veins. What did this mean? Had this witch seen me in a vision, or was this a mere coincidence? As the questions swirled in my mind, I felt a strange energy emanating from the drawing, as if the very essence of the past was reaching out to connect with the present.

Suddenly, the lights flickered, and the air grew thick with anticipation. Something was shifting, and I could feel the magic in the room responding to the energy of the journal, ready to unravel its secrets. My heart raced with the knowledge that I was on the cusp of something profound, an awakening that could change everything.

The room pulsed with a strange energy, as if the very walls were holding their breath, waiting for me to uncover the truth woven into the pages of the journal. I gripped the sketch tighter, my fingers trembling slightly. There was something about that image—something that felt like a mirror reflecting not just my face but the very essence of my being. The flickering light cast shadows that seemed to whisper secrets, igniting my curiosity and fear in equal measure.

With a shaky breath, I turned my focus back to the journal, the pages practically humming with anticipation. The ink, dark and bold, seemed to shift under the dim light, revealing new insights. The witch wrote of a gathering—a convergence of magic and destiny, where the power of the past was summoned to aid the future. Each word pulled me in deeper, weaving an intricate web of connection that spanned time and space. I could almost hear the crackle of the fire from her gatherings, feel the warmth of camaraderie and purpose wrapping around me like a shawl on a chilly evening.

A sudden knock at the door jolted me from my reverie, causing the journal to slip from my hands. It landed softly on the floor, the sketch still in my grip. I glanced at the clock; Ben should have been here by now, bringing his usual charm along with his coffee.

"Coming!" I called, slipping the drawing under the journal as I stood up. A strange thrill coursed through me as I opened the door, half-expecting to see him leaning against the frame with that easy smile.

Instead, I was met with an unexpected visitor—a figure cloaked in shadow, standing just outside the glow of my doorway. My heart thumped loudly in my chest, the warmth of the earlier moment replaced by a chill that crept through my bones. "Can I help you?" I managed to say, my voice steadier than I felt.

The figure stepped into the light, revealing a young woman with raven hair that cascaded around her shoulders like a waterfall of midnight. Her eyes, a vivid green, sparkled with an intensity that held both curiosity and something deeper—something akin to recognition. "You don't know me," she began, her voice soft yet resonant, "but I know you. You're the one who found the journal."

My mind raced. "And you are?"

"Call me Lila." She leaned closer, and I could feel the energy shifting between us, a current of magic that thrummed with urgency. "I've been searching for you."

"For me?" I echoed, trying to mask my bewilderment. "Why?"

She hesitated, as if weighing her words carefully. "Because you're part of something significant. The journal you found—it's not just a relic; it's a map of your destiny."

The weight of her statement settled around us, thickening the air. "A map? For what?"

"Power. Connection. The continuation of an ancient magic that has been waiting for someone like you to awaken it." Her gaze pierced through me, and I felt a strange compulsion to believe her. "It's time for you to step into your role."

My heart raced with a cocktail of exhilaration and trepidation. "You can't just drop something like that and expect me to—what, leap into some ancient sorceress's shoes? I'm still figuring out how to brew a decent cup of tea!"

Lila smiled, a hint of mischief playing at the corners of her mouth. "Trust me, there's more to you than just tea. And it's not about replacing anyone; it's about realizing the potential that's always been within you."

"Potential? Right. I was just told I look like a witch from centuries ago, and now you're telling me I'm part of some grand design." I threw my hands up, pacing the small confines of my apartment. "What if I mess it all up?"

She stepped forward, her intensity grounding me. "We all have doubts, but your journey is already unfolding. The journal has connected you to a legacy that stretches beyond time. You don't have to carry it alone; we can guide you."

"Guide me?" I repeated, my mind racing. "What does that even mean? And what if there are others—"

"Others like us," she interrupted, her tone serious. "Yes, there are. Some who wish to keep the magic hidden, who fear its return. But you can't shy away from what's calling to you. It's your choice, and it's time to make it."

A surge of uncertainty washed over me, a tidal wave of questions crashing against my resolve. But beneath the fear lay an undeniable spark—one that whispered of adventure, of embracing my identity, of stepping into the role I was meant to play. "And if I refuse?"

Lila's expression softened. "Then you might lose the chance to explore a power that could change everything—not just for you, but for the city, for everyone. It's not just about magic; it's about connection, community, and reclaiming what's been lost."

I met her gaze, searching for any hint of deception, but all I found was a fierce determination mirrored in her eyes. "Okay, let's say I'm intrigued. What do we do now?"

"First, we need to gather the others," she said, glancing over her shoulder as if expecting someone to appear. "There's a gathering tonight—a convergence of our kind. You have to be there."

"Tonight?" The urgency in her voice made my pulse quicken. "What if I'm not ready?"

She reached out, gripping my arm gently. "You are more ready than you think. Just trust in the magic that flows through you. It won't lead you astray."

Before I could respond, a loud crash echoed from the street below, followed by a string of frantic shouts. My heart lurched as I turned to the window, peering through the curtains. The world outside was suddenly chaos; figures darted past, and the air was thick with fear. "What's happening?" I asked, panic rising in my throat.

Lila's expression hardened, and she stepped back, her focus sharpening. "They've found us. We have to go, now."

"Who's found us?" I exclaimed, my mind racing. "What do you mean?"

"Those who want to silence the magic," she said urgently, her voice low but firm. "They know you've found the journal. They'll do anything to keep it from you."

As the shouts grew louder, a wave of adrenaline surged through me, a primal instinct urging me to act. I grabbed the journal, tucking it under my arm, and glanced back at Lila. "What do we do?"

"Follow me!" she commanded, and without another thought, I stepped into the unknown, following the stranger who claimed to know my destiny.

As we burst into the hallway, the chaos outside intensified, and I felt a rush of energy surrounding us, a sense of impending fate closing in. We raced toward the stairwell, the weight of my decision hanging heavy in the air. I was about to step into a world filled with magic and danger, and for the first time, I felt the exhilaration of what it truly meant to embrace the unknown.

But just as we reached the door leading to the street, a figure stepped into our path, blocking our escape. My heart dropped as I recognized the fierce gaze—the very eyes I had seen in the drawing. "Not so fast," the figure said, a smirk playing on his lips. "You're not going anywhere without me."

Chapter 27: Rising Tides

The sun dipped low in the sky, casting a molten glow across the rooftops of Vesper City. I stood on my balcony, the air thick with the scent of impending rain, mingling with the city's own peculiar perfume—a heady mix of burnt sugar, asphalt, and something green and alive that always surprised me. As the magic pulsed beneath my feet, it felt like the heartbeat of the earth was thrumming in time with my own. Each beat echoed with the urgency of what lay ahead, a symphony that filled the silence left by the corporate witches who had vanished like shadows at dusk.

I leaned against the wrought-iron railing, its coolness a stark contrast to the warmth of my skin, and closed my eyes. I could almost see the magic swirling, tendrils of shimmering light creeping through the alleys and up the sides of the buildings, drawing closer to me. It was like an old friend reaching out, beckoning, yet there was something distinctly ominous in its embrace. The ritual we had performed—what I had thought would be the culmination of our efforts—now felt like the quiet before a storm.

"Are you going to stare into space all night, or are we going to do something about this?" Grant's voice cut through the growing hum of the magic, his tone a playful jab that I knew concealed genuine concern. He emerged from the shadows of the doorway, his expression as earnest as it was exasperated.

I turned to face him, the soft light framing his features, making his tousled hair look like a halo of chaos. "Maybe I'm just enjoying the view," I replied, a smirk dancing on my lips. "This is prime balcony real estate, after all."

"Right, because watching the magic rise like a bad soufflé is the most scenic view you could ask for," he quipped, crossing his arms over his chest. "I can practically hear the city laughing at us."

"More like we're the punchline of a cosmic joke," I muttered, my playful demeanor slipping for a moment. The weight of the magic felt heavier, pressing against my chest. "We were supposed to fix this, Grant. Not make it worse."

"Hey, don't sell us short just yet. We're resourceful," he said, the corners of his mouth lifting into a smile that made the storm inside me calm, if only briefly. "Remember the time we managed to trap a rogue pixie in your kitchen? If we can do that, we can certainly handle whatever ancient magic is trying to knock down our door."

"That pixie was a nightmare," I shot back, a chuckle escaping despite the tension. "But I see your point. We've faced worse."

With a sigh, I pulled my hair into a loose bun, feeling the familiar ritual ease my mind. My fingers brushed against the nape of my neck, a habit I had picked up during my years of studying. Magic had always been a companion, but lately, it had morphed into something far more unpredictable. "We need to find out where this new surge is coming from. There has to be a focal point."

"Let's hit the archives. If anyone knows the roots of this disturbance, it'll be the dusty old books," Grant suggested, his eyes glinting with enthusiasm. "They might even reveal some dark secret that makes us feel like we're in a magical noir film. Just imagine it: shadowy figures, cryptic messages, and a cliffhanger ending!"

I rolled my eyes but couldn't suppress the grin tugging at my lips. "Right, because ancient tomes are notorious for their cinematic flair."

"Don't knock the classics," he retorted, feigning a dramatic expression. "Besides, think of the adventure. Who doesn't love a bit of risk?"

"Only if it's not me getting chased by eldritch horrors," I shot back, a spark of mischief lighting up my tone.

"Okay, but imagine how cool it would be if it were you leading a heroic escape."

I shook my head, laughing as I pulled on my jacket. "You'd make a terrible director. Come on, let's see if those dusty pages have anything to say about our lovely predicament."

As we descended the stairs to the library, the atmosphere shifted, like the city was holding its breath in anticipation. The old building creaked underfoot, the shelves lined with books that had witnessed centuries of secrets. Grant and I split up, his playful banter fading into the whispers of parchment and ink as I navigated through the maze of texts.

Each title I scanned felt like a tantalizing mystery, the air thick with anticipation. The soft rustle of pages echoed in the silence, drawing me deeper into the past. I finally pulled a hefty volume off the shelf, its spine cracking as I opened it to reveal ornate illustrations of spells long forgotten. I could almost feel the magic flicker around me, as if it were alive, swirling and beckoning.

My fingers brushed over the words, but just as I began to decipher the archaic script, a sharp gasp broke through the stillness. I turned, heart racing, to find a figure looming in the doorway.

"Can I help you?" I asked, my voice steady despite the pulse of adrenaline in my veins. The shadows hid their features, but the glint of something metallic caught my eye, sending a shiver down my spine.

"Do you know what you're playing with?" they asked, the voice low and laden with a gravity that sent chills racing through the air.

The atmosphere shifted, crackling with tension, and for a moment, I could feel the tide of magic swell behind me, as if waiting for a signal to surge forth.

The figure in the doorway shifted, a silhouette framed by the dim light filtering through the old glass windows, illuminating their expression as something between intrigue and caution. I took a tentative step back, my instincts flaring. "Look, if you're here to sell me on a new kind of insurance or something equally terrifying, I'm not interested."

"Insurance?" They chuckled, a sound like gravel crunching underfoot. "Not quite. I'm here to warn you. You're treading on dangerous ground, and it would be wise to turn back before you're swallowed by it."

I felt the prickle of unease snake up my spine, intensifying the hum of magic that had been building inside me. "And you are?" I shot back, feigning nonchalance. "The neighborhood watch for rogue magic? I didn't realize we had such dedicated volunteers."

"Names are of little importance in matters like this. What matters is what you're trying to uncover." They stepped further into the light, revealing a face that was both familiar and unsettling—sharp cheekbones and dark, watchful eyes that seemed to bore into my very soul.

"Finn," I breathed, recognition striking like a bolt of lightning. He had been a fleeting acquaintance during my time at the Academy, known for his talent in divination and his knack for showing up when things were at their most chaotic. "What are you doing here?"

"Following the threads of fate," he replied with a wry smile, his voice smooth and measured. "And trust me, they're tangled. I felt the shift in the energy when you performed the nexus ritual. You've stirred something ancient, and it's awakening."

"Yeah, that's what I was afraid of," I admitted, a frown creasing my forehead. "But I can't just sit back and do nothing. If there's a deeper disturbance, I have to find out what it is before it consumes the city."

Finn tilted his head, studying me with an intensity that felt both unsettling and oddly comforting. "And what makes you think you're ready for it? This is not just another spell gone awry. The magic you've unleashed has roots that dig deep into the city's very essence. You're not playing with fire anymore; you're dancing with a wildfire."

I squared my shoulders, the determination that had fueled my every decision surging to the surface. "I've faced worse things than fire, Finn. If there's a chance to help, I have to take it. Otherwise, it's not just the magic that'll burn; it's everyone I care about."

"Spoken like a true heroine," he replied, an edge of admiration creeping into his tone. "But even heroines need allies. You can't fight this alone. If you truly want to uncover the source, you'll need to understand the history—the sacrifices made to keep it at bay."

Grant's footsteps echoed from the back of the library, drawing closer. I glanced over my shoulder, silently gauging his reaction. Finn and I had an undeniable spark, a tension thick enough to slice through the air, and I didn't want my partner to feel sidelined.

"Looks like we have a guest," I said, raising my voice slightly to summon Grant. "Care to join the party, Finn? I think we're going to need every bit of knowledge we can gather."

"Let's hope I'm not the only one who brings something to the table," he said, his smirk returning, but it didn't escape my notice that his gaze shifted to Grant with a hint of calculation.

"Grant, this is Finn," I introduced, trying to keep my tone light. "A self-proclaimed expert on the ancient and arcane."

Grant stepped into the room, his brow furrowed as he took in the scene—the two of us standing too close, the charged energy in the air palpable. "Right. So, are we having a seance or what?" He leaned casually against the nearest bookshelf, arms crossed, though I could see the glint of competitiveness in his eyes.

"More like a strategy session," Finn replied, unperturbed. "If you're willing to listen, that is."

"Great, because we all know how much I love taking orders from charming strangers," Grant replied, a teasing lilt to his voice. "But if you've got some sage advice on how to deal with the magical apocalypse, I'm all ears."

"Consider this your initiation," Finn said, his tone slipping into something more serious. "The magic you unleashed has stirred forces that have lain dormant for centuries. To truly understand its nature, we need to look at the old archives—not just the books, but the history embedded in the very stones of this city."

I glanced at Grant, and his expression mirrored my own—a blend of skepticism and curiosity. "And how exactly do you propose we do that?" I asked, turning back to Finn.

He stepped closer, lowering his voice as if sharing a secret. "There's a hidden chamber beneath the library, an old sanctum where the founding witches stored their most dangerous spells. If we can access it, we might find answers—or at least the key to controlling what you've unleashed."

"And how do we get there?" Grant asked, his skepticism softened by intrigue. "Because I'm assuming it's not marked on the tourist maps."

"No," Finn said, a flicker of a grin playing at the corners of his mouth. "But I might know a way. The entrance has been concealed by wards, but I can break them. You two just need to follow my lead."

"Lead the way, oh fearless leader," I said, sarcasm dripping from my words, but the thrill of possibility surged within me. We were stepping into the unknown, diving deeper into a mystery that threatened to engulf us.

Finn shot me a sidelong glance, the weight of his attention both exhilarating and unnerving. "Keep your wits about you. What lies beneath this city is not for the faint of heart."

"Please, my heart's been through worse," I replied, feeling the energy of our surroundings pulse in agreement. With a nod, Finn turned, leading us deeper into the library, the air thick with anticipation.

As we followed, shadows flickered along the walls, the scent of aged parchment mingling with something darker, more foreboding.

The stakes had risen, and the tide of magic continued to swell, a tempest threatening to break upon us at any moment. The hidden depths of the city awaited, a labyrinth of secrets just beyond our grasp, and I was ready to face whatever lay ahead.

Finn led us deeper into the bowels of the library, the shadows thickening as we descended. The air was heavy with the scent of dust and secrets, each step echoing in the dimly lit corridor like a heartbeat of its own. The atmosphere felt charged, crackling with energy that made my skin tingle, as if the very stones beneath us were alive and listening.

"You're sure about this?" I whispered to Finn, trying to pierce the murky uncertainty that shrouded our path. "You know where you're going?"

"Trust me," he said, glancing back over his shoulder, his dark eyes glimmering with an excitement that was almost infectious. "This place holds more than just dusty tomes. The founding witches poured their magic into the very walls, binding their power here. If we're going to understand what's happening above, we need to tap into what lies below."

Grant walked beside me, his expression a mix of skepticism and curiosity. "So we're heading into the witchy underworld to find answers about the magic that's gone rogue. What could possibly go wrong?"

"Besides everything?" I replied, trying to lighten the mood, but the weight of the situation pressed heavily upon me. "Let's just hope we don't run into any disgruntled spirits or something worse."

Finn smirked, clearly enjoying our banter, but there was an edge to his demeanor that suggested he was well aware of the dangers we faced. "You'll want to be on your guard. This chamber was designed to protect its secrets, and not everyone who enters is meant to leave."

Just as he spoke, we reached a heavy wooden door adorned with intricate carvings of serpents entwined around a staff. It seemed to pulse with its own energy, a rhythmic thrumming that resonated in my bones. Finn raised his hand, fingers poised above a series of glyphs that glowed faintly in response to his touch.

"Stand back," he said, and I felt a rush of adrenaline as I took a step away from the door, instinctively moving closer to Grant.

With a swift motion, Finn pressed his palm against the wood, and the air around us crackled. The glyphs flared to life, casting an eerie green light that illuminated the chamber. I could almost taste the magic in the air—sharp and electric, like biting into a fresh apple.

The door creaked open, revealing a cavernous room beyond. Inside, shelves lined the walls, filled to the brim with tomes that looked as though they had been there for centuries, their spines cracked and worn. In the center stood a stone altar, ancient runes etched into its surface. A dull, pulsing light emanated from it, beckoning us forward.

"Welcome to the heart of Vesper City," Finn said, a note of reverence in his voice. "This is where the power was harnessed, contained to protect the city from itself."

As we stepped inside, I felt the atmosphere shift, thickening like molasses. It was intoxicating, yet laced with a fear that crawled beneath my skin. I approached the altar, entranced by the light that seemed to resonate with the very essence of magic itself.

"What do we do now?" I asked, trying to focus through the haze of excitement and apprehension.

"We need to read the runes," Finn instructed, moving closer. "They hold the key to understanding the source of the magic rising in the city. If we can decipher them, we might find a way to control what you've unleashed."

I knelt beside him, brushing the dust from the surface of the altar, and leaned in to examine the ancient carvings. The symbols were both beautiful and intricate, twisting together in a dance of power. The moment I touched one, a rush of energy surged through me, pulling me into a vision.

I was standing in the same chamber, but it was alive with people—witches dressed in flowing robes, their hands raised as they chanted in unison. The air hummed with magic, vibrant and fierce. Then, suddenly, I was thrown into chaos. The ground shook, and dark tendrils of shadow began to creep in from the edges of my vision, swallowing the light and the witches whole.

I gasped, the vision breaking as I pulled my hand back, heart racing. "We have to be careful," I said, breathless. "It's not just about control. There's something dark here, something that wants to be free."

"What did you see?" Grant asked, concern flickering in his eyes.

"A warning," I replied, shaken. "If we don't figure this out, the magic could turn against us."

Finn's expression darkened. "That's why we need to decipher these runes. They'll tell us what was sealed away and why it was hidden."

Together, we worked to translate the symbols, my mind racing with possibilities. The runes whispered secrets, and I could feel the magic coiling around us, wrapping us in its embrace. But with each deciphered line, the weight of dread settled deeper in my stomach.

"Here," Finn said, tracing a particularly intricate symbol. "This one speaks of a 'veil'—a barrier that keeps the dark magic at bay. It's been weakened, perhaps by the nexus ritual. That's why the city feels alive, why the magic is rushing in."

"What happens if that barrier breaks entirely?" I asked, the implications sending a shiver down my spine.

"The darkness will flood in," Finn replied, voice low. "We could face something beyond our comprehension. We have to act quickly."

Just then, the ground trembled beneath us, a low rumble that felt like the city itself was awakening. The lights flickered, and I could feel the energy in the room shift violently, as if the very walls were protesting our presence. I exchanged glances with Grant, his jaw set with determination.

"Let's finish this," he said, his voice steady despite the chaos brewing around us.

We leaned back over the altar, focusing on the runes. The magic pulsed in time with our racing hearts, a rhythm that felt both exhilarating and terrifying. The air grew thick, and a sense of urgency washed over me.

But then, without warning, the altar flared with blinding light, and a surge of power knocked us backward. I landed hard against the stone floor, gasping for breath, as shadows writhed at the edges of the chamber, hungry and restless.

"Stay together!" Finn shouted, his voice cutting through the chaos. "We need to hold the energy! Focus on the runes!"

But as I scrambled to my feet, I felt a presence shift behind me—a chilling sensation that froze me in place. I turned slowly, dread coiling in my gut, to see a figure emerging from the shadows, cloaked in darkness, their face obscured.

"What have you awakened?" the figure hissed, their voice a slithering whisper that sent a chill through the air.

Panic surged as the realization settled in. We weren't alone. The very darkness we sought to contain was here, and it was ready to reclaim what had been lost.

Chapter 28: The Final Ritual

The night stretches across the skyline like a velvet blanket, speckled with stars that twinkle like scattered diamonds, each one holding a secret of its own. The moon hangs low and full, casting a silver glow over the East River, illuminating the waves as they ripple like liquid mercury beneath my feet. I stand on the rooftop, the wind whispering against my skin, carrying with it the salty scent of the ocean mingled with the earthy aroma of rain-soaked asphalt. This night, heavy with expectation, feels alive, as if the city itself is holding its breath, bracing for the weight of what is to come.

I clutch the candles in my hands, each one a labor of love, crafted with painstaking care. They are not just wax and wick; they are vessels of my magic, infused with the essence of my emotions, hopes, and fears. The vibrant colors swirl through the candles—deep indigos, fiery reds, and soft, shimmering greens—each hue resonating with a different part of my soul. As I arrange them in a perfect circle, my fingers tremble slightly, a mixture of excitement and apprehension. There's a fragile beauty in this ritual, a rhythm that demands respect and reverence.

Beside me, Grant stands like a lighthouse in the storm, his presence grounding me. The flickering flames cast playful shadows across his chiseled jaw, highlighting the determination etched into his features. He glances at me, a hint of a smile playing on his lips, and I feel an unfamiliar warmth bloom in my chest. There's a connection between us, forged in the fires of our shared struggles, an understanding that transcends words. "You ready for this?" he asks, his voice low and steady, laced with an undercurrent of concern.

I nod, though my throat feels tight, as if the words are caught somewhere between my heart and my lips. "As ready as I'll ever be." The honesty in my reply hangs in the air, mingling with the scent of smoke and magic. He takes my hand, a simple gesture that sends a surge of energy through me. It's reassuring, a reminder that I'm not alone in this moment. Together, we step into the circle, and I can feel the energy shifting, swirling around us like an unseen tide.

With a deep breath, I close my eyes, letting the world around me fade into the background. I focus on the flickering candles, the way the flames dance and sway, their light reflecting the myriad emotions swirling within me. I extend my hands, palms facing down, feeling the pulse of the earth beneath my feet. The magic is there, simmering just beneath the surface, eager to be unleashed. It whispers to me, seductive and demanding, promising power beyond my imagination. But I know better. I've learned that magic comes at a cost, and the more I give, the more it takes.

As I begin the incantation, the words spill from my lips like a long-forgotten melody, ancient and familiar. Each syllable resonates with the energy around us, weaving a tapestry of light and shadow. The flames flicker violently, and I sense the power responding, stretching and straining against the restraints I've placed upon it. My heart races, a wild drumbeat that matches the rhythm of the city below, a cacophony of life and energy thrumming through my veins. I push through the initial resistance, grounding myself in the moment, reminding myself of why I'm here.

"Just let it flow, Mia," Grant urges, his voice a calm anchor amidst the tempest brewing inside me. I steal a glance at him, and for a fleeting moment, the chaos melts away. His eyes are locked onto mine, filled with an unwavering trust that ignites a fire within me. I swallow hard, allowing that trust to guide me deeper into the magic, deeper into the storm.

The candles flicker brighter, their flames intertwining, casting shadows that twist and writhe around us. It's exhilarating and terrifying all at once. I can feel the magic demanding more, pleading with me to surrender completely, but I resist, holding on to my strength. I draw upon the energy of the city, the pulse of life that has become a part of me, channeling it into the candles. One by one, they respond, flaring to life with a brilliant intensity that sends sparks dancing into the night.

A sudden gust of wind sweeps across the rooftop, extinguishing a few of the flames, but I don't falter. "We're not done yet," I declare, determination surging through me. I reignite the flames with a snap of my fingers, the energy crackling with renewed vigor. The wind howls, swirling around us, as if the very elements are testing my resolve. I can feel the tension building, a charged current thrumming beneath the surface, threatening to explode at any moment.

"Hold steady," Grant advises, his voice a steadying force amidst the chaos. "We've got this." And somehow, those words embolden me, fortifying my resolve. I focus, letting the magic pulse through me like a living entity, shaping it with intention, pouring my heart into the ritual. Each candle represents a piece of my journey, the struggles I've faced, the battles I've fought, and the love I've found along the way.

As the final incantation rolls off my tongue, the energy surges to a crescendo, enveloping us in a cocoon of light. I can feel the magic merging, swirling together like a storm ready to break free. My heart races, and I grip Grant's hand tighter, feeling the warmth of his skin against mine. This moment is everything—the culmination of my journey, the risk and reward intertwining in a beautiful dance.

And then, as if the universe has decided to intervene, a crack of thunder reverberates through the air, shaking the rooftop beneath our feet. The city lights flicker in response, a symphony of illumination and shadow. My heart skips a beat, and for a moment, doubt creeps in. What have I unleashed? But I push it down, anchoring myself in the strength of our shared purpose.

"Don't let go," I whisper, my voice barely audible over the roar of the wind. Grant squeezes my hand, his grip firm and unwavering, a silent promise that we will see this through together. With one final push, I release the energy, allowing the magic to explode in a brilliant display of light and color that bathes the rooftop in a kaleidoscope of brilliance.

The moment of release sends a shockwave through the air, a burst of energy that feels almost tangible, like a vibrant thread weaving itself into the fabric of the night. I watch in awe as the light from the candles dances in time with the rhythm of my heartbeat, swirling and shifting like a living entity. It's a breathtaking spectacle, but I can't let my awe distract me. There's work to be done.

"Okay, Mia, focus," I whisper to myself, though my eyes keep darting to Grant, whose steady gaze remains fixed on the center of the candlelit circle. The way he stands, resolute and unwavering, reminds me of an ancient oak tree weathering a storm. There's a fire in his eyes, an understanding that goes deeper than mere words. As I channel more energy into the ritual, I sense a pulse—a heartbeat—rising from the very ground beneath us. It thrums in harmony with my own, the essence of the city merging with my magic.

"Can you feel that?" I ask, a mix of wonder and fear threading through my voice. "It's like the whole city is... alive."

"It's not just alive, Mia. It's awake," Grant replies, a sly smile tugging at the corners of his lips. "You're not just summoning the magic; you're igniting the spirit of Brooklyn."

His confidence bolsters me, fueling my resolve. I let out a breath I didn't know I was holding and press forward. The ritual demands my full attention, and I draw the energy into me, weaving it like fine silk through my fingers as I recite the incantation with deliberate precision. The words seem to echo off the walls of the surrounding buildings, reverberating in the stillness of the night.

But the wind has different plans. It picks up suddenly, swirling around us like an unpredictable dancer, pulling at my hair and stinging my cheeks with a playful ferocity. The candles flicker wildly, their flames now a chaotic mess, threatening to extinguish under the onslaught of nature. I grit my teeth, pushing back against the force.

"Did someone order a storm?" I quip, trying to infuse levity into the tension. "I thought we were just lighting candles here."

Grant chuckles, his deep voice resonating amidst the chaos. "Maybe the universe decided it needed a little extra drama for your big finish."

My heart pounds, exhilarated by the banter and the wildness of the moment. "You know I prefer my drama with a side of caution."

"Caution has never been your style," he counters, his eyes glinting with mischief. "Just don't blow us off this rooftop while you're at it."

I shake my head, laughter bubbling within me, breaking the seriousness of the ritual just enough to give me a needed boost. But then I return to the task at hand, centering myself amidst the tempest. I focus on the candles, feeling the heat of their flames kissing my skin, reminding me of the warmth of hope. I begin to weave a protective barrier around us, pulling on the energy of the city and my own magic, forcing it to bend to my will.

As I draw the barrier tighter, the wind howls, and for a split second, I fear I may have overreached. The air thickens, crackling with tension, and I can almost hear the city's heartbeat quickening, as if it senses the impending storm. The candles flare, their light illuminating the rooftop in a blinding array of colors, swirling like a painting come to life.

"Mia, look!" Grant points, his expression shifting from amusement to awe.

My gaze follows his, and I gasp. From the circle of flames, tendrils of light begin to rise, twisting and turning, reaching up toward the sky like the fingers of a giant awakening from slumber. They pulse with an energy that feels ancient and wise, and I know, in the depths of my heart, that I'm tapping into something far greater than myself.

"Holy—" I stammer, and then cut myself off, realizing that swearing might not be the best addition to this moment of magic. "This is incredible."

Grant nods, his expression serious now, the light from the candles reflecting in his eyes like shards of glass. "Just remember to keep your focus. We're on the edge of something powerful, and it can easily turn on us."

I nod, a twinge of apprehension sparking within me, but I can't allow fear to take root. "Right. I've got this." With renewed determination, I dive deeper into the incantation, each word flowing more freely than the last. The energy surrounds us, filling the air with an electric hum, vibrating through my bones.

Then, just as I begin to feel the tide turning in my favor, the candles sputter violently, their flames flickering as if they're caught in a battle of their own. I bite my lip, panic flaring. "What's happening?"

Grant steps closer, eyes narrowed. "You're pushing too hard. You need to ease up."

"Easier said than done!" I shout over the howling wind, frustration bubbling to the surface. "This is a delicate operation!"

"I know," he replies, voice steady and calm, a soothing balm against the chaos. "But you can't force it. Magic responds to intention, not aggression."

His words hit home. I remember the moments in my life when I'd fought against currents only to find peace in letting go. Taking a deep breath, I allow the tension to drain from my shoulders, releasing the grip I've had on the energy. I breathe out, my exhale mingling with the wind, and with it, I send my intention into the night.

The candles respond instantly, flames steadying as the wild energy shifts, swirling instead in a harmonious dance. Light cascades around us, enveloping us in a cocoon of brilliance. The wind begins to calm, settling into a gentle breeze that carries the warmth of summer, and for a heartbeat, it feels like the world has stopped.

"I think we're getting somewhere," I say, my voice trembling with excitement.

Grant smiles, a grin that lights up his entire face. "Now that's the spirit."

As the final words of the incantation slip from my lips, the tendrils of light reach higher, coiling around us like a protective embrace. The city breathes in unison with us, the air thick with magic and possibility. I can feel the essence of Brooklyn surging through me, a connection that runs deeper than the pavement underfoot.

And just when I think I've mastered the rhythm, a shadow flits across the rooftop, a figure materializing from the darkness like a specter summoned by the magic itself. I freeze, a chill racing down my spine as my heart stutters in my chest. Who—or what—was intruding upon my ritual? The world, once bathed in light, suddenly dims, and I'm left grappling with an uncertainty I hadn't anticipated.

The figure looming at the edge of our candlelit circle sends a chill racing down my spine, cutting through the warmth of the ritual like a knife. It's as if the shadows have taken form, twisting into a shape that is both familiar and foreign, cloaked in a darkness that feels alive. I can hardly make out the features, but the presence is undeniable—intense, almost suffocating in its intensity.

"Who goes there?" I manage to call, my voice surprisingly steady despite the adrenaline coursing through my veins. Grant tenses beside me, his protective instincts flaring.

"Just a friend," the figure replies, the voice smooth as silk yet laced with an undercurrent of mischief. "Or perhaps an old acquaintance."

Recognition slams into me like a tidal wave, and I squint against the candlelight, struggling to comprehend what my instincts are screaming at me. "Lila?" I gasp, disbelief making my heart race faster than ever.

She steps into the light, and the flickering flames reveal her—an apparition from my past, with dark curls framing her face and an enigmatic smile that used to make my heart flutter. But there's something unsettling in her gaze, a glimmer that suggests she's changed in ways I can't quite fathom. "Miss me?"

"Not exactly on my list of priorities," I retort, fighting to maintain my composure. "What are you doing here?"

"Oh, you know," she shrugs, feigning nonchalance. "Just popped by to see how my little sister's big night was going. It's a family affair after all, isn't it?"

"Family?" Grant echoes, eyebrows raised, the protective barrier between us seemingly tightening. "You two are related?"

"Half-sisters," I clarify, not taking my eyes off Lila. "Though I use the term loosely."

Lila rolls her eyes, stepping further into the circle, and the energy shifts. The candles flicker ominously as though reacting to her presence, shadows dancing wildly around us. "Always so dramatic, Mia. But I'm not here to reminisce. I've come for something far more important."

"Great, just what I need tonight—more drama," I mutter under my breath, shifting my weight to prepare for whatever curveball she's about to throw my way.

"Isn't that what this whole ritual is about?" Lila says, her tone suddenly sharp. "You're playing with forces you don't fully understand. I thought I'd save you from making a colossal mistake."

"And what makes you think I need saving?" I counter, feeling my pulse quicken. "I've come this far without your help."

"Oh, but you're wrong." She leans in closer, her eyes glinting with a dangerous mix of excitement and something darker. "I know exactly what you're about to do, and believe me, it's not just magic you're unleashing tonight."

My breath catches in my throat as the weight of her words settles around me. The candles flicker more violently now, and I can feel the protective barrier I'd erected starting to waver. "What do you mean?"

"It's not just about you anymore, Mia. You're connected to something much larger, and you may not be the one in control."

I glance at Grant, whose expression is a mix of confusion and concern. "What is she talking about?" he asks, keeping his voice low, as if afraid that raising it might shatter the fragile balance of power we've just built.

"She's just trying to get into your head," Lila interjects, her voice dripping with mockery. "But you don't have to listen to him. You know what you need to do. Let go."

"Let go?" I challenge, indignation sparking in my chest. "Letting go is exactly what got me into this mess in the first place."

She chuckles, a sound that sends a shiver down my spine. "Ah, but think of the freedom you could gain. All that power—just waiting for you to grasp it."

The air thickens with tension, and I'm torn, the allure of her words weaving through the resolve I've worked so hard to cultivate. I can feel the pull of the magic thrumming beneath the surface, whispering promises of power and liberation, tempting me to dive deeper into its depths.

"Just because you're my sister doesn't mean I trust you," I say, my voice steadier now. "What do you really want, Lila?"

She steps closer, the light of the candles illuminating her face in a way that feels almost ethereal. "I want what's best for you, dear sister.

I want you to embrace your true potential, to stop hiding behind your fears. The city is alive, and it needs someone like you to harness that energy. To do what must be done."

A bolt of apprehension strikes through me, mingling with anger. "And you think I'll just take your word for it? After everything?"

"I'm not asking you to trust me; I'm asking you to trust yourself." Her voice softens, an almost soothing lilt that makes me want to believe her. "Think about it—what if you're stronger than you ever realized? What if you could change everything?"

The flames flicker wildly in response to her words, and I can feel the energy in the air shifting, bending to her will. The tendrils of light I summoned earlier pulse, threatening to unravel at the seams.

"Don't listen to her!" Grant urges, taking a step forward. "Mia, you know better than to let her in. She's playing you."

"I'm not playing anyone!" Lila snaps, her voice rising. "I'm offering you a chance to finally break free from all the limitations you've placed on yourself. I can help you."

"Help me?" I echo, incredulous. "You've always been more interested in what you can gain than what's best for anyone else. Why should I believe this is any different?"

Lila smiles, but it doesn't reach her eyes. "Because I'm tired of being in the shadows, tired of letting you have all the fun. I want in on this. Together, we could reshape everything—just imagine!"

"Imagine what?" I challenge, feeling the tension in the air thickening like a brewing storm. "Your idea of reshaping things involves a lot more chaos than I'm willing to unleash."

The energy pulses around us, the candles flickering as if caught in a brewing tempest. I can feel the magic responding to my emotions, urging me to make a decision, to take a leap into the unknown. It's tempting. So very tempting.

"Join me, Mia. We can be unstoppable," Lila urges, her voice a silken whisper that coils around my resolve, trying to draw me in.

"All I'm asking is for you to take my hand and embrace the power that's waiting for you."

In that moment, the wind howls, a fierce gust that sends the candles wavering dangerously. I feel the ground beneath my feet shift, as if the very earth is shifting to respond to our standoff. Grant's grip tightens around my hand, a silent reminder of the strength we share.

"Choose wisely," Lila warns, the glimmer in her eyes shifting to something colder, something calculating. "This is your moment, Mia. Don't let it slip away."

And in that charged silence, I realize that whatever decision I make could alter the very fabric of my reality, sending ripples through the city and beyond. But as I stand on the precipice of choice, uncertainty looms like a dark cloud overhead, and the weight of the moment hangs heavy, ready to shatter everything I know.

Chapter 29: A New Dawn

The city sprawled beneath us, a canvas splashed with colors both vibrant and muted, where shadows danced playfully with the morning light. I breathed deeply, savoring the crisp air tinged with the scent of fresh coffee and the lingering essence of last night's rain. It felt like the world was waking anew, each sound more pronounced—the distant honking of taxis, the soft hum of conversations, the rustle of leaves stirred by a gentle breeze. I turned to Grant, who stood beside me, his silhouette a comforting presence against the backdrop of a city that had become a character in our story, rich with layers and secrets.

"Do you think it's always going to feel like this?" I asked, my voice barely above a whisper. There was an anticipation in the air, a sense of something precious and fleeting, and I wanted to hold onto it for as long as I could.

He looked at me, his dark eyes glimmering with a warmth that melted away any remnants of doubt. "I hope so," he replied, his voice steady and deep. "But I think we'll have to keep reminding ourselves that it's okay to feel everything—to embrace the chaos, the quiet moments, and everything in between."

I smiled, feeling a flutter in my chest, like the softest caress of a butterfly's wings. His words wrapped around me, a cocoon of comfort. We both knew the road ahead wouldn't be easy, but standing there, hand in hand, it was as if we had cast aside the burdens of the past and stepped into the sunlight with a newfound resolve.

As we descended the rooftop stairs, the city's heartbeat echoed in my ears, a steady thrum that felt in sync with my own. Each step felt deliberate, a promise to myself that I would not shy away from the challenges that lay ahead. When we reached the street, the bustling energy of Brooklyn embraced us, and I couldn't help but marvel at how vibrant the world felt. The sidewalk shimmered with the remnants of rain, reflecting the sunlight like a thousand tiny diamonds scattered across the pavement.

We meandered through the streets, past familiar haunts and hidden gems, our fingers entwined, a silent declaration of unity against the uncertainties of life. A street performer strummed a guitar on the corner, his soulful melody weaving through the air, drawing me into a moment of joy and spontaneity. I found myself swaying to the rhythm, my heart light, as if the worries that had clouded my mind were melting away with each note.

"Want to join in?" Grant teased, his eyes sparkling with mischief.

"Are you suggesting we dance in the street?" I shot back, arching an eyebrow, half-serious but ready to indulge in a bit of recklessness.

"Why not? We've survived chaos before; a little public dancing seems tame in comparison." He grinned, and the infectious lightness of his spirit pulled me closer.

With a playful tug, he led me into the small crowd gathering around the performer. There we were, two souls intertwined amidst strangers, swaying and laughing as the world spun around us. It was absurd and beautiful, the kind of moment that felt like it belonged in a storybook. I closed my eyes, letting the music wash over me, forgetting everything else—worries, responsibilities, even the shadow of doubt that often lingered at the edges of my mind.

After what felt like a blissful eternity, we stepped away from the crowd, breathless and exhilarated. The world around us was alive, and it was intoxicating. As we wandered further down the street, the aroma of freshly baked pastries wafted through the air, drawing us into a quaint little café. Inside, the atmosphere was warm and inviting, with cozy nooks perfect for lingering over coffee and conversation. We settled into a corner booth, the sunlight streaming through the window, painting our faces with golden hues.

I leaned back, my heart still racing from the dance, and gazed at Grant, who was busy scanning the menu. "So, what's your plan for today? Any grand adventures on the horizon?"

He looked up, a thoughtful expression crossing his face. "I was thinking we could go to that new art exhibit at the gallery downtown. It's supposed to be spectacular, and I know how much you love getting lost in a painting."

My heart swelled at the thought. Art had always been my sanctuary, a place where I could escape into worlds crafted by the hands of others. "That sounds perfect," I replied, my excitement bubbling over. "I've heard whispers of a piece that's supposed to change your perspective on everything."

"Good," he said with a grin, "because I think we could both use a little perspective shift after the week we've had." His voice dropped into a conspiratorial tone. "And who knows what else we might find in the chaos of the city?"

As we placed our orders, I felt a current of anticipation coursing through me. It wasn't just about the art; it was about everything that lay ahead, the possibility of new experiences, the unpredictable journey of discovery that awaited us. With Grant by my side, I felt emboldened, ready to explore not just the vibrant streets of Brooklyn but the intricate landscapes of our lives intertwined.

With coffee steaming between us and laughter bubbling up like the rich foam of a cappuccino, I felt the weight of the past begin to shift, replaced by a delicate sense of hope. The sun bathed the café in a warm embrace, and for the first time in what felt like an eternity, I allowed myself to believe that this was only the beginning.

The café buzzed with the comforting hum of conversation, the clinking of cups, and the rich scent of roasted beans wrapping around us like a soft blanket. I cradled my mug between my palms, the warmth seeping into my skin, grounding me in this moment. Across from me, Grant studied the walls adorned with quirky art pieces that seemed to share the same spirit as our impromptu dance earlier. They reflected a chaotic yet beautiful tapestry of life—a reminder that every brushstroke tells a story, just like us.

"What do you think those paintings are trying to say?" I mused, nodding toward a wild splatter of colors that made my heart race and my head spin all at once. "Is it a celebration of chaos or an existential cry for help?"

He laughed, a deep, melodious sound that turned heads, and I felt a warmth blossom within me. "Probably both. Maybe that's the beauty of it; life is a jumbled mess of celebration and despair, and we're all just trying to find our place within it."

"I like that," I said, tilting my head as I considered his words. "Finding beauty in the chaos. I think I'll adopt that philosophy, especially if it means I can dodge a few of my responsibilities."

"Ah, the classic avoidance technique," he teased, a playful glint in his eye. "I've heard it's an effective coping mechanism."

We shared a knowing look, both of us acutely aware of the delicate threads connecting our lives—the worries about the future, the weight of unspoken fears. As our laughter faded, a comfortable silence enveloped us, punctuated by the occasional sip of coffee and the soft murmur of other patrons. It was in this sanctuary of warmth and familiarity that I felt the flicker of something profound—a connection deeper than I had ever experienced.

"Can I ask you something?" I ventured, breaking the silence like a fragile bubble.

"Of course," he replied, leaning forward, his expression earnest.

"What if we—" I hesitated, the words feeling heavy on my tongue. "What if we found a way to keep this feeling? This moment, this connection? How do we ensure we don't lose ourselves to the chaos of everyday life?"

His brow furrowed in contemplation, and for a heartbeat, I feared I'd veered too far into treacherous waters. "You're asking the big questions today," he said slowly, a hint of a smile breaking through his seriousness. "But I think it comes down to being intentional. Choosing each other every day, amidst the chaos, no matter how mundane or messy it gets."

I nodded, the idea resonating within me like a melody I had yet to fully understand. "So, you're suggesting we start a daily ritual? Coffee dates, spontaneous adventures, and maybe the occasional dance-off in the middle of a busy street?"

"Exactly!" he exclaimed, his enthusiasm contagious. "And who knows? Maybe we can even create our own little chaos. A beautiful mess that's uniquely ours."

The weight of my worries lightened further, and I could almost see the framework of our shared life taking shape—a vibrant collage of laughter, challenges, and spontaneous moments, piecing together our story with each passing day.

Just then, a sudden commotion outside interrupted our reverie. A loud crash echoed, followed by the frantic shouts of an unseen crowd. I glanced toward the window, curiosity piquing. "What on earth is going on out there?"

"I think we should investigate," Grant said, his eyes sparkling with mischief.

We quickly slipped out of the café, the cool air hitting us like a refreshing wave. The street was alive with activity; a small crowd had gathered around a fallen vendor cart that had overturned, scattering fresh produce and bright flowers everywhere. It was an unexpected spectacle, the chaos of humanity spilling into the streets in a burst of laughter and concern.

"Look at this," I laughed, gesturing toward a young girl gleefully trying to catch a wayward apple that rolled past her. "The chaos just got a little more colorful."

Grant's gaze turned serious as he watched the scene unfold, and I could see the wheels turning in his mind. "You know, sometimes these moments are the best. Life has a way of forcing us to pause and enjoy the messiness."

I nodded, watching as the vendor, a stout man with a thick mustache and an infectious smile, began to collect his wares with the help of enthusiastic bystanders. It struck me then how life, with all its unpredictability, could weave threads of connection even in chaos. "Should we help?" I asked, suddenly feeling that familiar tug toward community involvement that had defined my earlier days.

Grant grinned, and without a word, we rushed over to lend a hand. I bent to pick up a squashed tomato, the bright red juice staining my fingers. "Guess this one is a casualty of chaos," I quipped, tossing it aside. "But it could still make for a decent sauce if we get creative."

"Now you're just being optimistic," he chuckled, handing a sprightly bouquet of daisies to the vendor, who was watching us with a bemused expression.

As we worked alongside the vendor and the crowd, laughter and shared stories flowed freely, binding us in an unexpected camaraderie. It was as if the universe had conspired to remind us of the beauty in community, in coming together despite our differences. With each passing moment, I felt my heart swell, not just with joy but with a sense of purpose.

After what felt like an eternity of joyful chaos, the cart was uprighted, and the vendor beamed at us. "Thank you, thank you! I don't know what I would have done without you two!" His gratitude was palpable, a warm embrace that wrapped around us like the afternoon sun.

"Just doing our part," I said, grinning widely. "Consider it a community service—next time, maybe save the performance for the street fair!"

With a playful wink, I watched as the vendor went back to arranging his goods, the vibrant colors of fruits and flowers standing proudly against the backdrop of an ever-bustling Brooklyn.

As we stepped back, Grant and I shared a knowing glance, a spark of realization passing between us. The chaos, the spontaneity—it was all part of the life we were beginning to craft together. In that moment, I understood that love didn't require perfection; it thrived in the messy, unpredictable bits of life where we dared to embrace the unexpected.

The moment was electric, a mingling of excitement and uncertainty that wrapped around us like the soft tendrils of steam rising from the vendor's cart. I glanced at Grant, whose face mirrored my own mix of exhilaration and newfound purpose. The streets had turned into an unexpected stage, and we were the leading players, dancing in the chaos of the city, unafraid to seize the day.

"Okay, what's next, partner in crime?" I asked, a teasing lilt in my voice as I nudged his shoulder. "Do we take this show on the road or maybe plan a flash mob for the weekend?"

Grant laughed, the sound brightening the air around us. "Only if you promise to wear something fabulous. I won't be outshined by your dance moves." He gestured dramatically to the vibrant flowers strewn across the pavement, clearly relishing the moment.

"Fabulous? Oh, darling, you have no idea how fabulous I can be!" I replied, placing my hands on my hips in mock defiance, then swirled around to grab a handful of daisies. "Here, these are my contribution to your wardrobe." I tossed them at him, the petals catching the light as they floated through the air.

"Perfect! I always wanted to look like a walking flower shop," he deadpanned, catching a few blooms before they fell. "But in all seriousness, we should find something more exciting to do. The city is full of surprises just waiting for us."

"Lead the way, oh fearless leader!" I gestured grandly, and he took my hand, pulling me along the street. We wandered through the lively market, our laughter echoing in the spaces between vendors hawking their wares. Each stall was a treasure trove of oddities—handcrafted jewelry, colorful fabrics, and artisan cheeses, creating a tapestry of culture and creativity that felt invigorating.

We stopped at a stall draped in vibrant fabrics, where an elderly woman with wise eyes and a welcoming smile offered us samples of her homemade jams. "Try the lavender peach," she encouraged, her voice rich with warmth. "It's a taste of summer in a jar."

"Sounds perfect," I replied, savoring the delicate sweetness on my tongue. It felt like a tiny celebration, a reminder of the simple joys that life could offer amidst the chaos.

"Now you're just playing with my heart," Grant said, eyeing the jars hungrily. "What's next? Are we going to start a jam-making business? I could see it now—'Kleszcz and Co.: The Jam That'll Change Your Life.'"

I laughed, nudging him with my shoulder. "Oh, absolutely. Just think of all the flavors! Chaosberry, Heartbreak Lemonade, and maybe even Tangled Hearts Raspberry. A true culinary adventure."

We reveled in our ridiculousness, exchanging playful banter as we made our way through the market. But beneath the laughter, an undercurrent of tension remained, a subtle reminder that while the moment felt bright, shadows lingered just beyond the periphery. I couldn't shake the feeling that something significant was on the horizon, a twist waiting to unfold.

Just then, my phone buzzed in my pocket, jarring me from my reverie. I fished it out, and my heart dropped as I saw the name flashing on the screen. It was Sarah, my older sister. Our relationship had always been complicated, a patchwork of love and misunderstandings woven together over years of history.

"Uh-oh, your sister?" Grant asked, noticing the change in my demeanor.

"Yeah, she rarely calls," I replied, biting my lip. "Should I answer?"

"Why not? Could be a sign." He raised an eyebrow, encouraging me with that cheeky grin that always seemed to lighten the mood.

Taking a deep breath, I pressed the answer button, putting the phone to my ear. "Hey, Sarah."

"Thank goodness you picked up!" Her voice was frantic, urgency lacing her words. "I need you to come home. It's about Mom."

My stomach twisted into knots, a thousand questions racing through my mind. "What do you mean? Is she okay?"

"It's... complicated," Sarah hesitated, her words tumbling over one another. "There's something you need to see. Just promise me you'll come."

"Okay, I will. Just tell me what's happening!" My pulse quickened, anxiety creeping in, but I could hear the trembling in her voice, the fear that clung to her like a shadow.

"Just come home, please. I can't explain over the phone," she insisted. "I'll be waiting for you."

Before I could respond, the line went dead, leaving me holding the phone, confusion and worry swirling inside me like a storm. I looked at Grant, whose expression shifted from playful to concerned in an instant.

"What did she say?" he asked softly.

I felt the weight of uncertainty settle on my shoulders, heavier than before. "It's about Mom. I have to go home."

"Do you want me to come with you?" he offered, his voice steady, grounding me amidst the chaos.

I hesitated, torn between my desire for his support and the heaviness of the situation. "I don't know if it's a good idea. Things have always been complicated between us. I'm not sure I want to drag you into that."

"Hey," he said, reaching out to hold my gaze, "I'm not going anywhere. You don't have to face this alone. Whatever it is, I'll be right beside you. Just say the word."

His unwavering support sparked something inside me, but the fear of what lay ahead churned in my stomach like a tempest. "Okay. Let's go," I finally said, determination creeping into my voice.

We set off toward the subway, the vibrant energy of Brooklyn fading into the background as my thoughts spiraled with unanswered questions. My mind raced with memories of my mother—the warmth of her laughter, the wisdom in her eyes, and the strained moments that often felt like unspoken chasms between us.

The subway was crowded, the clatter of wheels against tracks echoing my unease. Each stop felt like an eternity, the walls of the train closing in as anxiety thrummed beneath my skin. Grant stood beside me, a steady presence as I wrestled with the uncertainty of what awaited us.

When we finally emerged into the familiar streets of my childhood neighborhood, the air felt thick with tension. I could see the outline of my family home in the distance, the house that had seen so many memories—some joyful, others tinged with sorrow.

"Ready?" Grant asked, his voice a soft anchor amidst the rising tide of my anxiety.

I took a deep breath, steeling myself for whatever awaited me beyond that door. "Ready as I'll ever be."

As we approached the house, my heart raced, the echoes of the past ringing in my ears. Just then, the front door swung open, revealing Sarah standing there, her expression a mixture of fear and resolve.

"Julia, you need to see this!" she called, urgency lacing her words.

But before I could step inside, a figure emerged behind her—a shadow from my past I had never expected to see again. I froze, my breath caught in my throat as reality crashed over me like a wave.

"Surprise!" my estranged father exclaimed, a wicked grin stretching across his face.

My world tilted on its axis, the chaos of the day shifting into a whole new realm of unpredictability.